George Alfred Lawrence

Blanche Ellerslie's Ending

George Alfred Lawrence

Blanche Ellerslie's Ending

ISBN/EAN: 9783337279974

Printed in Europe, USA, Canada, Australia, Japan

Cover: Foto ©Andreas Hilbeck / pixelio.de

More available books at **www.hansebooks.com**

Blanche Ellerslie's

Ending.

BY THE AUTHOR OF "GUY LIVINGSTONE," ETC.

Author's Edition.

WITH ILLUSTRATIONS.

CHICAGO:
HENRY A. SUMNER & COMPANY.
BOSTON: CHARLES H. WHITING.
1884.

LIST OF ILLUSTRATIONS.

CONTENTS.

CONTENTS.

BREAKING A BUTTERFLY

OR

BLANCHE ELLERSLIE'S ENDING.

CHAPTER I.

ALL IS VANITY.

Those three words come often home to many who never willingly listen to sermon ever so short, or sit under preacher ever so winning—ay, and to many of creeds, nations, and languages other than ours, who have not so much as heard of the name of Ecclesiastes. The world's kaleidoscope may shift as it will, with myriad changes of form and color; but the center-point of the prisms bides steadfast and unaltered, round which is inscribed the trite old dreary text. Frequent among the illustrations of its truth are those trifling disillusions— scarcely amounting to disappointments—that affect us when we confess that the reality falls somewhat short of the ideal; that the substance is something coarser in outline, or meaner in proportion, than the foreshadowing.

Said a friend to me, the other day,—

"I have tramped and sailed over three parts of the globe now; and I never saw but one thing, alive or dead, that thoroughly answered its warranty; and that was a cyclone. You must remember that, being an indifferent sailor at all times, I was just then in a state of mortal fear."

Now, the man who thus expressed himself was of a temper neither somber nor sanguine; not given to philosophy—cynical or otherwise; but one who went his way about the world in a quiet Odyssean fashion; taking the rough and the smooth as they came, and keeping, so far as I know, his heart whole and his digestion unimpaired.

Most of us—putting cases of exceptional luck aside—have thought, or will think, nearly the same. The mountain is lofty, yet not quite so stupendous—the river is romantic, yet winds not quite so picturesquely—the face is fair, yet not quite so lovely—as had been set forth by fancy or word-painting. In the after-time we may come to dwell in the shadow of that same mountain, and wax so jealous of its honor that we shall scarce allow there is its peer among the everlasting hills; we may float on that same river till we know and love every rippling eddy and quiet pool, and swear that there flows seawards no pleasanter stream; we may look on that same face till we are ready to maintain against all comers its sovereignty in beauty. But, if we go back honestly to our first impression of any wonder of nature or art that we have approached with expectation on the strain, we shall remember a faint reaction, like the slackening of a damped chord.

In the commonplace amusements and pleasures of life the apothegm holds specially good. Indeed, when some five hundred people, of different ages or sexes, attend any entertainment whatever that has been announced with a certain flourish of trumpets, the odds against some few of the number coming away disappointed are such as would puzzle Mr. Babbage, or the subtlest in the Ring, to compute.

On these premises it would seem a fact not less worthy of record than many set down in the *Annual Register*, that the first ball given at Nithsdale House, after the bride was brought home, was pronounced a thorough success by each and every one who assisted thereat, from the royal Personage who, with infinite grace and agility, opened the first quadrille, down to the linkman without, who, with a hoarse and unctuous blessing, sped the very last of the parting guests.

The host himself would scarcely have claimed any share in the social triumph. Hugh, tenth Earl of Nithsdale, was a grave, gentle person, now somewhat past middle age. He did not shine in ordinary conversation—though he could speak sensibly enough at need from his place in the House—and was too shy to be a general favorite. Nevertheless, few were better loved or esteemed by such as knew him thoroughly. In his nature there was not an atom of arrogance or self-assertion; but he was thoroughly imbued with the pride of caste, being more careful of the obligations than of the privileges of his order. From his youth upwards he had striven, in his own quiet fashion, to the uttermost of his power and light, to discharge his duty both to God and to his neighbor; and kept the fifth not less religiously than the other commandments. So when his mother—widow of the ninth Earl—found a helpmeet for her son soon after he came of age, Nithsdale showed no signs of rebellion or reluctance; though the damsel was something hard of feature and meager of frame, and, to say the least of it, acidulated in temper. But then she was of stainless descent, and had wealth enough to parcel-gild richly a faded coronet.

For many years that couple plodded on together, peacefully if not happily. Indeed, after they had once settled down into their places there was little chance of domestic jars: fretfulness was simply wasted on Nithsdale's grave, placid temperament; and for domestic jealousy neither gave cause. The earl never—so far as the nearest of his intimates knew—suffered his fancy to wander beyond bounds; and the countess carried down to her grave a virtue absolutely unsullied.

There was born of this marriage only one sickly boy, who died in infancy. The lack of an heir perhaps troubled Nithsdale more than he cared to confess, even to himself; to such as are free from all taint of avarice, it is weary work laying up riches without knowing who shall gather them. Nevertheless, he slackened not a whit in the skill and care that he had displayed since he came of age in administering a vast encumbered patrimony; mortgage after mortgage was cleared off, acre after acre drained, farmstead after farmstead repaired, till the great Nithsdale estates not only were set free of burden, but in such order as to become an agricultural ensample far and near.

When he was left a widower, Hugh of Nithsdale felt his bereavement heavily. He had never himself cared for country sports, though he took care to provide them plentifully for his guests; his own relaxations were chiefly sedentary, of mildly scientific kind; so that most of his time was spent within-doors. Naturally, the absence even of that hard-featured face and spare angular figure made a dreary blank, both at fireside and board-head; and just as naturally, after a decent interval, the earl began to reflect how that blank should be filled.

Perhaps he had never absolutely regretted the first alliance; yet he may have considered that in contracting it he had discharged all his duty to his house; and he determined, in wiving again, to please only his own fancy. Moreover, there was no privy-councilor, to insist on state-policy and the like, since his lady-mother went to her rest.

The union of January and May is so common nowadays that no one thinks of inditing epithalamia thereon, satiric or otherwise. Nevertheless there was a certain stir of wonderment in the great world when it became noised abroad that Lady Rose Marston was to be the second Countess of Nithsdale. In truth, there were disparities betwixt the affianced pair seemingly more serious than that of age, though the bride was barely in her twentieth year.

She came of rather a wild stock, and her bringing-up had been none of the staidest. Her mother, Viscountess Daventry, once a famous beauty, had not ceased to be dangerous and enterprising; and her father, though too lazy to be vicious, had never cared himself to practice any virtue, domestic or otherwise, and devoted all the energy he could muster to the mismanagement of his racing-stable, taking no thought as to the training of his olive-branches. From him the Lady Rose inherited the long, sleepy brown eyes that never grew eager or troubled when a race on which a year's income hung was being won or lost by the shortest of heads; and the soft, rich auburn hair, the envy of Lord Daventry's bald or grizzled compeers. There was much beauty in her face, but of the stillest, quietest kind; and it might have been inanimate but for the perfect little mouth, which, smiling often, smiled never unmeaningly. She was not particularly clever, and not a whit ambitious; hereditary indolence would have prompted her to glide listlessly down the social stream, accepting such flowers as floated into her hands, yet not straining after such as grew out of her reach. But, early in her first season, a large mixed jury of natives and foreigners pronounced Lady Rose Marston one of the best *valseuses* in Europe.

In these days, most demoiselles endowed with lithe, light figures, and a fair ear for music, dance—as our forefathers would have said—more or less "divinely;" so that one should be singled out and set above her sisters, involves some marked peculiarity. And Rose Marston's waltzing *was* very peculiar. However rapid the whirl, she never lost the languid grace that distinguished her in repose. But all the while a practiced eye, to say nothing of a practiced arm, could detect, in all her movements, a latent energy and suppressed power. Men found they could go on longer with Lady Rose without feeling the exertion than with any other; as for tiring her—a month after she was presented there was no question of such a thing.

"She's always going so thoroughly within herself," Regy Avenel remarked; "that's about the secret of it."

His opinion in these matters was worth having; for he was the crack cotillon-leader of that year.

Every man or woman who has a reputation to keep up, however flimsy or trivial, has a certain object and interest in life; and, after all, there seems no reason why there should not be choregraphic as well as athletic champions. The girl became imbued with a kind of artistic enthusiasm, and looked forward to her balls as a successful actress looks forward to her scenic triumphs. She was too lazy, perhaps too frank, ever thoroughly to flirt; yet she would do much in an innocent way to win or retain an eligible partner, and was not niggardly of looks, words, or smiles, in rewarding her special favorites. These were found naturally enough in a fast, though not a very vicious, set. They were too young, for the most part, to be thoroughly depraved; for among Lady Rose's attachés there was scarce one whose beard was fairly grown.

Nevertheless, certain matrons, and maids whose "snoods" had lost their gloss, looked askance as she passed by, whispering bitter words ; even as Rebecca, on the day after she cheated her first-born of his birthright, may have wagged her head, and scowled from under her brows, at some laughing daughter of Heth.

Whatever may have been her temptations, the Lady Rose must have kept herself heart-whole, if not quite fancy-free. When she first heard of Lord Nithsdale as a suitor, she showed no signs of repugnance or terror, but said placidly to her mother that she liked him as well as she liked any one else ; and she was sure he would be kind to her. Speaking on the subject to the most intimate of her male and female friends, she consistently declined to be looked on as a martyr. It was true that she had known the earl from childhood upward ; for one of his diverse estates, on which he had of late resided frequently, marched with her father's property at Daventry Court.

Perhaps, among their mutual acquaintance, more pity was felt for the bridegroom than for the bride ; though none of these amicable impertinences were expressed aloud. Despite his homely bearing and quiet manner, none, gentle or simple, dreamed of taking liberties with Hugh of Nithsdale ; and pity, real or feigned, was utterly uncalled for.

The earl had no mind to cage or clip the wings of the beautiful bird that had perched so willingly on his shoulder, and knew right well he could trust her not to range too far. Though there was no verbal compact, Lady Rose understood that she was free to follow her own inclinations in any reasonable way ; that she was still free to indulge her own taste, to plan and carry out her own amusement, and to gather her own friends round her, when and where she would. It was a very blithe bridal ; and when the honeymoon had waned, the bride did not scruple to confess, to whom it might concern, that she was perfectly—I believe her own words were "awfully"—happy.

In the shape of this same ball, her first matronly anxiety came upon her. The ordinary cares of preparation troubled her not a whit ; she left all such things in perfect confidence to her housekeeper and house-steward, and to the tradesmen, whom she had learned to look upon as trusty Slaves of the Ring. Neither was she nervous; though she would have to play hostess for the first time before a critical audience, and in presence of royalty. She had other causes of disquietude; and these were solemnly discussed one day at luncheon by a council of three, whereat assisted her mother and Reginald Avenel of choragic fame. The chiefest trouble, as may be imagined, was the revision of the invitation cards.

The countess had set her delicate foot down on one point—that, come what would, her first ball should not be overcrowded—a just and pleasant resolve, but not so easily carried out in the face of a visiting-list of portentous dimensions, when people congregated from the uttermost parts of the earth for the express purpose of showing themselves—if they had the chance,—on that especial night at Nithsdale House. The worst of it was, that friends, who had made their own election sure, declined to be content therewith, and persisted in pleading for others who seemed likely to be left in the outer darkness. Lady Nithsdale was at her wits' end. She had calculated, by the help of some cunning in such matters, how many her rooms would hold comfortably; and she was on the very verge of such a limit now. Yet still the letters came pouring in, and her carriage could not halt for five minutes in the Mile, without being beset by petitioners. She was too good-natured to like vexing anybody, and too wise in her simple way to make needless enemies thus early in her career. Even while she sat at luncheon two notes were brought in, of which she guessed the import so soon as she glanced at the monograms.

"One can't even eat a poor little plover's egg in peace," the countess said, pouting. "I declare it's a thousand times worse than Christmas bills!" And she tore open one of the envelopes quite viciously.

Avenel looked at her with a half smile—a little sad and a little envious. He had been trying for some time now to make a younger son's fortune square with expensive tastes, and had come to the conclusion that there are not many things worse than Christmas bills, when the patience of creditors waxes threadbare.

The first note contained only one of the ordinary petitions; for the countess threw it carelessly across to her mother, after a glance at its contents, saying,—

"Lady Blakeston wants to bring that plain prim niece. Quite impossible, isn't it, mamma? What can M. de Fonteyrac want?" she went on, as she opened the other envelope. "All the embassy, except those two who don't dance, have got cards already."

But the second note seemed to touch the countess more narrowly; and, as she passed it to Avenel, she clasped her hands in comic despair.

Yet there was nothing very alarming on the face of the document, couched in the courtliest of diplomatic styles. Therein M. de Fonteyrac, referring himself to the angelic goodness of Madame la Comtesse, prayed permission to bring with him to her ball his especial friend Gaspard de Sauterel.

Now, Lady Nithsdale, as you know, was, in a certain way, imbued with an artistic spirit; and all real artists are more nervous in exhibiting before a single *maestro* than before five hundred *cognoscenti*. Gaspard, Marquis de Sauterel, was a European celebrity. Filling a high post at the Imperial court, he held another office, quite as well recognized and defined, though betokened by no outward insignia. For the last four seasons he had reigned without a rival over Parisian cotillons. The haughtiest of the female *noblesse* altered the date of their entertainments to insure his presence; and the lightest feet in France were only too proud to follow in his wake.

"Oh, Regy, what is to be done?" the countess asked, half pettishly. "Something is sure to go wrong; and, then, can't you fancy his going back to Paris and talking compassionately about insular ambition?"

Before he answered, Avenel finished slowly a goblet of weak claret-cup. He was very temperate, both in food and drink—training, so to speak, for his work—and from mere condition would have run into a place in any ordinary two-mile handicap. Then he read the note through carefully, lifting his brows : he was not a handsome man, but his eyebrows were unexceptionable, and he made play with them accordingly.

"Don't you flurry yourself, Lady Rose" (to the Countess of Nithsdale's intimates her maiden name seemed to come always most naturally); "we're not beat yet, and I don't see why we should be, either. De Sauterel isn't running in his old form, so Dolly Forester says, and he ought to know, for there never was more than seven pounds between 'em. Baccarat after balls, and absinthe before breakfast, are beginning to tell. The marquis is as quick on his legs as ever; but, I hear, he can't stay."

What might have been a dark speech to others was intelligible enough to his hearer. Turf metaphors were scarce likely to offend the ears of Lord Daventry's daughter. Her sweet face cleared somewhat, though doubt still lingered there.

"Besides," Avenel went on, placidly, "it's very easy to make things quite safe. Why don't you let De Sauterel lead in his own fashion? He can't find fault then. Don't mind me; I'll abdicate with pleasure. I've always said my life is one long self-sacrifice."

Rose Marston by many of her acquaintances was called capricious and fickle—and not without reason. Her preferences were often wonderfully short-lived, and the first favorite of one night would become the extremest outsider the next. Indeed, sometimes after supper her card became so terribly involved that she was forced, so to speak, to take the benefit of the Act, and start afresh; paying her creditors nothing whatever in the pound. But in her real friendships she was stanch as steel. She had known Reginald Avenel long before she came out, and had always looked upon him as one of the family—their ancestors *had* been related in some very remote age : it was strange, but perfectly true, that their cousinly familiarity had never ripened into the cousinly flirtation which is almost *de rigueur.*

"Don't be so utterly absurd, Regy," she said, with a flush on her cheek and a flash in her lazy brown eyes. "Throwing one's old friends over for people one has never seen, isn't the way to bring luck about the house.

If you say two words more, I shall think you want to change me for the Firefly; I always thought her step suited you best."

He held up his hand in deprecation.

"*L'Empire, c'est la Paix,* Lady Rose. So said a greater than De Sauterel. Always remember that, before you begin to quarrel. If your majesty won't accept our resignation, it's easily withdrawn. We'll pull through somehow, never fear. Only don't fret any more about these things. You're beginning to look quite fagged already."

Lady Daventry was in no sort of way a model of matronhood; but she was foolishly fond of her children, and specially of this, her eldest-born daughter. She was a better listener than talker, and up to this time had taken little part in the family council; but she got up now, and wound her arm around her daughter's neck caressingly.

"Regy is quite right, darling," she said; "you mustn't fret, and there's no earthly reason for it. I saw a good deal of M. de Sauterel last year in Paris. There's not a more good-natured little creature alive; and, if he were given to fault-finding, he would scarcely practice it here." Lady Daventry's smile was full of memorial meaning. "I'll take care that everybody knows to-day that your list is full; so you shall be bored with no more begging letters. That's settled."

Then the conclave broke up.

Is it likely that, in this hard workday world, many should be found who could throw themselves seriously into a discussion frivolous as that set down here? Truly, I know not. The statesmen's plans probably were no less deep, the swords of soldiers no less sharp, the quibbles of lawyers no less astute, the song of poets no less musical, the lash of critics no less sharp, in Liliput than in Brobdingnag. Insects, as well as carnivora, are integral parts of creation; and Ephemeris, setting things in order for her bloodless banquet, has cares just as real, though less truculent than those of Megatherium, who shakes the forest-land with his roaring as he seeks his meat from God.

CHAPTER II.

So Lady Nithsdale's ball was a success—*teres atque rotundus*—without a single flaw. The Dieu de la Danse was thoroughly propitious, sanctioning everything and everybody with the benignest of smiles, and before daybreak became the merest mortal in his readiness to lay down his divinity at a mortal's feet. Indeed, when Gaspard de Sauterel returned to his own place, he created great scandal and discontent among the faithful beyond the seas by what they were pleased to call his Anglomania. It was months before he ceased to rave about Lady Nithsdale's waltzing, which he was wont to characterize as "a poesy."

But no triumph can last forever: so Lady Nithsdale's ball was over at last. Carriage after carriage drove away with its cloaked and hooded freight; while the men for the most part strolled off by twos and threes through the fresh spring morning. But only one brougham we need follow. In it sat two women, both fair to look upon, though neither was in her very first youth, and their beauty, such as it was, differed essentially in style.

The first thing which you would probably have remarked was, how wonderfully both faces stood that trying after-dawn light, under which few damsels, even in their first season, willingly linger. It only seemed to soften becomingly the exceeding brilliancy of Laura Brancepeth's coloring; and it did not bring out a line or deepen a shadow on Blanche Ellerslie's cheeks—soft, smooth, and white as the leaves of a tropical lily.

On neither countenance was there trace of weariness; and they were not too sleepy, it seemed, for a little quiet talk, opened by Lady Laura Brancepeth—better known in her own set as "La Reine Gaillarde."

"Thoroughly well done, wasn't it, Blanche? The rooms just full enough to look their best, and not a particle of heat or crowd.   Anne Daventry has a specialty for these things, when she will only give herself the trouble. Those leaf-screens round the fountains in the conservatory were the prettiest things I ever saw; and you admired them even more than I, apparently, for you spent about half the night there.   By-the-by, that reminds me—I should just like to know where you were all the cotillon?   I missed you after the first figure."

"I was tired," Mrs. Ellerslie answered   "I should certainly have got one of my headaches if I had gone on: you know what my headaches are?   The fact is, I am going down fast into the vale of years; after this season, I don't mean to waltz any more."

Few and faint were the signs of age on the delicate face just then, and so Laura Brancepeth thought, as she gazed at her companion with a mischievous flash in her broad, black eyes.

"Yes : I know what your headaches are, and how they come and go, and how easily tired you are sometimes. As for that excuse about your age, I consider it positively rude.   I'm two years older than you are, but I've no idea of wall-flowering just yet.   You wicked little *comédienne!*   I never saw you act better than you did to-night; you know very well you only slipped away to take another long lesson in botany from Mark Ramsay. Why; Blanche—is it possible?   I can't believe it : you're actually blushing!"

If an aurora borealis had blazed forth suddenly in the clear gray sky above them, Lady Laura could not have spoken with more astonishment.   She was, in truth, looking on a natural phenomenon.   The practiced coquette was no more likely to betray signs of discomfiture at the mention of any ordinary name than a charger is likely to start at a pistol-shot.   Yet there was no mistake about the tell-tale flush—rather deepening than fading under the other's searching gaze.

"Oh, Blanche! Was it not acting then, after all?" Lady Laura went on, in quite a changed tone, and the mockery died out of her eyes.   "You can't mean that you have been in earnest to-night.   The worst of your flirtations would be better than such fearful folly."

Mrs. Ellerslie's look of injured innocence was scarcely so successful as usual.

"You are too tyrannical, Queenie," she said, plaintively; "there's no possibility of contenting you. Well, allowing that you are right in your suspicion—which I don't—is it not better to be foolish once in a way than wicked always?"

But the other was not to be put off with a jest.

"I am quite serious," she said. "You and I are very old friends, fast friends too, though you'd provoke a saint sometimes, and I own I'm rather apt to bully you. Though I often tease you about men, I never really pity them much. But I should pity *you* awfully if you came to grief; and I'd sooner hear of your breaking half a dozen honest hearts than giving the least bit of yours to Mark Ramsay."

"What fresh story have you heard against him?"

The low voice was quite steady; but the down trimming fluttered, though there was no breeze to stir it.

"Are not the old ones enough?" the other answered, gravely. "If I had never heard a single word against him, I should take warning from his face; wonderfully handsome, I allow, and gentle too, when he chooses to let it soften. But when it is in repose, I think it the cruelest face I ever looked upon. It would be rather nice to be lorded over by some people, I know; but I don't like to think of any woman as that man's slave. And slave she would be; depend upon it, there would be no half-measures there."

Blanche laughed, quite naturally now.

"What a vampire you have made of poor Mr. Ramsay! If you knew him better, perhaps you wouldn't think him so fatal in any way. It's rather refreshing to talk to him, after the platitudes one has to listen to as a rule; though he neither talks politics nor scandal, and doesn't seem to consider flirting a matter of absolute duty. But—so far— Queenie, he has done *me* no harm."

Neither capitals nor italics, nor any other device of type, could do justice to Blanche Ellerslie's "me." *Du*, issuing from the tenderest lips that have murmured love-whispers in Rhine-land, never sounded half so cosy and caressing. Very few men heard it for the first time, without feeling a new sympathy awaking within them, and a kind of prescience that some confidence was coming.

Lady Laura's wiry night-slaves scuffled over the ground quicker than the best pair of steppers in town; and they were so nearly at home now, that she had only time to say,—

"I'm too sleepy to go on preaching; only, Blanche, do pray take care."

So the two women embraced, and parted for the night.

With a sinful indifference to beauty-sleep, Mrs. Ellerslie sat musing long after her maid had left her. Self-examination was not much in her line; but in the solitude of her own chamber she did not affirm to herself quite so confidently as she had done to Laura Brancepeth, that "no harm has been done to me."

CHAPTER III.

Now, what manner of man was he whose name had made Blanche Ellerslie flush and flutter like a girl, and the reckless Reine Gaillarde earnest in warning?

Not a wonder in any way. Yet one who would certainly have achieved some notable success in life, if he had turned to any account his gifts and chances.

Mark Ramsay came of an ancient Scots house that had once been very powerful in the Lowlands, but whose fortunes had ebbed steadily for centuries, and rapidly at last, till the present generation was well-nigh stranded. Instead of having a voice in the councils of the realm, Ramsay of Kilmains could scarce get hearing at petty sessions; out of demesnes vast and fertile, there were left now only a few hundred acres of poor, hungry land round a hideous red-brick barrack, tacked on to a gaunt, gray peel-tower; and of all the wealth amassed by wrong and rapine there was not enough left to keep a creditable balance at the county bank.

The family met with singularly little sympathy in their downward career. From time immemorial these Ramsays had been hard, despotic tyrants, apt to oppress the poor and needy, whether vassals or neighbors, and only lavish of their gold when it was a question of selfish vice. The present Laird of Kilmains, Mark's father, was quite as unpopular as any of his ancestors, though he had been guilty of none of the excesses for which they had been evilly renowned; being, indeed, exceeding miserly in his habits, and in religion a gloomy fanatic. Though he looked so keenly and carefully after the pence, the pounds, somehow, took to themselves wings, and flitted one by one out of his covetous fingers. He had an unhappy turn for small speculations, and each of these seemed fated to prove more or less unprofitable; so that, after pinching and saving for a score of years, he found himself rather poorer than when he came into his heritage. Ill luck may have done much to embitter a temper naturally morose and sullen; but certainly among all his forbears there was not found a more thorough tyrant, though his tyranny, perforce, was on a petty scale. A hard master, a merciless landlord, an austere father, and a brutal husband—though of actual violence he was never guilty—he seldom lost a chance of vexing any living thing that could safely be oppressed.

Two children were the issue of a most unhappy marriage; and Marcia Ramsay went to her rest—gladly enough, no doubt—within a month after Mark's birth.

The heir of Kilmains, both outwardly and inwardly, very much resembled his father: perhaps for this reason the two got on well enough together, in a sort of way. From his boyhood upwards, Gilbert Ramsay had always yielded to dictation, however unreasonable, a stolid acquiescence with which it was next to impossible to quarrel; and when he grew up to manhood, from mere force of habit he continued docile, with occasional fits of the sullens, that never opened into ripe revolt. All this the elder man accepted ungraciously, as his mere due; yet it is certain that he liked his first-born better than he liked any other creature.

With Mark it was very different. To say that "there was no love lost" betwixt the two does not at all express it. There was positive antipathy. Kilmains hated his second son almost from his birth; he hated him for the haughty beauty that always reminded him of the woman whose spirit he never could cow, though he broke her heart, and who died long before she was tamed. Mark's mouth and eyes were the counterparts of his mother's; and James Ramsay's violence of word or deed was soon met over again by the same disdainful smile and glance of cool defiance that had often galled him in the old days. He would never own it to himself, but it was quite true that he never felt thoroughly easy in the boy's presence. He hated him for this; he hated him worst of all because, before Mark was ten years old, he was made virtually independent of his father.

When Duncan Cameron came back with a fair fortune from the East, where all his youth and manhood were passed, almost his first visit was to his favorite sister's grave. He had heard enough of the manner of her life and death to keep him from ever setting foot under her husband's roof; and when he made his will in favor of her child, he took special care that not a doit should be handled by the Laird of Kilmains, much less pass into his clutches.

The guardians of the child were well chosen—two shrewd, sturdy, sensible business men; ready to do their duty without fear or favor, and as little likely to be bullied as beguiled. If Duncan Cameron had designed to work out a posthumous revenge on him who had made his sister's life miserable, he could scarcely have devised a more ingenious plan. From the day that he heard the will read, to that on which Mark attained his majority, James Ramsay lived in perpetual fret and discontent. The property was not so very large—a little over a thousand a year, all told—but the sum allowed yearly for the boy's nurture and education would more than have discharged all the household expenses at Kilmains. Of this, beyond a meager allowance for actual maintenance whilst Mark lived at home, the father could touch no part; for education, the guardians provided as it seemed to them good.

When it was decided to send Mark to Eton, Ramsay did make some show of resistance, and threw every possible impediment in the way; but there loomed in the distance the terrors of the High Court of Chancery; and, though he had never read Sophocles, he knew well enough what usually befalls those who

Hurl themselves violently against the footstool of Justice.

So he was bound to swallow the bitter pill, and wreak his ill humor on such as were compelled to endure it.

Mark's school-days passed very pleasantly. He was a great favorite with his masters and his mates. He did not show much energy, either at work or play, but got through a sufficient amount of both creditably enough. The vacations spent at Kilmains were terribly dreary. James Ramsay never lifted his hand against his son— perhaps he feared whither one act of violence might lead him — but he did not seek to dissemble his dislike. Though the boy was wonderfully intrepid by nature, and had unhappily grown quite careless of such things as domestic affections, he could scarcely help starting sometimes as, looking up suddenly, he met those hard, haggard eyes. His brother was no sort of companion for him, for they had not a single taste in common; so it was no marvel if Black Monday was a day to be scored with the whitest of chalk in Mark's calendar.

When he went to Oxford he became practically his own master; and his first act of independence was a refusal to spend any part of his first vacation at Kilmains. From that day forth he was no more under his father's roof-tree; and no communication by word or mouth passed betwixt the two.

Thus no foundling was ever more absolutely free of all home-ties than Mark Ramsay. How fraught with danger is such isolation, all men know—many to their cost. Some hearts there are of such rare material that, under such proving, they grow strong and self-reliant, but never hard. Mark was none of these. His selfishness, such as it was, lay not on the surface, but deep in grain. He did not object to benevolence on principle, and would do a good-natured action readily enough, if it led him not too far out of his way; but would help a mere acquaintance just as readily as an ancient comrade, expecting no gratitude in return. If he had confessed his real sentiments, he would probably have told you that friendship was a thing as much out of date as brotherhood-in-arms. He was liberal and hospitable to the outside limit of his means—*that* his worst enemies allowed—but was neither reckless nor prodigal. He was fond of playing his part in the battle of life; and had no mind to be invalided for lack of the sinews of war.

So he never got into any serious money-scrape on his own account. As for involving himself for another, the man was yet to be found, confident enough in his own persuasive powers to ask Mark Ramsay for the use of his name. Nevertheless he was quite as popular at Oxford as he had been at Eton; not a general favorite, simply because he did not care to mix much in general society; but the men of his set swore by him. His personal advantages may have had much to do with this. You may sermonize till you are weary about these things being but skin-deep, and the rest of it; but you never will prevent them being a passport to the favor of men, to say nothing of womenkind. The credentials may be false, or forged, of course: till their falsity is proved, they stand.

Mark's beauty was of a very rare type—slightly effeminate, perhaps, but none the less attractive for that. An old Venetian painter would have reveled in the rich soft coloring of his hair, eyes, and lips, each the darkest of their several shades of chestnut, blue, and crimson; and all harmonizing, instead of contrasting, with cheeks of clear pale olive. His frame was well knit and put together, though on rather a slender scale. And it was a good lasting figure; for at five-and-thirty neither gauntness nor coarseness marred its outline. His manner, too, was very winning: more perhaps at first than after long acquaintance; for sometimes its exceeding quietude almost irritated you. But of his voice, with its subtle variations of semitones, you never grew weary.

Any one thus endowed, unless exceptionally weak in intellect or strong in principle, or furnished with a special safeguard, is scarce likely to reach manhood without working some great harm to himself, if not to others. The safeguard I mean, is the having won the love of a true, beautiful woman; and the being able to hold fast that most precious pearl—never hankering after other men's jewels.

Now, Mark Ramsay was neither very simple nor very seraphic. Of boyish romance he never was guilty; indeed, before he left Eton he could theorize with dangerous glibness on certain subjects, and was an advanced Fourierist in matters feminine. Guilty passion or lawless caprice, when they have once fairly laid hold on a man, will leave their traces behind, however thoroughly they may seem to be shaken off, like any other malaria. Years after the patient has been pronounced perfectly whole, there will come back, without rhyme or reason, the hot thrills and the cold shivers. Nevertheless, there are degrees in maladies, and Mark Ramsay had curiously ill luck in his first fever-fit.

Frederic, Graf von Adlersberg, was a very famous diplomatist. The truces he obtained, and the treaties he cemented, when war, or discord at the least, seemed inevitable, are written down in history. Ermengild, his wife, was almost better known for the domestic contracts she had severed, and the family revolutions she had caused. There was scarcely a capital boasting an embassy on which she had not made her mark. In six European tongues at least, anathemas or complaints might have been heard at the mention of her name; and matrons, mothers, and maids would have joined in the chorus. She had served her master more earnestly and successfully than ever her husband served his earthly sovereign. But she never wrought a more thorough piece of the devil's work than when she "formed" Mark Ramsay.

There are crimes that no lawgiver, from him of Horeb downwards, has ever set down in his calendar; crimes concerning which the acutest legalist could never draw an indictment. Yet to expiate lesser offenses, men—ay, and women to boot—have come forth through a low dark door into the cold gray morning, and stood under a black beam, waiting for their shameful death, while ten thousand of their fellow-creatures looked on unpityingly. Many who are guilty of such deeds sit in the foremost places of our synagogues and the foremost rooms at our feasts, bearing themselves debonnairely or austerely after their fashion; either smiling with calm superiority at their neighbor's misdeeds and failings, or casting, with unerring aim, sharp stones at whoso shall have broken the least commandment in the Decalogue. Yet, I think, for these things there will come a reckoning, when the penalty shall be paid to the uttermost pang.

The Countess von Adlersberg was none of these smooth-faced hypocrites. She sinned with a high hand, and would no more have dreamt of draping herself in social virtue than of going to a masquerade as a wimpled nun. More than once blood had been shed, when she might have averted the calamity by a word or a sign; but she sat still, while it went on to the bitter end, with no more ruth than Faustina may have felt at the circus when she gave the death-sign with her little white thumb.

Yet Ermengild was never more thoroughly a murderess, in intent than when she dropped poison at the root of every frank, fresh, and generous impulse in Mark Ramsay's heart, watching them wither day by day, till only a dry waste was left on which flowers could never grow again.

It was at Baden those two met, in the summer of Mark's second year at Oxford. Myriads of handsome faces had passed under the review of the countess's critical eyes; but never one quite like Ramsay's. Almost at the first glance she determined on his conquest, very much as some wealthy bey may determine on the purchase of some new importation into the slave-market, and with no more doubt as to the result. There was no sort of difficulty in bringing him within her reach; for Count von Adlersberg then, and for some time after, was engaged in London on important diplomatic business, and Ermengild had a large English acquaintance. How quickly, rapidly, and completely Mark was subjugated need not be told; all the more rapidly, perhaps, for those theories aforesaid which had given him a hollow sense of security, and made him a sort of oracle among his fellows. Every one knows the trite old proverb about "a little learning." It is never more true than when applied to a moral or physical duel: the straightforward simplicity of utter ignorance has puzzled science ere now; but it is next to a miracle if one who flatters himself he has some cunning in fence escapes without a dangerous wound. All through that autumn and winter and the ensuing spring Mark Ramsay abode under the spell. The sorceress marveled sometimes at her own constancy in caprice; but this one, though it endured longer than most others, came at last to a rather abrupt close. Then —with little preamble or excuse—she cast open the gates of her prison-house, and told her thrall that he was free.

Such a freedom as it was! Freedom from faith; freedom from such old-world prejudices as reverence for woman's truth, or respect for her honor; freedom from all natural compunctions that cause a man to ponder for awhile, if not to hold his hand, when on the point of working bitter wrong, which may never be amended, on innocents or weaklings; freedom from ruth or remorse. And, in place of these things, only a vague desire to require on the many the harm wrought by the one, and a dogged determination to make his own pleasure the Lesbian rule of his life thenceforward.

In such a frame of mind Mark Ramsay went on his way through the world when he was not twenty-one; and a terrible parody of a noble maxim was his motto even to the end:—

Fais ce que voudras,
Advienne que pourra.

It would be unfair to impute all this to the influence— fatal as it undoubtedly was—which overshadowed him so early. Mark was born with a sufficient portion of the stubborn hardness which, for centuries past, if Fame spoke true, had run in the Ramsay blood. This had been fostered, doubtless, by his home-training, wherein natural affection was replaced by antagonism. If the Countess

Ermengild had never crossed his path, it is not likely he would ever have turned out gentle or good, or even wise in his generation.　Many there are—very fortunately for the well-being of this world of ours—who, had their first illusion been destroyed yet more rudely, would have remembered that there was much work left for them to do, and many prizes of all sorts worth the winning; and have braced themselves to the honest, healthy pursuit of these, instead of falling back long before their prime on the cynicism which ought to be the last resource of disappointed old age.　But Mark Ramsay—having said in his first haste, "all women are liars"—acted on the aphorism in bitter earnest.

For many years he led an odd wandering sort of life; spending much more of his time abroad than in England, and having nowhere a fixed abiding-place. He cultivated art in a desultory *dilettante* fashion, and his pursuits were rather of a quiet than an athletic order; though he was famous both with pistol and rifle, and had done some notable work with the big game in divers countries. The only restless element in all his nature was evinced in fondness for traveling.　There were few nooks and corners, indeed, of the civilized world that were strange to him; and fewer still, where he had tarried beyond a brief season, whence some tale might not have been gathered redounding little to his credit.　Wherever he went he made the same pitiless, unscrupulous use of his fair face and lissom tongue. With women, unfortunately, forewarned is not forearmed; and thus far his evil repute seemed never to have seriously hindered the accomplishment of his desires.　He was not a whit more reckless of the consequences to others than of the consequences to himself; but he had come out of the most serious scrapes scathless — though not always unscathing — with the strange impunity that seems to attach only to those who will play for their lives as readily as for any other stake.

Ramsay never paraded his conquests or boasted of them in after-days.　He would speak lightly enough of womankind, but never disparagingly of any single woman. Indeed, he would show a distaste for such converse plainly enough at times.　Few who sought to betray him into confession or confidence tried the experiment twice. This spark of chivalry, and a certain generosity at play—he was a bold and successful gambler—were the two bright spots relieving the darkness of Mark Ramsay's nature at thirty-five.

With all this, his evil reputation spread itself far and wide; the more so, perhaps, because there never had been imputed to him a single venial or vulgar intrigue. He confined his depredations exclusively to his own class; somewhat on the principle of those masterful thieves of ancient days, who, plundering priest, noble, and franklin without mercy, let peasant and pauper go scot-free. The demi-monde of foreign capitals knew him only by name; or, at the most, by meeting him occasionally at entertainments where their presence was only an accessory to high play; and not one of the "soiled doves," who flutter from tree to tree in the Forest of St. John, or build their nests in Brompton groves, had ever succeeded in perching, were it for an instant, on his shoulder.

Ermengild von Adlersberg had fallen back on feminine diplomacy when the cunning of cosmetics could no longer dissemble the retribution of Time the Avenger. Half the domestic plots that amused or scandalized Paris were hatched in her boudoir. Though those two met but seldom of late years, no *cancans* interested her so much as those concerning Mark Ramsay. She seemed, while she listened, to glow with a quiet satisfaction, and a kind of reflected triumph; like a venerable college tutor hearing of parliamentary successes achieved by some favorite pupil.

Two years before the opening of this tale, Mark's position had been entirely changed by a singular freak of fortune. During a winter spent in Paris, community of tastes, and, to a certain extent, of pursuits, brought him much into the company of a certain Sir Robert Kenlis. There was some sort of cousinship betwixt the two; but so entirely remote, that even a Scotch genealogist would have been puzzled fairly to unite the pedigree. Such as it was, it was enough to warrant the old baronet in gratifying a fancy and a dislike. The fancy was for his new acquaintance; the dislike was for each and every one of the relatives he had ever known.   So one day, about a week after Sir Robert Kenlis's sudden death, there was intense heart-burning in the large circle of expectants, and some wonderment in the world at large, at the announcement that Mark Ramsay had been left the dead man's sole heir.

It was a very goodly heritage, comprising some £8000 a year in improvable estates; and money enough in the Funds to buy another fair property; to say nothing of jewels and pictures, statues and furniture, stored away in half the capitals of Europe, enough to stock a vaster mansion than Kenlis Castle.

Ramsay was in no wise outwardly exalted by his great good luck, and seemed not in the least aware that from a comparative cipher in the world he had become an important unit, in whose well or ill faring the matronly part at least of polite society took an interest sudden and sincere.   Most of his time was now necessarily spent in England; otherwise there was little change in his habits, except that he indulged his taste in horse-flesh to the uttermost, and entertained in London oftener and on a larger scale than had been his wont.   Beyond a bachelor party in the grouse-season, he had made no attempt to keep house at Kenlis Castle.

Such was Mark Ramsay at the opening of this our tale.   Thus early in it I take leave to observe that he differs as widely from my private and personal idea of a hero, even of melodrama, as two created or imagined things can differ.   He is simply the chief actor in a company more or less indifferent; and such as he will, unluckily, often thrust themselves into such *rôles* whether it like the manager or not.

CHAPTER IV.

"Where are you off to, Ramsay? You'll come and have a quiet smoke and take a modest drink somewhere, surely? Platt's will be full in about ten minutes; and the big rubber at the Partington is in full swing just now; and—and there's lots of things to do before heading homewards."

The speaker was a big, brawny man, with a perfect aureole of light-red hair round a bale, weather-beaten face, that would have looked more at home on a purple moorland, or at the "down-wind" side of a gorse-cover, or under the steep bank of a salmon-river, or on the slippery deck of a cutter "going free," than among the delicate ferns and rare exotics lining the vestibule of Nithsdale House. Indeed, it was a miracle how Dick Calverly always contrived to look so fresh; considering that he was ready for "a quiet smoke and a modest drink" at any hour in the twenty-four, and had a perfect antipathy to taking his nightly rest at regular hours if he could find the most shadowy excuse for keeping vigil.

"That's the pull of Norway," he was wont to say. "You never need go to bed at all there, unless you like. Somebody's up all night long."

I believe his only objection to the English climate was that it could boast no midnight sun. People said he burned the candle at both ends; if so, it was a very tough taper, and seemed likely to outlast many that were consumed by miser's rule. He rather prided himself on his powers of seducing men into sitting up to unearthly hours; but on this occasion his simple eloquence failed. Ramsay shook his head as they went down the steps together.

"Your ideas of a quiet smoke are rather different from mine, Dick. If I had lungs like forge-bellows, or like yours, perhaps I shouldn't mind doing it in aa atmosphere that you might cut with a handsaw; but I haven't, you see, more's the pity; and my drinks already have reached the outside verge of modesty. We have done quite enough for our country to-night, I think; why shouldn't we try what a little sleep will do for our noble selves?"

Calverly laughed a jolly laugh in his huge ruddy beard.

"You're a pretty specimen of a patriot, Mark, you are! Gad! I shouldn't mind taking my turn at some of the duty-work you went through to-night. You didn't fag over it, it struck me. I don't wonder you're in such a hurry to get to bed: I suppose you're pretty safe to dream of the White Widow."

"I never dream," said the other, as they parted.

A short walk brought Ramsay home. He occupied the first floor of one of those pleasant houses that are to be found in certain quiet nooks of Mayfair, that, lying close to the stream of traffic, are never troubled by its rattle. The rooms were very large and lofty, and the rich furniture, though luxuriant to a degree, was subdued in tone. They had been bachelor's chambers from time immemorial, since the days of the Millamants and Wildairs; and no tenant had yet been tempted to mar the effect of the carved cornices and panels by any new-fangled devices of modern upholstery.

"I never dream."

It was a bitter truth. Neither waking nor sleeping did idle visions trouble Mark Ramsay. The deep-blue eyes, that seemed made for dreaming, rarely looked far into futurity—more rarely still into the past—but always straight and keenly at the goal set before them; never slackening in their gaze, or turning aside, till the race was fairly lost or won.

Despite the virtuous resolves he had expressed so lately, Ramsay seemed in no great haste to betake himself to rest, but sat down by his fire,—which was still burning, for the spring mornings were chill,—and began to build up the coals, in the slow mechanical fashion of one whose thoughts are busy elsewhere. At length he rose, frowning a little, and muttered half aloud these two words :—

" I will."

Now, when Mark Ramsay said, " I will," whether with a smile or a frown on his face, it meant a good deal. This is what it meant now.

Utterly vicious, cruel, and false,—for he was not more pitiless in pursuit than in abandonment,—he was not one of those tinseled Lovelaces who, on the strength of some few conquests, more or less easily achieved, are always dinning into your ears their noisy pæan,—

She is a woman, therefore to be won.

Mark was too good an engineer to conclude, simply because he had assisted at several victories by siege, sap, or storm, that no fortress was impregnable. Nay, more, he had learned to estimate very justly the precise strength, natural or artificial, of the place beleaguered. He had not known Blanche Ellerslie—intimately at least—very long; but he had known her long enough to be assured that there was but one way to win her. The austerest devotee in all Belgravia was not less likely to be beguiled into criminal folly than the dainty little coquette, who only rebuked audacity with a deprecating smile.

Now, Mark Ramsay—not only from the manner of his life, but from the bent of his inclination—had hitherto been exceedingly averse to wedlock. It had never entered into his head to divide the competence which barely sufficed his own needs with a woman no richer than himself. Liking luxury well, he liked liberty better, and preferred a dinner of potherbs to such banquets as purse-proud or wealthy heiresses purvey. That he was not often called upon to exercise self-denial you may well imagine. The fish must be hungry indeed that will rise at such baits as an evil reputation and a shallow purse; and more than one of the women who had sacrificed duty and honor and happiness for Mark Ramsay would have shrunk from finding him a wife among their own kith and kin.

The case was widely different now. Even Arline

probably slept infinitely sounder, after the first strangeness of novelty was past, under the fretted roof of Arnheim than ever she did under gipsy tent or cold twinkling stars; and Mark was never a thorough Bohemian. He was quite ready to admit that wealth, no less than nobility, obliges, and was quite ready to act up to his new duties, at least in outward seeming. Knowing that a *châtelaine* was sorely needed at Kenlis Castle, he had resolved within himself that the void should ere long be filled. But this was not to be hastily or rashly done.

Despite his antecedents, of choice there was now no lack. Matrons, however extreme to mark what is done amiss by paupers or detrimentals, are not prone to disbelieve in the penitence of Dives; and the sternest guardian of our sheepcotes will open the wicket readily enough to the wandering wether that carries fleece of gold. Also there are damsels always to be found, courageous and charitable enough to devote themselves so thoroughly to the good work of guiding the reclaimed sinner aright, as to be willing to walk on with him thenceforward through life hand in hand.

But over the ranks of the maiden battalion Mark Ramsay's eyes roved, admiringly perhaps, never longingly. He was not troubled either with scruples or remorse; but he would no more have thought of asking a young innocent girl to cast in her lot with him for better and for worse, than he would have sat down to play piquet with a boy who could not count the points of the game. Neither did the taming of a *lioncelle* tempt him a whit. He had seen such ventures turn out happily enough; indeed, there was fair promise of a like event in that very house from which he had just come; but he did not believe for an instant that such cases were parallel with his own. Insurance tables are not infallible; neither are years always to be reckoned by their mere number. Men like Hugh of Nithsdale, who have led from youth upward an honest, healthy life, taking duty and pleasure in their fair turn, have in them the moral, if not physical, vitality—very often both—of a dozen Mark Ramsays.

Though he was wonderfully self-reliant and confident in

his own resources, there was very little trivial vanity about this man. He had held his own—only too successfully thus far—against all comers; but he knew this could not last forever. Another victory or two, perhaps, and then he would be fain to stand aside among the veterans, and watch the feats of younger champions, with the mild satisfaction of criticism or comparison; for "age will be served." Years and years ago he had seen in Paris a sparkling little comedy wherein a choice specimen of the *ancien régime* was made to enter the lists with divers aspirants to his young wife's favor, and vanquish each and every one with tact, tongue, or sword. He remembered thinking at the time how much pains and ingenuity had been spent for small purpose—how unlikely it was that the gallant old marquis would repeat his triumph— how impossible he could repeat it forever. Having but faint.regard for most laws, human or divine, he believed implicitly in the *lex talionis.* He guessed with what malicious scrutiny his domestic life would be watched; and how little sympathy the assailant of others' peace was likely to meet with if his own were imperiled; what exultation, covert if not expressed, would be felt in certain quarters if it came fairly to wreck. It was odd enough, yet true, that he had never in all his life experienced one real pang of jealousy. What if this infirmity were to come, in the train of others, with advancing years? He had seen the faces of better and wiser men wax haggard and drawn under the slow torment; and he had no mind to see such a reflection in his own mirror. It was many years since he had read the *Betrothed;* but, if he had forgotten all other points of the tale, he had not forgotten the substance of stout Wilkin Flammox's speech to the constable :—

"Think her shut up in yonder solitary castle, under such respectable protection, and reflect how long the place will be solitary in this land of love and adventure! We shall have minstrels singing ballads by the score under our windows, and such twangling of harps as would be enough to frighten our walls from their foundations, as clerks say happened to those of Jericho."

Mark Ramsay shivered within himself at the bare idea

of such a charge as the captaincy of La Garde Doloreuse.

No.   The helpmeet for him was a woman who could sweep graciously and gracefully along the world's highway, not with prim precaution, yet keeping her dainty feet clear of mire and pitfalls; with a face still so fair that his own eyes might look on it long without wearying; with a charm of manner that would keep her attractive even if the face should fade; with tastes sufficiently in unison with his own to promise pleasant companionship in default of perfect sympathy betwixt them; a woman, in fine, who could take her place worthily among the beauties of many generations whose portraits lined the walls of Kenlis Castle.

Such a one Mark thought he had found quite lately.

He had long been familiar with Blanche Ellerslie's name; when they first met he felt only a languid curiosity, and desire to prove for himself whether fame had exaggerated the danger of her society.   But before the first hour was over he became sensible, with rather pleasant surprise, that he was becoming subject to the fascination that had enthralled so many, and recognized that there were fresh sensations still for his jaded palate.   As they were thrown together, her influence grew on him more and more.   He no longer watched her coquetries leveled at others with the calm amusement of a mere spectator.   Once or twice, when he found himself forestalled in attracting attention, he had stood aside, smiling a little disdainfully, yet conscious all the while of a sharp sullen pang that he could not account for.   You see, up to this time, Mark had never been quite certain that he had a heart, in the common acceptation of the term, and so could not be expected to be well up in the symptoms of cardiac disease.   At last he was fain to confess to himself that he was as firmly and fiercely bent on the winning of Blanche Ellerslie as he had ever been on winning any woman, living or dead.   He had given up, almost from the first, any idea of attaining this end in any way save one—the making her his wife.

And now you know what those two words meant that hovered on Ramsay's lips as he betook himself to his rest.

CHAPTER V.

Both in high and low places of this world there are found scores of homely, humdrum persons, who, plodding on through life in their own placid way, are always equal to any emergency whatsoever, and come out of such ordeals infinitely better than their flashy fellows.

Hugh, Earl of Nithsdale, was one of those. He was thoroughly bucolic in his tastes; never so happy as when jogging about on his quiet old cob, chatting with his tenants, or planning improvements with his steward and wood-reeve. He held Cowper to be the very chief of English poets, simply for having penned the words

God made the country, but man made the town.

That hackneyed line seemed to him the embodiment of one of the noblest truths that have ever been promulgated in prose or verse. He never breathed quite freely in an atmosphere laden with smoke and penned in betwixt brick and mortar, and felt far wearier after a lounge over pavement or trim gravel than after a trudge through the stiffest clay in the Midland shires. I believe, if the truth were known, he kept a private calendar in school-boy fashion, and marked off the days of the London season, congratulating himself, as he lay down each night, that his holidays were so much nearer. In general society he was not only silent and reserved, but shy to boot, and would flee from the face of morning visitors, to hide himself in the recesses of his library till such tyranny was overpast.

Nevertheless, when the saloons of Nithsdale House were full, the master of the mansion seemed thoroughly at home and at his ease, and essentially the right man in the right place. No critic could have found a flaw in the gentle, grave courtesy with which he received his guests and cared for their comfort. Having to welcome, for the first time in his life, certain august personages, he went through the ceremony, not with the tremor of one on whom unmerited or unexpected honor is conferred, but like a man whose ancestors, from immemorial time, have been deemed worthy of a place at the right hand of royalty, whether in feast or fray.

Not a few there present noticed this, and spoke of it afterward with a little wonder. The Countess Rose was not so busy but that she found leisure to mark how her husband bore himself, and to feel proud of him withal. When she had said "good-night" for the last time, she was too utterly weary to talk, even to him, and crept off to her pillow, whereon, till long after the sun was high, she slept the deep dreamless sleep that comes after toilsome triumph. But her first waking thought was a regret that she had not thanked her dear, kind Hugh for playing his part so well.

Nothing short of illness, or a social revolution, would have broken the even current of the earl's methodical ways. Late as it was when he lay down to rest, he rose at his usual hour, and was hard at work in his library— for business letters were unusually numerous that morning—when a message came that the countess meant to lunch in her boudoir, and begged that he would join her.

Only once before, since their marriage, had the earl been so favored. It was when Rose was kept for a day in her rooms, from the effects of a chill. He felt as pleased as a boy who has been asked to an impromptu picnic, and at the appointed hour he mounted the stair with an eager haste curiously contrasting with his usually sober gait. Yet he stood still for an instant in the doorway. Truly it was a picture worth pausing over that he saw.

The countess was lying, almost at full length, on a low, broad sofa. The Mazarin blue of the huge pillows in which her slight figure was half buried brought out in relief the soft tints of her face and hair; though her face was paler than usual, and there were dark circles under the long, brown eyes. A pair of dainty slippers, broidered to match her *peignoir*, just peeped out under the ample skirt of soft gray silk with broad cerise facings

LADY NITHSDALE.

Page 40.

Her husband thought—perhaps with justice—that he had never looked on anything so lovely, and his grave voice faltered a little with very tenderness, as he leant over her, saying,—

"Very tired, my darling? I am sure I don't wonder."

She wound her arm round his neck, and drew his head down, lower and lower, till his cheek rested on her lips.

"Only pleasantly tired, Hugh; and it was worth while, was it not? Fancy my going to bed without thanking you for all the trouble you took to make it go off well! You dear, patient thing! I was watching you all the time, and you never yawned once, though you hate late hours so."

The earl laughed quite merrily as he sat down on the footstool close to his wife's side, keeping her hand in his, and counting the jewels in her rings, one by one.

"You foolish child, did you think that all the burden of doing the honors was to be laid on your poor little shoulders? These things haven't been much in my line; you're right there. And I dare say I made some bungle that you never noticed; but I shall improve by practice. I wasn't bored for one single instant—I was too busy; and it was quite amusement enough for me to watch you enjoying yourself. You did that, I think; though you looked rather nervous at first."

"Yes, I did enjoy myself," she said. "But I think I am happier, now that I am quite sure you were not bored. My conscience is quite easy now, and—I do hope they've sent us something nice for lunch; I'm so awfully hungry."

It was a very pleasant meal—the pleasanter, perhaps, to one of the partakers thereof because there was not the faintest chance of its being intruded on; for the most familiar of Lady Nithsdale's friends—the few to whom the formal interdict of "not at home" had ceased to apply—would never have dreamt of breaking in on her repose till much later in the day. Lady Daventry herself was scarce likely to show before afternoon tea. When lunch was cleared away, and they were alone again, said the Countess Rose,—

"Now, Hugh, I particularly wish to know if you

noticed one single thing go wrong last night, or that you would have wished otherwise."

The earl pondered awhile. He was very loath to damp his wife's elation, were it ever so little; but he was too honest to keep back the truth.

"Well, there was one thing, Rose," he said, hesitatingly. "Don't be alarmed: it was a very trifling thing. Your invitation list was perfect, with one exception—I do wish you hadn't asked Mr. Kendall."

Lady Nithsdale raised her long eyelashes in languid surprise.

"Now you do puzzle me. Why on earth should you object to poor Horace Kendall? I fancied you didn't even know him by sight. I hardly know him myself; but I should have mortally offended Lady Longfield if I had refused him a card. From what I have seen of him, I should think him the most inoffensive creature alive, though he is so clever in his own way."

The earl bent his shaggy brows till they met.

"There's no more harm in Lady Longfield than in most other empty-headed women, I dare say; but she's too fond of patronage to be very careful where she bestows it. It's quite as well she has no daughters of her own to look after. I never saw Mr. Kendall, to my knowledge, till yesterday; but I have heard quite enough. It's the fashion to cultivate him now, of course. That don't make him, in my mind, a bit more fitting friend for your sister. And I don't believe, Rose, you'd consider him so perfectly inoffensive if you had watched, as I did, how completely he engrossed Nina last night."

Now, the earl—though about the last man living to wish to level or lower the standard of his order—was singularly unapt to stand upon its privileges. He would talk just as frankly and genially with one of his own farmers as with the inheritor of forty quarterings; and even the Radical solicitor who opposed him at elections, and strove in all ways to undermine his county influence, never hinted that Lord Nithsdale had a purpose in being, as he expressed it, "so infernally affable." Very seldom in all his life had he been heard to speak hardly or harshly to any fellow-creature. Indeed, he had sometimes scandalized his brother magistrates at Quarter Sessions by his ingenuity in finding excuses for criminals. No one knew this better than his wife; and she felt he must have good reason for so speaking, though she answered. laughingly,—

"Nina! You don't mean that puss got into mischief at her first ball? She ought to have been sent supperless to bed, at least. No, I noticed nothing; but I wonder mamma didn't, though she is so dreadfully short-sighted. She was too busy helping me, I suppose. The child shall have a real good scolding when she comes to tea."

Flirtations were things so entirely out of Lord Nithsdale's line, that it may be worth while to explain his reasons for interference.

CHAPTER· VI.

A **quarter** of a century ago few people, living beyond its immediate neighborhood, were aware of the existence of such a place as Swetenham. Lying somewhat out of the great highway to the West, it was scarcely possible to conceive any traveler being attracted there on business, and the country around was not sufficiently picturesque to tempt artistic explorers. Everything is changed now. Almost the sole relic of the quiet little hamlet is the gray old church-tower, that seems strangely misplaced among the red-brick street-rows radiating from the station on a well-traveled branch-line.

The great men of those parts, for many generations, had been the Vernons of Vernon Mallory. The then-time representative of that family was a very unpopular character; and deservedly so; for his manners and morals rather beseemed a Hungarian magnate than a decent English squire. Arrogant among his equals, he ground down dependents and inferiors to a dead level of servility; hunted poachers like wild beasts, with hound, if not with horn; and in more ways than one evinced ideas of feudal privileges, utterly out of date even in the earlier part of the nineteenth century. Several children had been born to him by a wife, endowed with a temper almost as haughty as his own, who was not inclined to condone his numberless infidelities. Horace Vernon was a profligate of the worst possible form; his victims were chosen usually from the class whose wrongs, by virtue of his station, he was bound to redress; and he was utterly unscrupulous as to the means of working out his will. His love, or the brutal passion that he dignified by the name, was more harmful than his anger; and it was better to see his cruel eyes set like black flint-stones, than melting into treacherous softness. Educational boards, and middle-class examinations, had not come into existence then; and radicalism had not spread far beyond the outskirts of towns: peasants and small yeomen, in many remote rural districts, were as stupidly patient and irrationally loyal as any Carinthian boor. Men would look up from their work and scowl as the wicked squire rode by, and perhaps growl a curse under their breath; but none murmured or complained aloud: even in the ale-house, when tongues were loosened by liquor, only a glum, significant silence followed the mention of his name. So long as Horace Vernon was not thwarted abroad, he cared little for being called to account at home; and went on the tenor of his way, reckless, if not rejoicing. Nevertheless, in the great house there was discontent always, and not seldom bitter word-duels.

If the dwellers in and about Swetenham were not lucky in their landlord, they could boast of one blessing not to be despised. It was the healthiest place possible. It lay in a broad valley, sheltered to the east and north, but athwart which there was free passage for the pleasant breezes that swept over the chalk downs. So the sanitary requirements of the neighborhood were easily satisfied; indeed, there was no more than work enough for a single practitioner.

For nearly fifty years this post had been filled by a certain Dr Thorner. All medical men were "doctors" in those parts and those days, without regard to their precise diploma or degree. You needed only to watch him jogging along behind his sober old pony, and coming to a stand-still wherever he got a chance of a gossip on the road or over a gate, to guess at once that there was seldom urgent need for his services. In truth, these were chiefly confined to bringing young folks into the world, and helping old ones to slide out of it comfortably. But the shadow on the dial kept creeping on—a little more slowly, perhaps, than in other places, yet still creeping on, even in Swetenham. Dr. Thorner felt less equal to his work, light as it was, and less patient of interruptions to his night's rest. He had saved more than enough to furnish thenceforward his modest needs; but was too wise to give up practice altogether, for the bread of utter idleness would certainly have disagreed with his digestion; so he determined to retire on half-pay for the present, and to take an assistant. One fine morning a new doctor appeared in Swetenham.

James Kendall was a man of about thirty, with a sharp fox face and foxy hair; a low though not a pleasant voice; and a manner that most people found disagreeably obsequious. The master of Vernon Mallory was not easily surfeited with servility: from the very first he seemed to take a fancy to the new-comer, and treated him with more courtesy—cold as it was—than he had ever shown to the honest, homely old man who had assisted at his own birth and the deaths of both his parents.

The discords and bickerings at the great house had waxed bitterer of late; indeed, ever since the establishment there of Mademoiselle Adèle Deshon in the quality of governess. She was a Provençale; rather piquante than pretty: perhaps her only real attractions were large velvety eyes, and a superb contralto voice, perfectly trained. The 'quire was really fond of music, and himself no mean performer; so perhaps it was only natural that he should take pleasure in Mademoiselle Adèle's performances, and, to a certain extent, pleasure in her society. But Lady Eleanor Vernon in no wise saw the matter in this light. She did not care to dissemble her dislike to the foreigner; and soon was not ashamed to put her suspicions into words. Ere long reports came to her ears that fanned the jealous embers into flame—reports of meetings, frequent and prolonged, not in her presence; and of words and actions that Griselda would scarce have looked on tamely. Then the Lady Eleanor took up the daggers in earnest; and there was a battle-royal—a battle such as the servants (unhappily used to such scenes) spoke of afterwards with 'bated breath—a battle that was bound, one way or another, to be decisive.

Oddly enough, the event was not such as might have been expected from the relative strength of the belligerents. At the moment when she seemed certain of defeat, Lady Eleanor, for the first time in her matronly broils, fell back upon "her family;" and that army of reserve turned the fortunes of the day. With all his violence, Horace Vernon was not blinded by passion; though he might utterly disregard the good or bad opinion of his poorer neighbors, he was by no means indifferent to the opinion of the county at large, or inclined to risk his own position therein. He knew very well that this would be jeopardized, and seriously too, if he were brought into open collision with the House of Arlington—a house thrice as powerful as his own, and not less unscrupulous than himself in the exercise of their power. If Lady Eleanor betook herself to her own people, insisting on a separation, with grounds of complaint just and grave, the squire guessed that place would no longer be found for him among the magnates of the land. Many who never troubled themselves to sift reports, or inquire into village scandal, would have been earnest enough in their partisanship when it was a question of Lady Eleanor Vernon's wrongs.

Though the squire cursed and stormed more savagely than his wont, evidently weakness was at the bottom of all that fume and fury. The wife kept her temper in a manner marvelous for one of her character—kept her ground too steadfastly—and at last carried her point, as she well deserved.

It chanced that James Kendall came to Vernon Mallory that same afternoon to visit one of the household. After leaving his patient he was summoned to the squire's study, and remained closeted there for a full hour. When he drove away, there was a great satisfaction on his cunning face, tempered by the momentary distaste of a man who has bound himself to perform some hard or unpleasant service on exceedingly remunerative terms. Immediately afterward Mdlle. Deshon was called into her master's presence. The interview was long, and, if domestic tittle-tattle is to be believed, very tempestuous. Some servants passing near the study-door heard the Provençale's rich round voice strained and shrill in plaint or reviling; answered by the deep harsh tones that, when Horace Vernon was angered, sounded like the growl of distant thunder. When Mdlle. Adèle came forth, she went straight to her own chamber, whence she emerged no more that evening; but one of the housemaids, who crossed her on her way thither, averred that "Mam'sell looked as pale as a turnip, and her eyelids were as red and puffed as ripe gooseberries." The next morning the village gossips—there were gossips in an out-of-the-way hamlet five-and-twenty years ago—were startled by the news that the new doctor had been for some time past engaged to the governess at the great house, and that the marriage would take place shortly.

A week later, it was noised abroad that Dr. Thorner had, for a liberal consideration, been induced to abandon his practice altogether to his assistant; and that thenceforward Swetenham and the neighborhood would be under James Kendall's sole medical care.

It was a very quiet wedding. The only person of any importance present was the squire himself, whose louring face would have suited a funeral better than such a ceremony; and neither the bride nor the bridegroom looked precisely like people whose uttermost happiness is crowned. Before Adèle had been long a wife, a weakness in her lungs displayed itself—at least, so her husband said, and he, of course, must have known best— that could only be arrested by removal to a warmer climate. So she went to her own people in Provence, and abode with them nearly twelve months. She returned to all appearance perfectly recovered, bringing with her a handsome dark-haired boy—extraordinarily forward for

a yearling—who had already been christened " in honor"
—Adèle was wont to murmur demurely—" of our good
friend and benefactor up yonder."   The precise nature of
such benevolence she never cared to define; neither into
such matters was it anybody's special business to inquire.

In the twenty years that ensued, Dr. Kendall certainly
prospered.   He was clever in his profession, and wrought
many cures in cases where honest old Thorner would
have thrown up his hands in despair; and his practice
had largely increased, especially since the branch railway
was begun; for the navvies were not only always cutting
and maiming themselves after their fashion, but also in-
fected the neighborhood with evil habits of debauch and
drink.   So grist flowed in fast to the medical mill—not
quite fast enough though for all the luxuries in which his
wife indulged, nor for the expensive education of his son.
Being an only child, it was perhaps likely that Horace
should be much indulged; but one or two of the more
sharp-sighted of Kendall's neighbors thought the doctor's
manner was scarcely that of an overfond father.   He
seemed to yield to the boy's whims, and overlook his insolence, rather because it was politic than pleasant to him
so to do.   With each year, Horace seemed less inclined
to cumber himself with putting on even a decent semblance of filial respect.   All the affection he had to spare
centered itself in his mother, who certainly deserved it by
her intense devotion: it was a great trial to both when
Horace left home to live permanently in London, on his
appointment to a clerkship in the Rescript Office.

Retribution for the sins of his youth had come heavily,
in more ways than one, on the master of Vernon Mallory.
He had plunged deep into speculation of late years, with
the headlong obstinacy of a man who will listen to no
counsels but his own, believing the rest of mankind to be
either fools or knaves.   He struggled out of the quag-
mire, not absolutely ruined, but crippled in income for the
rest of his life.   The expenses of his family—though he
grudged every shilling not spent on his own comfort—
added to his numerous ailments, caused the squire to
break up his establishment and reside almost always

abroad. His last act before leaving England was to exert his influence to obtain that clerkship in the Rescript Office for Horace Kendall. Competitive examinations were not as yet; and Vernon of Vernon Mallory had always shown himself a stanch adherent to the party then in power. It was not a great boon for a man to ask, who brought up as many votes to an election as he could count tenants; for none of these had yet been found bold or enlightened enough to run counter to their lord's will. Such a patriot would have been dismissed very speedily to ruminate in fresh pastures on the blessings of independence and the privileges of our glorious constitution.

Horace Kendall began life under auspices exceptionably favorable for a country apothecary's son. He had personal advantages of no mean order. His face was decidedly handsome, in the *jeune premier* style, with a delicacy of feature almost effeminate; and he had the full, eloquent Provençal eyes; his figure was, though long and loosely hung, one of those that make up well under the hands of an artistic tailor; his manner, though sometimes rather affected, was not devoid of a certain grace; and by some mysterious means there was provided for him an allowance more than sufficient.

Yet, for awhile, he seemed not likely to make the best of a good start, and among his immediate associates was decidedly unpopular. The Rescript Office men were not more fastidious than other civil servants; but they generally contrived to find out something concerning the antecedents of each fresh recruit to their small and select company. There were several among them not much, if at all, superior to Kendall in birth—according to his reputed parentage—who got on perfectly with their fellows, both in and out of office-hours. But then these men bore themselves modestly, not with the assumption in which Horace saw fit to indulge.

There are degrees and differences in conceit, as every one knows. There is the light, frothy conceit, easily blown away with a strong breath, which not unfrequently floats on the surface of a generous nature. There is the puerile conceit of the spoiled page, which provokes a not ill-natured laugh from manhood and often meets encouragement from women.   Lastly, there is the conceit in-grain,—at which none are inclined to smile, even if they chafe not thereat,—that betrays itself not so much by vaunting words as by subtle self-assertion.   This last, surely, never since the world began, has been known to leaven stuff out of which brave or wise or honest men are made.

"A natural curiosity," said Walter Rougemont, the heraldic authority of the Rescript Office.   "That super-cilious look of his yesterday, and the way in which he minced out 'Cheltenham' when Goodenough talked of having been at school there, were quite a study.   But when I want to see natural curiosities I go to a museum. If he knew his own interests, he would not always be provoking people to ask, 'who is he?'   I'm not quite clear about it yet, but I have more than a vague notion that, if he's any right to armorial bearings, it is as a 'Fitz'-somebody or other.   I vote we begin seriously to take the conceit out of him.   The man's a perfect nuisance, as he stands."

Now, this exhaustive process, however sanitary in the end, is intensely disagreeable to the patient.   Kendall's self-sufficiency was in no wise proof against the keen sharp-pointed shafts that ever and anon sought out the joints of his harness; and, when he was free from such annoyance, the sense of isolation was almost more intol-erable.   Ere long, Horace felt so thoroughly ill at ease that he was sorely tempted to resign, and seek fortune elsewhere.   While his first London season was yet young, all such notions vanished, and his social prospects bright-ened suddenly.

Kendall's visiting-list was, thus far, very limited; but he chanced one night to be present at a large musical party whereat most of the *cognoscenti* then in London were assembled.   He knew hardly any one there, and hovered rather disconsolately near the piano, where some-how he felt rather more at home.   It was not a set pro-gramme, and there was plenty of room for amateurs as well as professionals to display their talent; but it was rather late before the mistress of the house bethought her-self of asking Kendall to sing.

"He has rather a singing face," she thought, "and must be fond of music, or he would not have been hovering round the instrument all night."

Horace complied very willingly. He was not a whit troubled with bashfulness, and reckoned—not without reason—on some sort of a triumph, though most assuredly not on such a one as he obtained. His audience were fairly taken by storm. Professionals were not less enthusiastic than amateurs in their praise of the purest tenor voice that had been heard in London saloons for many a day; and those who understood such matters best affirmed that there was in it a latent power that only needed to be developed to surpass many of high renown on the stage.

Thenceforward Horace's immediate future was assured. On the morrow morning he woke and found himself The Fashion; what that terse and rather vulgar expression signifies, every one knows. Before long, as far as evening parties were concerned, he was only troubled by the embarrassment of choice. His fellows in the Rescript Office liked him perhaps not a whit better; but they could not help feeling a certain pride at counting among their subalterns such a celebrity; and they could not deny that he had some right to give himself airs now —the which privilege Kendall was not minded to neglect.

Adèle Kendall was not a model, either as a wife or a mother; but the wisest and purest of women need not have been ashamed of such tears as clouded her eyes as she laid down the letter in which her son's first success was set forth, and in a long sweet day-dream built up a stately air-temple, fit one day to be her idol's shrine.

Among those who cultivated the new celebrity most assiduously was the Lady Longfield mentioned above, concerning whom Hugh of Nithsdale spoke so irreverently. She was one of those wealthy worthy widows, with hearts even larger than their purses, who seem to thrive nowhere so naturally as on English soil, who always mean thoroughly well by their generation, even if they do not greatly contribute to its credit or well-being. Among all followers of that *haute vénerie* there was found no more intrepid "lion-hunter." "Lion-slayer" to boot she was called by her detractors; in truth, sooner or later, in one fashion or another, her *protégés* generally managed to come to grief. But, putting a little harmless vanity aside, she had no selfish motive in the pursuit; and, though her days of mourning lasted not long, no one regretted more sincerely the shortcomings or downfall of her favorites. For the time being, she spoiled them intensely, and no amount of disappointments could teach her discretion in patronage. She might be as plaintive as you please overnight; but the joy of a fresh and rarer discovery was almost sure to come with the morning; and her moan over the monarch of her affections was scarcely made, before on her lips resounded a jubilant "Long live the king!"

It was very pleasant to have the *entrée* at all canonical hours to that charming mansion in Mayfair, where every domestic detail was faultless, and visitors found themselves metaphorically, no less than literally, on velvet; but the atmosphere would have been pernicious to a healthier nature than Horace Kendall's. Very few men of his age can occupy the oracular tripod round which clouds of incense are always steaming, with senses sober and clear; and fewer still can feed on flattery daily, without waxing overweening as Jeshurun on the rich, unwholesome diet.

Lady Longfield did not scruple to suggest to her new favorite that he should abandon at once mechanical quill-driving, and seek fame and fortune on the operatic stage. To this plan Horace lent a not unwilling ear. Whilst it was yet immature, he wrote to Swetenham, setting forth this new project, in perfect confidence of its meeting with assent and encouragement. Had the answer rested with her alone, it is certain Mrs. Kendall would have tried to promote this like any other whim of her spoiled darling; but she was fain to take others into counsel. Within a week there came from across the seas a veto, curt, stern, and decisive, that neither mother nor son dared disregard; so for the present Horace was fain to content himself with private ovations, instead of aspiring to public triumphs.

There was a faint savor of bitterness in the luscious cup that day by day he drained so eagerly. His presence was sought by many melo-maniacs in the "upper ten:" yet his overweening vanity did not blind him to the fact that it was in a semi-professional capacity that he was welcomed in their houses. Only at Lady Longfield's he was thoroughly at home. His hostesses were civil and grateful to a degree; but after their most elaborate compliments and expansive thanksgiving, he felt as if he were being paid in kind, if not in coin. Their daughters were liberal of pretty speeches and smiles; but somehow he never found his way into a *coterie;* and, with every advantage of time and place, he could never bring off one of the "cosy two-handed cracks" contrived, even in the heart of a crowded assembly, by barbarians who had not so much as heard of the chromatic scale.

With men he was not a whit more popular than before he began to be famous. They had no purpose to serve in gaining his "most sweet voice ;" and troubled themselves very little with his whims or his ways—always excepting certain *parvenus* and their parasites, to whom notoriety was a sufficient attraction. Not many seemed to care for more than a nodding acquaintance with Kendall; and when he sought to be admitted into a certain club—not ill-naturedly exclusive as a rule—he was "pilled" pitilessly.

With all his fatuity, Horace had a keen cunning eye for his own interests, and very just ideas as to the wisdom of filling his garner whilst the sun shone. A marriage that by connection, if not by mere dowry, would assure his position thenceforth forever, was the aim set steadfastly before him. There was nothing wildly improbable in such ambition. Was he not, in common with other frequenters of the Mile, dazzled daily by the gorgeous equipages of Camille Desmoulins, who, not long ago, had been content with the modest salary of a second-rate tenor; and was it not known how the said Camille, with no other exertion—bodily or intellectual—had so warbled himself into the good graces of a wealthy widow, that she proffered him the guardianship of her venerable person and of her vast worldly goods? Kendall knew himself to be an adventurer, and felt no shame in avowing it to himself; reckoning his chances and resources quite coolly, he came to the conclusion that he had the pull of most of his rivals in the ignoble race.

Nevertheless, the curtain dropped on the summer season, the country visits that engrossed almost all his autumn furlough were over, the mild dissipations of winter were past—and his object as yet assumed no more definite form and substance than the shadows that cross magic mirrors or glide past the watchers on All-Hallows-eve. Horace waxed discontented, if not disappointed; but, before the spring was far advanced, there came a salve to his wounded vanity.

Gwendoline—more familiarily called Nina Marston—was, as the most indulgent of her friends and kinsfolk allowed, "a very odd girl." She was not eighteen yet, so that her character could scarcely have developed itself; yet even now it presented the strangest contrast of weakness and strength. In what manner Lady Daventry's children were trained has already been told. Nina was no exception to the general *laissez-aller* rule; indeed, being decidedly independent, not to say turbulent, by nature, she emancipated herself sooner than Rose had done from the light thraldom of the governess, and, being less a favorite with her mother, was left more entirely to her own devices. She was as different as possible from her sister, physically no less than morally. Till you remembered how such peculiarities reappear capriciously after the lapse of generations, and that within the last century and a half there had come a Spanish cross into the Marston blood, you would have been puzzled to account for the wavy black hair, and the eyes more intensely black that lit up the small, dark, resolute face. After being an hour in Nina Marston's company, and watching the play of her lips, you guessed that she was a woman already in willfulness and tenacity of purpose; yet impulsive withal, and romantic to a degree most uncommon in these days, when our very school-girls smile at the love-conceits which beguiled their granddames, even as *they* may have smiled at the philandering of Arcadia.

It was at the very beginning of Nina's first season, before her presentation dress was ordered, that she met Horace Kendall at a morning concert, and heard him sing. As she drove home she said to herself, "she had met her fate." Now, in the mouths of most girls, such words would have been a mere form of romantic speaking; with Nina, it unhappily was not so.

She was none of the little melo-dramatic heroines who talk by rote, but one of those who play out their parts, good or bad, only too naturally. They met tolerably often after that first day. Horace Kendall was no dunce in such matters; but it needed no expert to decipher the language of the great earnest eyes, that rested on him with such rapt attention while he was singing, and followed him afterward, till they hid themselves shyly under their long lashes if their pursuit was detected. He came from the Nithsdale ball with a pleasant conviction of "having made an impression in that quarter," and a firm resolve to work out the chance to the uttermost.

Lady Daventry did not bow down and worship before the newly-discovered star. She was quite content with her own set, and found her house sufficiently attractive without calling in the aid of talent, professional or otherwise. Nevertheless, Horace was sufficiently well acquainted with her to warrant his seeking an introduction to Nina early in the evening. Lady Daventry was not at the best of times a vigilant chaperon; and all her energies that night were engrossed in giving aid and encouragement to her elder daughter; she performed the presentation almost mechanically, and was too busy afterward to notice the flirtation which gave umbrage to Hugh of Nithsdale. Had she known of it, it is possible that haughty dame would not have lain down to rest without a single misgiving of the complete success of the entertainment.

Rose Nithsdale was too thoroughly good-natured to get any one, gentle or simple, into a scrape if she could possibly avoid it; and had a great horror even of the mildest domestic discussion. She stood in great awe of Lady Daventry, who was, in truth, anything but a stern duenna. Nevertheless, she resolved that the punishment-parade should be strictly private; and, on some pretext or another, carried Nina off into her own dressing-room before she said a word concerning the misdemeanor of overnight. When Lady Nithsdale did speak, she spoke very much to the purpose, and with most unwonted earnestness and energy; but the culprit was quite impenitent, and seemed inclined to justify, if not to glory in, her guilt.

"I never heard so much ado about nothing," she said. "If I had waltzed five times running, or sat out half the night, with Regy Avenel, or any of that lot, I shouldn't have heard a word about it; and I don't see why Mr. Kendall isn't as good as any of them, though he don't happen to be in your set."

"We know who 'that lot' are, at all events," Rose Nithsdale said; "and of Mr. Kendall we know absolutely nothing, except that he sings charmingly. Regy Avenel would never have dreamed of compromising a child like you at her first ball."

"No, he only compromises married women. So kind of him—isn't it? So kind of you, too, to sacrifice yourselves to keep us out of harm's way. I thought you were too well amused last night, Rosie, to watch other people amusing themselves."

"I didn't watch you; but Hugh told me this morning ——" the countess checked herself abruptly, biting her pretty lip; she saw she had made a false move.

"Hugh is more than old enough to be my father, I'm quite aware of that," Nina retorted; "but while papa's alive I don't see that he's any right to treat me paternally. He'll have quite enough to do in looking after one Marston, I fancy, without taking all the family on his hands."

It was hard indeed to ruffle Lady Nithsdale's easy indolent temper; but she began to be provoked at the stubbornness of the reckless little rebel, and that last thrust touched her nearly. She rose up with no bad imitation of matronly dignity, considering how seldom she had tried to assume it.

"You're very ungrateful, Nina, and you speak very improperly about Hugh. It's only too good of him to try to keep you out of mischief. I didn't mean to worry mamma with this nonsense, but as you are so self-willed I must tell her about it. Perhaps she will make you listen to reason."

The stubborn defiant face changed into a look almost of terror. Nina was not the least afraid of her mother's anger; but she was mortally afraid of being put under surveillance; that would materially interfere with the carrying out of divers ingenious schemes, floating since last night in her busy brain.

"Oh, Rosie, you won't do that!" she whispered, coaxingly, nestling close to her sister's side. "I didn't mean to be ungrateful either to you or to Hugh—I didn't, indeed. If you only won't speak to mamma, I promise to be as good as you please."

Lady Nithsdale was only too happy to accept the olive-branch; she hated the idea of haling any one before the judgment-seat. In her own heart, she felt she was no more fitted to play the monitress, even to that willful child, than to teach a class in a Sunday-school. So she consented readily enough to connive for that once at Nina's derogation, and, without actually becoming surety for her sister, contrive to persuade her husband that the offense should be repeated no more.

CHAPTER VII.

MARK RAMSAY was none of those over-eager hunters who mar their own sport by impatience in the stalk. Every footfall that brought him nearer to his quarry was cautiously planted; so that no rustle of leaf or grass-blade should startle in her fancied security the fair hind he had marked for his own. Yet day by day, almost hour by hour, the distance between them lessened.

To those who knew Blanche Ellerslie, it would have seemed impossible that any man—not standing in the place of her accepted suitor—should find the field clear of rivalry more or less dangerous. Mark Ramsay's attentions were never persecuting or obtrusive—seldom, indeed, so marked as they had been at the Nithsdale ball. Yet, somehow or other, the "old loves," whose name was legion, found that an invisible circle was being drawn around her, wherein there was no rest for the soles of their feet. The small ear that used to listen so readily had grown strangely deaf to whispers of late; the delicate lips answered kindly and courteously, but no longer with the old temptations of mockery or gibe; the soft, eloquent eyes had grown pensive, and sometimes full of an anxiety which the most confident admirer could not flatter himself *he* inspired.

Even Oswald Gauntlet, the famous and fatal horse-gunner (by the rules of the service he had been trans-ferred twice or thrice into a field-battery, but even the War Office hadn't the heart to keep him there), who, ever since their first flirtation on first principles—begun when Blanche was scarcely seventeen and Oswald a beardless *aide-de-camp*—had retained his post of high confidant at the capricious little despot's court, no matter how other ministers were changed, found himself, to all intents and purposes, shelved. He was a warning to all "scufflers" present and to come, as he stood apart, twisting his long tawny mustache in angry bewilderment; always beset by the same dreary doubt, "Whether it was worth while to come up all the way from Woolwich for *this*"—"this" meaning a passing fan-salute, or careless smile, or per-chance a few words, to which all the world might have listened and been none the wiser.

Now, the thought of making Blanche Ellerslie his wife had never dwelt for an instant in Major Gauntlet's mind. He was too poor a man to dream of such a luxury, and he had never in his life spoken to her passionate or over-earnest words; but he was really attached to her in his own fashion, and he felt their estrangement keenly. Fur-thermore, putting all jealousies aside,—he was fain to confess to himself that he was jealous at last,—Oswald happened to have heard more than most people of Mark Ramsay's past; and he would have been sorry to see any woman, for whom he cared ever so little, given over to that man's keeping. One morning, Major Gauntlet went to lunch in Gaunt Square, with the fixed resolve, if he found opportunity, to take heart of grace and say out his say.

La Reine Gaillarde had a fine instinct in such matters, and somehow guessed that it would not be disagreeable to one of her guests at least if she left them alone. Any ordinary flirtation she was rather inclined to countenance than to hinder; and she was only too ready to aid and abet in anything that might possibly weaken Ramsay's growing influence over Blanche Ellerslie. So, when they went up-stairs after luncheon, the fair widow found herself *en champ clos*, with no possibility of escape unless by absolute flight, which she was not cowardly enough to contemplate. Had she not been five hundred times before alone with Oswald Gauntlet, and was it not too utterly absurd to feel awkward now? In spite of all this, she felt so nervous that it was almost a relief to her when he actually broke ground.

"I have been waiting for this chance some time, Blanche"—she was quite a girl when he came on her father's staff, and he had called her ever since by her Christian name—"and I'm not going to waste it by talking nonsense now. You know pretty well how much and how little I like you; and you know, too, whether I have deserved to be dropped as I have been of late. Good God! you're not going to deny it?" he broke out, almost fiercely, seeing that she was about to speak. "Surely we're too good friends still to begin that kind of fencing. I'm not going to quarrel with you; and, what's more, I don't complain. If a woman chooses that old acquaintance should be forgot, she's only using her woman's privilege. It's of your new acquaintance I'm going to speak."

Mrs. Ellerslie had sat a picture of pretty penitence till now, with bowed head and drooping eyelashes; at those last words, she drew herself up, and looked straight into Gauntlet's face.

"You mean Mr. Ramsay, I suppose."

"Could I mean any other?" he retorted. "Now, Blanche, just be patient and hear me out. I sha'n't bore you any more, after to-day. If I had asked you to marry me, any time when you were free, you'd have said, 'No,' I dare say. That's neither here nor there: but why I never could ask you, you know as well as I do.

When I heard you were going to be married to poor Ellerslie, I didn't like it at first, but I never grudged him his luck; and now, if I heard that the same luck had befallen any true honest man, I wouldn't grudge it him—I wouldn't, by God! But I should grudge it to Ramsay; for I don't believe he's either honest or true "

They had known each other very long, and Oswald had often amused himself with teasing the pettish little beauty; but he had never before seen real anger in her eyes.

"And that is your idea of truth and honesty," she said, speaking very low—"to revenge yourself for neglect that was never intended, by coming here to say to me what you never would dare to say to him ?"

Major Gauntlet had won his Cross, not by a single act of foolhardiness, but by repeated proofs of disciplined valor; and he could well have afforded to pass over such a suspicion coming from a man's lips. Coming from a woman's, it only made him smile.

"Wouldn't I?" he said, simply. "You are a very clever woman, Blanche Ellerslie—accustomed to read men's hearts, and all the rest of it—and you know best, of course. Now, I fancied, as I lay awake this morning, that there was nothing I should like better than to say to Mark Ramsay what I say to you—that he's not a fit person to be trusted with the happiness of any woman alive. There's not the least necessity for your telling me I have no right to interfere between him and you. I'm perfectly well aware of that; and another taunt like that last one won't make me forget it; but I wouldn't talk too much about ' daring,' if I were you. It's bad form, to say the least of it."

Blanche was thoroughly ashamed of herself long before he had done speaking.

"Those were very base words of mine," she said: "try and forget them. I am not used to being taken to task, and every one seems to have had a special call to do it lately; I thought I was safe with you. I have never known you so hard on my *fredaines* before : you might look sulky at first, but you always laughed at last."

"HE HAS NEVER ASKED ME."   Page 61.

"I wish I could laugh now," he said. "I'm doing nc good here, I see; but, Blanche, for old acquaintance' sake, answer me one question; never mind whether I've a right to ask it or not. In spite of all you have heard or may hear, do you mean to marry Ramsay?"

"He has never asked me."

The sentence meant little, but the shy, conscious look, and the trembling of the voice, meant—all. The other knew that darker proofs of Ramsay's unworthiness than he was prepared to bring forward, would only embitter Blanche against himself, without turning her aside one hair's-breadth from the path she was bent on pursuing. He rose up, with both her tiny hands in his own; and his handsome face was very pale, though he strove to speak lightly.

"Don't let us part in anger because I was fool enough to think that my warning would not come too late. Perhaps you'll need a friend yet before you die; when you do, you'll not forget me, if I'm to the fore? I sha'n't see much of you for some months to come. I've been offered to go on this commission that is to visit all the great fortresses and camps of Europe—a good thing for me, in more ways than one, just now. I suppose everything will be settled before I come back. So—good-by, Blanche, and God bless you!"

Oswald Gauntlet was by no means a devout man. I fear he seldom attended public worship unless on duty or some such sort of compulsion, and perhaps was not always regular in his private orisons. But no fanatic, trailing himself from shrine to shrine, ever uttered a petition more thoroughly heartfelt and earnest than was contained in those last three words. Whether that prayer reached the base of the Mercy-seat, or whether, like many petitions formed by more saintly lips, it was borne idly away by one of the winds that never blow in heaven, you will know hereafter who have patience to read to the end.

Thus the lady was left in possession of the field, whereon, to say the least of it, she had held her own. Yet she did not seem triumphant or victorious, as she sat there with her face buried in the sofa-pillow for some minutes. after she was left alone.   When she looked up again, her eyes were wet.

Her best friends—Laura Brancepeth, for example—called her a cruel coquette; yet there was much of softness, if not of tenderness, in her nature.   That same inconsistency has been noticed in much more famous criminals.   Mohammed's cat, and Couthon's lap-dog, are matters of history; and Count Fosco's canary has always seemed to me one of the happiest touches in a very powerful picture.   Though she had wrought so much harm in her time, Blanche had never with malice or of aforethought injured any living thing.   Her repentance was not keen or durable enough to keep her from falling into fresh temptation; yet. each and every one of her victims might have been consoled by knowing that Blanche's heart wore for him a decent half-mourning.   In one respect Mrs. Ellerslie had exceptional luck.   Among womankind she had enemies not a few; but men —no matter what wrong they had suffered at her hands —seemed incapable of nourishing rancor against her; in almost any company there might have been found champions ready and willing to buckler her good name against whomsoever should presume to assail it.   She was really fond of her cage-birds, though she teased them so terribly; and it was not her vanity only that suffered, when one of these found the use of his wings and escaped from bondage.

Major Gauntlet was not an ordinary pet.   Till within the last two months, she had liked and admired him more than any one she had known.   A soldier's daughter and a soldier's wife, she was able to appreciate soldierly renown: she liked to think that she had at her beck and call one whom brave hearts were proud to follow, and to carry on light word-warfare with the man whose name carried terror with it wherever it was spoken along the northwestern frontier of India.   Many maids and matrons, since Una walked in forest-land, have found it pleasant pastime to dally with the mane of a couchant lion.   She knew that Oswald had left her not in anger, and that she might count on his friendship now and always; but she knew, too, that it could never be the same between them any more, and that the ancient intimacy—half sportive, half tender—had that day gotten its death-blow.

When, after discreet absence, Laura Brancepeth returned, she found Mrs. Ellerslie looking so sorrowful that she could not forbear questioning.

"There's nothing the matter," Blanche said, with a little sob; "only I do so hate saying good-by; and that is what Oswald Gauntlet came here to say. He's going abroad, for I don't know how long, on some stupid commission or another."

Now, La Reine Gaillarde had an implicit belief in the dashing horse-gunner—not in matters martial alone—and had reckoned rather confidently on him as a counter-agent on the present occasion. It was provoking to her that he had so readily beaten retreat and left the field clear for other invading forces.

"Rather a sudden resolution, wasn't it? It was only the night before last, that Major Gauntlet was talking to me about his summer plans; and traveling on the continent was certainly not one of them. I wouldn't worry myself too much about saying good-by, Blanche, if I were you. You'll have to say it, sooner or later, to more than one old friend, I fancy. It's to be hoped the new ones will make you amends."

It was not often that Mrs. Ellerslie was at a loss for a reply; but now she could frame none,—unless a low reproachful whisper, "Oh, Queenie!" could be called such, —and escaped to her own room.

Those two were very silent during their drive. When they drew up under their favorite tree in the Mile, the least observant of her courtiers saw that something had ruffled the quick temper of La Reine Gaillarde; and the most successful of those who strove to engross Mrs. Ellerslie's attention was scarcely rewarded with a languid smile. While that especial carriage halted, there was always a kind of circle round it; but, by some strange coincidence, one familiar face was missing—the face of Mark Ramsay.

CHAPTER VIII.

"And is this your last—your very last—answer?"

Mark Ramsay spoke quite calmly, almost unconcern-
edly; yet his thoughts were very bitter just then. He
had very seldom left on the board the stake in any game
on the winning of which he had thoroughly set his
heart's desire—so seldom, indeed, that nine men out of
ten, on the strength of their evil success, would have
grown overweening in confidence. But Mark was none
of these. He deemed that the devil's luck, like any other
luck, would run itself out at last, and was prepared at
any moment to see the intermittence set in. From personal vanity, pure and simple, he was, as has been aforesaid, singularly free; and he could calculate his own
chances of success or failure just as coolly as if he had
been looking over a third person's game. All this only
made him feel his present disappointment more keenly.
He had never been more sure of any one thing in his life
than of Blanche Ellerslie's assent whenever he should
ask her to marry him.

He knew perfectly well with what manner of woman
he was dealing, and was prepared from the first to meet
all the wiles of finished coquetry. But over the perfection of any art whatsoever, Nature will sometimes prevail. Smiles may be feigned, glances be tutored, and
voices be trained to tremble; but Cleopatra herself,
though she might counterfeit a blush, could not summon
up at will the faint, tender glow of happiness which, at
the sound of a certain footstep or the glimpse of a certain
figure, has caused ere now many ill-favored faces to wax
for the nonce pleasant and comely. For such signs
Ramsay's practiced eyes had watched often and earnestly of late, and had not watched in vain. He could not
accuse himself of being precipitate now in pressing his
suit. And what manner of answer had he just listened

to? It was not an absolute refusal; but still less was it one of those feminine Nays concerning which so many pleasant conceits have been indited both in poesy and prose. The plea for delay was too earnestly urged, and too steadily persisted in, to be set down to coy subterfuge.

That delays are dangerous, none knew better than Mark Ramsay. If a fortress to which he laid siege could not be carried at once, he guessed that its defenses were not likely to be weakened by the according of a truce. Nevertheless, within that same fortress much doubt and difficulty prevailed just now.

Mrs. Ellerslie was, in all ways, of the world worldly; yet the veriest country-girl, hovering on the verge of first love, could not be more single-minded in intent than Blanche had been of late. Not one mercenary motive entered into her preference for Mark Ramsay. She might have landed quite as heavy, if not heavier, fish ere now, if she had cared to work the waters where the big trout lie more patiently; but she had wealth more than sufficient to satisfy all her whims, and, as yet, had never been seriously tempted to exchange the freedom of the Allée des Veuves for any prison whatsoever, even if the walls were of jasper and the gates of wrought gold. As for ambition—that is another affair. Blanche was too thorough a woman not to savor triumph in holding at her discretion the "stag of ten," against whom younger and fairer huntresses had emptied their quivers in vain. She was well aware that many matrons, . who turned indignantly away from Mark Ramsay lingering at her side, would have found gracious glances for him, lounging in their own drawing-rooms; and that the pity they feigned to feel for her would scarce have been extended to their own daughters, had these been exposed to like temptation; she was keenly alive, too, to the delight of successful rivalry. But, putting all these incitements aside, she felt for Mark Ramsay what she had never felt for any man, alive or dead. It was not only a strong liking, but a growing sense of dependence which almost frightened her, intensely pleasant though it was. From her girlhood upward, she had scoffed pitilessly at the substance of Love, though she had ever been coquetting with his shadow; but she felt misgivings now, lest she should have been over-rash in her gay defiance. Yet, had the choice been given her, she would not have drawn back one step on the road that seemed to trend toward the house of bondage.

All this being premised, it seems hard to understand why she should hesitate and plead for delay when Mark asked for her hand. It was scarcely prudence withheld her; but rather one of those presentiments that are such true prophets, though they speak more darkly than the Oracles, whose utterances were whispered on the winds of Dodona or through the smoke of Delphi. All the warnings that she had put aside and tried to forget came back upon her now, and she could not drive them away. The friends who had spoken those warnings might not have been very safe counselors as a rule, and certainly were little apt to preach; but she knew that they had spoken honestly for her good—ay, and not without sound reason.

"Not fit to be trusted with the happiness of any woman alive."

How sharply she had checked Oswald Gauntlet when he spoke these words! But her heart heard them over again, sleeping or waking, often enough since. They rang in her ears like a church-bell, that never wearies of its message of truth and kindness to sinners, whether they will hearken or not. From the first moment when she looked on her suitor's face, she had tried to believe that much of the ill report concerning him was idle gossip or scandal: yet, at this very moment, she remembered that without fire there is no smoke; and that creatures more innocent than herself—innocent as the children that were burned before Moloch—might ere now have passed through the furnace of Mark Ramsay's evil passions.

It was very true that the love he now proffered brought with it no shame; nevertheless, the gift might be fatal. On men of his stamp, vows are not more binding because they have been spoken before an altar. Spirits so hard to tame stand in small awe of a simple wedding-ring. Moreover, if the Talmud speak true, the talisman whereby

King Solomon controlled the Djinns could not save him from betrayal by the fair Shulamite.

Warning and presentiment availed just so much as to make her hesitate—no more. For her life she could not have spoken the words that would have sent Mark Ramsay away from her forever. When he said, "Is this your very last answer?" she could only look up at him timidly, murmuring,—

"You must not be angry; you must be patient. If you knew all I have heard, you would not wonder."

His face began to harden.

"Rare tales, I dare be sworn. With all the talent for invention that is abroad, it's very odd better novels are not written nowadays. And do you think it is only about me that *fabliaux* are made? I find it so much pleasanter to take people as I find them, instead of on hearsay; and so much wiser not to trouble myself with what happened before my time. But if one were to believe half one hears—— Mrs. Ellerslie, as you are so fond of listening to stories, I'll tell you one. It's not very sensational; but it's true.

"When people told you so much about my past, did they tell you that some time ago I spent twelve months in India? No? It was so, nevertheless. I was a poor man in those days, and only too thankful to be set forward on my road, or helped in getting at the big game. I had heard a good deal of Indian hospitality before I started; I was not prepared for half the kindness I met with. With one regiment in particular, I lived nearly three months, at free quarters,—the —th Hussars, who were quartered at Meerut. The day before I was to leave them to return home, sitting alone with the Chief in his bungalow, I naturally offered to execute any commission for him or for any other comrade.

"'Well, there's one thing you might do,' Colonel Neville said, 'but I hardly like to ask you, though it would please several others in the regiment besides me. There's one of ours whom you have never seen yet, though you've heard him talked over often enough, for he's been on the sick-list since you came here. It's a very sad case. We liked what we saw of him immensely, when he joined, and thought we had got a real acquisition; but I don't think he has done ten days' duty since, nor dined a dozen times at mess. He was very shaky from the first, and he's never given himself half a chance since; for he does nothing but mope in his bungalow, smoking like a chimney, and, I'm very much afraid, drinking to match. He don't look fit to travel, and seems to hate the idea of going home; but the doctor says the sea-voyage is his last chance. He was very loath to move; so I got his sick-leave without consulting him, and he starts to-morrow. Now, if you are not in any great hurry—you haven't taken your passage yet, I know—I thought perhaps you wouldn't mind looking after him as far as Calcutta. You'll have to travel slower, of course; but otherwise he won't be much trouble: he's as gentle as a girl in his ways, spite of the drink.'

"An act of simple charity was not much return for all the kindness I had met with there. So I said; and so it was settled. I did not see my traveling-companion till I called for him at his bungalow next evening. I thought I had seldom looked on a handsomer face, though death was written on it very plainly; and I was quite struck by the pleasantness of his voice as he said good-by to his comrades; for every officer of the regiment was there to see him off. Beyond a few sentences of commonplace courtesy exchanged then, very few words passed between us that night; and, when we reached our first halting-place, he seemed so tired that I did not tempt him to talk.

"There were no railways in those days. Traveling was done by dâwk-gharries. You travel always by night, resting, if there's no necessity to push forward, during the heat of the day. I saw scarcely anything of my traveling-companion except at meals, at which he made a mere pretense of eating, and then betook himself to lie down again in his own room till it was time to start. He did not seem inclined to talk, but his manner was always winning, and he seemed very grateful to me for lingering with him on the road. So it went on, till we halted on the sixth day at a lonely station beyond Benares.

When he got out of his gharry, he seemed scarce able to walk into the dâwk bungalow, and said he would try to sleep, for he could swallow no food. So I breakfasted alone, and afterward began to doze. I woke up with a start—feeling sure that there was some one in the room near me, though I had not heard the door open.

"My companion stood there, resting his hand on the table and swaying to and fro. The sun-blinds were closely drawn and the room was very dark; yet I could see his face—deathly white—and the gleaming of his great black eyes. From certain significant words dropped by my bearer I guessed what his habits had been throughout the journey, and *delirium tremens* was the first idea that crossed my mind.

"'I'm not drunk!' he said, as though he read my thoughts; 'I'm dying, that's all; and I—I daren't die alone.'

"I sprang up just in time to catch him in my arms as he stumbled forward; and I laid him down on my couch, from which he never stirred again. There are times, I believe, when a man must speak—even to a dog or his worst enemy—rather than keep silence altogether. So it came to pass that I, a mere chance-acquaintance, heard his last confession, spoken slowly and painfully in the lulls between the heart-spasms. I dare say the story is very dry and old; but I never listened to one quite like it, and it made rather a strong impression on me. I remember it almost word for word.

"He had served, till he got his lieutenancy, in a heavy-dragoon regiment; and during those three years met a woman, who—unwittingly, as I thoroughly believe—turned all the current of his life awry. Neither did he accuse her. He accused only his own folly, for having been so bewitched.

"'She was only in play,' he said; 'and she could not guess that it was playing the devil with me. She would not have soiled the tip of her little finger for my sake; and there's no sin or shame on earth that I would not have worked out at the beck of that same finger. I never told her as much. I don't think I ever said a syllable to her that her husband might not have listened to. And this is how we parted.   I was going on leave to see after some of my mother's affairs, that ought to have been attended to long before: I should not have gone even then; but she knew how things stood with me, and would have it so.

"'To reward me for being "dutiful and obedient," I was to have as many waltzes as I chose at a dance that came off at barracks that night.   I had heaps to do; but I managed to get there just as the first quadrille was over. She was sitting in an out-of-the-way corner, talking very earnestly to a man whom I had never seen before, though I had heard his name often enough; for, to give him his due, I believe there's no better soldier.   I felt hot and savage, and then sick at heart, before she spoke.

"'I wasn't to be furious.   When she promised me those unlimited waltzes, she had reckoned without Oswald Gauntlet, who was a very, *very* old friend; and old friends were *so* exacting.   He had traveled a long way to be there that night; and she had been weak enough to promise him the first waltz and galop at all events.   *Après, on verrait.*

"'I felt very dizzy just then; yet not so dizzy, but, as I turned away, I heard him say, with a half laugh, "It's hard lines on him too, poor boy."

"'And she laughed too, as she answered,—

"'"You were always fond of children, Oswald—fonder than I am.   Shall I call back my pretty page?"

"'Those were the last words I ever heard her speak; and I never saw her face again.   I got away to my quarters somehow; and I got through the night—well, very much as I have got through most nights since, and the first thing I did after getting to London was to arrange an exchange into the —th Hussars.   I never went near the old regiment again; and I never answered the letter she wrote when she heard I was going to India, though I did answer the postscript her husband added. He was a rough old martinet, but he had been really kind to me.   I thought I should get rid of her by coming out here; but I haven't.   The drink that has killed me has only driven her away for an hour or two.   And now— well, there's my mother, who has petted me since I was born, and who will break her heart when she hears of this. If one of the two could come and sit beside me now, it would not be the mother I'd choose. Look here: you're a real good fellow, from all I have heard' (I am speaking by rote, you know, Mrs. Ellerslie), 'and I know I can trust you. You'll see *this* buried with me; and not let any of those black devils handle it.'

" He drew out from his breast a broad gold locket in a double case. There was a photograph in the front; at the back a tiny scrap of paper with the word ' Dear.'

" 'It's very absurd,' he went on, ' very childish, *she* would have called it. I cut it out of a common invitation-note: I thought it looked so well in her handwriting. Now you shall hear her name.'

" He drew my ear down close to his mouth.

" 'If ever you get a chance, I should like you to tell her that I said, ''God bless her!''—now.'

" Those were very nearly the last words he spoke intelligibly, for the spasms came on sharper and stronger till half an hour after he was dead. Mrs. Ellerslie, it's just possible you've guessed already that this man's name was Harry Armar; and whose face was in his locket; and why I have broken no confidence in telling you this story."

Guessed it? Yes, she had done that long ago. Eyes less keen than those that looked down on her might have read so much, even before she started at the mention of Oswald Gauntlet's name. She had often felt mild penitence and self-reproach; but real remorse, never till now. For a moment she was as much shocked and startled as if she had been brought suddenly into a chamber where a corpse was lying. She remembered the brave, handsome boy so well; remembered how she had laughed that night at what she deemed his pettish anger; how sure she had made of his coming back to her lure; how surprised she had been when she heard of his exchange to India; how vexed when no answer came to her farewell letter; how grieved when she heard of his death. How different all would have been, had she known then what she knew now! She bowed her head in silence for a minute or two; and when she spoke it was low and brokenly.

"I have done deadly harm, though I never meant it, God knows.   But I scarcely deserve that the pain should come from you.   Could you not have told me this sooner, or—later?"

"I never thought of punishment," Mark answered, "for I never thought that you deserved it.   Perhaps I'm not a fair judge; but, you'll remember, I believed from the first all the harm had been done unwittingly.   You were amusing yourself as hundreds of women do: the only pity was, that you found out a little too late with what a brittle toy you were playing. I should fancy poor Armar was not organized to stand the wear and tear of every-day life long, even if he had never crossed your path. Only think what gaps would be made in society, if men in general, on finding out they had mistaken jest for earnest, were to flee to the uttermost parts of the earth to drown their disappointment in strong drink!   I told you all this, partly because I was in a fashion bound to tell you some time or other; but more because I wished you to understand that I ask no more than I offer, when I ask you to let the past bury its dead.   For now—with this story, which some good-natured friends would work up into a 'sensation,' fresh from my lips—I ask you, once more, to cast in your lot with mine."

For the last few minutes Mark had kept his eyes averted from his companion's face, as though willing to give her time to recover herself.   Before he looked at her again, he knew that he had won the day.   As he finished speaking, a soft hand crept into his palm, and was content to be clasped; and, as their lips met, Blanche Ellerslie knew of a surety that she had found her heart at last.

When a woman of her experience—though she was comparatively young in years—makes this discovery so late, it is by no means certain that it is for her happiness it is made.   It is the old story, of the peasant suddenly made rich, by lighting on a treasure hidden in the ground that he has delved for years.   There is great joy at first over the new-gotten wealth; but the cares and fears of guardianship follow soon; and there will be heard never more the light-hearted lilting and ready laughter that made the cottage merry, when it held nothing that thieves would break through to steal.

Theirs was a strange wooing—strange even for these days, wherein sentiment does not greatly abound. Scarcely a word of tenderness passed between the two before they were irrevocably plighted; and such as believe in omens might have noted as an evil augury that sharp stings of remorse were tingling in Blanche Ellerslie's breast, when she betrothed herself to a man who brought her a message from the dead.

CHAPTER IX.

LAURA BRANCEPETH could not affect surprise at the news that greeted her when she came in from driving. Nevertheless, she was exceeding wroth, and, as was her wont on such occasions, spoke somewhat unadvisedly with her lips. Blanche was too happy just then to quarrel with any one—much less with a real friend. The sharp words only made her smile; and she answered as serenely as if she had received the warmest congratulations.

"I'm very sorry, dear. You'd have liked me to have married some great church dignitary, I do believe. But I don't know any bachelor bishop; and, though the Dean of Torrcaster is a widower, I could not have become bone of his bone even to please you. For my part, I think it's better for like to match with like—sinners with sinners, and saints with saints. Besides, Mark and I have sown all our wild-oats; and we shall do nothing henceforth but quiet family gardening."

Laura Brancepeth had the outline in her mind of a retort at once scriptural and severe, relating to seeds and tares, and reaping the whirlwind; but she got her metaphor into a tangle, and so gave it up; contenting herself with observing that "she didn't believe in sudden conversions, but that she was tired of preaching, and only hoped the other would not one day have cause to remember her sermons when it was too late."

Mrs. Ellerslie's face put on the caressing look that women, no less than men, found it hard to withstand.

"Too late to warn, perhaps," she said ; "but, Queenie, not too late to wish me happy. No one would be sorrier than you, I know, if your prophecies were by any chance to come true."

Lady Laura's gusts of temper never lasted long. She stooped and kissed her friend very affectionately.

"I do wish you happy, dear, from the bottom of my heart; and, if you should ever come to confess to me that it was otherwise, I promise you that I won't answer with 'I told you how it would be.'"

La Reine Gaillarde never could bear malice for having been worsted in fair fight. She had done her very uttermost to thwart and countermine Mark Ramsay ; but, now that he had finally prevailed, she was as ready to shake hands as if she had been throughout his warmest partisan. When they next met, she greeted him quite cordially, making him free of her house at all canonical hours, and entered with great energy and good will into all preparations for Blanche's marriage.

There was much lawyer's work to be done ; for Mrs. Ellerslie was by no means a portionless bride, and Mark's liberality in point of settlements needed rather the check than the spur. As a poor man he had always been free-handed to a fault ; and wealth had not made him miserly, or even careful to count the cost. In all this, beyond a few timid objections to excess of generosity, Blanche took little concern ; but, when she was asked to choose her trustee, she named, without hesitation, a cousin of the late Colonel Ellerslie, and principal executor of his will. She had seen comparatively little of George An-struther ; but she knew that her husband trusted implicitly in his judgment and honor, and more than once had sought his advice and assistance. Since she became a widow, she had always found him ready and willing to assist her in business matters, of which she was ignorant as a child.

Mr. Anstruther had gone out, when comparatively young, to a lucrative appointment in India ; interest was more powerful then than it is nowadays, and the cadets of certain families—unless actually deficient in ability— had a kind of hereditary claim to rapid advancement. He was a just and upright man, and would have scorned to exact a doit more than his due either from rich or poor; but saving withal, with a shrewd, sagacious eye for all legitimate chances of increasing his store, and well able to sift the chaff from the grain in the tempting specula- tions that even then were rife in the East. So it was not wonderful that at the age of forty-five—some six years before the opening of this story—he was enabled to retire with a fortune that, added to his pension, was affluence to one of his tastes.

From the morning when George Anstruther sailed out of the Downs, to the evening when he saw the points of the Needles glimmering white through the twilight, he had never once set foot on English ground. Absence of less than a quarter of a century will make most men feel aliens at first in their birth-land; with some, this feeling of estrangement never quite wears away. So it was with Anstruther. For many years he had lived almost entirely alone; for his station, though an important one, lay far up the country, out of the line of traffic; and the scanty European society that lay within his reach had rather repelled than attracted him. Solitude had not made him morose or eccentric; but it had fostered the shy reserve natural to him. His habits were too set now to be altered greatly by change of clime.

His living relatives were singularly few, and even with the nearest of these he had corresponded but rarely; so, when he landed in England, there were none who would have traveled far to bid him "Welcome home." An- struther did not feel this isolation as many would have done. Perhaps he rather rejoiced that absence of any family ties left him free to live after his own fashion, without seeming ungracious toward his kinsfolk. He paid a few duty-visits in the first few months after he landed; but these were made as brief as possible, and were never repeated. Before the year was out, he had established himself in a house on the northwestern bor- der of St. John's Wood—very modest in appearance, but sufficiently capacious to hold him and his belongings;

and with ground enough around it to prevent the possibility of being hemmed in or overlooked. Other reasons, besides a fancy for seclusion, guided Anstruther in the choice of a dwelling. For some time past chemistry had been his favorite pursuit; and he had no mind that any timid or sensitive neighbor should take out an "injunction" against his laboratory.

Most of his Indian contemporaries—less lucky or less prudent than himself—were still toiling on out yonder; so in London he found few personal friends. Nevertheless, he became a member without difficulty of the two clubs into which he sought admission—the Planet and the Orion. At one of these he was sure of a faultless dinner; at the other, sure of finding scope for the display of his rare skill at whist and piquet. Beyond some half-dozen fevers, that had left no seeds of disease behind, he had never known what sickness meant; but his daily routine was as regular as if he had been condemned to live by rule.

Winter or summer, he breakfasted always at nine; then came a huge cheroot, and the reading of the morning paper; then work in the laboratory till about noon. Then, no matter what the weather might be outside, he went out on horseback for two hours, neither less nor more; never through the streets or in the Row, but straight out into the country—not dawdling along on a leisurely constitutional, but riding quite as sharply as was good for the legs and wind of the cattle that carried him. He gave great prices for his hacks; and was too good a judge not to get his money's worth. When he came in, he changed his dress completely—solitude had not made him the least of a sloven—and drove down to the Orion, where he played whist or piquet till seven. After dressing again, unless there were special reasons for the contrary, he dined at the Planet. Though he never offered to join any other party, he seldom dined alone. There was generally some one ready to take the second place at the corner-table to which, ere long, he acquired a prescriptive right; for it was known in the Planet that Mr. Anstruther's talent in composing a *menu* —simple or elaborate—was exceptional, and that he could talk sensibly on most subjects without speaking *ex cathedrâ.*

"Not half a bad fellow, when you know him; and devilish shrewd, too; but wants drawing out"—was the club verdict,—a pretty just one, as such verdicts commonly are.

After his black coffee, he smoked one digestive cheroot —very slowly, and in silence, for choice—and then betook himself to the Orion again, where his brougham was always waiting at midnight. After that hour he could not be tempted to begin a rubber.

Though his acquaintance without the walls of the Planet and the Orion was so confined, when he was permanently established in town, invitations began to drop in; but these were one and all courteously declined; and when it became known that there was no exception whatever to Mr. Anstruther's rule of never dining out and never entertaining at home, the Amphitryons forbore to disquiet him. Only one or two very intimate friends could tempt him sometimes to slightly vary the even tenor of his life; chiefest among these was Walter Ellerslie. These two were not only kinsmen, but had seen much of each other in India. Each had learned long ago to value aright the sterling qualities of the other's nature —disguised in the one case under shy, cold reserve, in the other by a curt, incisive manner that at its best was anything but courtly.

Colonel Ellerslie was passionately fond of whist, and a hopelessly bad player. His errors sprang not from rashness, or want of thought; but from a combination, peculiar to himself, of a set of rules, of which all that were not absurd were more or less false in principle. He was one of the most intrepid men alive, and, not only in his profession, but in ordinary life, acted, whether for right or wrong, with singular promptness and decision. When he sat down to the whist-table, the whole nature of the man seemed changed. He became timorous and vacillating to a degree; avaricious of his trumps in season and out of season, and leading from his weakest suit, rather than from ace queen. He would certainly have chosen the "happy dispatch" of throwing up his hand, rather than lead up to an exposed honor.

Some years ago there flourished in the Shires a notable sportsman, from whom, it was said, many useful hints had been gained by such as had got a bad start and wished to know which way the hounds were turning. They watched the line that he was taking, and then took exactly the opposite one, and nine times out of ten were right. So, a beginner at whist might have greatly improved himself by watching Colonel Ellerslie's play whenever there was the shadow of a doubt, and thenceforth noting that card as the very last to be produced under the circumstances. Even had he been likely to take schooling patiently, he was so palpably incorrigible that few would have wasted reproach on him, much less argument. He lived and died in happy unconsciousness of the blundering that made him a very proverb among those who suffered thereby. The colonel had a great idea of playing "in good company," as he termed it—in no wise alluding to the social position of those who made up the party, but to their celebrity at the game. He was not a member of the Orion; for he was poor, and too prudent to pit himself constantly against men by whom he felt he was overmatched; but nothing pleased him so much as an occasional rubber there. If he lost his money, as was generally the case, he grudged it not a whit; if he won, were it ever so little, he went home prouder than Diomedes bringing back from the Trojan camp the fatal horses of Rhesus.

When Ellerslie first appeared at the Orion, it was as Anstruther's guest; and there was great marvel that he, who would often wait for an hour or more rather than cut in at a second-rate table, should have brought in a man to whom the veriest neophyte in the club could have given one point in ten. But Anstruther only shrugged his shoulders with a quiet smile—it was his way of declining discussion—whenever the anomaly was hinted to him, and would sit patiently for a whole evening conniving, so to speak, at the other's blunders; never once at the most flagrant of these lifting his shaggy gray eyebrows, that arched themselves readily enough over much more venial transgressions. Others too, less disposed to indulgence, deemed it better to suffer in silence; partly out of deference to Ellerslie's entertainer, partly because it seemed scarce safe to vent spleen, however justly provoked, on the grim old martialist.

Philosophers and politicians have ceased long ago to write treatises *De Amicitiâ;* and even Corinna finds graver or more passionate use for her pen than inditing sonnets to a female favorite. The romance of sentiment rarely survives our school-days; and surely these gray-beards had cast such follies far behind them. Yet I doubt if sincerer sacrifice ever was laid on .the altar of friendship, than the one just recorded.

For his hospitality George Anstruther never would take payment in kind. When his cousin's regiment was quartered within easy distance of London, he could not be induced to visit the pretty villa in which the other had set up his household gods. Before she became a widow, he had only met Blanche Ellerslie twice—each time by accident. The duties of executorship brought them more together, of necessity. Then, despite his reserve and shyness, Anstruther showed himself so thoroughly kind and considerate that Blanche conceived a great liking for and confidence in him, and thenceforth did not scruple to rest entirely on his advice in any important matters of business. These consultations were always made by letter.

CHAPTER X.

On a certain bright May morning, Mr. Anstruther walked in his garden, smoking slowly his after-breakfast cheroot. When he walked, his step was planted firmly, never springily; and all his movements were marked by a kind of mechanical slowness. His frame, naturally tall and spare, had grown gaunt and angular under twenty-five years' endurance of Eastern dust and sun. His features were roughly cast, but rather regular than otherwise; and though the cheeks and forehead were crossed by myriads of intersecting lines, none were as yet very deeply grained. His strong, short hair, carefully-trimmed whiskers, and thick eyebrows were all of the same dark-grizzled hue; and his eyes, of a paler gray, were steady without being searching, with a kind of look in them of judicial authority—not unbecoming one who had spent the better part of his life in winnowing grains of truth out of sheaves of falsehood, and from whose decision there had seldom been appeal. His feet were large and clumsy; but his long hands were well shaped, and the nails carefully trimmed, though dark specks here and there betrayed the nature of his favorite pursuit.

Neither in face nor figure was there a single point on which the eye of an artist or of a woman would have loved to linger; yet in a crowd of strangers you would probably have singled out George Anstruther as worthy of a second glance. You would have guessed that you looked upon a man whose strength lay rather in patient pertinacity than in daring genius or passionate impulse —a man not easily moved by avarice or ambition, but yet who would seldom fail to work out his own end by his own means—a man self-respecting, if not entirely God-fearing; who might possibly be goaded or beguiled into the commission of some great crime, but scarcely into any action merely base or mean—a man who would pass safely through toils and temptations in which others would surely be entangled, and over whom the Lust of the Eye and the Pride of Life had as yet seldom prevailed.

It was a morning to make one forget the many sins of English spring. A light breeze from the northwest came, without a taint by smoke or miasma, straight from green pasture-grounds and pink orchards and russet fallows. A morning that would have braced the nerves of a hypochondriac better than all the tonics of the faculty—a morning that might have tempted a would-be suicide to give the world another chance of making him amends for intolerable wrong.

Staid and sober as Anstruther was, he was by no means inaccessible to weather influences; and he was very happy, after his own fashion, as he paced to and fro, halting often to savor the fragrance of his trim parterres, with which mingled not unpleasantly the keener scent of the Manilla weed. He was no gambler, in the common sense of the word ; for his stakes both at whist and piquet were invariably such as could scarcely have damaged the fortune of a much poorer man ; but he felt success or defeat none the less keenly ; and the fact of the previous night having been an exceptionally good one may have contributed not a little to the pleasantness of his humor. The tenacity of his memory was something marvelous; and he could carry more than one whist-problem in his brain quite easily. He was work ing out rather a difficult case which had occurred on the previous night, and had just determined that his own and his partner's cards could not possibly have been played to more advantage, when his servant brought him out a note, saying that the bearer waited for an answer.

It was a dainty-looking missive. At the first glance Anstruther saw that it was a woman's ; and the second told him whence it came. When he was alone, he sat down and opened the envelope deliberately, taking care not to destroy the intricate monogram of violet and silver. Considering the brevity of the note, it took strangely · long in perusal.

Therein, for the first time, Anstruther was made aware of Mrs. Ellerslie's matrimonial intentions; and further entreated, if he was not weary of doing her kindness, to take charge thenceforth of her separate interests, as her trustee.

"But it is so much easier to talk than to write about some things," Blanche concluded; "and if you would only name an hour that would suit you best for calling here, I would be quite sure to be at home to you and to no one else."

Then she signed herself "affectionately," instead of "truly," as heretofore.

For a space that would have sufficed to get every word written on two pages by heart, George Anstruther sat musing; and, as he mused, he toyed with the delicate

F

note, passing it to and fro over his lips and nostrils, as though it had been a fresh May-blossom.

Mrs. Ellerslie's worst enemy would not have imputed to her such a vulgarism as using scented paper; and George Anstruther was little wont to give imagination the rein; nevertheless, he seemed to savor a suspicion of perfume. Other roses, besides those of Gueldres and Provence, have been known to impart fragrance to the meanest object they brush with their petals,—a fragrance the like of which exhales not from any herb or flower of earth, the like of which no cunning of chemistry can imitate,—a fragrance that will endure after those same roses are withered and dead. As Anstruther mused, his bushy gray brows were drawn together, and the lines on his forehead grew deeper and deeper.

"Married again!" so his thoughts ran. "A risk surely for one of her stamp; she's scarce likely to have her old luck over again. And to Mark Ramsay, too! There's more than risk there. It's the same man, of course, I heard so much of in India. He was not more than a twelvemonth out, and was keen enough after the big game; but he found leisure enough to do harm that could not be undone in a lifetime. Didn't he come into a great fortune a year or so ago? Not that that would have anything to do with it: she has more than she wants already. Well, I'm not her guardian, or even a very old friend; so there's no reason for my concerning myself with her future, beyond looking after settlements and investments. Of course I'm always ready to do as much for poor old Walter's sake. I'll write and tell her so, and call this afternoon. Congratulation-visits are not much in my line: I'd just as soon get this one over."

When he had written a few lines in reply, the hour at which he was wont to betake himself to his laboratory was past; but he went out into the garden again, muttering, while he lighted a fresh cheroot,—

"No use attempting to work; it's a broken day."

A forenoon passed in idleness was not the only infraction of the methodical habits which had become ingrained in Anstruther's nature. He had long been accustomed to destroy every letter that he received so soon as it was answered; but Blanche's note, instead of finding its way to the waste-basket, was dropped into a drawer in the writing-table, the key of which was always turned. The circumstance was trifling in itself; yet a physiologist might have found ominous significance therein. When a clock that for years has not varied a second, begins all at once, without any assigned reason, to indulge in ever so slight vagaries, it is a chance if any horologer will make it thenceforth keep quite correct time.

Whether Mrs. Ellerslie desired to show gratitude to her trusty counselor for his past services, or whether she desired still further to secure his future fidelity, or whether she was prompted by the mischievous devil of coquetry that had been her familiar so long, is a question not worth discussing. All these motives—the last for choice—may have influenced her that afternoon.

La Reine Gaillarde was once heard to say that Blanche would flirt with a baby in her arms rather than not flirt at all; and truly her conduct on certain occasions—like the present one, for instance—made the imputation seem not unfounded. A more unpromising subject for captivation than George Anstruther could scarcely be imagined. She had long had great respect for his judgment and confidence in his honor, and felt grateful to her late husband for having bequeathed to her so useful an ally. Nevertheless, she had always looked on him in a sort of professional light; and seldom thought of him except in connection with business of some kind. It was on business he came to speak now—ay, more than that, on business relating to her own second marriage.

Anstruther, to do him justice, after offering his brief good wishes, seemed disposed to keep the conversation on a correctly formal footing. It was not his fault that it assumed gradually a quasi-cousinly tone. It was not his fault if, while deeds were being consulted and vouchers verified, Mrs. Ellerslie, instead of sitting decorously at the table over against her adviser, chose to adopt a posture befitting a pupil of Gamaliel. Even that venerable rabbi might have found it hard to meet quite unmoved such confiding upward glances. George Anstruther was neither stock nor stone. He was originally, perhaps,

not colder of constitution than his fellows; but the se-
cluded life on which he entered at a very early age, added
to a shy reserve increasing with his years, had kept him
to a great extent clear of temptation : he was continent
rather by force of habit than for conscience' sake.   He
had mixed so seldom in society, from youth upward
until now, that a woman's voice speaking low and sweetly
was in his ears like the sound of some strange unearthly
music; and he felt like one scanning the alphabet of an
unknown language, as he looked down into Blanche
Ellerslie's eyes.

Soon his thoughts began to wander from dry business
details, and to dwell on such trifles as the fashion of a
skirt or the hue of a trimming.   He wondered whether
any two colors on earth could blend so harmoniously as
lilac and white, or were so fitting to be twined in bright
brown hair.   He was not unconscious of the growing
weakness, and strove to shake it off with inward self-contempt; but it fared with him as with the victims of
witchcraft in old time, who never could quite complete
the cross-sign that would have set them free.   And so
the weaving of the spell went on.   He became so absent
at last that Blanche noticed it.

"You have got quite tired over these dreadful papers.
It's such a shame of me to give you so much trouble.
Shall we put them all away till another day ?"

As she spoke, she laid her fingers lightly on his wrist.
If a spirit had touched him in his sleep, Anstruther could
scarcely have started more violently.

"I beg your pardon," he said; "but I was really
thinking of things concerning you, though not exactly of
your settlements.   I am not tired in the least, and these
papers are very simple.   I believe I quite understand
what has to be done; and I don't know that I shall have
to trouble you much more about this business."

"But you'll come again, and soon ?" she said.   "Do
you never mean to visit me, except as my trustee ?"

Before Anstruther could reply, the door opened slowly.
The Brancepeths' butler was an elder of infinite discretion.   Incapable of hurrying himself, he was not less indulgent to his superiors than to his inferiors, and far too

discreet to make sudden irruptions on a *tête-à-tête*, how-soever innocent in outward seeming.　He came now to inquire whether it was Mrs. Ellerslie's pleasure to receive Mr. Ramsay.　Mr. Ramsay had heard she was engaged, and would detain her for a few minutes only.　The lady did not stir from where she sat, but glanced up at her companion, rather doubtfully.

"I meant this afternoon to be all yours, and I mean it still.　If you don't mind my leaving you for a very little while, I'll go down and give Mark his audience.　I shall be back before you have finished looking through my photograph-book."

Anstruther rose up hastily.

"Don't think of such a thing.　You are only too kind; but I really must leave you, now that our business-talk is done.　I had no idea how late it was; and I have one or two engagements that I cannot break."

She pouted a little, as if half loath to be gainsaid.

"You know best, of course.　I didn't mean to be exacting; but at least you'll see Mark before you go?　I should not like to lose this opportunity of making you acquainted."

It would have needed a very keen observer to detect the shade of coldness and constraint in Anstruther's acquiescence; and the slight formality of manner after-ward, during the interchange of the few courteous com-monplaces with Ramsay, might be fairly set down to constitutional shyness.

"A quaint creature," Mark observed, as soon as the door had fairly closed behind Anstruther; "I have seen the very image of him in some old picture or another—ah, I remember now—it's the faithful steward in Hogarth's Marriage *à la mode:* only this one wears whiskers and no wig.　I hope he'll never have reason to hold up his hands at our extravagance, Bianchetta."

"Don't laugh at him," she said, gravely.　"You would not, if you knew how thoroughly kind and useful he has always shown himself to me; though I never had the grace to thank him for it, properly, before to-day."

"I don't laugh at him.　Lawyers who understand

their business, and work without fees, are too rare to be lightly entreated.　I would not have his manner thawed for the world.　If it were a shade more genial, it would not suit a model trustee."

She shook her head reprovingly, smiling nevertheless; and, five minutes later, they were speaking of matters with which conveyancing had little enough to do.

Whatever were the engagements for that afternoon that George Anstruther could not break, he seemed to have forgotten them before he left Craven Square far behind him.　Instead of turning his steps toward either of his clubs, or toward any frequented thoroughfare, he walked slowly away northward, through the Regent's Park, to the gardens of the Botanical Society, of which he had been some time a fellow.　The grounds were almost empty; and the solitary bench that he selected lay far out of the track of the few loungers who wandered hither and thither, mostly in pairs.　Minutes passed into hours, and still Anstruther sat a-musing, haunted by the echo of a voice, by the shadow of a face, and, most of all, by the memory of a look—the look with which Blanche Ellerslie, before she spoke ever a word, had greeted Mark Ramsay.

The names of Hafiz and Firduzi are strange to many; but we all have heard or read of the eloquence of Eastern eyes.　They gleam not less lustrously, be sure, on the banks of Indus or Ganges, than beside the waters of Shiraz.　No man could have dwelt for a quarter of a century, with almost autocratic power, in a remote Indian district, without having chances enough of studying such language.　Anstruther had seen eyes, compared with which Blanche Ellerslie's might seem dull, melting in entreaty, sparkling in provocation, and languishing sometimes in passion not wholly venal; but such a look as he had watched to-day—a look in which there was none of the guile of coquette or courtesan, but only the frank confession of a woman's love—he had never seen before. He felt somewhat despondent, as he thought that he had spent two-thirds of the span of human life without ever winning such a one for himself, and that to dream of winning such a one now would be the very madness of vanity.

His reverie was not rose-colored, yet it cost him a painful effort to break it. He forced himself back into the groove of his usual habits that evening; but the *chef* of the Planet failed for once to please his palate; and, in the first rubber that he played at the Orion, if his partner had not been one of those irrational loyalists who think that the King can do no wrong, exception might more than once have been taken to his play.

CHAPTER XI.

On that same forenoon, one of the opening scenes in another drama was being enacted in another garden—the garden of Kensington, to wit.

What a many secrets have been overheard by those ancient elms, since Heneage Finch built the boundary-fence of his pleasaunce! Could their experience be set forth for the behoof of modern lovers, would they be apt, I wonder, to encourage or to warn? If they said, " Forbear!" the word would be whispered very timidly, be sure, on such a morning as this.

In the Hamadryad there was ever a touch of human weakness that the daughters of Oceanus would have spurned, and from which the Naiads and Oreads were free. She was not immortal, you know; her fragile life might any day be cut short by the woodman's axe, withered by long unseasonable frosts, or blasted by cruel lightning. Some of the saddest and tenderest of ancient legends are those which tell of the sorrows of these poor nymphs, for whom no place was found on Olympus, and whom the greater gods seldom deigned to notice, unless it was to work them woe. So it was but natural that they should sympathize with the hopes and fears of mortals, and that the favorite spots for love-trysts, since the trees budded in Eden, should have been found in forest-land.

Mythology, in these practical days, is chiefly "for the use of schools;" and if any of those who loitered in Kensington Gardens that forenoon thought of such old-world fables, it was probably such a one as that sallow, gray-bearded man yonder—sitting apart and alone, seldom lifting his eyes from a dingy volume in antique binding—a bibliopole most likely, anxious to ascertain whether his purchase of yesterday was a veritable Elzevir or no. No such fancies, you might be sworn, crossed the brain of either of the pair with whom we are now concerned.

Horace Kendall was first at the trysting-place, as in duty bound. In the pleasant shadowy nook where he sat, any idler would have been content to lounge an hour away without such special object as a meeting with Nina Marston. But, before ten minutes of solitary expectation were gone, Kendall evidently began to think himself ill used, and a victim either of circumstances or caprice. His face —handsome enough in its own peculiar style—was something like a flashily-furnished room, that must be well lighted up to be attractive. Just now, with peevish fretfulness upon it, it was certainly rather the reverse of fascinating. He was chewing a second cigarette rather viciously between his teeth, when he saw Nina Marston approaching.

Few people would have called Nina beautiful—she had not enough regularity of feature or brilliancy of complexion for such a distinction—but fewer still would have denied that she looked wonderfully piquante and pretty, sweeping over the grass with the rapid grace inherited from her Spanish ancestry; while stray gleams of sunlight flickered on the ripples of her rich black hair— scarcely concealed by the excuse for a bonnet matching her dress of misty blue. Even Kendall did her that much justice; and his brow cleared involuntarily as he rose to greet her, though his first words were querulous.

"I began to think you were never coming."

"That is so like a man," Nina answered. "A man who has nothing to do but to stroll out after breakfast, without any danger of being questioned about 'whithers or wherefores.' I'm sure a cigarette must be much pleasanter here than in a hot, stuffy room. I'm not a quarter of an hour late, after all; and you are as plaintive as if I had no danger and difficulties to fight with. Yes, dangers—you needn't shrug your shoulders. It isn't very likely that mamma will come down or want me before I get back—we weren't home from the Broadlands till past four—and it isn't very likely she'll question Rosie as to whether I've been with her this morning or not; but she might do it, you know, and then——"

She pursed her firm, scarlet lips significantly.

Kendall did not repent being unjust; but he had tact enough to see that to persist in sulking was scarcely wise. He laid his lips on the gloved hand that he held with a grace that the girl thought perfect, though many women would have termed it theatrical.

"Cannot you guess what makes me exacting?" he murmured. "It is because the minutes I spend with you seem so short and few, and the hours I spend alone—I am always really alone when I don't see you—are so long and dreary; and yet I should be miserable, and hate myself forever, if you got into trouble on my account to-day. I fear your sister would hardly help you out of the scrape."

"Never!" Nina replied, decisively. "Rosie is the most good-natured thing alive, as a rule; but in this case she would not help me one bit. It was all I could do, on the morning after her ball, to prevent her putting mamma on her guard about you and me. I think it's partly on account of something Lord Nithsdale said—I do wish those grave elders would mind their own affairs—but it's not only that. She's got prejudices of her own, I'm certain."

His brow grew overcast again.

"Yes, it isn't likely that I shall ever have to be grateful to Lady Nithsdale for her good offices or her good word either. I suppose it isn't in her to be uncivil to any one; but her manner grows colder every time we meet, and that's seldom enough, God knows. So you weren't home from the Broadlands till past four? How you must have enjoyed yourself! It was so pleasant for me to sit alone and fancy it all—who were your partners, and what they said; and how you listened and smiled back at them; and all the rest of it."

He shut his lips quickly; but scarce quick enough to prevent the escape of a base, bitter word—such as must, indeed, grate on any woman's ears, unless, like the relatives of a certain potentate of the press, she has "grown steady under swearing" The girl looked at him with a little pained surprise, but without a particle of fear. If Lord Daventry's daughter was to be ruled by terror, another manner of man than Horace Kendall must have swayed the iron scepter.

"I wish very, very much that you could have been there," she said, simply; "and I didn't quite give you up till midnight; for I thought it just possible you might have got an invitation at the last moment. But when I saw that wishing was of no use, I tried to make the best of it; and I *did* enjoy myself after a fashion; I'm not a bit ashamed to confess it. You hardly expected me to sit sulking in a corner, or to waltz with tears in my eyes? I'm sure I can't remember what my partners said. Much the same as usual, I suppose; but I can remember their names, I dare say. Hardly any of them are friends or enemies of yours."

There was not a shadow of taunt in those last words; yet they stung him not the less sharply.

"That's very likely," he sneered. "All in your sister's set, I suppose,—a very nice set too. They live in a sort of Agapemone of their own, and don't think an outsider worth nodding to. They are the very partners I should have chosen for you, of course, if I had had to choose."

Gwendoline Marston was not by any means a literary young lady; and *Spiritual Wives* had not then been written. The long Greek word fairly puzzled her.

"I haven't an idea what you mean by Aga-something-or-other; something very severe, no doubt. I suppose I'm an outsider too; for very few of Rosie's set ever notice me much—unless it's Regy Avenel, who gives me a turn sometimes for old acquaintance' sake. You needn't be captious about my partners. Wait till I risk for any one of them one-quarter as much as I have risked for you this morning—something more than a scolding, as you know. But I didn't come out here to quarrel. Look pleasant this moment, or I'll carry back what I've brought for you. Cross-grained people don't deserve anything half so pretty."

"I ARREST YOU IN THE QUEEN'S NAME."

She opened a small case, holding a sort of armlet, like an Indian bangle; only the band of dead gold was flatter and broader, and it was closed with a spring-lock. On the outside, in bright raised Roman letters, was the word "Nina;" and within was engraved a date—the date of the Nithsdale ball.

"I arrest you in the Queen's name," she said, laughing delightedly at his look of surprise, "and resistance is useless: so sit still and be handcuffed."

As she spoke, she fitted the band round his arm, and closed the spring-lock with a snap. It was not so tight as to be galling, yet not loose enough to slip below the wrist-joint; so that under any ordinary circumstances the sleeve would hide it. Very wise or very morose he must surely be, who is not mollified by a present offered timorously by fair white hands. Men who would put aside such a thing, coming from one of their fellows, as though it savored of bribe, would no more reject the first proof of a woman's generosity than they would stay the dropping of the summer-dew; and might be inclined to doubt whether it is always more blessed to give than to receive. The consciousness that the natural order of things is for this once reversed, does not make the situation less pleasant. When Solomon sat in his glory, and peace-offerings were laid at his feet from Ophir and Arabia and the Isles of the Sea, I doubt if the richest of them all found such favor in his solemn eyes as the meanest gift of the dusky Sabæan beauty.

Kendall was neither a sage nor a stoic, nor at any time hampered by overmuch delicacy. His ill humor vanished instantly. He would possibly have preferred a trinket that he could have flaunted more ostentatiously—the plebeian drop in his blood showed itself in nothing more than in a garish taste in personal adornment; nevertheless, he was much gratified, and so eloquent in his thanks that Nina was fain to check them.

"It isn't worth speaking about," she said, with a bright blush; "but I'm so glad you like it, and that you should like the fancy, too. Whenever you get tired of it, you must come to me to take it off; for it can't be opened without the key, which I mean to keep."

Not worth speaking about?   Perhaps few women, un-spoiled by the world, think any homage paid to their first *suzerain d'amour* worth a second thought, much less a second, word.   Yet there are men, not especially high-souled or unselfish, who would have owned to a certain swelling of the heart, had they guessed with what infi-nite difficulty and risk Nina Marston had contrived to order that armlet, and at what cost, not only of self-denial, but of self-abasement, she had contrived to beg and borrow and save coin enough to pay for it.   If Horace Kendall had been aware of these details, he would only have smiled; and the smile would have been half contempt-uous of the girl's folly, half exultant over his own irresist-ible charms.

For a minute or two they sat hand in hand, quite silent; then Nina glanced at her watch, and rose up quickly.

"I must go now.   Don't try to keep me; I feel it isn't safe.   It's always bad luck to go against presentiments. You may walk with me to the gate, if you like, but you mustn't come outside.   I don't want to scandalize my respectable old cabman.   It was so nice of him to bring me here all through by-streets, just as if he guessed what I wished, and not to look in the least knowing when I told him to wait here.   I only hope he'll be as discreet in taking me back."

Kendall had studied his part of *jeune premier* very carefully; he thought it was his cue here to look mildly reproachful, and to heave a little, injured sigh; but he did not attempt to detain his companion either by word or gesture, and the two walked away together.

"I shall see you again soon—very soon?" Horace asked, when they were nearing the gate.

"I'm sure I hope so," she said, rather drearily. "Every day it seems more difficult to manage. We go to the opera to-night, of course; and to-morrow there's a great dinner at home, and a crowd coming in the evening. On Satur-day there's a hateful garden-party of the Chetwynds' at Twickenham. I do so wish it would rain, and spoil those horse-chestnuts they make such a fuss about. I don't see a chance of our meeting, unless it's in the crush-room to-night; and then you mustn't talk to me for more than a second or two."

His face lowered again, and he looked at her askance from under his bent brows

"I have always heard that where there's a will there's a way. The proverb don't seem to apply in our case. I suppose we shall not meet again till some one of your acquaintance gives a music-party at which I'm wanted. I have a great mind to go in for the regular professional game. Then, perhaps, Lady Daventry wouldn't mind my giving you some singing-lessons ; my terms wouldn't be exorbitant, and your voice is worth taking some pains about."

There was sorrowful wonder in her great black eyes, but no anger or upbraiding. Considering her quick, willful temper, the patience with which she met each fresh proof of his peevish ingratitude was something miraculous.

"I don't deserve that," she said. "Never mind; I'll forget it as soon as I can ; but I wish you wouldn't say things that it hurts one to remember. It isn't my fault, surely, that Lady Longfield has been crossed off our visiting-list, so that there's no chance of her bringing you to-morrow evening. I don't think mamma had any spe cial reason for doing it—she's too indolent to quarrel with any one—but she's rather a knack of dropping her acquaintances. Did you ever hear of a girl, in her first season, teasing people for invitations for a man—neither her cousin nor a very old friend? If you won't trust me, I can't help it. It will only make more up-hill work for us both."

Kendall had the tact to see that for once he had touched the wrong chord and pressed it too long; so he drew the contrition-stop at once. The first few words brought the light back into Nina Marston's face ; and, after the usual promises to write, and so forth, they parted amicably.

Horace Kendall's meditations seemed somewhat checkered in their kind; for, if he frowned twice or thrice as he walked back across the park, his lips wore an insolent smile, as he halted in a solitary spot, and, drawing back his sleeve, let the armlet shimmer in the sun.

CHAPTER XII.

WHEN the news of Mrs. Ellerslie's engagement was announced, there was in the world not a little wonder, and much diversity of opinion as to the chances of its turning out happily. The prophets of evil were to the prophets of good, as it were, ten to one; yet few of these were influenced by rancor, or anything beyond the purposeless spite of the hack-gossip, who is bound to be cynical if not scandalous.

The animosities that Blanche Ellerslie had provoked were all feminine, and not very bitter or enduring. Indeed, many who had watched jealously the going-out and coming-in of the dangerous little cruiser were not ill disposed to wish her "God-speed," now that she was to sail no longer under her own flag, and so could have less excuse than ever for molesting the stately caravels forging onward toward nuptial roadsteads and havens.

No man could follow such a career as Ramsay's had been for years past without laying foundation for more than one mortal feud; but, if Mark could not speak of his enemies in the words of the old Spanish statesman who has just passed away,—"*Ils sont tous fusillés*,"— he could comfort himself with the assurance that none of them was just now to the fore to witness against his past or augur maliciously of his future. It should be remembered that since the early meridian of life he had lived so much abroad that the untraveled part of English society scarcely knew him, except by hearsay.

On neither side were there any of those ill-used friends whose querulous voices mar the harmony of epithalamia. In the early and middle days of her widowhood, Blanche had not lacked suitors; but of late her disinclination to marry again had become such an established fact that no one had cared to incur an almost certain rejection, which might bring a restraint on the present freedom of Platonic straying. Others, besides Harry Armar, had carried away from her presence the sting of her coquetry, and had striven, more or less effectually, to deaden it by one or other anodyne. But, of all that had known her intimately, Oswald Gauntlet was perhaps the only one who had never quite ceased to think of her in the light of his possible wife.

Since Mark Ramsay's name was first quoted in the marriage-market, his demeanor had been so carefully guarded, and his courtesy so justly apportioned, that no *chaperone*, howsoever exacting or sanguine, could complain of his having trifled with the affections of their charges.

If on the present occasion there was not much of envy or uncharitableness, doubt and infinite curiosity were expressed as to the result of the match. It could not exactly be called an ill-assorted one; for the several ages of the two affianced were suitable enough, and they might be supposed to possess a certain similarity of tastes. Nevertheless, their contract seemed to rouse in the world a kind of buzz of expectation—such as pervades the gallery when two renowned *ecarté* players face each other. If any of these whispers reached, as is not likely, the ears of the parties chiefly concerned, neither surely bestowed on them a second thought; for Mark had walked too long after his own devices to care a straw for the world's wisdom when it criticised his private concerns; and, though Blanche had hesitated, as you are aware, before taking the final step, all the preachers in Christendom would not have persuaded her to repent it when once taken.

All things were soon ready for the marriage. Even legal charioteers have no excuse for driving heavily when their well-oiled wheels meet with no impediment; and it is known with what a will milliners will work for a favorite customer, in whose order there is the ring of ready gold. If any had been disposed to question Mrs. Ellerslie's popularity, they would have been compelled to acknowledge it after reviewing her wedding-presents. This was not a case of contract between financial or social magnates, where the gifts, as a matter of course, are gorgeous and numberless. Very few of Blanche's intimates could really afford to be generous; yet day by day offerings came pouring in, till Laura Brancepeth's back drawing-room became all ablaze with *bijouterie.* Among these there was a gift that attracted much attention, though several that lay around were much richer in appearance, if not in intrinsic value—a fire-opal, of great size and brilliancy, set in the midst of a square amulet of the soft pale gold worked only by Eastern jewelers. Round the upper edge ran an intricate mixture of dots and curves, that ninety-nine out of a hundred would have mistaken for a pattern in arabesque. A very accurate observer might have noticed that the graving of the signs was of later date than the ornament itself.

This was Mr. Anstruther's present, and he brought it himself. He had written to Blanche several times about her business-matters, which he managed with his usual skill and earnestness, but had never shown in Craven Square since the day you wot of. On the present occasion his manner was stiff almost to ungraciousness; and, if Blanche had not been taken up in admiring the amulet —for the quaintness of the design, even more than the beauty of the gem, captivated her fancy—she must have noticed this at once. And when she thanked him, not only for his pretty present, but also for the trouble he had taken on her behalf, he answered, quite chillingly,—

" I cannot accept thanks that I have not earned—at least, from you. A little business is quite a godsend to a perfectly idle man who has worked in his time; and the little I have done for you I would have done twenty times over, unasked, to please Walter Ellerslie. And he *did* ask me, in the last letter I ever had from him, to serve you whenever I could. If I have carried out his wishes, I am glad; but I can claim little gratitude from you, you see, any more than I can for devising that trinket, which I got, honestly, I assure you, years and years ago. The change I made in it—it's hardly worth naming—was only adding these letters."

He traced with his finger the inscription round the edge.

She was surprised, and a little hurt, at the change in

his demeanor. He seemed so bent on ignoring entirely their last interview—so determined to make her feel that familiar confidences between a grave personage like himself and a light-minded bird like her were misplaced, and that for her own sake she was not worth looking after. Nevertheless, she felt somehow that no real unkindness was meant, and deemed it best to let it pass for the present.

"Those letters?" she said; "I had no idea they were letters. And what do they spell?—some terrible cabalistic word, I dare say."

"No; a very plain and simple one, whether it is written in English or Sanscrit: the word is 'Ready.' I had it engraved there because I wished you to be reminded sometimes that though the trust, if you can call it so, that Walter Ellerslie left me ends on your marriage-day, I am always ready with any help that I can render. If I had ever been romantic, Mrs. Ellerslie, I should have outlived that long ago. I mean literally what I say ; and I shall not go back from my word if we don't chance to meet for years after next Wednesday—not a very unlikely thing, either—and the service I refer to has nothing to do with the duties of a marriage-trustee."

"I will not forget," she said, softly ; "but, if I ever ask you for help, it will be in my own name—not even in that of the kind, brave soul who trusted me to you—and then I may thank you for myself, and in my own fashion. But I cannot understand what you mean by its being likely that we should not meet. Wherever I am, you know you will always be welcome ; and I'm certain you will like Mark when you become better acquainted."

Was she so sure of that? Little as she was to be trusted when trifling, Mrs. Ellerslie was seldom insincere. She felt a disagreeable consciousness, just now, that those last words might just as well have been left unsaid, and that George Anstruther deserved something better than a hollow form of courtesy. Possibly some such thought may have crossed his mind likewise. If his manner had thawed a little, it froze now more rigidly than ever.

"You're very kind. I'm not likely to be troublesome

to you; and I fear I've little chance of improving my acquaintance with Mr. Ramsay. I never mix in general society, as perhaps you have heard, and my bad habits are past mending. When I accepted your invitation for Wednesday next, I accepted only for the church, you remember."

With all her tact in such matters, Blanche felt at a loss how to break the awkward pause that ensued. She had always considered Mr. Anstruther very abrupt and eccentric; but his manner now fairly puzzled her. That he still meant kindly by her was clear; but, then, what signified the harsh coldness for which she had given no sort of fresh cause? While she was in this state of perplexity, the door opened, infinitely to her relief, and Laura Brancepeth entered—from whose presence, so soon as he could decently escape, Mr. Anstruther made precipitate retreat.

Lady Peverell herself—hating La Reine Gaillarde as only Puritans can hate—was fain to attribute to her some slight good nature and generosity; but the warmest of her admirers scarcely gave that reckless dame credit for so much delicacy as she had evinced since the engagement had become an accomplished fact. Her one object seemed to be to make Blanche forget all that she had said while warning was of avail; and she would not hear of the wedding-breakfast taking place elsewhere than in Craven Square—devoting to the celebration of that select banquet more time and zeal than she had ever spared to the most important of her own entertainments. She was not fickle, either in her likes or dislikes. At first it was rather a trial to be always cordial to Mark Ramsay; and she had to set a watch on her free-spoken lips, lest a sharp word should escape them unawares. But this restraint soon passed away. She could not deny that Mark's demeanor toward his *fiancée* was simply perfect; and as, day by day, she came to acknowledge that report had not exaggerated the fascination of his manner, she ceased to wonder at Blanche's infatuation, or even to call her choice by such a name.

"Devils are not often quite so black as they are painted," she confessed. "And this one's complexion certainly improves on acquaintance. I don't feel the least inclined to exorcise him now when he appears; and I have quite left off pitying Blanche; though I don't think it's likely I shall ever quite come to envy her. There's room for improvement, of course; but I'm not sure that's a bad thing. Mr. Brancepeth is never so happy as when he's 'improving' some piece of land or another; and Blanche can try her hand in the same line. Perhaps she will get some good crops out of her new property, after all, if she's any luck in husbandry."

Her confidant—*vieux routier* himself—smiled approvingly.

"Metaphorical, as usual," he said. "I don't suppose any one else would have got Satanic and agricultural similes into the same sentence. But your charity covers even such a sin as that very old joke about husbandry. I do hope things will turn out better than the wiseacres would have it. It's such a comfort to see the talent wrong sometimes."

When Blanche Ellerslie lay down to rest, on the eve of her second wedding-day, she could not help comparing her sensations with what she had felt at a similar season once before. Though she was very young then, she had tasted, in all innocence, of the fruit of the tree of knowledge of good and evil, and she was not much overcome by the vague terrors that beset guileless maidenhood just about to cross the frontier of an unknown land. Left motherless in her childhood, she had managed a household at an age when most girls are still in school-trammels. General Norman, when off duty, was too busy with his own pursuits to keep strict watch and ward over the proceedings of his charming daughter. He was only too glad to see her amusing herself in her own way; and, though he told his friends in confidence, sometimes, that "such an arrant little flirt never breathed," he said it rather pleasantly than complainingly, and never dreamed of the possibility of her coming to harm.

The old soldier, though not very wise in his generation, was right so far. Blanche, before she was far advanced in her teens, was well able to defend her own heart. Love-whispers not a few had been poured into her ears, before Walter Ellerslie's deep, grave tones made the offer of marriage; but she had never been hampered by a serious attachment, or even by a fancy that survived a week; neither had she any repugnance to overcome. Perhaps she would have preferred a husband whose

locks were like the raven's,
Whose bonnie brow was brent.

But this was a mere matter of taste, not worth insisting on; and she felt somehow that she would be safer and happier, and freer to boot, in the long run, under the guardianship of the stiff, stern soldier, than under that of the gay gallants whose lissom knees would bend each night before a fresh beauty. She fully intended to make Colonel Ellerslie's home bright and cheery; and that resolve she worked out to the letter, after her own fashion. At least, he thought so who ought to have known best, and said so when he lay a-dying.

She had sat on her first husband's knee, and played with his sword-hilt, when she was quite a child; he gave her the first ornament she ever wore,—a waist-belt of regimental gold lace; and she had got so thoroughly used to him, that, on the eve of the day when she was to take his name, she hardly felt as if she were going to enter a strange home. It was very different with her now. She had known Mark Ramsay scarcely four months, and there was no reason why she should feel safe in trusting herself implicitly to his mercy: indeed, now that she was about so to trust herself, there were less grounds, as she knew full well, for confidence than for fear.

To his mercy. That was the only true way of putting it. That she had firm and fast hold on his affection now she could not doubt; but, if that hold were ever to be loosened, or cast off altogether, she felt she would have nothing else to cling to in this life, or—if truth must be written—in the next. Blanche was not absolutely a heathen, but she had never been taught to say a prayer except by rote, and hers was but a lip-religion at the best. Her perishable wealth, such as it was, was all locked up in treasure-houses that, if they keep out the robber, cannot for long keep out the canker-worm. She had made a plaything of love till now; suddenly the laughing child had waxed into a giant's stature, and stood before her—dark-browed, armed, menacing. Into the fair house so long tenantless, though swept and garnished, the strong spirit had entered; what manner of spirit it was, could be proven in the future only.

She felt somewhat like a gamester who, having always till now played for the merest trifle, finds himself lured on to deeper and deeper stakes, till at last all his fortune is set upon one cast—a cast yet to be thrown.

Pondering on these things, it is no wonder if Blanche Ellerslie's heart fluttered strangely; but she never repented for an instant, or wished the morrow deferred, and the tremor only gave a keener zest to the delight of anticipated happiness. She would not have set the shadow of the next morning's sun one hair's-breadth back on the dial. A smile lingered on her lips long after her eyes were closed; and, if her sleep was not dreamless that night, it was haunted by no visions of warning.

CHAPTER XIII.

Few men, if they told truth, would not own to having experienced some curious sensations when they came to realize that with another round of the clock the thread of their bachelor life must be cut in twain.

It is not a very terrible death, certainly. The Wielder of the shears wears a fair white robe, all beribboned and purple-fringed, and over her features there falls the brightest of saffron veils; but, mask it as gayly as she will, we know it is Atropos, and none other, that cometh in the morning. Even the impetuous lover—who for the last month past has quarreled with the tardiness of time— may, without treason, at such an hour indulge in two or three retrospective sighs. These last hours are spent differently, of course—often very differently from what one would expect from previous knowledge of the person; but I think they are not often spent alone.

Not long ago, a man, who has since turned out a perfect prize husband, was found, very late on the eve of his wedding-day, wandering through the groves of Cremorne. He was no roistering Alsatian; the place had never been a favorite haunt of his; and I dare swear there was not a single wish or regret then in his honest heart that his bride might not have known and approved. When put upon his defense there and then by certain acquaintances, who pretended to be scandalized at lighting on him there, his sole excuse was that it was too hot for any smoking-room, and he came there for company. It was the simple truth, I have no doubt. He had less reason, perhaps, than most people to dread being left alone with his own thoughts; but he preferred any society to theirs just then.

Mark Ramsay was not given to sentimentalize, and—troubling himself not a whit about the past—was nearly a fatalist as to the future He had a presentiment, as has been hinted before, that retributive justice, in one shape or other, would lay hands on him some day; but he felt no awe of the distant shadow. Whether the sword over his head swung by a steel wire or a silken thread, he cared not to inquire, and fully meant to take his ease after his own fashion till the blow should fall. He was no surface Sybarite: his thoughts were so thoroughly drilled that, if he could not always regulate their flow, he could at least draw them out of any disagreeable channel; so that they were scarcely likely to give him much trouble now. Nevertheless, he had been careful to provide against solitude on the last evening of his bachelorhood; and another beside himself heard the clocks chime midnight in those same chambers where his musing-fit after the Nithsdale ball had ended with the words, "I will."

Mark Ramsay had a very large acquaintance, and, in despite of his misdemeanors, was rather popular than otherwise in general society; but if he had lived from youth upward the life of a recluse he could not have had fewer intimates. Such a term certainly would not apply to his present companion; though since he first knew Vere Alsager he had been much in his company, and each could have told curious tales of the other, had they been given to babbling.

Some people thought Alsager's face singularly handsome. Picturesque it certainly was—with its keen aquiline contour, set off by a blue-black beard, whose massive lustrous waves might have made an Osmanli envious. His deep-set eyes were quiet enough as a rule; but now and then there came into them rather a truculent look, after seeing which once, you ceased to wonder at the man's story. It was a simple and not a very uncommon one.

He was bred to diplomacy; and was on the fair road to advancement, when an unlucky accident—as his friends called it, though the world in general gave it a harsher name—turned him adrift without a career. Half a dozen different versions of this were given at the time; none of which, perhaps, were absolutely correct. No one believed that the first cause of offense arose out of the difference of opinion at the Casino; or that Agnello Salviati, the sweetest-tempered of voluptuaries, would have made a few careless words, dropped by the other, the pretext of a mortal quarrel. One thing was certain—that Alsager might easily have avoided the unhappy issue, had he been so minded, without impeachment of his honor. This told heavily against him. There was a rumor, too, more generally believed than disbelieved, of a woman, thickly cloaked and veiled, who visited him late that night; and of agonized entreaty, and bitter wailing, overheard by some who lodged under the same roof; and people would have it that other reasons, besides natural grief for her only brother, drove Maddalena Salviati soon afterward into the shelter of the cloister. If it was she who came to plead, that night, for herself or another, she might have spared herself the trouble and the shame. There was no more compassion in Vere Alsager's eyes, than if he were there to avenge a wrong, when he took his place next morning for the barrier-duel; and his hand was steady enough to send a bullet through his adversary's lungs, before the forty paces betwixt them were shortened by three.

Looking at it in its most favorable light, it was a very ugly story—so ugly that all the family interest, used unsparingly in the delinquent's behalf, could make no head against it. The chief of the Foreign Office in those days was no purist; but his bitterest political foes avouched him a high-minded gentleman; and the black cross, set by him over against Vere Alsager's name, none of his successors was tempted to erase. It was years and years ago when all this happened; and Alsager—who since then had lived a quiet *dilettante* life, addicting himself chiefly to painting, wherein he had acquired no mean skill, and giving no further grave cause for scandal — had been gradually taken back into the world's good graces, till now he was not in much worse repute than many of whom it is vaguely whispered that "they have been a little wild in their youth." His own memory was not quite so accommodating. He never thought of *that* night —and he thought of it often—without intense bitterness; the bitterness of an eager, ambitious man by whose own act and deed a promising career has been marred, with which mingled, perhaps, certain black drops of remorse. But then, you see, he knew all the rights of the story; wherein he had the advantage of any living. Even Mark Ramsay, who paced out the ground from the barrier and measured to a grain the charge of the fatal pistol, was only partially taken into his principal's confidence at the time; and since then, by tacit consent, the subject had been ignored betwixt them.

All the circumstances considered, one might have thought that Ramsay, lacking a groomsman, would have chosen some other than Alsager. The parallel of one good turn deserving another would scarcely apply here. Yet both seemed to think the arrangement perfectly natural: when Vere said, "Of course, I shall be very happy," the other thoroughly understood the meaning of his smile. And so it was settled.

It was characteristic of the two men that, though they had dined and spent all the evening together, neither had made the faintest allusion to the event of the morrow. They had analyzed the racing of the past week, and the chances of certain of their fellows surviving the next great meeting—for plunging was much affected by the set to which they both belonged—decided that the great Ethiopian opera was a delusion and a snare, and that its *impresario*, through age and overfeeding, had become incapable of judging whether voices were cracked or legs crooked—discussed the latest alliances, legal or illegal, of their mutual acquaintances; but of Mark's marriage not one word.

"Perfect chambers, certainly," Alsager remarked, after a long pause, making a blue smoke-wreath curl round the bronze torso of a dancing faun; "quite ornamental enough, and not overdone. I hate, when I'm sitting in a man's room, to be always reminded of a boudoir in the Quartier Breda."

"Yes. Clinton had very chaste notions of furnishing," the other assented, "which is odd enough, remembering what his other tastes were. I took this place off his hands just as it stood, when he was obliged to make a moonlight flitting. There was no valuation; and I gave him his own price without chaffering; but I fancy I got a real bargain. Nothing you see is really mine, so far as choice goes, except a few pictures and statuettes; and I haven't been long enough here to feel thoroughly domesticated: so there's no great reason why I should be plaintive about changing my quarters."

A little, incredulous laugh stirred the black waves of Alsager's beard.

"You're improving," he said. "Till now, I never guessed that you would undervalue a pretty thing because another man owned it, or that you could not be comfortable unless you felt thoroughly domesticated. *Macte novâ virtute.* The will-o'-the-wisp will be a steady, shining light, before all's done. What do you mean to do about these chambers?—to let some one else have them, all standing? That's the simplest way. I wish I could afford to take them, I know."

"I've hardly made up my mind," Mark answered. "I'm in no particular hurry about it There's nothing here I should care to move all the way to Scotland; and I sha'n't look out for a town-house till next spring. I'll tell you what, Vere; you may live here till then, if you like—rent-free, of course. It's no favor. I'd infinitely sooner leave my things in your charge than at the old housekeeper's mercy. Will you come?"

" I should like it, of all things," the other said; "though, if it isn't a favor, I've very vague ideas of benevolence. The worst of it is, one would never be able to go back and settle down in dingy lodgings again. Never mind. Unto the day, the day. I accept all the same. I'm very disinterested, you see; for I can't understand why you don't clear out at once. You could easily put your nick-nacks in safe-keeping somewhere; and it's so utterly impossible that you could ever use these chambers again."

"Highly improbable, certainly; but—as for impossible, it's a very big word; too big for my dictionary, I know."

They looked at each other; and Alsager smiled.

"Ah, I understand. A wise general always provides for retreat. Your provisions are made in good time. Mark,—the devil's in it, if we two can't speak frankly,— you'll own, it is a leap in the dark you are taking, after all ?"

"Very much in the dark," the other answered, coolly. "But the landing is likely to be as safe, or more so, than in most of the jumps that we have taken with our eyes open. One thing I am certain of,—if I'm not comfortable it will be my own fault or misfortune; and so you'll see when you come to know Blanche better. There are dozens of women all round us prettier and wittier and better than she is, I dare say; but she is simply the most sociable creature I ever met with; her voice and manner, let alone her face, grow on you quite curiously."

"I never doubted Mrs. Ellerslie's attractions," Alsager said, "and I dare say you could not have made a luckier choice. What I did doubt was—whether you should have chosen at all. But we're creatures of circumstance much more than of habit, I do believe; and, perhaps, if any one left me a big property and a big house, I should begin to feel matrimonial immediately, as a matter of course. It isn't likely such a good part will ever be cast to me; but, I confess, I look forward to seeing *you* play the Head of the Family."

"Mind you do come and see it, then," Ramsay retorted. "There's no disease in the Kenlis moors so far, I hear: they are only overstocked, and want shooting down. I shall reckon on you early in August, mind."

He stretched himself as he spoke, pitching the end of his cigar away. The other took the hint, and rose.

"Yes; it's full time we went to bed. It's no question of steadiness of eye and hand to-morrow; but the breakfast is an awful trial of nerve; I'm not afraid of the church-work."

"Very brave of you, I must say. Now, I think it's just as well, for your sake, there's no sprinkling of holy water in our marriage-service over the assistants; there's no knowing what the effect might be. Good-night: mind you're ready when I call for you."

"'The assistants,'" Vere Alsager thought within himself, as he strode away. "And how about the principals? *They* have no need to shrink from holy water, of course —particularly St. Mark yonder. I've done some queerish things in my time; but, if his past were weighed against mine, I know which side would kick the beam. It's kind of him, too, to lend me these chambers; though I question if it's quite disinterested kindness. Bah! I'm always questioning; and what's the use of it? Perhaps it will be longer than next spring before he wants to make use of his *petite maison:* perhaps he never had the idea, after all. I like what I have seen of her. Those dainty, delicate women are piquant long after they cease to be pretty; and hers is a face that will last. I shouldn't mind painting it. I'll book Kenlis for August, at all events: it won't be half a bad place to stay at, as long as things go on smoothly."

CHAPTER XIV.

Did you ever chance to read *Firmilian*—the most complete literary mystification of modern times? You may be sure it has not been forgotten yet by the ill-used critics who sat in judgment on its merits and demerits, wagging their heads over its spasmodic vagaries (though some, tempering judgment with mercy, held out hope of amendment to the hot-brained offender, if he would but profit by their monitions), and who found out, when it was too late, that they had but fed the laughter of the veteran humorist, who, having spread the net, never stirred tongue nor finger till the grave Palladian birds were fluttering in the meshes.

Truly, the mock tragedy deserves to be remembered on other grounds besides these. After all, the spasmodic element was not much more glaringly developed than in parts of *Festus*, and others of the same school; and many dramas, worked out in sober earnest and profusely sprinkled with the midnight oil, lack the rhythm and power of the pasquinade penned for pastime in the summer forenoons by Spey-side.

There is great pomp and festival in the church of St. Nicholas. The sun streams full and fair through the gorgeous window; sweetly and slowly rises and falls the chant of the trained voices:—

> There rolls the organ anthem down the aisle,
> And thousand voices join in its acclaim.
> All they are happy—they are on their knees;
> Round and above them stare the images
> Of antique saints and martyrs; the censers steam
> With their Arabian charge of frankincense;
> And every heart, with inward fingers, counts
> The blissful rosary of pious prayer.

It is very still and dark in the vaults below, where the powder-barrels are stored, and where waits the busy mocker, holding the slow-match that will anon send the souls of all those good worshipers above flitting hither and thither. After a while comes the last triumphant antiphon—

> Nicholai, sacerdotum
> Decus, honor, gloria:
> Plebem omnem, clerum totum—

And then—

[*The cathedral is blown up.*]

Not long ago, I heard a man confess—he was not given to quaint fancies, nor specially sardonic or somber of temperament—that he never listened to a marriage-service without thinking of that same cathedral scene. His experience of life, it appeared, had forced him to believe that under the feet of most couples standing face to face before the altar there is stored up more or less of combustible elements, the firing of which is merely a question of time; though the explosion may be long deferred, and, when it occurs, may be attended with nothing more harmful than a little noise and smoke.

But even this foreboder of evil would have been puzzled to discover anything very threatening in the aspect of things, if he had been present on the morning when Mark Ramsay took Blanche Ellerslie to be his wedded wife. Though neither the bride nor the bridegroom had turned the corner of middle life, they were quite old enough to know their own minds; and neither was likely to make a false step through impulse or from rashness. If there was little likelihood of intense devotion on either side, there was fair promise of the pleasant companionship which unites people endowed with similar tastes and facilities for indulging the same.

Against this were to be set, of course, Ramsay's antecedents, which certainly were the reverse of encouraging; but he had been more than twelve months, as it were, on his probation, and, so far as the world knew, had shown no signs of relapse. Society in general was disposed to give him credit for having turned over a new leaf. If he had not intended henceforth to do all things decently and in order, there was no earthly reason why he should have hampered himself with a wife or a regular establishment. Kenlis Castle was a fine place, to be sure;

but there were others quite as majestic on either side of the Border, the honors of which were done by bachelors in bachelor-fashion—in the most liberal sense of the word. Mark's was one of the exceptional faces that never look weather-beaten, after a youth ever so stormy; and any one, seeing him that morning for the first time, would have found it hard to believe that half the stories told of him could be true.

It was meant to be a quiet wedding, and the invitation-list was purposely limited; but the concourse of spectators, larger than was common in that fashionable church, proved that others besides the intimate acquaintance of the contracting parties were curious to witness their espousal. Several of the wedding-party, to whom seats were allotted in the pews nearest the altar, may have felt like the Pope at Paris, when he said that "the greatest wonder of the town was to see him there." But not one of them seemed so thoroughly out of place as Mr. Anstruther.

The color and fashion of his garments, more funereal than festive, would not have been so remarkable (for Anglo-Indian attire is apt to be eccentric, especially when the wearer is not on speaking-terms with his tailor); but the settled gloom of the man's countenance was not so easily to be accounted for; and the nervous discomfort of his manner could hardly be attributed to mere lack of familiarity with the forms and ceremonies of the Church as by law established. In his eyes, usually so hard and cold, there was a haggard look, not pleasant to meet. Perhaps he was vaguely conscious of this; for during the delay before the service commenced, and throughout it except when he was compelled to stand up with the rest, he kept his face always shaded with his long, bony hand.

Yet, when Blanche Ramsay turned away from the altar and descended the steps, leaning on her husband's arm, it so chanced that the first glance that met hers, as she raised her eyes rather shyly, was George Anstruther's. His tall, lanky figure could scarcely fail to be prominent anywhere; and he stood close to the aisle. A superstitious person might have taken the omen somewhat to heart; and Blanche, who believed in the *jettatura* no more than she did in second-sight, was half inclined to regret she had so pressingly insisted on the presence of this especial wedding-guest. She never suspected for a moment that any one there present could take more than a friendly interest in the ceremony just concluded; and, as for any malice or uncharitableness being stirred in the breast of so staid a personage as George Anstruther, she was just as likely to impute such emotions to Mr. Brancepeth, who gave her away. If she had been forced to answer the question of Oswald Gauntlet's searching eyes, she might possibly have felt rather timid, and just the least bit remorseful. But he would never have glared at her in that uncanny fashion.

Men, out of Bedlam, or off the stage, very seldom do glare nowadays. Those that she has jilted most cruelly, instead of confronting the bride at the church-door in the antique ballad fashion, bow their heads meekly and courteously as she passes out, even if they do not hum under their breaths Béranger's gay wicked refrain :—

> Un doux espoir
> Me sourit encore
> De la couronne de la mariée.

Nevertheless, the glimpse of that face did affect Blanche Ramsay with a faint presentiment of ill luck; and she shivered ever so slightly—even as Horace's fair mistress may have done when, stepping daintily toward her litter, she caught sight of the snake

> Qui per obliquum similis sagittæ terruit mannos.

The wedding procession had scarcely passed down the aisle, when Mr. Anstruther began to make his way out of the church, muttering some excuse to his nearest neighbor about the heat. It was an odd pretext for him to choose, who had lived so long where 90° in the shade was the normal state of the thermometer, and who had often, in old times, stirred the ire of portly *baboos* by looking comfortably cool in an atmosphere that caused them to pant and perspire. Yet it was not, perhaps, altogether a false one; for there was a dark flush round either check-bone; and if you had touched his hand, as he dragged his gloves off impatiently, you would have thought there was fever in his veins. But no one in the crowd, through which he elbowed his way, noticed anything strange in his demeanor; and the idlers outside never turned their heads to watch the gaunt, ungainly figure hurrying away with long, uneven strides through the glaring sunlight.

The breakfast in Craven Square was not nearly so dreary as such entertainments are wont to be. The table was not crowded, and almost all who sat round it were in the habit of meeting each other daily. Formal speech-making would have been utterly out of place there—so, at least, thought every one except Mr. Brancepeth.

This honest gentleman had not so many opportunities of airing the eloquence on which he rather prided himself, as to lose one when it presented itself. He had been a hard-working member of the Commons' House for many years, but his maiden speech was yet unspoken. The "whip" of his party regarded Mr. Brancepeth with an immense respect and affection, as a model that hair-brained, garrulous legislators would have done well to imitate. He never asked importunate or impertinent questions, and when he was wanted was sure to be found in his place, ready to vote exactly as the keeper of his political conscience directed, listening always—or seeming to listen—with impartial patience to the declamation on either side, but never to be biased in the faintest degree by argument, persuasion, or diatribe. Surely he had a perfect right to indemnify himself elsewhere for his silence at St. Stephen's; and few grudged him that simple satisfaction. At quarter sessions, agricultural meetings, and all manner of county gatherings, Mr. Brancepeth was always listened to with greater attention than more brilliant orators could command, while he glozed on through one smooth period after another, enouncing truisms like startling verities, and winding up with a peroration in which there was seldom any definite conclusion.

On occasions like the present he was great. The facetiæ that formed his stock-in-trade were rather trite and mild; but from long practice he had acquired a knack of setting them forth so that they did not seem so *very* threadbare; and the fumes of champagne, consumed at abnormal hours, are apt to make an audience rather indulgent than critical. During the long, purposeless afternoon, when the idea of dinner is as it were an abomination, we wax more captious, to be sure, and wonder how we could have been weak and base enough to smile at the platitudes floating in our memory. But this is a mere question of digestion, after all. If any of Mr. Brancepeth's hearers felt bored or weary, they were polite enough to suppress all outward and visible signs thereof. So, in perfect charity with all man and womankind, he drank to the health of the bride and bridegroom, and finished with the comfortable conviction of having achieved no mean social success.

La Reine Gaillarde had a keen sense of humor of her own; and you may guess that the exhibition was not particularly agreeable to her. But she was not inclined to be hard on any innocent weakness: her sigh of relief was not too audible, nor her smile too satirical, when the orator sat down. Her lord and master had shown himself so very amiable about all arrangements that she considered he had quite earned the license of making himself ridiculous if it so pleased him. Most men think they have done enough if they play father to a comparative stranger at the altar, without placing their mansion at her disposal before or on the marriage-day.

Mark Ramsay replied in half a dozen sentences; and this was the only other interruption to the flow of general talk that went on pleasantly enough till breakfast broke up.

Availing herself of the widow's privilege, Blanche had dispensed with bridesmaids: so the cynics—if any such were present—were balked of the treat of hearing the acknowledgments of innocence and beauty spoken by the lips of Vere Alsager.

Among the advances of civilization made in this our century ought to be reckoned the shortening of honeymoons. Very few conversationalists can talk quite up to their mark if they know they are expected to be amusing; and the effect of being expected to be amative for a certain definite period must often be much the same. If our grandsires would confess the truth, we should hear, I fancy, that the sun drove his chariot somewhat heavily before the twenty-eighth day of enforced seclusion closed in; and, long ere that, there had been certain misgivings as to the perfect truth of the ancient adage, "Two are company: three are none." We have changed all this, most assuredly. Even Mrs. Malaprop, whose matrimonial ideas were somewhat in advance of her age, would lift her brows in wonder over the curtness of some wedding-trips.

Dropping into a certain club on a murky afternoon in this very spring, to my great wonderment I lighted upon an ancient acquaintance in his accustomed place, smoking his cigarette, and sipping his *perroquet,* in the contemplative fashion that is usual with him when the day is almost done. I rubbed my eyes, so to speak, thinking that I saw a vision, or that, at the least, I must have been dreaming when I read, not twenty-four hours before, the announcement of his marriage. Inclining to this last opinion, I expressed it in so many words.

"There's no mistake," Randal Lacy said, placidly. "We were married all right enough; and we went down to ——" (the precise locality of the Arcadian hostel doesn't signify): "but it rained all yesterday, and our windows were on the ground-floor, and the people walking under the veranda *would* stare at us; and so—and so—we came back to-day, you see; and I'm going to take Nellie to the Prytaneum to-night. We've got the stage-box; and she can sit back behind the curtain. Will you come? There's lots of room."

I don't know a happier *ménage* than this has been, up to the present moment of writing, in a quiet, domestic way, or one that holds forth fairer promise of so enduring.

Now, Ramsay did not apprehend that either himself or Blanche would grow weary of each other in a *tête-à-tête,* even if it was somewhat prolonged; but he had an objection on principle to crucial tests, and opined that sufficient solitude for all reasonable purposes could be found in the skirts, if not in the heart, of a crowd. If Kenlis Castle had been habitable, he would have gone thither straightway; but there was much still to be done there before the bride could fitly be brought home.   He might have found shelter in the country-houses of half a dozen friends; but Mark was not minded to begin his married life by trusting to the mercies of another man's household.   On the whole, he thought that Paris would be as good a lounging-place as any; and Blanche, when the idea was suggested to her, adopted it quite eagerly.   So it came to pass that their second domestic dinner was eaten in the Place Vendôme.

It was one of the close sultry evenings, more trying to natural complexions than the glare of lamp or sun. Blanche was quite refreshing to look upon in her pale-gray dress—relieved at the neck and wrist by trimmings of filmy lace—not a braid of her smooth soft hair ruffled or awry, and with just the faint flush on her check that an artist would have chosen to see there.   Mark's critical eye took in every point of the picture with profound satisfaction, as he realized how much more suited to his taste was that demure little person than any brilliant beauty of the Fornarina type, magnificent in redundant outline and gorgeous coloring.

Two days of Blanche's exclusive society had made him more fully aware than he had ever yet been how thoroughly pleasant a companion he had found.   There was nothing impulsive, or demonstrative, or expansive about her: though it was evident that she liked being petted above all things, she was not exacting, or lavish of her own caresses.   It would have needed a very subtle analysis to discover a single acid drop in all her composition; but there was no danger, with her, of being cloyed with too much honey.   The very sound of her voice would have been a specific for more irritable nerves than Ramsay's; and the most indolent of talkers deemed it worth while to be amusing only to provoke one trill of her low laugh-music.

With these thoughts in his mind, said Mark, after sitting silent awhile—

"Is there anything you care particularly about seeing here, Blanche? or are any of your commissions very pressing? If not, I think we might as well move into cooler quarters while this heat lasts.   Fontainebleau isn't half a bad place: there's always shade in the forest, and generally a breeze somewhere, if you know where to look for it."

"I've never been at Fontainebleau," she answered; "but it must be quite charming in this weather. My commissions can wait; and as for sight-seeing, I went through that penance long, long ago, when——"

Her face was a little grave as she stopped: the next instant, in spite of herself, she smiled.

She always thought kindly, if not tenderly, of honest Walter Ellerslie. It was with him she had lionized Paris when they had been married about a year; and she remembered how each morning at breakfast he used to pore over *Galignani* as if it had been a new drill-book—wrinkling his forehead, and knitting his brows, while he mapped out that day's work—conscientiously making a toil of every pleasure, after the fashion of a thorough-going British tourist. She had plodded through the weary round quite patiently then; but she had not forgotten her thankfulness when it was over. It was partly those memories that made her smile, partly the contrast of the present with the past. Truly, there was not much fear of any woman, traveling under Mark Ramsay's escort, being driven against her will into the performance of any duty whatsoever, much less an irksome one.

Thus the wise and worldly resolves of this pair went for naught, after all; and a full week of their honeymoon was spent, not only in solitude, but "under the green-wood tree."

It was the very happiest week of all Blanche Ramsay's life. Even had she visited it alone, the place would have had great attractions for her. She liked intensely the slow drives through forest-land, and the long halts under the great oaks and beeches, that are just as liberal of their shade now as when the beauties of the old time rested there after the "*hallali!*" had been sounded over a hart-royal; she liked the ugly, formal gardens, that can scarcely have changed since the *reines mères* rustled along their alleys; she liked the quaint, low-browed courts better than if each had been a model of architecture. In this fancy she was not alone.

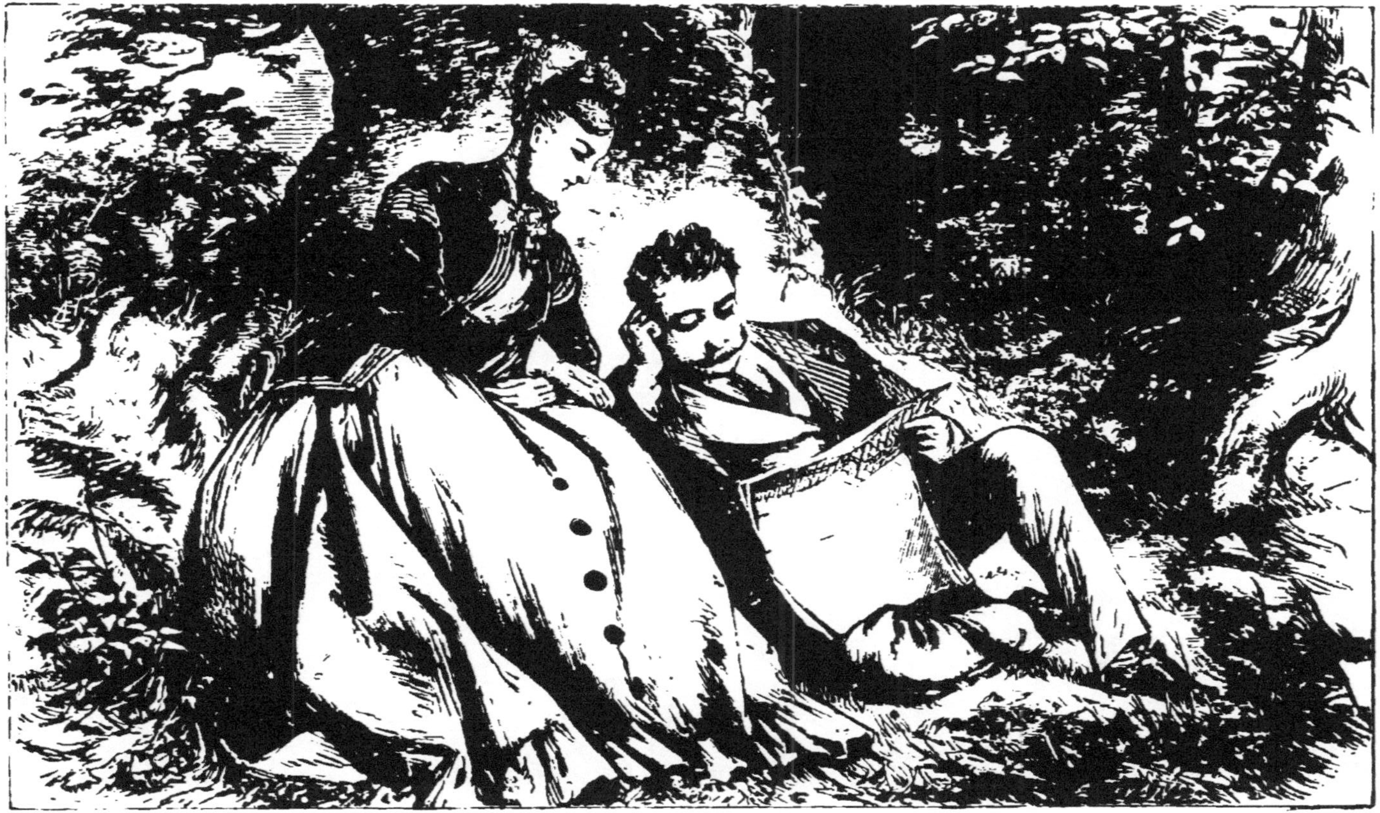

"UNDER THE GREENWOOD TREE"

There are few places that bring up the past more vividly, to others besides antiquarians, than Fontainebleau. Though time, and neglect, and revolution have left their marks plainly enough there, a pleasant *rococo* savor still hangs about the place, heightened rather than marred by the restorations of the Citizen King. The double initials, "H. D.," intertwined so tenderly, still look almost as fresh as when they were first set up to the glory of the superb courtesan who carried the garment of infamy as if it had been a robe of honor. In the Galerie des Cerfs you can stand on the very spot where Monaldeschi was done to death under the eyes of the Swedish Messalina. Leaning out of the window of the Queen's boudoir, you touch the *espagnolette* wrought by the cunning hand of Louis the locksmith ; and you can fancy the smile—half kindly, half scornful—with which the haughty Austrian paid the labor that proceeded of love. Altogether a place fitter to dream in, than many to which Art and Nature have been more kind.

Blanche had no drawback to her pleasure, in a suspicion that her husband was bored. He had seen all these things before, of course ; but, if they had no fresh interest for him now, it was excellently feigned. Blanche could have stayed another and another week there, without a chance of growing weary ; yet, when the hot weather broke up in rain that looked like lasting, it was she who suggested a move back on Paris. It was just the instance of womanly tact that Mark could appreciate ; and that he could do so he showed plainly enough, though his approbation was not uttered in words.

CHAPTER XV.

THERE have been many changes in Paris of late years, besides those for which the Prefecture is accountable: old types, no less than old streets, have been swept away; and the British resident has not been exempt from the spirit of change.

A quarter of a century ago, he was a decent domestic creature, usually of a certain age; not absolutely in embarrassed circumstances, yet under necessity of retrenchment; and always bent on ministering to the educational demands of a growing family at a reasonable rate. *Cœlum non animum mutabat.* After the first bustle of removal was over, he went on contentedly enough in his old humdrum way—the right of grumbling, of course, always reserved—looking out for his special corner-seat at Galignani's, as he was wont to look for the club arm-chair; indulging but rarely in the dissipation of a *café* dinner at his own charge; and frequenting theater or opera not much more sedulously than he was wont to do during a trip to London in the old days. Little versed were these quiet spirits in the *chroniques scandaleuses* of the day; an *émeute* in the Quartier Breda interested them no more than a revolution in Ashantee. They seldom sought to master the intricate idioms of the foreign tongue; and, if they could steer clear of glaring faults in grammar, were no more ashamed of their fine broad British accent than of any other proof of their nationality.

Among them there were always to be found, of course, certain roisterers, doing penance for past sins and follies in enforced exile; and not hankering the less after Egyptian dainties, since they were forbidden to taste the flesh-pots. But these were the exceptions to the rule; and regarded with little favor by their fellows, who gave these black sheep as wide a berth as was consistent with courtesy—by no means encouraging them to frequent the pastures in which their own lambkins strayed.

That modest colony is utterly broken up and dispersed now. The remnants thereof have migrated to Tours, Toulouse, and provincial towns yet more remote from the costly capital, where the space left for the poor and needy is narrowed hour by hour. In their places sit another generation of aliens, differing from those sober sojourners as widely as Rochester and his crew from the worthies of the Commonwealth; scarcely alien, either, if taking art and part in all the vices of his adopted country can make out a man's claim to naturalization.

The Anglo-Gaul at present is a jaunty gallant—usually in the flower of his age; with a full, if not a fathomless, purse; lisping out impurities with the purest of accents, and able to answer the *argot* of the *coulisses* in kind; found at all races within the jockey-club *enceinte;* and, when *baccarat* is afloat at the Cercle des Crèvés, holding his own undauntedly against all plungers—Jew, Turk, Christian, or infidel; in fine, hurrying down the broad slope of ruin in all respects with as easy a grace as if he traced his descent from Grammont or Montmorency. No wonder that the fair city accords to these strangers within her gates a very different welcome from that which she deigned to bestow on their modest predecessors.

In this especial clique Ramsay could not exactly be reckoned. Till quite lately he had been too poor to live their pace, and too prudent to hazard a certain breakdown; and since he became wealthy, business of one sort or another had kept him chiefly on the other side of the Channel. But he was thoroughly at home here, and at two Cercles his face was better known than in any London club.

The season was virtually over, and each day the trains starting for frontier or seaboard carried away a heavier freight; but the Bois was not a solitude as yet, and a score at least of ancient acquaintances greeted Ramsay the first time he appeared there. The news of his marriage had gone before him; and Blanche had to run the gauntlet of many curious glances before their carriage reached the turning-point at the head of the lake. On the whole, she came out of the ordeal very cleverly.

" *Un peu pâlotte; mais gentille à croquer, avec un*

morbidezza délicieuse—" said Amédée de Beaumanoir, a veteran *viveur*, whose valuation of fresh faces carried as much weight as the Admiral's judgment of a yearling.

Coquettes of a certain grade know by instinct when they have achieved a success, before a compliment—ever so delicately veiled—has reached their ears. Despite this satisfaction, it was not without a sinking of the heart that Blanche realized, during that first drive, that she must not expect to have her husband entirely to herself for some time to come. She was not discontented or disappointed; for their *tête-à-tête* had lasted already longer than she had hoped; and she did not feel—much less look or express—surprise when, after dinner that evening, he left her "to look in at the Cercle for an hour." A very elastic hour; for it slid into another day, and Blanche was sleeping placidly before it ended. At breakfast next morning it was so evident that she expected no excuse, that Mark never thought of composing one. Nothing could be more prettily saucy than her smile as she listened to his epitome of the congratulations offered him over-night.

Mrs. Ramsay had a long list of commissions to execute for herself and others, and she preferred going about this business alone, she said; so they did not meet again till the evening. After an early dinner, they went straight to the Bouffes, where a famous operetta was being played for about the four hundredth time.

You know the operetta and the fashion thereof. Not a very potent or generous liquor fills the jeweled cup that the wicked princess waves before us so deftly. It has plenty of froth and sparkle, and flavor enough to please a not-too-curious palate; and there is small danger of the weakest head being turned thereby. Feet and hands— to say nothing of eyes—have quite as much to do as the lips here: the *prima donna*, if only she be perfect in such arts of provocation—though a singer whose compass and sweetness of voice could hardly vie with a Bayadère's— need seldom despair of triumph.

What would Beaumarchais have said of the public that can assist nightly at such a performance as this—never craving for novelty, and by their persevering enthusiasm giving the *claque*, after the first week, a sinecure ? If he were in the flesh again, he might, with some justice, have been severe on the derogation of Parisian taste ; but wherefore we insulars should shrug our shoulders thereat would be rather hard to say. How many times, I wonder, have you and I sat through a sensational drama, waiting patiently for the leap into a fathomless abyss that would break the long dead-level of dullness? And how often have we gone, with a laugh ready cut-and-dried, to reward the one dance tacked on to a patter-song, that gave vitality to the weakest of burlesques? Go to ! Faith, hope, and charity shall flourish, for many a day to come, no less benignly on the hither than on the farther side of the narrow seas—faith in our playwrights, hope in their prolific talent, charity to their shortcomings.

The sort of thing was quite new to Mrs. Ramsay, and amused her intensely ; indeed, in the opening scenes there was nothing that need have called up " the blush on the cheek of a young person," unless the equivocal jokes of the libretto had been carefully studied beforehand. It was a crowded house ; but one double *baignoire*, exactly opposite the Ramsays' box, remained empty till the middle of the first *entr'acte*. Then, with some bustle and flourish—as if willing to announce their presence to all whom it might concern—two women occupied it.

In the appearance of one of these there was nothing remarkable. Her face in the very first freshness of youth might possibly have been tempting ; but now, in spite of cosmetics and carefully-disheveled false hair, it was simply ignoble. There was a cowed, servile look about this woman. The flourish of her entry was palpably rather in imitation of her companion than an act of self-assertion ; and she hesitated about seating herself in front, till an imperious sign from the other bade her do so.

In this evil trade, as in others, there are bankrupts. When Lolotte Lalange's scanty stock of beauty failed, she had not wit enough to be either dangerous or attractive : she had just sense enough to know this ; and to know furthermore that, if she would find food and shelter and clothing thenceforth, she must cease to traffic on her own account, and take wages—ever so nominal. Being of a torpid, pliable nature, by no means sensitive of affront, and always open to a peace-offering in any shape whatsoever, she had thriven thus far tolerably well on the bread of dependence.   In that same bread—especially, I fear, if it be dispensed by female hands—there must always be a bitter leaven.   Those who are bound to truckle to the caprice of crabbed old maids or purse-proud widows do not sleep upon roses; but—setting ignominy altogether aside—the unluckiest of "companions" may well feel thankful to the Fates that have spared her the endurance of a harlot's tyranny.

The other woman was a striking contrast, and would have been remarkable in any place or company; though, after looking at her once and again, you might have been puzzled to decide where the secret of her famous fascination lay.

There was a good deal of character certainly in her face, with its low, broad brow, which the strong crisp curls half covered without shading—in the great, hard eyes, that seemed as if they never would blench or soften—in the firm, well-chiseled nose, with nostrils always dilated as if they scented prey—in the full, crimson lips, curling outward, so that the level, gleaming teeth were never quite hidden—and in the square, cruel jaw scarcely tapering toward the chin.   But it was essentially an unlovely face—one that wearied the eyes that dwelt on it, like a garish picture.   If they had been asked to name its antitype in the animal creation, nine men out of ten would have pitched upon the tigress.   She was *forte femme* in every sense of the word.   There was physical power in every line of the straight throat, the round arms, and ample bust—white and firm and cold as Carrara marble; but a wasp-like waist only just saved her figure from coarseness.

Such as she was, Delphine Maréchal had wrought damage enough with her enchantments to become a byword in a land where such sorceries are rife.

The world first heard of her as the wife of a captain of Spahis in the army of Algiers.   Of her birth and parentage, and of the manner of her wooing, nothing certain was known; but that Eugène Boisragon, on his return from furlough, brought back a lawfully-wedded wife, there was no reason to doubt. Before the second year of their marriage was half spent, there were many scandals afloat concerning her. It was whispered that long good service, and hitherto stainless repute, did not save a certain general of brigade from sharp rebuke in high quarters, where such trifles as a *liaison* are seldom noticed. Eugène Boisragon, after a few outbreaks of jealous fury that his wife laughed utterly to scorn, had taken to desperate drinking, and was seldom seen sober off parade. Men all said that something worse than absinthe was working in his brain; and that he was off his head long before the last frenzy-fit possessed him, when he rode down alone, yelling like a maniac as he was, on the thirsty Kabyle yataghans. His widow went through no farce of mourning, but "made her packet" with the briefest possible delay, and betook herself to Paris—not without male escort. From that day forth, she threw off the thinnest disguise of respectability, and went on her wicked way rejoicing.

Whether it was some faint scruple of remorse, or only a wild whim, that prompted her to drop the "Boisragon" and fall back on her maiden name—Heaven save the mark! —none could guess; but on any note or quittance she signed herself Delphine Maréchal. She was much better known, though, as "La Topaze." Looking at her yellow lustrous hair and tawny gleaming eyes, you were struck at once with the aptness of the *sobriquet*. She was no hypocrite, and disdained the common stratagems of her trade. She never affected softness or sympathy, and conquered without troubling herself to be winning. When her phantasy—and phantasies she had not seldom—was past, or when the purse that supplied her reckless caprice was drained, she dismissed her lover just as she dismissed her lackey; and it would have been as vain for one as for the other to look for charity or compassion at her hands in after-time. Threats or complaints or entreaties were all met with the same hard, ringing laugh; and none, so far, had fared better than his fellows—from Achille, Prince de Senneterre, who for her sake left a fair young bride to pine before the orange-flowers had time to wither, down to Léon Gondrecourt, the struggling sculptor, with a face like an old Greek statue, who left her presence for the last time with scarcely *sous* enough in his pocket to buy the charcoal that stifled him. She was not particularly clever, and passably ill educated; but was endowed with a rude mother-wit, and a certain readiness of repartee. This, added to the known violence of her temper and utter unscrupulousness in revenge, made her much dreaded among her sisterhood; so that in most companies she took and kept the lead— queening it like a thorough usurper.

Rather royal, in her own fashion, La Topaze looked to-night, in a dress that few of her complexion would have dared to wear—a superb maize *moiré*, trimmed with priceless lace—with emeralds flashing in her tawny hair, and round the carved column of her neck, and all over her ample white breast. The contrast of color, that would have shocked any civilized taste, only seemed to enhance her quaint, barbaric splendor. Any one fond of such parallels would surely have been reminded then of the famous Czarina whose loves and wars, more than a century ago, kept all Europe on the alert.

As she entered, there was a stir through the parterre, and a murmur that might have been mistaken for subdued applause; and, before she had been seated three minutes, a hundred glasses leveled at her box answered the challenge of her audacious eyes. To nine-tenths of the men present hers was a familiar face. To provincials, who saw her for the first time, their neighbors pointed out the celebrity with the sort of pride that a Javanese might feel in the exhibition of a flourishing upas-tree.

On this personage Mrs. Ramsay gazed with an eagerness of which she was more than half ashamed. She was no country-bred girl looking for the first time on the world's wicked ways. She had seen Pelagia flaunting in different guises in divers places, ere now, without shrinking aside in holy horror at the sight, or feeling any special interest therein; but such a specimen of the sisterhood as this she had never looked upon, and she was attracted by it as she would have been attracted by any other animal curiosity.

While Mark, laughing outright at her eagerness, was answering her questions with a brief sketch of the antecedents of La Topaze, the door of the *baignoire* opposite opened again, and two men came in. One, a pale, boyish-looking Frenchman, came to the front at once, and evidently began some explanation or excuse, to which La Topaze gave no sort of heed—dashing it aside as it were with an insolent wave of her fan; while she glanced over her shoulder, as if waiting to be addressed by the other cavalier, who, after he had closed the door, remained leaning against the wall, in the shadow. He came forward at last, and proceeded to take stock of the house through his glasses, in a lazy, leisurely way, before he troubled himself to reply to a remark from La Topaze, which was evidently either an angry question or a sharp reproach.

A man of proper presence, decidedly, with a tall, martial figure, and a face that must have been strikingly handsome once, and had not ceased to be picturesque since it grew hard and haggard and marred by a kind of lowering that told of evil temper not often controlled. It was a face, though, that few women would easily forget when they had seen it once. That Mrs. Ramsay had not forgotten it, was abundantly clear; for, as she caught sight of the new-comer, she started, and drew back hurriedly, saying, in a whisper,—so low that her husband hardly caught the words,—

"Good heavens! It is Vereker Vane."

11*

CHAPTER XVI.

IN the storehouse of almost every woman's memory—
whether it be bare and poverty-stricken, or crammed to
the threshold with treasures varied and manifold—there
is kept a special corner for her "old loves." I do not
speak now of those who, having been interwoven to a
greater or less extent in a woman's life-skein, have colored it with deep joy or deep bitterness—of those whose
names never recur without a reminder, regretful or reproachful, of

> How close to the stars we seemed
> That night on the sands by the sea.

I speak of those who in the old time could scarcely
be distinguished from the rank and file of her friends and
acquaintances; who never caused her pulse to flutter uneasily, or her cheek to flush unbecomingly; but who,
nevertheless, proffered to her once, without stint or limit,
the richest gift that was in their power to bestow, albeit
it found no favor in her eyes—I mean, the wooers that
wooed in vain.

If it be a weakness to wrap up these memories rather
tenderly, it is one to which women of every shade of
character are prone. It is just as likely—rather more
likely, indeed—to be found in the gravest prude as in the
most frivolous coquette; nor does the state of their domestic relations seem to have much to do with it.

The historic Helen was probably not a much more conscientious personage than Schneider represents her. Yet
her heart may have melted a little when, from the tower
over the Scæan gate, she looked down on the Achæan
array and remembered that each and every one of the
chiefest there was expiating, by exile from home and peril
of limb and life, the madness of having once aspired to
her hand.

For an opposite example, take Lady Gatacre. That model matron for years has ruled every household in her parish with an iron rod—a merciless allopath, both in religion and medicine; forcing her doctrine, her physic, and her charity down the throats of the poor, whose cottages she carries at the point of the parasol. She regards all works of fiction as more or less emanating from the father of lies, and romance in real life as a folly almost within the pale of sin. An upright woman,—*s'il en fût,*—she dresses the character to perfection, and towers at her board-head darkling and stately, not to be lighted up by sconce, lamp, or luster. But, on certain evenings, you may see gleams of scarlet breaking the sable monotony of her attire; and you recognize, with a certain astonishment, that the dame may have been admired once by such as look favorably on somber, severe beauty. On such occasions there sits always on her right hand the head of a certain Chapter hard by. The dean is a rabid Protestant, prone to take up his parable, in season and out of season, against the abominations of the Seven Hills; but my lady remembers what was his favorite color in the old, old times—the times when a patient, hard-working curate asked a proud, penniless girl to share his fortunes, and took meekly, if not contentedly, "Nay" for an answer. Good Sir John stands in far too great awe of his spouse to banter her on this or any other subject; but you may see by the twinkle in his merry, moist eye how thoroughly he appreciates her rare concessions to the vanities of this wicked world, and rejoices over these vulnerable points in the tough Amazonian harness.

The last time that Vereker Vane stood face to face with Blanche Ramsay, he had urged his suit for her hand as eloquently and earnestly as it was in his nature to speak; and had gone out of her presence in bitter anger. If she had ever regretted her answer then—and I believe she never had done so—she surely would have known no such misgivings now, in the flush of her own fresh happiness, and meeting him—thus. Nevertheless, the very proof before her eyes of how far he had gone astray, made her remember that she might have moulded his life otherwise had she so willed it; and a kind of self-reproach mingled with the natural pity of a woman who, having parted from an old friend in good estate, finds him again, brought very low.

It may be that something of this showed itself in her voice and manner; for Mark's smile was very meaning, as he answered her exclamation recorded above.

"Vereker Vane, without doubt. So he was another of your victims, Blanche? Why, you are nearly as bad as Miladi, in *Les Mousquetaires:* the traces of poison tell us *elle a passé par là.*"

His tone did not quite please her; though why she misliked it she could hardly have told. They had mutually agreed to pass lightly over the past, and to let by-gones be by-gones. Nothing, in theory, could be more convenient and comfortable; but she would have preferred a little more susceptibility—even a little captiousness—to that easy indifference.

The green-eyed monster is troublesome to deal with always, and a perfect pest sometimes; yet there be beasts abroad noisomer, or at all events more difficult to tame, than he. *Mesdames*, are you sure you would approve of his utter extinction? Would it not be a pity if there were use no longer for all the sweet sops and potent charms that are now employed to lull him to sleep? The zest and subtle attraction of danger you know just as well as the boldest *malamore* of us all. The rambles of those who walk abroad after their own sweet will—unchecked and unwatched—are dull as an enforced "constitutional," compared with the stealthy, albeit innocent, sallies of those whose footfalls are planted within earshot of a dozing dragon.

It is of masculine jealousy only I have been speaking. Feminine jealousy is, as we all know, not a ravenous wild beast, but a virgin, severe if serene,—Justice, in fact, under another garb,—who never smites unreasonably, unrighteously, or on insufficient grounds.

So, as was aforesaid, Blanche felt ever so slightly discontented, and answered, rather more coldly than her wont,—

"Not a victim, in the least; but I saw a good deal of him at one time; and I liked him very much in his way;

and he liked me well enough to ask me to marry him, and too well to keep friends with me after I said 'No.' There's the whole story. It wouldn't make a chapter in the meekest romance that ever was written."

He shook his head, always with the same smile on his lip.

"The poison works all the same; but it affects different constitutions differently, of course. What drives one man to drink drives another to the *demi-monde.* Whether of the two is worse, the immortal gods alone can tell. Either remedy is worse than the disease, I should fancy. Vane's face has awfully changed, even since I saw him last; and that's not long ago."

Mrs. Ramsay shrugged her shoulders impatiently.

"It's not a pleasant or improving spectacle. I'd rather look at the stage, I think; though I'm not inclined to rave about *Herodias.*"

Just then the second act began. Vane had recognized, even more quickly than Blanche had done, who sat over against him. He scarcely checked the sweep of his opera-glass, and his left hand, that held it, remained perfectly steady; but his right, resting on the back of La Topaze's chair, grasped it so hard and nervously that the chair slightly rocked. He had become almost domesticated— if the term could be applied to such a life as his—in Paris, of late, and took little heed of matters on the other side of the Channel. Nevertheless, he had heard of Mrs. Ellerslie's engagement to Ramsay soon after it was made public in England. He took the news with an outward unconcern that rather chagrined the purveyor thereof— a worthy gossip, who considered agreeable intelligence not worth the trouble of carrying. He was an ancient comrade of Vane's, and well acquainted with this episode in the other's life; furthermore, he had a grudge of long standing against him, and rather reckoned on the effect of his little *coup.* The colonel only laughed boisterously, and swore with a great oath that a better match was never made up down below, and that the devil himself could not tell which had the best of the bargain.

He had been drinking deeply already, or he would have scarcely spoken lightly, much less coarsely, of

I

Blanche Ellerslie; but he drank deeper yet before the "little supper" was done, and contrived to make himself intensely disagreeable to all who assisted thereat—the news-bearer above mentioned being especially set upon and overborne. The thought of the engagement, whenever it recurred since, had always chafed him; but, as he had not read the announcement of the marriage, he never realized till this moment that the prize he had coveted was actually another man's chattel.

With men of Vereker Vane's temper, these "realizations" are no jest. Not being endowed with a very vivid power of fancy, they are less tormented than their fellows by the spectral foreshadowing of grief or pain; but, when set face to face with the substance of these, they suffer more keenly. It is no figure of speech to say that for the moment Vane was fairly blinded with passion: though he swept his glass mechanically backward and forward along the crowded boxes, they were all blanks to him, save one in which those two faces were framed. Yet it was a vague, purposeless rage, leveled rather at fate and the force of circumstances that had balked him, than against a flesh-and-blood enemy. If some one had succeeded where he had failed, as well this one as any other. He bore Mark no greater grudge than a loser does the winner, where the stakes are ruinous and the play perfectly fair.

So, in just the frame of mind to relish the antics of *Herodias*—they had made him yawn the third time he witnessed them, and this was about the fortieth—Colonel Vane sat down far back in the *baignoire*, whence he thought he might watch his opposite neighbors unobserved; for a certain savor of good manners, despite of evil communications, still clung to the sometime Chief of the "Princess's Own." The avowed protector of the most famous courtesan in Paris, he was inconsistent enough to have scruples about "staring."

La Topaze was in no placable humor that night. The highest-born dame of the Faubourg was not more arrogant or exacting than she. She had got a grievance cut and dried: her cavalier had presumed to dine without her, *en ville*—an *outrecuidance* only to be atoned for in the usual course of things by much contrition, rich bribes, or unlimited indulgence of her next whim. But the offender did not seem in haste to make his peace, or even to apologize for being late; but had handed over that trouble to smooth-tongued Adolphe,—a conscientious parasite, always ready to take any troublesome thing, or person, off his friends' hands—for a consideration. To be sure, she had learned already not to look for any abject submission from Vereker Vane, and had learned, too, that it was scarcely safe to provoke him beyond a certain point. His fierce, overbearing temper had a kind of attraction for her. She was sick, even unto death, of the mincing ways, petty fractiousness, and languid love-making of *les Crèvés*, and liked her bear's growlings and roughnesses a thousand times better than their monkey-tricks. Nevertheless, she had no notion of letting neglect pass unpunished; and determined, if she could not make Vane contrite, she would at least make him uncomfortable.

Facing round with this intent, she marked in what direction his glasses were leveled. Indeed, he did not disturb himself, or seem to notice that she had turned toward him, till she spoke. The woman's instinct, always on the watch for rivalry, added to the cunning of her craft, set La Topaze on the scent at once.

"My faith, Bruno" (for some time past the *cocottes* had called him by no other name), "thou art charming this night! Since when hast thou the wine taciturn? I marvel why thou camest here—*Nenni;* I marvel not. It was, apparently, to devour the little pale woman yonder. The morsel does not seem to me dainty; but perhaps thou hast found it to thy taste ere now. *Hein?* Art thou touched? Answer, at least, without blushing."

Blushing! It is the fashion nowadays to christen ugly things prettily; but he must have been a euphemist indeed who would have given so tender a name to the dark flush on Vane's cheek. In truth, the aggression was singularly inopportune. Since that first access of jealous rage, his thoughts had turned into a milder channel. The sight of the quiet pale face opposite rather soothed than irritated him: he was trying to recall the cadences of some low, caressing tones, just as one tries to

piece together the fragments of a half-forgotten tune
Here his reverie was broken.

Now, the most besotted admirers of La Topaze were
fain to confess that her voice was not one of her chiefest
attractions.   It was a good serviceable organ; clear,
though not flexile, and proof, so far, against the effects
of late hours and hard living; but its steely ring—which
gave such effect to sarcasm or retort—the toughest nerves
found, after awhile, rather fatiguing. How that voice
grated on Vane just then, would be impossible to describe.

He frowned heavily; and, as he glanced down on her,
you might have seen the blood mount to his eyes.

"Leave me in peace, I counsel thee; and leave yonder
lady in peace also. Are there not *cocottes* enough here for
thee to dissect, that thou must fall foul of honest women ?"

Her broad nostrils dilated; and she showed her white
teeth—not smiling.

"Honest women !—Fine guarantee, my faith, for a
woman's honesty, that she should have been an ancient
acquaintance of M. le Colonel Vane. Our tongues are
free to speak of the greatest dames in France: I would
know why they should spare *une petite chipie d'Anglaise.*"

The phrase is not easily translatable ; nor could any
verbal insolence be half so expressive as the gesture of
her lithe fingers.

Dare-devil as she was, a minute later she wished her
words unsaid, as Vane rose up, with such a darkness on
his countenance as she had never seen there. She had
reason to know that time and place could put no check
on his passion when it was fairly roused, and shrank
within herself in mere physical fear. If any mad temptation to violence assailed him, he controlled himself after
one glance at the box opposite, and, taking down his
overcoat, went out without uttering a word, flinging off
the hand that La Topaze would have laid on his arm as
if it brought contagion.

Vereker Vane's worst enemy might have pitied him a
little, reading his thoughts as he walked away through
the empty corridor out into the air. He had begun to
hate his paramour with the sudden intense loathing that,
unlike most rapid emotions, does not lightly pass away.

He ha,ed and despised himself yet more ; and desiring earnestly, for the moment at least, to escape, saw no way out of the shameful maze in which he had wandered for some time past. He did not walk straight away, but, though a fine rain was falling, paced backward and forward in front of the theater, so persistently as to excite the suspicions of certain police-agents hovering about. They concluded, from his manner, that he must have a worse object than a mere assignation in lingering there.

Standing back in the shadow, he heard, after awhile, the *coupé* of Madame Maréchal summoned, and watched her come forth, followed by her frightened "sheep-dog"— her very robes rustling with passion—and fling herself into the carriage with an energy that set the springs a-quivering. He waited till they had driven off; and began to pace to and fro again, retreating into the dark nook when each fresh carriage was called up. Ere long a continuous stream succeeded the straggling departures ; then Colonel Vane thrust his way forward till he stood just without the principal doorway, so that he was within arm's-length of all that passed out.

It was an odd anomaly—one that might have furnished a text to a homily-writer, or a sketch to a humorist. From youth upward this man had been wont to work out his purpose by mere strength of will or hand, cutting all manner of knots without attempting to unravel them ; from sentiment, properly so called, Witikind the Waster was not more exempt; in his breast, specially after the life he had led of late, it was no more likely that pathos or tenderness should be found than that lilies should bloom on sea-sand. Yet his heart fluttered like a bashful boy's as he stood there, waiting to see whether, as she passed out, Blanche Ramsay would appear conscious of his presence or not. He no more dreamed of addressing her first, than of offering her any other insult. More oddly still,—considering of what manner of man we are speaking,—passion had little or nothing to do with this longing to hear her voice and touch her hand again. Rather, it was such a hankering after the better and pleasanter days now past and gone, as might beset any outcast reminded of these things suddenly by the sight of an ancient friend.

Before very long the Ramsays came out. Blanche chanced to be on the side nearest the pillar against which Vane was leaning: as he was just outside the doorway, she did not see him till her dress brushed his foot. She started and shrank back a little, clinging closer to her husband's arm. It was no wonder. Vane's face was not pleasant to look upon just then ; and hair and beard dank with rain made it more haggard and wild. He marked the effect he produced, and was not a whit angry ; only it was something like a groan that he gulped down as he stepped back a little to let her pass, slightly moving his hat, as if he had made way for an utter stranger. But, after a second's hesitation, Blanche held out her hand, with rather a nervous laugh.

"Is it *de rigueur* to cut your old friends, Colonel Vane, when you are living abroad? You are become quite acclimatized, they tell me; but I had no idea you were in Paris. I wonder, at least, that you and Mark have not met somewhere."

It was a falsehood, of course—such a one as certain moralists would find it very hard to condone—and that it was a falsehood the man to whom it was spoken knew perfectly well. He knew that she had recognized him hours ago, and that she had been made aware long ere this—even if she had not guessed for herself at the first glance—who and what were his companions. But he did not thank her the less; and let us hope that this white lie was covered, like a multitude of other sins; for assuredly it was conceived in charity.

The colonel just touched the little hand, with a timid half-pressure—very unlike his usual grip

"No, I've a pretty good memory for old friends, Mrs. Ramsay, even when they have new names; and as for cutting, that would come well from me, wouldn't it? I seldom look at an English paper, somehow, except the sporting ones, and I didn't know that you were actually married, much less that you were in Paris, or I'd have hunted you out and sent the regular congratulations, if I hadn't brought them. You must take them now in the rough—both of you. Ramsay and I, at least, needn't stand on ceremony."

"Not exactly," Mark answered, "even if pretty speeches were your *forte*, Vereker. It *is* odd we haven't met. Never mind; better late than never. We're at the Bristol; will you breakfast there to-morrow?"

Vane accepted at once. Three minutes later he stood on the pavement alone, watching the lamps of a certain *coupé* gleaming away through the mist and rain.

There were high jinks in the half-world that night. Mdlle. Frétillon had lately so far honored M. Bonasse, the famous financier, as to accept from him a modest mansion hard by the Barrière du Trône,—the price of which would have bought twice over a château and appanages in Touraine,—and called her friends and neighbors together to rejoice over *la pendaison de la crémaillère.* Over the Babel of tongues at the supper-table La Topaze's laugh rang out, and she was unusually brilliant in her pitiless sallies—leveled impartially at friend and foe—and none entered with keener zest into the *lansquenet*, that raged till dawn. But the door never opened without her tawny eyes were turning toward it—defiantly at first, then wistfully, hopelessly at last—in search of some one who never appeared; and she did not carry it off so successfully as to prevent every one there present being aware that there had been something more than a love-quarrel betwixt her and Bruno.

"You did that very well, Blanche," her husband remarked, as they drove homeward. "I should have been sorry if you had cut Vane outright. He felt himself in a false position this evening, I do believe; and that's a point gained, at all events. He'll never be thoroughly respectable; but he's too good still to swell the returns of killed and wounded that La Topaze publishes yearly. He certainly left her in the lurch to-night. I shouldn't wonder if he were to break with the whole lot, if he had a little timely encouragement. Shall we be benevolent, and try what we can do?"

Blanche assented very readily. But as, lying awake, she thought over these things, she was haunted by misgivings as to whether her hands were strong enough to deal with such a good work; and, more than that, if a blessing was likely to attend benevolence prompted by Mark Ramsay.

CHAPTER XVII.

On a certain forenoon toward the close of that London season, a party of eight sat down to breakfast, in a pleasant bachelor house in Charles Street, just as the latest church-bell ceased to chime.

The host was rather a character in his way. With every disadvantage of a start, and retarded by more than one early failure, by dint of energy, patience, and calculation he had contrived, while still in middle-age, to climb to one of those high places in the mercantile heaven, which having attained, an adventurer may thenceforth lie beside his nectar, smiling at the toil and turmoil below. But Olympian *idlesse* would have been irksome to Richard Garratt. He was not a whit ashamed of his business, and applied himself thereto at certain seasons with the same cautious sagacity as heretofore ; but he treated commerce as a master, not as a 'prentice, now—taking his pleasure when and where he would, and taking it, too, right royally. He was quite aware of the weak points in his own breeding, and earnestly desired to amend these. From the commonplace weaknesses of the *parvenu* he was singularly free ; but he affected—and did not scruple to confess it—the company of men likely, directly or indirectly, to help him upward in the social scale ; and contrived to minister to their amusement—their profit sometimes—without ever truckling to their caprices or submitting to contumely, however covert or polite. A natural tact prevented him from presuming on good nature or forcing on familiarity.

The " swells," as he *would* call them, soon found out that Mr. Garratt was ready to meet his friends cordially on club-ground without insisting on identifying himself with them in all places and at untimely seasons ; and that he would cast the bread of hospitality freely enough on the waters, without expecting it to return in the shape of invitation-cards to the houses of their mothers and sisters. So the circle of his acquaintance widened daily, till it became quite as large as was convenient. Men rather plumed themselves than otherwise on being asked to one of the Sunday breakfasts in Charles Street. In truth, they were very agreeable entertainments.

However vagrant in his other habits, it must be a strong temptation—sport or business out of the question—that will draw any thorough-paced Englishman, possessing a fixed abiding-place, many yards from his own hearth-stone fasting. And in this case there was a very strong temptation. Richard Garratt was a born *gourmet*, though his taste had only of late years been cultivated as it deserved; neither was his *chef* altogether unworthy of his large hire; and his guests, culled from very different sets, amalgamated, as a rule, very fairly. On a Sunday forenoon in London, few idle men, who are not church-goers, have anything better to do than to sit in judgment on the savor of delicate meats and wines. No one at these entertainments descended to tea—or to coffee, unless of the blackest, backed by a *chasse*.

On the right of the host sat Lord Morecambe, the intrepid and insatiable traveler, who had thrust his ferret-nose into more out-of-the-way corners of the earth than perhaps any other man living. Exploring was his profession; and he was just home from Patagonia on a short furlough, recruiting for an expedition which was to start from the southern shores of the Caspian, and end—indefinitely. A pale, puny, parched personage; and, like many others of his build, a voracious feeder. Indeed, his appetite was his chief encumbrance on his wanderings; supporting all other hardships cheerfully, he waxed desperately despondent under famine.

Next to him was Harry Polwarth—more at home, certainly, on the boards than in the barrack-ground; yet he was no carpet-soldier either, and none grudged him his brevet step after Inkermann. He had been stage-manager to the Brigade for years, and each winter made a starring-tour through country-houses where amateur theatricals were carried out on a grand scale.

Right opposite to him sat his subaltern and crony, and

butt to boot—Terence Tiernan, with the same bloom on his round, smooth, pink face, and the same mystified look in his innocent blue eyes, as when he first joined the battalion; though how he has contrived to preserve any outward signs of innocence is wonderful indeed. Rather prone to take offense, as a rule, he stands any amount of bullying from Polwarth "like a lamb," and in all respects plays the faithful henchman to perfection.

"I'm awfully fond of Terry," the other once averred; "I wouldn't travel about without his photograph for any consideration. To look at it in the morning quite picks one up after a night spent in indifferent company. There never were so many good qualities compressed into the same space of flesh and blood, and—God never made such a fool!"

Besides these, there were Jack Raymond,—most cheery and urbane of vintners,—who, having got through one fair fortune in the exercise of boundless hospitality, is trying, not unsuccessfully, to build up another by filling other men's cellars; and Pierce Llewellyn, editor of the *Scorpion;* with two others whom you have met before,—Reginald Avenel and Horace Kendall.

If you could assist invisibly at the assemblage of seven or eight of the cleverest men you like to name, brought together for purely convivial purposes, do you think you would often listen to sustained talk worth taking down? I fear *Noctes Ambrosianæ* are nearly as imaginary as *Arabian Nights;* and, when they do occur, "the crack" is generally three-handed, or four-handed at the outside. Richard Garratt could discourse sensibly enough on many subjects—with a lead; but he rarely took a decisive line of his own, much less attempted to cut out the work for others. On the present occasion his guests seemed to incline rather to the consumption than to the utterance of good things; and, though Polwarth was fonder of chaffing than of eating, as a rule, breakfast was half over before he opened fire on his left-hand neighbor.

"You don't like those sweet-breads *à la Monarque,* Morecambe, I can see; for you've only managed half the dish. You really should conquer your dislike to civilized viands: as it is, you don't take enough to support life

Never mind: when I come into mine inheritance, and you come to stay with me, I'll kill a fat buffalo, and you shall have the hump all to yourself. I dare say Garratt would have provided a bear-haunch this morning if you hadn't taken him rather by surprise."

"They are both very good things in their way," the other said, seriously; "but you must be careful to bake the hump under a very slow fire; and the bear ought to be killed early in the spring, before he gets lean. After all, I think the paws are the best part of him."

"Tell us some more secrets of the *cuisine sauvage*," the other went on. "What's the best way of dressing a guide, for instance? *En chasseur*, I suppose? Don't look modest about it: you know very well you ate one when you lost your way in the Dolichoschian Mountains."

Most of the men laughed; but Tiernan made rather a wry face, as he set his fork down without touching some *aspic* which he had just taken on his plate.

"It's quite true, Terry," Polwarth continued; "and they read a short burial-service over the poor Iroquois before they put him down to roast, just like they do over sailors before they give them to the sharks. It was very considerate of you, Morecambe; I've always given you great credit for it. It shows how, under most trying circumstances, a real Christian can keep up appearances."

"It's very well to joke about it now," Morecambe said, frowning slightly; "but the real thing isn't so comic. No; I never was in the strait of having to draw lots for a life; but I don't know what might have happened once, if we hadn't lighted, by God's mercy, on a lame deer, that was half dead with famine itself when we got up to it in the snow. The night before, the men looked at each other very queerly—so queerly, that I see their eyes still, sometimes, when I have bad dreams."

There was not a particle of wounded vanity in the speaker's manner; only the gravity of a man remembering thankfully his escape from great peril. No one laughed now; and Polwarth, for a moment, looked contrite.

"You're a game old bird," he said; "and we stay-at-homes are not worthy to unloose the latchets of your moc-casins.   Haven't you done enough in your generation in search of the Great Unknown?   I'd give something to see you settled once for all.   You wouldn't be hard to please in a squaw; and More Court would be a comfort-able wigwam, if it was made weather-proof."

"Well, there are one or two other places I want to see," the other returned, placidly, making steady play with some Reform cutlets the while.   "Besides, I'm too poor to mount an establishment properly at home; and, though I don't much care where I sleep, I don't know that I should approve of roughing it under one's own roof.   I shouldn't approve of my wife's roughing it, I'm quite sure "

"Too poor?" Llewellyn interrupted, shrugging his shoulders.   "What's that got to do with it?   You may take your oath your coronet has been fresh-gilt already, at some time or another.   Why should you be nicer than your forbears?   A plum taken in season, how good is it! And there are several Golden Drops just now, about fit for plucking.   What do you think of Mary Welsted— goes about with Lady Mandrake?   Jekyl christened her Maria Maggiore—not a bad name, either.   She's substan-tial enough, in all ways, to prop up a principality, much less a peerage."

"A cut above my mark," Morecambe said,—"morally, financially, and physically.   I don't pretend to know much about domesticities; but I fancy any husband must sooner or later be in a false position who gives more than three stone weight away.   I've no idea of tying myself up yet, either for pleasure or profit, unless I find a stray Peri somewhere between the Caspian and Cash-mere."

Quite lately, by the merest chance, as if he had picked up a purse in the street, Tiernan had discovered he had rather a good bass voice; and since then he had become a perfect melomaniac—ready "quidvis facile, aut pati," the better to cultivate his organ.   Kendall, of course, could be very useful in this way; and this was enough to account for their sudden intimacy.

When the name of Miss Welsted was mentioned, Horace had looked up quickly from his plate; and as the last words were spoken, he glanced across the table at Tiernan, who nodded and smiled in answer.

"What are you grinning at now, Terry?" Polwarth asked. "It's a most extraordinary thing that grave matters can never be discussed in your presence without that indecent levity breaking out."

"I wasn't grinning," the other retorted, rather rebelliously—he didn't approve of his *fin sourire* being so stigmatized—"I was only thinking that perhaps the Welsted Cup ain't quite such an open race as you imagine. How do you know the entries aren't closed already? Ask Kendall, there: he can tell you something about it, I dare say."

An awkward pause ensued; for no one seemed inclined to put the question into words, though several asked it plainly enough with their eyes. At last Polwarth spoke.

"I suppose Terry means we're to congratulate you, Mr. Kendall, if he means anything at all: it's never more than even betting. Rather sudden, isn't it?"

It was a perpetual chafe to Horace, that men who seemed to be hail-fellows with all the rest of the world would persist in addressing him formally. Furthermore, there was sarcasm, if not incredulity, in Polwarth's tone; yet he answered, sweetly and smoothly,—

"You won't make me responsible for Terry's indiscretion, I hope." (Polwarth's by-play on the stage was one of the best points of his acting; his start of surprise and shudder at the familiarity were perfect.) "What I said to him was in confidence, to begin with, and didn't go half so far as you infer. I'm very good friends with Miss Welsted, I'm happy to say; but I don't know that I should care to be more. She's rather an overpowering person, as Morecambe says; perhaps she'd be too much for my weak mind. Don't you think so, my lord?"

The peer was a cosmopolite in the largest sense of the word. He had the faculty of becoming promptly handand-glove with any fellow-creature, utterly irrespective of race, color, or degree; but he could assert himself pretty decisively on occasion, as others besides Kendall had found out to their cost.

"I said nothing about Miss Welsted's being overpowering. I simply said she was above my mark; it doesn't follow that she's above yours; and as to what your strength of mind may be equal to, I know absolutely nothing. I judge no man's character on short or slight acquaintance."

The taunt went right home, through the triple brass of Kendall's self-conceit; but, instead of teaching him caution, it made him vicious.

"A thousand pardons," he said, with bitter humility, "for asking your opinion about what couldn't interest you. You'll remember it was not I who mentioned Miss Welsted's name; I simply answered a direct question. I have a perfect right, I presume, to disavow any present intentions in that quarter. Indeed, to form any such, one ought to be quite fancy-free."

The fatuous smile, and the still more significant sigh rounding off the sentence, were so intensely exasperating that more than one of his hearers felt a keen desire to arise and smite the speaker on the cheek. Avenel, who sat next to him, could not repress a movement of impatient dislike.

Kendall did not seem to notice the effect of his words, but went on nibbling delicately one by one the grapes from a bunch that he held in his left hand, leaning his elbow on the table. The sleeve, loose after the fashion of that year, fell back naturally from the wrist, leaving the armlet that you wot of nearly bare. It may be that Tiernan desired to show that his new intimate was a person of more consequence than the rest of the company gave him credit for; or he may have been prompted only by an ultra-Irish propensity to thrust in an importunate oar just when rocks and quicksands were ahead.

"Fancy-free?" he said, nodding his head again still more sagaciously. "How can a man be free at all who goes about manacled? It's a pretty ornament, too, and a pretty idea. Let's have a look at it closer."

With a faint show of remonstrance, hardly masking covert exultation, Horace stretched out his wrist over the table. There, in bright relief on the dead gold, glittered the word "Nina"—legible as ever was record of female folly since the days of Cadmus. Not half, certainly, of those present guessed at the story linked with the word: yet all, save one, guessed that there was something base and boastful in the action, and despised it accordingly. Even jovial Mr. Garratt looked on his guest with disfavor and some apprehension: he smelt the storm a-brewing; and this was the first time that quiet digestion had not waited on appetite at his entertainments. But Tiernan's blundering head was fairly loose, and, utterly disregarding the warning frown from Polwarth, he floundered on deeper into the mire.

"Nina—eh? Not a common name, is it? I think we could put a surname to it, if we chose. Perhaps we needn't go far from N to find the other initial. I should like to know how you came by it, though?"

"Stole it, most probably."

If Reginald Avenel had wrought no notable good in his generation, he assuredly deserved all the blessings that rest on peace-makers. The first article of his creed was, that to float on placid waters was absolutely essential to his personal comfort; and he had shown considerable tact, more than once, in healing disputes that might have rankled into quarrels. The most insolent and iniquitous of cabmen had never been known to provoke him to anything beyond banter—serene, if severe. If a maroon had exploded in the midst of them, his friends could scarcely have been more startled than by such an interjection proceeding from him.

Kendall's outstretched hand dropped on the cloth sharply, as he faced round on the speaker, flushing to the roots of his hair.

"That's meant as a joke, I suppose," he said, with rather a lame attempt at a laugh. "I confess I don't quite see the point of it; and I'll ask you to spare me those jokes in future."

"It's meant as nothing of the sort," the other retorted; "I never was more serious in my life. A man who's capable of parading such a thing as that before half a dozen comparative strangers, and, so to speak, thrusts his confidences down their throats, is perfectly capable of petty larceny, in my humble opinion. It's a mere question of opportunity."

Despite the Provençal blood in his veins, Kendall was too cunning to embroil himself, if he could possibly avoid it, unless the chances were heavily in his favor; but no choice was left him here. He rose up, pushing back his chair in great heat and haste.

"I didn't come here to be insulted," he cried.

"No; you came here to sing, after you had finished your breakfast," Avenel interrupted, beginning to peel a peach scientifically; "so don't strain your voice, whatever you do."

"I—I tell you," Kendall gasped out, fairly hoarse with passion, "I could account—nothing easier—for how I became possessed of that armlet, if you had any right to ask for an explanation."

"But I haven't a right, you see," the other answered, coolly; "and, if I had, I don't know that I should care to press the question. Single-handed testimony don't go for much—under certain circumstances."

Here the host interposed.

"Look here: we've had more than enough of this. It's an unlucky misunderstanding from first to last. You'll promise me, both of you—I know you will—that this shall go no further."

Avenel arched his handsome brows in genuine surprise.

"My dear Garratt, are you dreaming? You talk like Polwarth when he plays the heavy father. Nothing ever does go further in these days. I had very slightly the honor of Mr. Kendall's acquaintance before; and that little I choose henceforth to decline. I'm awfully sorry that I've broken up the harmony of the meeting; and I'll do penance now, by calling on an invalid aunt. When I'm gone, you can listen to love-stories as long as you like."

"No; don't *you* go, Avenel."

Richard Garratt was one of the most good-natured creatures breathing, and would have gone out of his way rather than tread on a worm; but, for the life of him, he could not help laying an emphasis on the personal pronoun that would have been significant to a duller comprehension than Kendall's.

"*I'll go*," he said, sullenly; "indeed, I'd much—much rather."

Beyond the faintest of formal remonstrances from the host, no attempt was made to detain him; and Tiernan, who had assisted at the scene with as much astonishment as if he were utterly innocent of having provoked it, did not think it necessary to bear his *maestro* company.

The after-breakfast talk in Charles Street was often prolonged into the afternoon; but to-day no one seemed to have energy enough to shake off the wet blanket that had fallen on the company; and the smoking-room was deserted a full hour earlier than usual.

Quoth Polwarth to his subaltern, as they walked away together,—

"I tell you what, Terry; we'll have to take measures with your music-madness. I don't so much mind being driven wild at all hours of the day and night by your native wood-notes" (they lodged in contiguous chambers); "but if your tongue leads you into bad company it'll have to be slit, and that's all about it. A pleasant sort of 'pal' you've picked up lately—a creditable sort of creature, to be Terry-ing you all over the place, and making you his confidant. All that happened this morning was more than half your fault. What the devil did you mean by trotting him out for a show? Aren't you thoroughly ashamed of yourself?"

And the subaltern was constrained to confess that he had indeed "made a regular hash of it," and that "Kendall had come out in rank bad form;" and, furthermore, to promise that he would not lightly entreat this tuneful person to a dinner on guard.

.

CHAPTER XVIII.

Avenel's charitable resolve went the way of many other good intentions.   His invalid aunt waited in vain that afternoon for the visit which was none of the least of her "consolations;" for that devout lady—though she would have been exceeding wroth had such an idea been suggested to her—did in truth prefer the company of this graceless nephew to that of more strait-laced relatives. Regy went to his chambers, and shut the door upon the outer world, in a frame of mind very unsabbatical and unsatisfactory.   He was thoroughly discontented, not only with the aspect of things in general, but also with himself.   In the first place, he held it unworthy of a literate person to lose his temper, under any circumstances whatsoever, to the extent of speaking unadvisedly. Though he had maintained a decent outward show of coolness, he could not deny that his anger had passed boiling-point more than once—a gross mistake, to say the least of it.   But there was worse behind.

Without wearing his heart actually on his sleeve, Avenel was more truthful than most men who have lived his life.   His moral law was sufficiently elastic; but the saving of a woman's credit was, in his eyes, about the only excuse which could turn a lie into a venial sin; and in such a strait he had seldom been placed.   Now, this morning, if he had not spoken a falsehood, it is most certain he had acted one.   He pitied Kendall no more than any other venomous creature on which he had chanced to trample; but the fact of his having come out of the encounter with flying colors did not make his cause the stronger.   As a mere question of justice, what right had he to hold up the man as a vain braggart, not to be believed on his oath, knowing all the while that, base as the hint might have been, the other was only hinting at the truth?

Avenel had seen that armlet before in a certain jeweler's shop that he was fond of frequenting, having a great taste for cunning goldsmith's-work. He had been first struck by the device of the fetterlock, then by the name embossed on the gold; and, hearing it was for Lady Gwendoline Marston, who was expected to call for it herself, had bestowed on the damsel a waltz that same evening, with the express purpose of questioning her.

"It's for Helen Tyrconnel," Nina said, coolly, though her color flickered as she spoke. "She's my pet friend, you know, and she's to be married next Thursday. No one but her is to know where it comes from. Regy, you won't get me into a scrape by telling any one? I hear sermons enough about extravagance as it is; and this one would be an awful homily. I'll keep a secret for you whenever you ask me; I will, indeed."

A pretty woman's confidences are not, as a rule, burdens grievous to be borne; and Avenel, though a philosopher in his way, had never studied in the Stoic school. He considered himself almost as one of the Marston family. All the platonic devotion that he could spare was engrossed by Rose Nithsdale; and he would no more have dreamed of flirting with Nina than with any other child-cousin. But she looked too bewitching just then to be refused anything; and it would have been too absurd for Avenel to have taken up his parable against extravagance: so he gave the promise readily enough, and had never given the matter a second thought since.

Now, with his real regret at the girl's folly mingled a twinge of injured self-esteem, as he remembered how easily he had been fooled. Hoodwinking is not pleasant, even when performed by a mistress of falconry; but it is more aggravating still to be blindfolded by a mere chit, who ought to be busy with her broidery-frame, instead of meddling with lures and jesses.

Over all these things Avenel meditated, smoking sullenly the while; but, beyond a vague impression that it behoved him to do *something* without delay, he arrived at no conclusion. He generally found Nithsdale House within the limits of a Sabbath-day's journey; and went straight thither on leaving his chambers, purposing, if opportunity should serve, to propound the difficulty to the countess.

Of whatsoever shortcomings in respect to the Decalogue this lady may have been guilty, she carried out thoroughly at least one of its precepts—that of making the Seventh Day a day of rest. The attractions must have been exceptional that would have tempted her to dine abroad; and not above a dozen names were exempted from the general orders of "Not at home" on Sunday. Her boudoir was nearly as full as it could hold, according to Lady Rose's idea, when Avenel entered: that is to say, three besides herself were there assembled. Two of these were men, pleasant to look upon and to listen to, or they would not have been sitting where they were, and as it chanced—for this was by no means a *sequitur*—no less eligible as *partis* than as partners. The third person was Gwendoline Marston.

Avenel knew the habits of the house well enough to be aware that a coterie such as this did not break up in a hurry, and saw no present chance of consultation with Lady Rose; however, if his interest in securing a *tête-à-tête* had been purely personal, he never would have dreamt of sulking at its being deferred. Nothing could exceed the air of domestic comfort with which he settled himself into his favorite corner.

The concentrated wit of all assembled there would scarcely have furnished forth one brilliant conversationalist; but they were very pleasant in their own way, and relished their mild jokes and harmless repartee quite as keenly as sager and sourer people relish highly-spiced epigrams or venomous satire. If the laughter was not very discriminating, it rang none the less musically.

Lady Nithsdale was too indolent to take her proper share in the talk; but Nina more than made up for her sister's deficiencies. It almost seemed as if the girl had some presentiment of approaching danger, and guessed too from what quarter the danger came. If she had meant beforehand coaxing Avenel into a good frame of mind, she could hardly have laid herself out more assiduously toward that object, or, to speak the truth, more successfully. Regy was not so often really amused but that he could feel grateful to any one, male or female, who purveyed him such entertainment. Before he had sat there an hour, he said within himself,—

"She shall have another chance, though she don't deserve it."

And he resolved to bring Nina to confession, before betraying her delinquencies even to Rose Nithsdale. The opportunity presented itself sooner than he had reckoned on. Tea was scarcely over, when Gwendoline said,—

"Will some one put me into a cab and pack me off home at once? I'm dreadfully late as it is. We have to dine at Richmond—at seven, of all unchristian hours! And the Buckhursts are so awfully punctual."

"You'll walk home in about half the time," Avenel interrupted; "and I'll take care of you. I've overstayed my time here too, considering what I have to do before dinner. You'll trust her with me so far, won't you, Lady Rose?"

Lady Nithsdale's eyes opened rather wonderingly. She was the least jealous and suspicious of mortals; but she was not wont to see Avenel so ready with his offers of escort; and she was rather puzzled as to the nature of the business which could call him away from her boudoir so peremptorily on a Sunday afternoon. She bit her lip ever so slightly, as she answered,—

"Oh, yes; I can trust you—so far. I dont think either of you will get into mischief between here and Carrington Crescent. What you'll do afterward——"

So those two went off together. When they were fairly in the street, said Avenel,—

"Have you heard from your pet friend lately, Nina? You know who I mean, of course—Helen Irnham, *née* Tyrconnel. Do you know where she is now?"

"I haven't heard very lately," she replied; and once again her color flickered; "but I know she's in Paris. They went over before the Grand Prix, and won't be back for another ten days at least."

"You think so? Then you'd be very much surprised if I told you that I met her at breakfast this morning—at a bachelor-breakfast, too, in the Albany. Odd place to meet a bride in—wasn't it? Irnham's an easy-going creature; but I doubt if he'd approve."

In a bewilderment that could scarcely have been feigned, she stopped short, gazing up at him.

"What utter nonsense you are talking! What can you possibly mean?"

"Don't strike an attitude," he retorted. "You can hardly have learnt to be theatrical—already. I'm talking perfectly good sense, though in rather a roundabout manner. You gave that armlet to Helen Irnham, you know. Well, I met the wearer of it, precisely at the time and place I have mentioned. I recognized it directly. If I hadn't, I and half a dozen more might have examined it at our leisure. It has changed owners, perhaps you'll say. No; I don't think you *will* say that, though, or that you will say that you don't know now what I mean."

Walking on by his side, she looked up again—very pale this time, but without a sign of flinching. Her lips moved before she spoke aloud. An ear laid close against them might possibly have caught three syllables :—

"How could he?"

"You're quite right, Regy," she said, aloud. "I'm not going to tell you any more falsehoods. I know what you mean very well. The bracelet has always been where it now is. I'm not sorry for that; but I'm very sorry that you have seen it, and seen it—so."

She could scarcely have gone on, for the choking in her throat; but Avenel broke in here,—

"You didn't reckon on his parading it, then? Why, those *novelettes* you're so fond of might have given you a better insight into the *jeune premier* form. He didn't steal it, after all? I'm rather glad I suggested the possibility, though."

The fire, slumbering always in the depths of the Spanish eyes, flashed out.

"You said that, knowing all the while it must be a base, cruel falsehood. How dared you?"

"There wasn't much daring required," he said, rather scornfully; "and if there had been—though I don't pretend to be a champion—I'd have tried to screw my courage up to the sticking-point, to stop the name of your father's daughter being made a shuttlecock for the amusement of such a company."

The girl laughed insolently.

" My father's daughters are infinitely obliged to you. Such disinterested kindness is quite touching. I don't know what we can have done to deserve it. Don't you think the taking care of Rosie's reputation is about as much as you can manage? What is the disgrace if my name was coupled with his—just as if he were not better —cleverer—dearer in all ways—than the best of you !"

Her passion moved him no more than if Lady Niths-dale's pet lory, whom he was always teasing, had pecked him rather sharply.

" I wouldn't take the passers-by into my confidence, if I were you, however proud you may be of your secrets. That respectable couple nearly dropped their prayer-books, and looked quite scandalized. Child, all your heroics won't make a hero of Mr. Kendall. Troubadours are at a discount, even in Provence, just now. I don't abuse him, mind. I know nothing of who he is or whence he comes; and, if what I've heard is true, per-haps he couldn't give us much information on those points himself. But I know that if he were all you say, and more, he's not a fit person to be flashing about *gages d'amour*—or *d'amitié* either, for that matter—from Gwen-doline Marston. However, we won't discuss the question any further. It isn't likely we shall agree; and, as you very properly observe, it's no concern of mine. I suppose it does concern slightly your mother and father, though. We'll refer it to one or both of them, if you please."

She stopped short once more—luckily the street was nearly deserted just there—clasping his arm with both her hands; so that, without actual violence, he could scarcely have stirred from where they stood. The same terror was in her face; but the threat of betrayal worked far more powerfully now than when, two months ago, it brought her, outwardly at least, to submission; for with the dread of being separated from him there mingled a vague apprehension of insult or injury imminent over Horace Kendall. The big drops gathered slowly in her eyes; and there came into them the expression—at once piteous and desperate—that may be seen in those of a deer brought to bay on a crag's edge, where the sole chance of escape from the hounds is a leap into air.   An old, old simile, that; but an apt one, nevertheless. Those who have ridden straight from the find under Dunkerry Beacon to the finish on the Channel Cliffs, and were up at the finish, can bear witness that the first half of the parallel is no flight of fancy; the second, I fear me, will hold good so long as womanhood has sorrows.

"You won't do that, Regy," she said, at last, in a faint voice; "not just yet, at least. You'll give me a week; well, then, three days—just three days. I promise—I swear I won't do anything rash—anything anybody need mind; and I'll tell you honestly what I have done.   Of course you are right; of course they'd lock me up rather than let me see him; and I'm so helpless; but I must, I must tell him in my own way that it's—that it's all over."

To Avenel's consternation—for, under the most favorable circumstances of time and place, he dreaded a scene —she fairly broke down here.   How at that moment he regretted ever having meddled at all, is not to be told. His first impulse—rather a cowardly one, it must be owned—was to calm Nina at any price; but he really pitied her besides.

"For God's sake don't do *that!*" he said, imploringly. "I don't want to bully you, if you'll only be reasonable, or to get you into a scrape, either.   I never told tales of man, woman, or child yet.   There, I'll take your word, and keep your secret; but you'll set all straight, like a good, sensible girl, won't you? You'll thank me for this one of these days."

As she dropped his arm, and moved on again, she smiled up at him through her tears—a quaint, sad smile.

"Perhaps I may.   I thank you now, at all events; and you sha'n't repent trusting me, Regy."

Not another word was spoken till they reached Lord Daventry's door.   As her escort was about to ring, Nina laid her hand on his wrist.

"Only one thing—you won't do or say anything that could hurt him?"

Avenel prided himself, with great reason, on the evenness of his temper; but, for the second time that day, it was fairly ruffled. The obstinacy, and wanton waste of solicitude, were a little more than he could bear. He shook off the little hand with a certain roughness, and rang the bell sharply.

"I'm not in the habit of abusing people behind their backs; and Mr. Kendall and I are not on speaking terms."

He walked away without further ceremony, leaving the damsel planted somewhat disconsolately there. A lively Richmond dinner, I suppose, is rather the exception than the rule; but few of us have undergone such a penance as that evening's entertainment proved to Gwendoline Marston.

CHAPTER XIX.

Morning in Kensington Gardens again; but mornings follow, and resemble not each other. On such a day— for it was not summer always even in Arcadia—the Loving Shepherd's pipe could hardly be attuned to sonnets, nor would Daphne have shown much indulgence to his lagging muse. Not a break or gleam in the dull leaden sky—not a breath of breeze to clear the murky air—not a whisper from the sullen elms.

I think we hardly realize sufficiently the effect of atmospheric influences in this curious climate of ours; nor how they affect persons to whom "nerves"—in the common acceptation of the word—are things of theory. Years and years ago, when, during the decline of the P. R., there still were fights without crosses, on the eve of a famous battle I heard a gladiator say, speaking of what the morrow would bring forth,—

"I hope it'll be gay weather. I'd chance the sun in my eyes for a real heartsome morning."

To the criminals pacing to and fro in the prison-yard for a half-hour on their enforced constitutional, do you suppose it matters nothing whether the square patch of sky above be bright or lowering? There are days on which good news, however agreeable the surprise might be, would come to most of us colored with a certain inconsistency.

On this especial morning it is more than doubtful if Horace Kendall would have received the pleasantest news gratefully or graciously. It was just twenty-four hours since that breakfast-party in the Albany broke up. He had been gnashing his teeth, so to speak, ever since, over the recollection thereof. One of the attributes of natures such as his is a proneness to shift their own burdens on to any other shoulders whatsoever, and never, by any chance, to blame themselves for any mishap or mistake while it is barely possible to throw the responsibility on friend or foe. In Horace's composition there were no such things as "fine feelings;" but, from mere personal vanity, he felt contumely quite as keenly as many endowed with more delicate sensibility. If he had looked the matter fairly in the face, he must have acknowledged that all that befell yesterday was the result of his own Juanesque posing, and that the display of the armlet was no more accidental than any other planned stage-trick. But looking things, or people, in the face is precisely what men of his stamp will not or cannot do. He hated his host for not taking his part; Tiernan for the unlucky question that provoked the debate; each and every one of the assistants thereat for being witnesses—not illpleased witnesses either, he fancied—of his discomfiture: most savagely of all, of course, he hated Avenel; but he would sooner have accused Gwendoline Marston of bringing him to grief with her romantic whims than imputed to himself a tittle of blame.

Yet, if he were not troubled with self-reproach, Kendall spent about as uncomfortable a Sabbath afternoon as can well be conceived. He too went straight to his own rooms, and did not stir forth till the evening, when he was engaged to dine out. It was a large party, made up of an exclusively musical set. It was any odds against any one there present having been made aware of his misadventure in the morning; nevertheless, Kendall felt as if every glance that dwelt upon him for more than a second's space was either inquisitive or derisive. When there was low talk and laughter at the farther end of the table from where he sat, he grew hot at the suspicion that he himself furnished matter for the jest. He could not well refuse to sing; but one attempt showed so plainly that his plea of not being in voice was no formal excuse, that the mistress of the mansion forbore to press him further. Horace was right glad to get back to his own rooms again. Intemperance was not among his vices; but his "night-cap" that evening would have fitted a much more seasoned head; and even this procured only feverish and broken sleep.

Few men, indeed, reach their life's end without having cause to remember what it is to wake with the consciousness that trouble is lying in wait just beyond the threshold of the day. Most of us know only too familiarly that "evil quarter-hour," and the manner thereof: how there comes at first a vague impression of something having gone very wrong; and how that something looms nearer and larger, like the images of the phantasmagoria, till it confronts us in full, it may be in exaggerated, proportions. Certain adventurers, they say, in the course of warfare with the world, become proof against this, among other human weaknesses; but, fortunately for society, such mighty Adullamites are rare. A racking headache did not improve the color of Kendall's morning meditations. Not without a misgiving of what the post might have in store, he reached out his hand for his letters Only one, as it happened, was of the least moment, and was brief enough in all conscience.

"*At eleven, in the old place. You must be there. N.*"

That was all. Nothing, one would have thought, to make his hand shake as he read the note and cast it down beside him with an oath. With what, or with whom, he was angry he himself could scarcely have told you; that curse was not leveled at any one head in particular; but things in general seemed going contrary; and, with men of his kind, blasphemy is the readiest panacea

That the note had something to do with the occurrences of yesterday morning he felt sure. How could she have heard of it, though? Avenel had told her, probably—this time the malison *had* a mark. If it were only Nina's anger, he could set that square easily enough; but suppose Lady Nithsdale had been told too? This would complicate matters considerably. It would come to Lady Daventry's ears next, and then—— Well, he would bear the worst or the best of it soon; and there was not much time to spare, if Nina was not to be kept waiting, which, under the circumstances, might be hardly advisable. She might just as well have made it an hour later, though.

Grumbling to himself in this wise, Kendall arose, made a careful toilet, though not quite so scientific as usual,—he had become a thorough *petit-maître* of late,—swallowed a cup of coffee, more as an excuse for the *chasse* than for its own sake, and reached the trysting-place a minute or so before the appointed hour. As he put his watch back after ascertaining this, he saw Gwendoline Marston approaching. Kendall's perceptions, when his own interests or inclinations were not immediately concerned, were not very keen; but, as the girl drew near, even he guessed that it was not only to upbraid him that she had summoned him thither. Her head, instead of being lifted in eager expectancy, as it was when they met there before, was bowed dejectedly; and her step, as she came slowly across the grass, was liker a sick woman's than that of a girl with Spanish blood in her veins.

"What has happened?" Horace asked, as he took her hand in both his own. He had intended to treat the matter in a light, off-hand way; but, when it came to the point, his nerve failed him. It was evident enough, from his manner, that he divined the nature of her news.

"Can't you guess? Have you forgotten yesterday morning already?"

In her tone there was nothing of reproach or scorn, only intense sadness: nevertheless, he dropped her hand at once, and his countenance fell.

" So you have heard of it—his version, too—and you have come to take his part now? His conduct, of course, was chivalrous, and all the rest of it ; and mine——"

"You are quite wrong," she interrupted, always in the same quiet, sad voice. "So little was told me, that I can only guess at what was said or done ; and you would not say that I took his part, if you had heard me speak yesterday. That fetterlock was a very foolish fancy of mine.

I know; but I never thought that any one besides you would have laughed at it."

"I never meant to show it. I can't help it, if you choose to make an unpardonable sin out of a mere accident."

His eyes were bent sullenly downward as he spoke; but it needed not to look into them to know that he was lying. Some such conviction, perchance, was borne in upon Nina, despite herself, for she answered only the last words.

"I have nothing to pardon, dear; you have not sinned against me. It was not because I am ashamed of caring for you that I begged you to be cautious. It was because I felt there would be dreadful danger if any one else were taken into our secret. I didn't hear who else besides Regy Avenel were present; but we are at his mercy, at all events. Now you know what has happened."

"Curse his insolence!" he said, viciously. "What right has he to dictate to me, or to set himself up as your protector? He shall suffer for this somehow, by ——!"

She shrank away from him now.

"Hush! I should hate to hear such words from you, even if they could help us in the least. I don't say he's any right to interfere; but, if he thinks he has, it comes to the same thing. He won't be frightened into silence, I'm very sure. It was all I could do to get three days' grace. He won't betray us till I've seen him again. He won't betray us at all, if I act, as he calls it, 'sensibly.'"

"Sensibly! That means giving me up for good and all. Well, it's a modest condition, and not hard to fulfill. That's what you are driving at, I suppose?"

As she gazed up at him, her eyes brightened, not with the gleam of quick excitement, but with the steady light of resolve.

"So hard—that I think I would die before I would promise any such thing. We must have patience and faith, dear; that's all. We must not meet again, except by accident, for a long, long time. Indeed, indeed, we have no choice. I've not been very carefully watched, hitherto; but, if this were known at home, I should be simply a prisoner, till they had made sure that we were parted forever. You know this as well as I do—don't you, now? I'm miserable enough as it is, without your being unjust and unkind."

He stood silent awhile, debating what he should answer. A strong temptation just then assailed him; the temptation to test his power over Nina there and then—to try whether he could not induce her to cast in her lot with him at once, by consenting to an elopement so soon as opportunity should serve. He did not mistrust his own eloquence, and Nina had never looked so attractive as at this moment. To a man of his vainglorious temperament, the notoriety of such an adventure was in itself a strong inducement: nevertheless, he forbore. Thinking over these things afterward, he took infinite credit to himself; yet pity or generosity had wonderfully little to do with it. The safety of his own precious person was with Kendall the chiefest of all earthly considerations. He had a strong impression that the law might call his romantic escapade by some uglier name, that would render him amenable to all manner of penalties. Furthermore, he argued within himself that he and his bride would have to feed almost literally on crusts, till such time as it should please the Daventrys to condone the offense; and after all, now and then, such monsters as parents indefinitely relentless will sometimes outrage dramatic proprieties. If the whole truth must be told, there was in the background of his meditations a certain figure—not a comely one, albeit a woman's—whose stout forefinger was first raised in warning, and then pointed to a goodly pile of money-bags. On the whole, he came to the conclusion that the forward game was scarcely suited for his resources, and that the best policy would be to yield as gracefully as might be to the *force majeure.* While he thus reflected, his anger had full time to cool. The charlatan was himself again now, and fell into his theatrical mannerisms quite naturally. His facial muscles were remarkably well drilled; and his plaintive expression of self-sacrifice might have imposed on a keener critic than poor Gwendoline Marston.

"It was too bad of me to speak so," he said, almost in a whisper. "But this is such very sharp pain; and it has come on me so suddenly. Not to meet again for a long, long time; so long that we can put no limit to it now. Do you know what that means—for me? It means that the aim is taken utterly out of my life; and that I wander on henceforth without hope that to-morrow will be brighter than to-day. It means that I must not think of you as mine any more, except in my dreams; that I ought not to wear this any longer,"—he stroked the armlet tenderly,—"because, before I see you alone again, some one else may have a better right to wear it. It means all this. I don't murmur or rebel; I would bear a hundredfold more sooner than bring any trouble on your head. I will not even blame you if you forget me. For you will not be like me; you will often be tempted to forget."

It was a pretty recitative enough, and gracefully delivered too. Nevertheless, not a few women, deeming the sentiments something too sublime, and the periods something too neatly turned, to have come straight from the heart, would have requited the effort by a smile. But every word came to Nina's ears with the golden ring of truth. The last three months, measured by their influence on her character, might count for years; but, though she was a woman now in energy of purpose and strength of mind, both to dare and to endure, she was in many ways the veriest child still—just as prone to invest her tawdry idol with all manner of godlike qualities, as when she first bowed down before him. As she listened to Horace Kendall, it seemed to her that she looked on the sublimity of devotion; and the tears, that had gathered more than once during the interview under the long dark lashes, began to rain down fast. She bowed her face upon his arm, murmuring, as she pushed the armlet back on his wrist,—

"You will always keep it; you will not forget?"

"I never will. I never can."

The spot of their meeting was well chosen. The trunk of a huge elm screened them from most passers-by; and on such a morning there were few loiterers in the gardens.

Nevertheless, there is a time and place for all things; and the cavalier, even if the lady had lost her head, might certainly have remembered that the pose was such as ought only to be rehearsed *intra muros.*

But Horace took no heed of such trifles, as he launched forth into a fresh tirade. Perhaps the girl's passion was really to some extent infectious; but Kendall dearly liked the sound of his own voice; he was in the vein that morning; and it was not likely that so fair a chance of airing his eloquence would soon again present itself. Moreover, though he judged it politic not to put his hold on Nina to the breaking-strain, he had no mind it should be loosened except in his own good time. So he poured forth a string of promises, consolations, and endearments, much to his own satisfaction, and greatly to his hearer's comfort; for, while he was still in mid-career, Nina lifted her head half smiling, as she dried her eyes with an absurd little filmy kerchief, that never was meant for such serious work as the stanching of tears.

"Practicing for private theatricals, I presume, Nina? Will you present me to your dramatic friend?"

As the words were uttered, the speaker unmasked himself from behind the trunk of the elm.

Horace Kendall was fond of stage-effects, as you know. But in his programme it was not set down that he should find himself face to face with Raoul, Earl of Daventry.

A RENCONTRE.

Page 160.

CHAPTER XX.

SOME one—an eminent divine, if I mistake not—once valued a thoroughly good temper at £500 a year. If such things were marketable, Lord Daventry's ought to have commanded a fancy price. His had not been one of the level, uneventful lives that cause men to laugh and grow fat. Almost all his pleasures, from youth upward, had been more or less fraught with danger, moral, physical, or financial; and he had generally indulged his fancy without counting the cost or consequences. Nevertheless, few could say that they had seen the peace of his great calm eyes troubled by impatience or anger : as for fear, the Marstons, male or female, had not been hampered by that weakness for some generations past. It was quite a treat to see him go in to back one of his own horses for a stake at a large race-meeting. The layers of odds knew pretty well when Lord Daventry meant business, and, before he opened his mouth, would gather round him ravenously. Amidst all the turmoil and uproar there he would stand, a perfect picture of repose; reminding one of the beautiful sea-birds that, in wild weather, may be seen rocking betwixt purple billows. Through the clamor of many voices, hoarse and shrill, you would catch sometimes his clear, quiet tones :—

"In hundreds? Yes, you may put it down again.— And once more with *you*, Mr. Irons.—An even monkey to finish with? Thanks, that will do; no more."

And then he would close his book, and saunter off to look at the race; with less apparent interest in the result than any man on the ground. He was not at all nice in the choice of his company, and, if he had any purpose to serve, would just as soon be seen in earnest converse with a clever outsider as with the most venerated of turf magnates; but somehow he seemed to have acquired the secret of touching pitch without being defiled. He never

L14*

dreamed of keeping any one, gentle or simple, at a distance; yet perhaps not twice in his life had he had occasion to repress insolence or familiarity.

"I wish I'd your knack of keeping people in their places. It's all that infernal quiet manner, I suppose; but that ain't so easy to master."

Thus would grumble Sir John Pulleyne—envious, and not without cause; for that blatant baronet, when he cursed jockey-trainer or professional, not unfrequently got to the full as bad as he gave. Even at whist, the earl never visited the most atrocious fault in his partner more severely than by a slight shrug of the shoulders and a compassionate smile. Once—the blunder was an exceptional one, and had cost him something over two hundred sovereigns—he was heard to say, reflectively,—

"I've been at it now for about thirty years; and I've come to the conclusion that play rather tells *against* one than otherwise."

But this remark was not made till the rubber had been some time over, and it was murmured too low to reach the ears of the offender. Neither was he one of the "angels abroad and devils at home," that seem to be less uncommon since cigarettes and absinthe came in. His wife had always had quite as much of his attention and his society as she cared to claim: though he never interfered with the actual management of his family, he liked to have his children with him, and, when he had leisure, was always willing to minister to their amusement.

Of all the unlucky coincidences in life, the most frequent certainly is the unwelcome presence of the "very last person one expected to see." Lord Daventry's presence here was purely accidental. He had business to transact that morning with a famous turf commissioner, and, for reasons best known to himself, had chosen to confer with this potentate at the latter's own house in Tyburnia. His nearest and pleasantest way back from the interview lay through Kensington Gardens; and, as it chanced, it led him within a few yards of the trysting-spot. His friends were wont to deny that anything could possibly surprise Daventry; but this opinion might have been modified by whoso had read his thoughts when he first recognized the female figure in the interesting group over against him. It was a breach of delicacy, of course, to approach unobserved, and to listen to sentiments never intended for his ears; but I think few British parents, under the circumstances, would have acted more chivalrously.

Being such a manner of man, you may guess that there was nothing very awful in the demeanor of Nina's father, though his appearance did savor of the *Deus ex máchiná;* but if he had descended from the clouds with all the attributes of Jupiter Tonans, the pair before him could scarcely have been more startled. The first impulses of surprise were thoroughly characteristic of the two. Horace stepped a full pace backward; Nina drew ever so little closer to her lover's side. She spoke first, too, though it was in a very faint, unsteady voice that she named—

"Mr. Kendall."

The earl lifted his hat. With whomsoever he was dealing, he could not, for the life of him, omit any form of courtesy. If, during the Reign of Terror, he had been forced to pass through Sanson's hands, when they first met face to face he would not have failed to salute the headsman.

"One of the west-country Kendalls?" he said, interrogatively. "No? That is the only family of the name with which I'm at all acquainted. Ah, now I remember! I have heard of a Mr. Kendall with a wonderful voice. Have I the pleasure of speaking to that—person?"

The pause before the last word was just long enough to give it point—no longer. Horace's scattered thoughts had not rallied sufficiently to enable him to do more than bow an assent to the suggestion.

"Exactly so," the earl went on. "This daughter of mine seems to have a good deal of dramatic talent, and I suppose you're assisting her to cultivate it. We're infinitely indebted to you, I'm sure. But, Nina, my dear, I think you've had about enough rehearsing for one morning. You found your way here alone, I presume, and I have no doubt you could find your way home just as easily; but there's no necessity for that. Will you be kind enough to sit down there"—he pointed to an unoc-cupied chair about fifty yards off—"till I'm ready to escort you? I sha'n't detain Mr. Kendall ten minutes; but what I have to say to him I don't choose you to hear."

Very keen, according to the poets, are the perceptions of hate and fear; yet are they much keener than those of any true woman when it is a question of pain, or peril, or even discomfort, impending over the man who has the keeping of her heart? What caused Nina to apprehend that her lover might fare ill, if left unsupported to the tender mercies of her urbane sire, would be rather hard to say; but, having such a misgiving in her mind, her first impulse followed as a matter of course. The wound may be but skin-deep, and he for whom it was incurred is not always cognizant thereof; but wonderfully often, in the tragedies and comedies of this life of ours, that scene is enacted which gave Kirkconnell Lea a name in story.

"It was all my fault, papa," the girl cried out; "it was, indeed!"

The earl smiled compassionately.

"My dear Nina, I have no doubt that your first French governess taught you that *qui s'excuse s'accuse.* I didn't say any one was in fault. I only said, 'Sit down there till I am ready to take you home.' Will you do so at once?"

The steady brown eyes quelled the rising rebellion in Nina's breast. Very slowly and reluctantly, like one who yields to the mesmeric will, she did as she was bidden. She looked back once over her shoulder; and then her lips rather formed than uttered the single word "good-by." The earl's glance followed his daughter till she sank down on the chair he had pointed out. When he turned again on Kendall, his brow was still smooth, but the smile was off his face.

"Now, perhaps you will explain the meaning of all this."

Kendall had expected some such interrogation for the last five minutes, and was prepared to reply to it after a fashion. He began a pretty set speech, wherein he was aware that he was scarcely worthy, etc. The earl cut him short before the second period was scarcely turned.

"Ah, we'll leave all that out, if you please. I prefer to listen to that sort of thing from a stall in the third row. I want a plain answer to a plain question. All clandestine meetings have some object, I presume. What was yours this morning?"

Kendall was a craven to the marrow of his bones; yet something in the other's manner goaded him into a show of spirit.

"My object?" he said, doggedly; "the same object that any man might own who loves a woman in truth and honor, and hopes to win her in spite of some differences of station. It may sound presumptuous, of course; but I have yet to learn that I have anything to be ashamed of."

The earl bent his head in quiet assent.

"I think you *have* a good deal to learn, Mr. Kendall. I'm obliged to you for coming to the point, though. Perhaps the less said about truth and honor the better; our ideas are not likely to coincide. Mine are old-fashioned, I dare say. The set I've lived with are not very straitlaced; but they're plain people, who would call compromising such a mere child as that one yonder little better than kidnapping. No; I'm not prepared to say that there's any particular presumption about it. Intellect marches on so fast, that very soon any man within the franchise will be entitled to ask any other elector for his daughter. I suppose, however, the said elector will retain, for some short time to come, the right of saying 'yes' or 'no.' You are good enough to allow that there exist some slight social differences between yourself and Lady Gwendoline Marston. Never mind that; I'm speaking to you now as if your birth and breeding were on a par. You know best what your own resources and expectations are. I don't want to hear a word on that subject, for the simple reason that neither now nor at any future time can it possibly interest me or mine; but, before you think seriously of winning any woman, gentle or simple, wouldn't it be better to consider how you are going to support her?

Now, listen to me. There's a certain sum settled on my younger children, of course; but Lady Daventry and myself have the 'power of appointment.' Perhaps you don't know what that means. Well, I can tell you. It means just this: that I can prevent any one of those children from being one shilling the better by that same settlement during my life or after my death. Now, this power, in case of need, I intend to exercise to the very last letter. If a daughter of mine marries without my consent, she is cut adrift from her family from that day. I would rather thenceforth help with my purse or my influence the merest stranger than her, her husband, or her children, however sore their strait might be. I shouldn't waste breath in cursing; it would be much simpler to leave her alone to bear her own burdens. Under the circumstances, so long as I lived—and I have a very fair constitution—I don't think the 'connection' could be turned to much account. I can't answer for Lady Daventry, of course; but I have an idea that her feelings would not be easily worked upon. You have heard what I say—speaking for myself I will never alter or abate one syllable, so help me God! Are you in the same mind still?"

In the same mind? No, certainly not that; but the precise state of Kendall's sensations at that moment could not be easily set down in words. He was quite clever enough to distinguish between vaporing menace and substantial warning. He acknowledged within himself that the man who had uttered those words would be more likely to die than to relent; and—standing there with scarcely a wrinkle on his white forehead or a silver fleck in his chestnut curls—Lord Daventry looked provokingly full of vitality. Weighing the certainty of heavy risk against the faint chances of remote gains, the speculation was hardly such as to tempt a prudent pauper, with his way to make in the world. Nevertheless, Horace could not bring himself at once to relinquish it. To begin with, Nina had strong attractions for him—social and mercenary considerations apart. He knew that to many others besides himself her face seemed very fair. There was incessant food for vanity in the thought that men who scarcely favored him with a careless nod, and who would have blackballed him from head to heel in any ballot whatsoever, might have labored long to secure one of the smiles that for him had ceased to be rare. He liked the girl's wayward daring, perhaps all the better because it contrasted so strongly with his own cautious, calculating nature. Furthermore, there was working within him—though this, perhaps, he was utterly unconscious of—the black, acrid poison that, since the world was young, has leavened the ferment of so many revolts—the spleen of social inferiority.

Without some sort of gloss, that last sentence might easily be misconstrued. I do not mean to claim for the "blue blood" immunity from meannesses, or to assert that the guinea-stamp is the best voucher for purity of metal, or to deny that, setting the influence of circumstance aside, high and healthy impulses are not as likely to be found in the gipsy-child, swaddled in haybands, as in the daintiest porphyrogenete. If the prophecies of the meek and amiable "Historicus" are to be fulfilled, we will wish the working-man good luck with his honor, appending thereunto the hope that his right hand will not teach him *too* terrible things. I was not alluding just now either to the peasant or artisan; much less to those unhappy creatures who seem predestined to ramp in the mire at the foot of the World's Ladder, with no particular interest in any schemes mooted above that do not bear more or less directly on the subversion of order or alteration of the penal code. Neither had I in mind the vast middle class, taken as a whole, but only certain specimens thereof—people who, instead of doing their duty in the state of life to which it pleased Heaven to call them, like the honest men who begat them, are always wriggling up a rung higher, utterly careless as to how unsteady their footing may be, or how their hands may be soiled in climbing—people whose aspirations have furnished food for ridicule ever since pencil of caricaturist or pen of satirist was wielded; those who brought into vogue surely the most odious word that ever sprang from a musical root—"gentility." Mark this too: wherever it is a question of class-jealousy, the envy of the plebeian born and bred is the very milk of human kindness compared to the malice of the parvenu.

For some time past, Kendall had kept steadily before him one object—the securing a recognized position in what is called society. In the furtherance of this, there is scarcely any contumely from which he would actually have recoiled; but partial success only made him more keenly alive to slights and repulses; albeit many of these, perhaps, only existed in his own morbid fancy. He was always tormented by the misgiving that his pretty little affectations must seem to others, as well as himself, like sham jewels set side by side with heirlooms. The very type of the "set" that Horace hated and envied about equally was before him now—languid, self-possessed, thoroughly at ease, and thoroughly determined to abate not an inch of his vantage-ground. Overt insult or coarse abuse would have been infinitely easier to endure than the amenities he had just listened to. Kendall vowed to himself that his adversary should not carry the matter quite so smoothly through; nevertheless, he answered with touching humility, after an instant's pause,—

"My wishes would never change, even if I were forced to give up hope. Do I understand that you require that Lady Gwendoline and myself should be strangers henceforth—strangers always—and that this can never be altered? It sounds very, very hard; almost too hard."

The earl drew himself up ever so slightly, and the fashion of his countenance was changed. Even now there was no anger in his eyes; but the softness had gone out of them utterly.

"Unquestionably you may understand that much," he said; "but you'll understand something more before we part. I have been arguing on grounds of expediency so far, as if there were no such things as social distinctions. As the argument don't seem to be convincing, we'll take the other side of the question—the kidnapping side. If you suppose for a moment that I'm going to turn that poor child into a prisoner, or my house into a jail, to keep her safe from you, you labor under such a mistake as few men make twice in a lifetime. You have ample warning now; it won't be repeated. If, after this, there comes any annoyance from you, directly or indirectly, by word, deed, or letter—more than that, if I hear of your making a good story out of any folly that you may have entrapped her into already—*I'll stop it*—not by fair means, but by foul. Rather a hard sentence to construe, isn't it? But the right of translation is reserved. We live in the midst of law and order, of course, and the Coventry Act has been a dead letter this long time past; but, if they were communicative down at Scotland-yard, they could tell you one or two curious stories about 'East-ending.' I shall give you no further hints: the unknown is always the most terrible."

Many men, finding themselves in Kendall's position, would have turned the tables at once in their own favor by laughing the menace to scorn; but, by dint of making experiments *in corpore vili*, Lord Daventry had acquired a tolerably sharp insight into the weaker and worse side of human nature. On the present occasion it seemed he had gauged very accurately the character with which he had to deal; and his bolt was not shot at a venture. It was evident that Kendall was thoroughly frightened. His clumsy attempt at bluster would not have imposed on a child.

"I—I'm not to be intimidated," he said, in a thick, unsteady voice. "Are you aware, my lord, such threats are actionable?"

"Perfectly aware," the other replied, placidly. "You can lay an information if you like; but I doubt if you'll get any magistrate to take it. I've got a reputation for good temper, and I haven't been in a quarrel since I left school. I doubt still more if you came to harm hereafter —if your beauty were spoiled in a street-row, for instance—whether you'd bring me in as accessory before the fact. East-enders are too well paid to peach. I can spare you no more time, I'm sorry to say: you can think over all this at your leisure."

A man bold enough to set the earl's warning utterly at naught could scarcely have failed to be impressed by the contrast between his *débonnaire* manner and the purport of his words. Truculence would have been infinitely less effective. Such a contrast might have been seen at some of the banquets in the wild old times, where none wore garb more warlike than what is wrought in velvet, miniver, or lawn, but where, if a guest stirred overhastily, an ominous rattle would have been heard, and gray steel would have glimmered under rochet or robe of estate. There was an awkward pause. Then Horace spoke with some faint show of spirit: it was like the last melancholy ruffle of the drums when the garrison of a surrendered fortress is forming to march out.

"I have no wish to annoy any one, or to thrust my company where it is not welcome. I would have said as much five minutes ago. Nothing I have done, my lord, justifies such language as you have seen fit to use. I will pass my solemn word not to communicate in any way with Lady Gwendoline Marston without your knowledge or consent; and I need hardly say that her name shall never suffer through me. I presume this will satisfy you?"

Without going deep into decimals, it would be hard to set down the precise value at which the earl estimated Horace Kendall's word; but he thought he had a more material security against any future breach of the peace than that gentleman's own recognizances; and it had always been his policy to provide the broadest of bridges for a flying foe. "Never pen 'em, if you can help it," he was wont to say. So he answered with edifying gravity, just as if he were accepting the most substantial of guarantees.

"Perfectly satisfied. And now, as we understand each other thoroughly, and I happen to be rather busy to-day, I think I shall wish you a very good-morning."

And once more the earl lifted his hat. The other returned the salute mechanically without looking up; then he stood quite still, his hands crossed before him, and resting on the handle of his walking-stick. A few seconds later Nina passed him on her father's arm, and her piteous glance was unanswered, even if it was noticed, by those sullen eyes.

"What did you say to him, papa?" the girl asked, when they had gone about a hundred yards. "You *will* tell me, I know."

Her lips were very white, but they scarcely trembled at all. She was a thorough Marston; and that family had a knack of taking their punishment quietly, in whatsoever shape it might descend.

"Well, there's very little to tell," the earl answered, in his airy way. "I explained to Mr. Kendall that there must be an end to all this nonsense—utterly an end—and he perfectly agreed with me."

"He—perfectly—agreed—with you?"

The dull, heavy syllables dropped out one by one. Then her lips were pressed tightly together; but she could not keep them from quivering a little now.

Raoul Marston was not devoid of natural affection, though he seldom went out of his way to display it. He felt very sorry for his little daughter, and very loath to add to her pain. It cost him no small effort to answer her cheerily.

"Of course he agreed with me; and so will you, my dear, when your foolish little head gets straight again. I hope it won't be so easily turned in future, or we shall have to send you back to the school-room and have that last Gorgon of a governess back again. I'm much too old to turn detective, and you're too young to be turned into a prisoner at large. Now you'll just give me your word that there shall be no further communication between yourself and Mr. Kendall that I don't sanction—it's no more than he's done already—then all this shall rest a secret between you and me. I sha'n't even tell my lady about it."

A real heroine would have avowed herself willing to be incarcerated there and then, and to eat the bread-and-water of affliction indefinitely, rather than resign her heart's desires; but we do not often even read of such in the romances which profess to mirror modern society, and probably neither you nor I ever encountered them in the flesh. Nina Marston was able and willing to bear up her full share of the burden of the battle; but, now that her natural ally had signed terms of surrender on his own account, she was not minded to fight to the death—alone. It may be, too, that one of the misgivings that she had never been quite able to smother, as to the real character of the man for whom she had risked so much and with such poor return, came back upon her just then. Moreover, you will remember she had come to the trysting-place that morning with the settled purpose of saying "Good-by." She looked up bravely in her father's face.

"Let me write to him—just one little note—that he may not think me cold and cruel, and then I will give you that promise, papa, and keep it too."

Gwendoline Marston's parole was a very different thing from Horace Kendall's. A strong-minded parent would assuredly have rejected that condition: perhaps it rather strengthened Lord Daventry's confidence.

"I oughtn't to listen to such a thing," he said, half grumblingly. "I feel like an accomplice as it is. Well, you may write just that once, and I trust you—do you hear me, Nina?—I trust you not to write a word that either you or I need be ashamed of hereafter, and then all this shall be as if it had never been. But there won't be an end of it, as far as I'm concerned, if I see you look pale and moping."

"You needn't fear," she said.

Glancing around first, to see that nobody was near—he was exceeding circumspect in such matters—the earl stooped and kissed his daughter's brow. If the compact had been duly engrossed, attested, and signed, it could not have been more effectually sealed.

That same evening Nina and Avenel met—in a crowd, of course—but there was space and leisure enough to serve their purpose.

"Well?" Regy asked, lifting those expressive brows of his, which did almost as much service as Burleigh's nod. There was bitterness enough still clinging about the girl's heart to make her feel triumph in being able to defy, at all events, her self-appointed guardian.

"Well?" she retorted; "that means that you want a full and correct account of all my sayings and doings to-day, on pain of being brought before the judgment-seat if I refuse. I do refuse, then, and you can make the best or worst of it!"

Avenel was really chagrined, and showed it.

"So you haven't come to your senses yet? And I so hoped you would. I must speak to them at home, then: God knows how I hate it."

He looked so pained that Nina's enmity was disarmed. He had meant kindly by her throughout, after all: she knew that.

"No, I've nothing to tell you, Regy," she said; "but you needn't go to papa, for all that. He knows everything, or nearly everything; for he came up—quite by chance, I'm certain—when I was talking to *him* this morning. It's all over—quite over. Papa's satisfied about that, so I suppose you'll be. Don't speak of it any more, please, and take me up-stairs directly. I wouldn't miss this waltz on any account. I'm just in the humor for dancing to-night. Can't you fancy it?"

And so the first romance of Gwendoline Marston's life died and was buried—decently, if with no great pomp of funeral honors. Well, when on such sepulchers there is not written

Resurgam.

CHAPTER XXI.

"A THOROUGHLY satisfactory place," said Vere Alsager.

A better epithet could not have been applied to Kenlis Castle and its belongings. There was nothing either of savage grandeur or soft luxuriance in the landscape; but no one would have thought of calling it tame, and it embraced most of the best features of ordinary Scotch scenery. The topmost peak of the long hill-ranges, stretching away till purple faded into misty blue, was far from kissing heaven; yet the traveling of them was no mean test of wind and muscle. The pines in the hanging woods were mere dwarfs compared with the "shadowy armies" that line Norwegian or Alpine heights; but they made up a rich background, and a fence withal, through which the northeast winds, though they strove hard and often, could not force a passage. The loch,

widening gradually as it trended seaward, was scarcely
more than a rifle-shot across over against the castle; yet
its shores were broken by more bays and promontories
in miniature than are often found in more imposing lakes;
and in calm weather you felt as if you could almost cut
out the shadows of birch and oak resting on the clear,
deep water.

As for the castle itself, no one with proper ideas of
comfort would have wished to add a cubit to its size or
a year to its age. Some additions to the original fabric
had been made from time to time—always in the same
solemn granite, that looks not much more hoary after the
lapse of a century than when fresh from the quarrying.
However, for two generations, at least, the sound of
mason's hammer had not been heard there; and the general aspect of the building was little changed since Sir
Dugald Kenlis, with his own hands, fixed the last battle-
ment of the central tower.

After the fall of the leaf, when the trees were bare,
and the hill-sides bleak, and the loch fretted with foam,
the castle would doubtless look somewhat somber and
eerie. At such a season, without some strong antidote
to melancholy or morbid fancies, even a strong-minded
skeptic might have caught himself speculating, oftener
than was agreeable, whether it were absolutely certain
that the legend of the Brown Lady was such an idle
tale. For Kenlis, be it known, possessed a ghost, the
existence and occasional appearance of which could be
attested by several living witnesses—chiefly by a certain
ancient ex-housekeeper, who, in a cottage just without
the demesne-wall, lived in much ease and dignity on her
pension and peculations. A pitiless Presbyterian was
this ancient dame, and—on the principle of truth being
generally disagreeable—implicitly to be believed.

But, with autumn weather overhead, and wealth of
greenery all round, there was no excuse for such vain
imaginings; and there was justice in Blanche Ramsay's
self-reproaches when she called herself ungrateful and
fanciful, and a dozen harder names, for feeling so constantly out of spirits there. Her first impressions of the
place had been most favorable, and these, to a certain.

NESTLED IN A COSY NOOK   Page 175

extent, had not worn off. She liked water, and wood, and heather, to the full as well as when she looked on them first, and while in the air she was happy enough in her own quiet way; but directly she came in-doors a heavy weight seemed to oppress her that she could not shake off, try as she would. She began to feel dull and chilly, and disinclined to talk or even to move unnecessarily.

Very clever upholsterers, with *carte blanche* given them, had refurnished the castle, and few appliances of modern luxury were wanting there; nevertheless, the interior was certainly somewhat gloomy. After sunset, even at this season, Night and Echo would have their way in the long corridors, in despite of frequent sconces and thick-piled carpeting; and, when not a leaf was stirring outside, a breeze seemed always soughing among the black timber-work of the vaulted hall. Yet this could not account for it; for her own special rooms, looking to the south, were airy and lightsome as she could desire, and she felt it there just the same. To be sure, all her arrangements hitherto had been on rather a tiny scale; and, when she first began to play the *châtelaine*, it was only natural that she should feel somewhat overawed. Domestic cares or anxieties she had none; for Ramsay had no small economies, and would just as soon have thought of brushing his own clothes as of allowing his wife to trouble herself with any matters falling within the house-steward's or housekeeper's province. Perhaps it might have been better if Blanche had been forced to exert herself in some way that would have kept her thoughts busy while she was alone; and she was a good deal alone at first, for business, chiefly connected with outlying portions of the estate, had accumulated during Mark's long absence; and during the week following their arrival at Kenlis he was seldom in-doors between breakfast and dinner.

On one of these afternoons, Blanche strolled down to the loch-side, and nestled herself, with her novel, into a certain cosy nook that she had discovered in one of her earliest rambles. There she sat, reading and day-dreaming in about equal proportions—for the book rather bored her than otherwise—till she was startled by a rustling in the birch-boughs overhead that could not have been caused by the breeze, for the water at her feet was smooth as steel. Before she could look up, Mark had swung himself down from a jutting crag above, and dropped lightly on the sand beside her.

"So this is your notion of doing the honors of Kenlis, Bianchetta? Don't you know that you ought to be sitting up there in state to receive visitors? These are the very first that have called since we came into our kingdom. I've no doubt the worthy creatures came famishing with curiosity to see what Mrs. Ramsay was like; and, lo, they are sent empty away!"

He threw a couple of cards into her lap, whereon was inscribed

CAPTAIN IRVING.

MISS IRVING.

Drumour.

"I'm a true penitent," Blanche said. "If you'll believe me, the possibility of a morning visit never once crossed my mind. Conceive there being a neighborhood somewhere beyond our hills! I wonder what these people are like, Mark; the name sounds rather nice, doesn't it?"

"Don't found pleasant conclusions on that," Ramsay said, with a laugh, as he settled himself on the rocky ledge on which his wife was reclining. "I know nothing about the Irvings,—I've a sort of notion they were away when I was here last autumn; at all events, they didn't deign to notice graceless grouse-shooters,—but I dare say my fancy portrait won't be half a bad likeness. The father—a regular half-pay 'heavy,' with an ancient War-Office grievance, always ready to be brought in when he has said his say about Kirk and Session—shoots with one muzzle-loader over slow setters, and won't allow that any one but himself can tie a fly. The daughter—

or sister, as the case may be—of the 'bitter bar-maid' type, gaunt and rather grim, wears good serviceable boots and a tartan petticoat, and writes short tales with long morals for Family Journals. Before you have been ten minutes in her company, she will find out something about your 'state of grace,' Blanche, depend upon it."

Mrs. Ramsay shuddered slightly.

"And you call that portrait-painting? I wonder what your caricatures would be like. Now, I've no doubt that they are just what you said at first—very worthy creatures. It was a great stretch of charity to drive out at all on such a sultry afternoon. We shall appreciate it better when we return their visit, I dare say."

"I rather admire that 'we.' Is it absolutely necessary that I should take part in the ceremony? I think I must stay at home and look after Alsager, who comes to-night, you know. It wouldn't be civil to leave him to his own devices quite so soon "

"How truly considerate!" Blanche said, demurely. "It's quite refreshing in these selfish days to find any one so alive to hospitable duties. Now, I think that both you and Mr. Alsager, if you made a great effort, might possibly survive the pilgrimage to Drumour. If you can't, I think I shall defer mine till the Brancepeths come next week. I'd give anything to hear Queenie questioned as to her state of grace."

"Well, we'll see about it," Mark replied, picking himself up leisurely. "I haven't the slightest doubt, when it comes to the point, you'll manage it your own way. Suppose we stroll slowly home; it's too hot to hurry, and it must be close on dressing-time. These long rides give one a savage appetite, and Isidor's *entreés* are too clever to be kept waiting."

It was on the following morning that Alsager made the remark recorded above, while he and his host were smoking the after-breakfast cigar on the broad terrace-walk that ran along all the western and southern sides of the castle.

"Yes, it's a liveable place enough," Ramsay acquiesced; "but I'm happy to say there's plenty of room for improvement still. I don't seem to care for things that are absolutely perfect."

M

"No, I shouldn't think you did," the other retorted. "You're not exactly a 'character,' Mark; but I never saw any one quite like you, all the same. Now, if I'd been making both ends of a pittance meet, so long—that's just what a thousand a year is to a man of your tastes and habits—and found myself one fine morning a Carabas, I couldn't for the life 'of me take it so coolly as you do. I think I should always be calling my neighbors to rejoice with me, or making myself ridiculous in one way or other, for at least another twelvemonth to come."

"The neighbors come without being called—at least, a couple of them have," Mark said; "I'll tell you about that presently, though. But you are wrong there; I don't take what's happened all as a matter of course; indeed, I wonder at it as much as I can wonder at anything."

"Ah, it never rains but it pours!" the other went on. "I'm not at all sure that your last stroke of luck wasn't as good as the first. You don't think I'd flatter you at this time of day; but I don't know when I've seen anything so nice as Mrs. Ramsay. You ought to be too happy, Mark, that's the truth of it. If I were you, I'd contrive to drop something very valuable into the loch occasionally, on that Greek tyrant's principle of throwing a sop to Fortune."

"Polycrates, you mean. It wasn't such a very bright idea, either. They crucified him soon afterward—served him quite right, too—for fancying that he could satisfy the envy of gods with a jeweler's toy. What would you have me throw away, Vere? Not my wife, I presume? She's about the only portable treasure I should care very much about losing—just now."

Alsager was not more malicious or envious than his fellows; nevertheless, as he repeated the last words to himself, he laughed a little inwardly. While the world lasts, he whose garden is barren of herb, fruit, or flower will not seldom console himself with the thought that a canker-worm may be coiled round the root of his neighbor's gourd.

"You were mentioning some neighbors just now," Vere asked, after smoking silently a minute or two. "What of them?"

" Well, a Captain and Miss Irving left their cards yesterday, and it's a question of returning their call. Morning-visits in desert-life are too absurd ; but Blanche is so plaintive about going alone, that I hardly like to send her. She's cruelly out of her element with stiff, uncouth people, such as these are certain to turn out. Would you mind very much going over to-morrow afternoon ? We can make up a scratch team for the break ; and, as they want putting together, they'd just suit you. It's a fair, hard road, I believe, and goes through some good scenery."

" I don't want bribing," the other said ; " I rather like the idea than not. How do you know that these are such rough diamonds? The country is fairly civilized hereabouts, and the name don't sound uncouthly. There was an Irving made a great stir in Florence just before our time. Though domestic duties are very elastic out there, I don't think he *could* have been a family man. To be sure, ' Miss' stands for sister as well as daughter ; but it's long odds against it's being the same. We'll see Mrs. Ramsay through it to-morrow, anyhow. We shall have a rare sail this evening if the breeze holds—a leading wind both ways—and we're sure to pick up something, ' trailing.' "

The drive next day quite answered Ramsay's warranty. The ground was not such as most people would have selected for the trial of a scratch team, but Alsager was a thorough workman of the " fast" school. He hustled his horses a bit too much, some critics said ; but he never let them get out of his hand. Even the stubborn near leader was fain to realize at last that he had not come out for his own amusement that day, and settled down doggedly to his collar up the last steep slope, in the valley beyond which lay Drumour.

An exclamation of pleased surprise broke from Mrs. Ramsay as they rose the crest of the hill.

" Do pull up for an instant, if it's possible, Mr. Alsager ; I didn't reckon on such a view as this."

" Nothing easier," Vere said, as he brought his team up with a long, steady pull ; " they'll be all the better for a breathing. That's worth looking at, certainly."

It was one of the bits of scenery not uncommon in

Scotland—which, lying out of the beaten track, are better known to stalkers than to tourists—where Nature has shown what she can do when she sets her hand in earnest to landscape-gardening. It would not have been easy to improve on the grouping of cliff, wood, and water at Drumour; though everything was on a miniature scale—from the loch, that looked as if no gust had ever ruffled it rudely, to the velvet lawn, on which a few gorgeous flower-beds lay like jewels. The house itself was in perfect keeping with the rest—a low, irregular building, abounding in nooks and gables, and mantled in creepers to the base of its quaint, twisted chimneys.

"Do half-pay officers usually live in such quarters, Mark?" Mrs. Ramsay asked, rather triumphantly. And her husband was fain to confess that his fancy portrait might not turn out such a faithful one, after all.

A few minutes later they had drawn up before the porch, and had been informed by a very correct-looking man-servant that Miss Irving was at home, and her father within call. Blanche's own boudoir at Kenlis was not more dainty to look upon than the drawing-room into which the visitors were shown; yet the furniture was not specially costly, and, setting aside some rare china, the nick-nacks scattered about were more valuable for their workmanship than for their material. And the mistress thereof—was she of "the bitter bar-maid" type? You shall judge.

A tall, very tall figure, and superbly developed; yet so supple and delicately moulded that even a rival would not have ventured to speak of it as "fine;" glossy nut-brown hair, rippling low over a broad Egyptian forehead; gray opaline eyes, rather deeply set under strong arched brows, shaded by lashes much darker than the hair; a mouth too large to please an artist, but to ordinary mortals, with its firm scarlet lips, and teeth faultless in shape and color, tempting past the telling; features of the subdued aquiline; a complexion pale on the surface, with subtle, faint rose-tints beneath, when you looked more narrowly. Such was the *signalement* of Alice Irving, *æt.* 22.

In the fashion of her dress there was nothing apparently beyond the scope of ordinary waiting-maid's skill; but I doubt if the high-priest of the fashionable temple in the Street of Peace, after an hour's devout meditatioa, could have ordained anything more suggestive than the modest *foulard*, which might have been chosen to match her eyes. Her beauty was of that peculiar stamp which is certain to provoke enmity and envy, howsoever meekly it be used, simply because other types, differing ever so much betwixt themselves, suffer almost equally in comparison. Unluckily, it happens that women endowed with this perilous pre-eminence seldom *do* use it wisely or well. Nothing could be quieter than her voice and manner; but, before her few simple words of welcome were spoken, Alsager, whose ears seldom deceived him, thought within himself that it would be worth walking more miles than they had driven to hear that woman sing.

Mrs. Ramsay, whose presence of mind was equal to most social emergencies, was fairly startled by the apparition. She thought, perhaps, like Christabel in the wood,

> 'Twas fearful there to see
> A lady richly clad as she—
> Beautiful exceedingly.

Mark himself took the whole thing in his wonted matter-of-course way, and did not even answer a meaning side-glance from Alsager.

"Yes, Drumour is charming, even in winter," Miss Irving said, in answer to au admiring remark of Blanche's; "at least, I find it so; but at this season every one is fascinated with it. I have seen little of it lately; we've been abroad the last four years, and the place was let."

"Traveling abroad?" Mark struck in. "I have been such a wanderer myself that it is strange we have never met. We never did meet, I'm quite sure."

A faint smile showed that the subtle flattery of the last words was not lost upon Alice Irving.

"Not so strange," she said, "when you hear that our head-quarters were at Darmstadt, and that I, at least, was almost always a fixture there. It's not an out-of-the-way place, certainly, and birds of passage often perch there for a single night; but I can hardly conceive any one lingering longer, without strong and sufficient reasons, such as ours were. Everything and everybody is so deadly-lively, from the Grand Duke downwards; and when one gets thoroughly torpid, even Shakspeare in German won't wake one up."

"Well, I hope you are quite established here now," Mrs. Ramsay said, kindly; "and that's not a very disinterested hope. Kenlis can't have many such neighbors, and within such easy distance, too; the drive is a mere nothing."

"I'm sure I hope so," Alice answered; "but we're the most uncertain people. I think papa rather piques himself on making no plans beyond the week. Ah, here he comes; he will be so glad not to have missed you!"

There was little, if any, family likeness betwixt father and daughter. Captain Irving's figure was wonderfully proportioned, and his features nearly faultless; but it was diminutive perfection, and the general effeminacy of his appearance was heightened by an evident coxcombry of attire. He was the sort of man that you could fancy, in case of shipwreck, appearing without a trace of disorder half an hour after he had been cast on a desert shore. He doffed a broad-leafed hat of Panama straw as he entered through one of the open French windows; and, as he crossed the light, it was plain to see that either Time had dealt very gently with his glossy curls, or that Art had balked the old Avenger.

If there was little outward resemblance betwixt father and daughter, their voices, at least, were remarkably alike. Both had the same rich flexible intonations; and you could fancy Captain Irving's white taper fingers straying over the keys of an instrument and working wonderful things thereon. His manner was very quiet and gentle, though there was no lack of warmth in his welcome; and he settled himself down by Mrs. Ramsay with the matter-of-course ease of a man who, rightly or wrongly, considers he has a prescriptive right to the attention of a pretty woman.

Altogether, it was a pleasant quintette; and the conversation, such as it was, did not flag a whit, till it was full time to order the break round.

" I suppose it's no use asking you to shoot with us just yet ?" Mark said to his host, as he rose to depart. " A man's own birds have the first claim on him for a good week after the 12th. But we shall be too happy, whenever you can spare a day—or, better still, two days—sleeping at Kenlis, of course; and perhaps Miss Irving might be tempted to accompany you."

" A thousand thanks," the other answered. " I should like it of all things ; but—it's a very humiliating confession—I haven't fired a shot-gun for years. A little feeble fly-fishing is my best attempt at fulfilling the Whole Duty of a Hielandman ; and all my ground, except one beat that supplies the house, is let. I'll drive Alice over one morning, though, in time to escort Mrs. Ramsay, if she chooses, to meet you at lunch. Those are the only circumstances under which I ever take the hill. We'll stay that night with pleasure. How time passes! I was an ensign and lieutenant when I slept at Kenlis last."

And so it was settled.

A vote of confidence in Drumour and its tenants was passed unanimously by the committee of three sitting in the break ; but the homeward was more silent than the outward drive had been, and before the hanging woods of Kenlis were in sight, one of those fits of depression that had vexed and puzzled her so much of late began to creep over Blanche Ramsay. They would not have seemed so unaccountable, if she had thoroughly believed in presentiments. But her life hitherto had been so free from storms that she had not learned to read the meaning of the innocent-looking white flecks in a cloudless sky ; and had never been forced to realize that a small inner voice oftentimes speaks more soothly than all the prophets that, since the time of the Tishbite, ever have threatened " Woe !"

CHAPTER XXII.

The men were scarcely alone together till they settled down to their evening smoke.   Then said Alsager,—

"It's the Florentine celebrity, after all, you may depend upon it.   'Never shoots with a shot-gun'—that's likely enough ; but I dare say he could give either you or me a lesson with hair-triggers.   His pistol-practice used to be something miraculous, if I remember right ; and it pulled him through one or two awkward dilemmas.   It's an agreeable surprise altogether, isn't it ?"

"Very agreeable, particularly if the rest of the neighborhood comes up to the first sample.   That isn't likely, though.   I've seen the father before—it's a sort of face that dwells on one's memory ; it was at Baden, three years ago ; he was playing fearfully high, with the luck dead against him.   Navaroff used to point him out as the only Englishman who could lose in real Russian fashion.   I quite understand their living at Darmstadt now : it's within hail of every hell in Germany."

"How about the daughter's face ?   Don't you think *that* would be likely to stay by one too ?   There has been, or will be, the frame-work of a sensation-piece in that young woman's history, unless I'm much mistaken."

"Too thoroughbred for the stage, I should say," the other answered ; "and Darmstadt isn't exactly a dramatic place.   It's odd that she hasn't married, though."

"Odder still that she should not have got into some scrape of one sort or another.   There's a quiet devilry in those eyes that ought to take her far."

Ramsay shrugged his shoulders somewhat impatiently :

"I'm not going to argue the point.   You're a scientific oculist, Vere ; but even science is wrong sometimes.   I can see nothing in Miss Irving but a highly ornamental young person, likely to make a pleasant companion for Blanche whenever we're alone here."

" *That* of course," Alsager said, with his low laugh—
"a perfect godsend for Mrs. Ramsay in every way."

And all the while he thought within himself, half compassionately, that it would have been better for his hostess,
a thousandfold, to have found at Drumour a hard-featured,
harsh-voiced virago than such a one as Alice Irving.

Two days later the Kenlis party was completed for the
present by the advent of three fresh guests—the Brancepeths and Colonel Vane; and the following morning,
being the Feast of S. Tetrao, four guns were at work
betimes, pairing off on separate beats. Mr. Brancepeth
was a steady, methodical performer, but could not stand
being hurried or flurried, and, setting jealousy aside, had
a wholesome horror of long-striding companions like
Alsager and Vane. With his host he felt a comfortable
certainty of being allowed to go his own pace and pick his
own shots ; for Ramsay, like many others who have gone
in heavily for the big game, was by no means keen in the
pursuit of feathered fowl, though he shot in remarkably
good form. When they ceased firing, the leisurely couple
were found to have contributed rather more than their
quota to a fair mixed bag of over two hundred head

There was no luncheon-party that first day; for La
Reine Gaillarde was just tired enough by her long journey to incline rather to a quiet lionizing of Blanche's new
home than to the climbing of a hill-side on pony-back,
even with the chance of seeing a certain stalwart figure
standing in relief against the sky-line. She and Vane
were ancient acquaintances, and might have been familiar friends—to put it mildly—if in those days the
colonel of the Princess's Own had had eyes or ears for
the service of any but Mrs. Ellerslie. It was not in
Laura Brancepeth to bear malice, much less to pine over
any discomfiture ; especially if, as in this case, she had
never seriously addressed herself to the conquest. Certainly, she had no need to go out into the highways and
byways to recruit the ranks of her adherents. Nevertheless, her black eyes flashed with pleasure when she heard,
on her arrival, who was expected hourly. Vereker was
about the last person she had reckoned on meeting at
Kenlis, at least so soon. Of one thing she felt sure—that

Mark had invited him there, and was thoroughly safe in doing so; and, further, that if Vane should show signs of better taste than heretofore, Blanche would not be likely to interfere with their innocent amusements.

There was a good deal worth looking at within-doors at Kenlis Castle; but before luncheon Laura Brancepeth had rambled through the whole of it alone, and had penetrated into more passages and recesses than Blanche herself had ever discovered. After luncheon, the two women loitered together through the gardens and wood-paths beyond, till they ensconced themselves at last in that tempting nook by the loch-side whereof mention has before been made.

"I declare, it's the most perfect place I ever saw," La Reine said, in her hearty, genuine way. "This is only the second time I've been over the border, it is true; but I don't think it could be matched in Scotland. Blanche, don't you love it already?"

"Yes, it's quite charming," Blanche answered, after a second's hesitation, "and I like it, of course—who could help liking it? But somehow I don't think it quite suits me, Queenie. You can't imagine how languid and depressed I've felt at times, particularly when I'm alone. I've been a good deal alone since we came down. There were an infinity of things for Mark to look into all over the estate; and there's a terrible creature—a factor they call him—who won't be denied. Perhaps the air is rather too relaxing."

"Absurd," the other retorted. "The air's simply faultless. It has given me a fabulous appetite already."

Even while she spoke a light breeze ruffled the bright water at their feet; and the veriest hypochondriac must have acknowledged gratefully the briny freshness it brought from the open sea.

"Mark says just the same thing," Mrs. Ramsay answered, with a slight sigh, "and you are both right, I'm certain. I haven't an excuse for moping either, now you're come. Indeed, I feel ever so much better since yesterday. We'll take their lunch out to the hill to-morrow. There are plenty of available ponies, and you'll enjoy the scramble. I shouldn't wonder if the Irvings drove over in time to go with us. They're our nearest neighbors—the only ones, indeed, that have given signs of their existence—quite a *trouvaille* in such a wild country. The father looks like a statuette of white Dresden, and the daughter—well, I won't describe her, Queenie; but I think you *will* be surprised."

"O, I do hope they'll come," Lady Laura said, eagerly. "Fancy lighting on a pair of Phœnixes so far north ! It's a wonder that none of you mentioned the female bird, at all events, sooner."

"I had so many things to talk about, I suppose," Mrs. Ramsay said, blushing a little. "It's dangerous to rest too much on first impressions; but I wish I was as sure of fine weather to-morrow as I am of your being just as favorably impressed with the Drumour people as we were."

Then they fell to talking of other matters, interesting to themselves, but of no moment to the world in general.

The next day was one of those that Scotland occasionally produces to confute the sulky Southrons who assert that "there's no climate there, only d——d bad weather." The air was so clear that with a good glass you might almost have counted the heather-sprays where they cut the sky-line. There was just breeze enough from the northwest to prevent sultriness and to help the setters, without any of the gusts or flaws that make the packs lie uneasily and carry them when once on the wing far out of bounds. There was firing enough to satisfy a glutton on both beats that morning; and the luck or skill on either side was so nearly level that no man's appetite was spoiled either by self-upbraiding or envy of his fellow. Alsager halted for a second on the crest overlooking the hollow where lunch was already preparing—the other party were half-way down the opposite brae.

"Drumour is to the front, you see" (there had been speculation on this point the previous evening). "I wish we had a photographer here—with a painter's eye, of course, to throw in color afterward."

In truth, the group beneath them was worth reproducing. The rich heather—crimson rather than purple just here—toned down, instead of contrasting with, the bright hues of the kirtles, peeping out below upper-skirts kilted *à la* Lindsay. The soberer tints were supplied by . the plaids on which the women reclined, and the neutral gray of Captain Irving's shooting suit. He leaned against a rock a little in the background, in precisely the attitude that a sculptor would have chosen as best adapted to display the points of his slight, graceful figure.

The luncheon, of course, was a success, for—putting the Irvings aside, who evidently came determined to be pleased—everybody had more or less sufficient reason for being in special good humor. To begin with—seventy brace of clean-killed birds, with scarcely a "cheeper" among them, is a fair forenoon's work for men shooting for their own amusement, with no idea of newspaper renown or the puffing of their moor. Mr. Brancepeth, having differed in opinion from the head-keeper as to the best way of beating the ground, had not only carried his point, but afterward proved himself to be thoroughly in the right, to the conviction, if not satisfaction, even of the stubborn official. Lady Laura, after some sharp *badinage* at breakfast, had backed Alsager against Vane for a fair stake in gloves, and was now rejoicing over having landed her bet by the very short head of a single bird. Her champion to a certain extent went shares in the triumph. As for Vereker, he was thinking how much pleasanter it was to lose in this fashion than to win—even with the probability of being paid—at Vincennes or La Marche, and how differently sounded Laura Brancepeth's healthy merriment from a certain hard, cruel laugh that he hoped to hear never again.

The last two months had wrought a wonderful change in him, outwardly no less than inwardly. At his worst, he had never altogether lost his taste for the field-sports among which he had been born and bred; and he came back to them now with a keener zest than ever. His face would never look otherwise now than battered and worn; but the haggard fierceness which had deformed it was there no longer; and it was now quite possible to believe that those who had known him long ago had not overrated his personal advantages. In many respects he had waxed wiser of late, notably in this one. He could eat of Mark Ramsay's bread and salt with a clear conscience; for he coveted his wife no more. On that night at the Bouffes there was worked a cure—sharp, complete, and lasting. The ex-dragoon's code of morality was rather vague; but he had his own notions concerning equity, notwithstanding. He felt, somehow, that the Ramsays had held out their hands to help him shoreward, when others would have passed by and left him wallowing in the slough; and, since then, the idea of troubling their domestic peace had never once crossed his mind. He stood quite firm on the friendly footing now. When passion such as his is once slain outright, it passes the skill of sorcery itself to put life again into the evil dead.

Blanche herself was, perhaps, in better spirits that morning than she had been since she lunched under the sandstone rocks of Fontainebleau. The keen, pure mountain air had produced a tonic effect already. Also, she felt somewhat elated at having accomplished a formidable feat successfully; for she was a timid horsewoman, and, though she kept her tremors to herself, had seen great fear in the beginning of the ascent. But misgiving lapsed gradually into implicit confidence in the sure-footed beast that bore her; she began to think that it was not so absolutely necessary she should always stay moping at home when her husband rode over the hill; and this in itself was enough to make her happy.

The special cause of Mark's contentment would not be so easy to define; but that he was satisfied with the general aspect of things was very clear. From his welcome of the Irvings, you would scarcely have guessed that their acquaintance was but four days old.

Altogether a cheerier repast is not often partaken of; and an hour was nearly up before Mr. Brancepeth—who in his amusements never lost sight of a stern sense of duty—thought of looking at his watch meaningly.

"Yes, you're quite right to call 'Time,'" Ramsay said, answering the other's glance of appeal; "but it so happens that we needn't hurry. Cameron wants us to try a drive, you know. Some of the men are left back with the flags; but it'll take him nearly half an hour to get his

beaters in line. He has shown me where to post the
guns; it won't take us ten minutes to get there."

"How lucky!" Lady Laura cried; "it's the very thing
I wanted to see. I'd rather look at a partridge-drive
than a 'hot corner' any day; and this must be twice as
exciting. We sha'n't be in your way, Mr. Ramsay, if
we sit where we are told as still as mice. Henry will go
bail for my good behavior, I know."

Mr. Brancepeth smiled sedately.

"You couldn't be very mouse-like under any circumstances, I'm afraid, Laura; but I've never yet seen you
spoil sport."

"You won't be the least in the way," Mark answered;
"indeed, to speak the truth, the drive was organized as
much for your amusement as for ours. It isn't a long
pull either up to the stand; but it's rather steep in
places."

"Beyond Punch's powers, I'm afraid," Blanche interrupted, "and so beyond ·mine. I never intend to part
company; I don't feel safe anywhere on the hill, as yet,
off his back. As for Queenie, she's a perfect Anne of
Geierstein; and I think Miss Irving is nearly as brave."

"I've quite forgotten my mountaineering," Alice said;
"but I'm not in the least tired, and I own I should like
to see the drive; yet it seems so selfish to leave you here
alone. Perhaps you won't be alone, though; for, as far
as I can see, papa looks too comfortable to move just
yet."

"Infinitely too comfortable, my child," Captain Irving
said, serenely. "I wouldn't climb a hundred feet higher
to see a drive of golden eagles. I can't promise to amuse
Mrs. Ramsay; but I promise to take all care of her till
you return: I suppose nothing more terrible than a hill-
fox is likely to come near us."

The rest of the party set off, making for the head of
the hollow. It was a steep and broken ascent, but nowhere an absolute escalade; and—with the exception of
Mr. Brancepeth, who plodded onward slowly and soberly,
taking a line of his own—not one of the climbers was
fairly out of breath when they reached a broad neck of
table-land, with higher ground on either side, about the

center of which the guns were to be posted. There had been built across here a rude stone wall, about breast-high, with loop-holes through which the birds could be marked some sixty yards ahead. When the four men had aligned themselves under this at regular distances, they nearly covered the pass. Brancepeth and Vane had the midmost stands, and to the latter of these went La Reine Gaillarde. She was going double or quits of all her winnings on the event of this drive, and chose, she said, to see with her own eyes that the colonel shot fair, without claiming other people's birds. The *demoiselle* seemed to be hesitating under whose protection she should place herself, when Ramsay said,—

"Will you come to my stand, Miss Irving? You won't see such good practice as if you were at Alsager's, for my hand is rather out for this work; but I suppose I'm morally responsible for your safety till I bring you back to your father."

Judging from Alice's face, the arrangement seemed to her also the most natural one. Neither did Vere Alsager look a whit discontented, as he moved away to his post; indeed, he laughed a little, as he muttered to himself,—

"Moral responsibility!—that's rather a neat way of putting it. There's no story in those eyes, is there, Mark? I wonder if you'll say as much to-morrow. It must have come sooner or later; but it's hard lines on the other that it should come so soon, d—d hard!"

And Vere bit off the end of a cigar with vicious emphasis; but a minute later he was smoking tranquilly, and listening with all his ears for the first "Mark over."

"You needn't be a mouse just yet," Ramsay said, as his companion seated herself on a broad flat stone; "the beaters can hardly have got round. And this is your first experience of grouse-driving, I believe?"

"My first of any kind of shooting. I've never yet been close to a gun when it was fired: so if I start you must not be too scandalized. I'll promise not to scream."

"No, you won't scream," he said. "I fancy your nerves don't often fail you. It'll be rather deafening at first, I'm afraid; but you'll soon get steady under fire."

"One soon gets used to most things," she said, with

an odd sort of smile.   And then there was silence; for a
shout, barely audible, gave warning that the drive had
begun.

A few seconds later, even Alice's inexperienced ears
caught a whirr and whistle of wings.

"They're coming our line," Mark whispered, peering
through his loop-hole.   "Shall I shoot this time?"

Her eyes flashed eagerly.

"Shoot?   Of course!   How can you ask me?"

Eleven grouse came sailing low over the neck, right
before the wind, scarcely swaying their pinions, though
they were at top speed.   When they were within fifty
yards or so, Mark showed his head and shoulders over
the wall.   The wary old cock who led the pack, having
no time to swerve, towered upward with a startled cry;
but the best part of an ounce of No. 5 breasted him as he
rose, and he left his life in the air, though the impetus of
flight carried him within a fathom of the wall. Mark was
equally lucky with his second barrel—an easy cross-shot
to the left.

"A good beginning," he said, smiling—not so much at
his own success as at his companion's satisfaction, for
Alice fairly clapped her hands in triumph,—"and you
never even started, I do believe."

"No; I—I forgot to be frightened," she said, half
penitently.

"Well, mind you don't remember it next time.   There
are more coming; but to the center guns.   Ah! I think
Lady Laura is not quite so mouse-like as—you are.   I've
no doubt she's accountable for Vane's only getting one
barrel in, and that when they had passed him."

For some moments afterward, and indeed till the
beaters came up, the firing was so sharp all along the
line that there was no leisure for talking.   Out of twenty-
six grouse gathered there and then, besides three more
stone dead just below the brow, Alsager—as Ramsay
had predicted—claimed the largest share.   So La Reine
landed her *paroli*, though Vane submitted with a laughing protest.

"I do admire your idea of 'seeing fair,' Lady Laura.
How on earth do you expect a man to shoot, when some

one always offers to back the bird just as he's covering
it ? It's much more nervous work than standing opposite the pigeon-traps with the Ring behind you."

"You're very ungrateful," she retorted; "you ought
to thank me for furnishing you with excuses for all those
misses. Pearl-grays, six and three-quarters, mind; and
I have a weakness for Melnotte."

"Well, I suppose I'd better pay and look pleasant,"
the colonel said, resignedly. "I only hope I shall live
to see them worn out; but I decline to plunge any
more."

Then they descended again into the hollow, where Mrs.
Ramsay and Irving were reclining contentedly; and the
non-shooting members of the luncheon-party started off
homeward. Mark looked after them rather wistfully. If
he had followed his own inclination, he certainly would
have struck work there and then; but he had a certain
conscience in these matters, and felt himself bound to see
Mr. Brancepeth through the day. That methodical person had a great horror of any alteration in the programme, and would have considered himself more than
shabbily treated if he had been left to finish their appointed beat alone.

"What do you think of them, Queenie ?" Mrs. Ramsay asked, as the two women came down-stairs together,
after changing their walking-dress. "Are they not quite
as clever and agreeable as you expected ?"

"Rather more so," the other replied; "but I'm not
quite so wrapped up in them as you all seem to be. I
don't know how it is, but I can't look at either of them
without thinking of the old Scotch proverb, 'Fair and
false.' There's too much gloss about the father quite to
please me; and the daughter—handsome as a picture, I
admit—is rather too much like one's idea of Cleopatra."

"Don't be cynical," Blanche interrupted; "it isn't
like you. I dare say they are just as honest as humdrum
people, though they have much more to say for themselves. I was quite sorry when you all came back this
afternoon. You have no idea how amusing Captain
Irving can be when he chooses."

"Well, you'd better go on with the flirtation," La Reine rejoined; "meanwhile I'll submit to be fascinated by the Signorina."

Fascinated Lady Laura was not; but before dressing-time came she accused herself more than once of lack of charity in her first impressions of Alice Irving.

It was in the evening, however, that Drumour achieved its crowning success. All the Kenlis party were more or less musically inclined, though perhaps only Alsager was thoroughly able to appreciate the vocal powers of the father and daughter. One duet especially roused Mr. Brancepeth himself into something like enthusiasm. The great drawing-room was a trying place for singing; but their voices, single or blended, seemed to fill it without an effort or the straining of a note, and a marvelous softness pervaded the rich volume of sound. Lady Laura and Vane were as vehement in their admiration as Blanche herself could desire; and Alsager — himself no mean performer, and quite aware of the fact—did homage in his own fashion to superior talent; for, though he never left the piano after the Irvings came to it, he could not himself be prevailed upon to utter a note. During all the singing Mark sat a little apart, shading his face with his hand, and, when it was over, paid his acknowledgments in courteous commonplaces. But their glances met for two seconds — no more — as he wished Alice good-night; and the lady's rest was broken by no misgivings as to the completeness of her triumph. She had been complimented on her voice ere now by those whose favorable verdict carried with it fame ; but Ramsay's look flattered her as she had never been flattered before.

There are vanities and vanities, you see. Even in her failings Alice might have boasted—without any special cause for thankfulness—that she was not as other women.

The smoking-room held four that night; for Mr. Brancepeth, living by rule, seldom allowed his feet to stray into such unhallowed places. As for Captain Irving, he "never touched tobacco," he said, "but, keeping regularly late hours, did not choose to risk his night's rest by seeking it too early." Before long the conversation turned upon play, *apropos* of some recent Parisian scandal.

"I've given up heavy wagering," Irving said, "or rather it's given me up. But I own I've missed my picquet dreadfully since I've settled down here. I could have taught Alice, for she's quick enough to learn anything; but I'm too old to play for love. I don't think I should ever have left Darmstadt if Bernsdorff hadn't died. You never knew him, I dare say. He had a perfect passion for the game; and he won two hundred points of me—we played the Russian rules—within twenty-four hours of his end. He was the Grand Duke's favorite chamberlain, and a great loss to society in every way; but I doubt if any one regretted him as much as I did. I've never slept 'on both ears' since. I should be quite happy at Drumour if I had my *partie.*"

"Then I hope you'll be tempted to come oftener to Kenlis," Mark answered, ringing the bell at his elbow; "you'll always find it here, and the least we can do is to try to amuse you after the treat you gave us this evening. It's my favorite game, and I used to fancy myself at it; I've no doubt you'll take the conceit out of me."

To Alsager the change on Irving's face was quite a study; and Vane too—not near so keen a physiognomist —remarked on it afterward. Listless languor had given place to hungry eagerness; yet, to do the man justice, it was not the eagerness of greed, but rather that of the thoroughpaced gambler, to whom losing at play is the second pleasure in life. Not less strange was it to mark how, by mere force of habit, while the cards were being dealt, his face settled down again into statuesque calmness—only the eyes glittered still.

The match, to all outward appearances, was so even as would have interested both if they had been playing for stamps instead of sovereigns. It was only a run of luck just at last that brought off Mark the winner of the odd game.

"I'm not a Crœsus," Captain Irving observed, as he opened his purse; "but I should not grudge losing *that* every night for a week to come. You play, I think, a shade better than Bernsdorff."

The other shook his head.

" I doubt if I could quite hold my own in the long run; though I do think, between us, it's very much a question of cards."

" I hope he will sleep well," Mark observed, as the door closed behind Captain Irving. " That estimable person has ministered more to my amusement to-night than any one has done for years past; I'm rather tired, though. What do you say to a regular driving day to-morrow? The women would like it."

"'Two of them would, no doubt," Alsager answered, " and I dare say Mrs. Ramsay wouldn't mind. So the 'moral responsibility' wasn't too much for you to-day, Mark? I'm glad of that. Considering how short a time you've been head of a household, you take pretty kindly to your burdens. What an organ she has, though! I quite forget to look at the woman, in listening to the voice."

"Ah! you're a *fanatico*," Mark said, not noticing the thrust at himself; "that makes all the difference. Good-night, and musical dreams."

CHAPTER XXIII.

THE women certainly *did* like it when the programme for the day was propounded at breakfast. The ground to be driven lay nearly opposite the castle, on the other side of the loch, and it was easily to be reached by the help of the ponies sent round to await them on the farther shore. Nevertheless, Captain Irving elected to stay at home, declaring himself not equal even to that exertion. He had rather better health than the majority of his compeers; but his *maladive* appearance was always a convenient excuse for laziness. The weather was perfect again, and before noon the guns, "with the fair spirits, their ministers," were duly posted under stands built up of turf and heather. Two of the pairs were the same as yester-day ; Mrs. Ramsay was under Alsager's charge.

"It rather went against my conscience to leave your father at home alone," Mark observed to his companion as he made a seat for her on a folded plaid, "particularly after his good nature last night. It's not often you find a man of his age so willing to exert himself for other people's pleasure. It was so perfectly evident, too, that there was no vanity about it."

"No, papa isn't vain," Alice assented. Considering his habitual courtesy, it was odd that Mark still so per-sisted in ignoring her share in the performance, and odder still that the omission did not seem to disappoint her in the least. "And he's generally very good-natured, though rather inclined to be capricious. I have known him re-fuse to sing a note when most persons would have been glad of the occasion for display, and where requests passed for commands. He was disinterested, too, last night, for he could scarcely have reckoned on his reward so soon. I never asked him a question, I assure you ; but I guessed by his face this morning that he had his picquet before going to bed. Was I wrong ?"

"Perfectly right. And perhaps you guessed, too, that he left off a good winner?"

"No ; my gifts don't go so far. I have asked the ques-tion of his face often ; it has very seldom answered me. I am afraid he would not be less grateful to you—or who-ever it was that made up his *partie*—if he got up a loser. It was you, I feel certain."

"Right again," Mark answered ; "but why do you say afraid ? I rather admire the *grand seigneur* way of accept-ing bad luck, you know."

She smiled very sadly, and her head drooped a little.

"I have good reason to say 'afraid.' We are too poor to play the *grand seigneur* either at home or abroad. I'm not a bit ashamed of speaking frankly to you, Mr. Ramsay, though I suppose I ought to be. I have no idea what stakes you were playing for last night—nominal ones, I dare say. It always begins so."

Her head drooped lower and lower.

"I don't ask you not to tempt him to play deep—I'm

sure you wouldn't do that—but I do beseech you—oh, so earnestly!—not to be tempted yourself. Can you promise me this? You can't imagine what a rest it is to lie down at night not in fear and trembling; and I did hope for that rest here."

"I would promise a much harder thing," Mark answered, bending over her. "We only played for sovereigns last night: the stakes shall not be increased if I can help it; and I can help it, I feel sure. I always used to avoid high play under my own roof, even in the old days; and Captain Irving can't have much worse gambling-sins to answer for than I, though he may have more."

Her face as she lifted it was grave still, though not sad.

"There are very, very few like him. I would almost as soon—don't ask me why—that he should lose as win heavily. Gambling runs in the blood, like any other madness, I suppose; it runs in ours, assuredly. If it had not been for the law of entail, Drumour would have passed away from us long, long ago. Did you ever read, or hear of, that horrible story of a man setting his wife's honor on a cast when he had no other stake left, and losing—and paying? Duncan Irving did all this when he was in exile in Holland with Charles II., and added a double murder to the shame. The direct line ends with us; for my father has no child living but me: so perhaps the curse will be abated. Let us drop the subject, please. I'm so glad I had courage to speak out; I shall feel quite safe now both at Kenlis and Drumour."

"Yes, you are quite safe with *me*," Mark said, very quietly; nevertheless, there was something in his look that brought the color out brightly on Alice's cheek, and sent her eyes earthward again.

Neither, so long as converse was permissible, was there silence in the other stands, save in that one where Mr. Brancepeth sat with his loader—he still stuck to his favorite Purdey's—a saturnine Scot, whose garrulity was limited to "Mark right," "Mark left," or a gruff "Gude wark," after a peculiarly creditable shot.

La Reine Gaillarde and her cavalier were in great amity this morning, and were talking of old Marlshire times quite confidentially.

"What an utter fool I made of myself," the colonel confessed, with a pleasant frankness, "and what a nice example I set my youngsters! It must have been great fun for you all to watch me, though. Do you remember the meet at Pinkerton Wood?"

"I should think I did remember it. You quite spoiled our hunting that day—Blanche's, I mean, and mine—with the fright you gave us. I have never looked at the Swarle since without a sort of shiver. What became of The Plunger, by-the-by?"

"He went up to Tattersall's with the rest," Vane answered; "and I got a plaintive note soon afterward from the man who bought him, asking me how he was to ride him. Cool, that, wasn't it? I wrote back that the brute only wanted humoring, but I didn't give my horses characters for anything but soundness. So she was frightened a little? I shouldn't have thought it likely. Well, I bear no malice, God knows, to her, or her husband either. Perhaps it was for the best, after all. If she had said 'Yes' instead of 'No,' I should never have suited her as he seems to do. They are perfectly happy; don't you think so?"

"Wonderfully happy, if it only lasts," she answered, rather gravely. "So you actually did propose? I always guessed as much, though I never could make that little wretch own it. It's pleasant to be able to talk over old times comfortably ; but we mustn't chatter any more. If you don't shoot quite up to the mark, it won't be any fault of mine : my sympathies are against the birds to-day."

For the first time since his arrival, Alsager found himself alone with his hostess. He was rather glad of the opportunity of improving their acquaintance; for his first liking for Blanche had much strengthened of late, and he fancied that the favorable impression was to a certain extent mutual.

"Wouldn't that make a good sketch?" Vere observed, after they had duly complimented the weather.

He pointed to a ravine on their right, widening into a glen as it trended down to the loch, so that a broad strip of clear water filled up the background.

"I was just thinking so," she returned; "but I can

only admire points of view, unluckily. It's very different with you, Mr. Alsager. I'm sure you have not left your paints and brushes behind you in the South."

"They would be of little use here. I, too, can only admire still life. I never could accomplish a landscape worth the framing, and I can't afford to spoil canvas. I can manage a recognizable portrait now and then, for I've a sort of knack of catching expressions that please me, though I may fail in bringing out the features. Do you know, Mrs. Ramsay, I thought of asking you to indulge me with a sitting on the first hopelessly bad day ? The rain-gauge will come to its level before long, depend upon it."

"I'm very much flattered, of course," Blanche answered; "but it would be rather a waste of talent while such a much better model is available."

Alsager smiled as he followed her glance till it rested on a figure in the extreme left-hand stand.

"You're quite right; it is a superb model for a master *du genre.*—Boulanger, for instance, would go leagues to paint her. But I'm not a master—only a mild amateur, with more than my share of professional whims. I said, if you remember, that I could sometimes catch expressions that please me. I'm not quite sure that Miss Irving's comes into that category."

The wonder in her face was not affected.

"What can you find to cavil at? I was quite struck by the sweetness of her expression the first time we saw her; and it is a beauty that grows on you."

"Very sweet," he said, still smiling, "and perhaps a little—ever so little—subtle. At any rate, it's beyond me. I could listen to her—or, better still, to her and her father—for hours with my eyes shut; and it would be ungrateful to caricature her. So, if you don't condescend to sit to me, my brushes will lie idle—no great loss, either, to the world in general."

Much of the coquettish leaven that had made Blanche Ellerslie so dangerous lingered still in Blanche Ramsay. She was pleased by the preference, assuredly, and showed this; but the next minute her glance reverted somewhat wistfully to that group on the left.

"Artists are not to be contradicted," she said; "so I suppose you must have your way; but I think that even Mark would pity your taste. He *must* admire her, I'm certain, though he's never fairly owned it yet."

It was a question, though not a direct one, and so Vere interpreted it. For a little while he doubted within himself whether those words were spoken in simplicity or with a purpose of entrapping him. Taking the charitable view at last, he answered, quite frankly,—

" Yes, I fancy he must admire her; though I only speak in conjecture. Mark is not expansive at any time, and on the present occasion I haven't detected even a spark of enthusiasm. He called me a fanatic only last night for speaking of Miss Irving's voice—well, not a bit more highly than it deserved."

There was a long pause. Then Blanche said, softly,—

" You are such a very, very old friend of Mark's, Mr. Alsager, that I can hardly realize you and I were strangers six months ago. That is why I am going to ask you something that you need not answer unless you like. Do you think I make him really—thoroughly—happy ?"

Vere Alsager had little charity for his kind to spare ; but if, without power to help or warn, he had been forced to watch the hungry sea swallowing up, inch by inch, the rock on which a fair woman lay sleeping, it is likely that he would have been affected by some such thrill of compassion as he felt then, looking down on Blanche Ramsay. Nevertheless, he answered as cheerfully as if he saw no peril in the future.

"Our oldest friends don't carry windows in their breasts ; but, speaking according to my own light, I think you may feel quite at ease on that point. You have read that old story of Polycrates' ring? Well, I actually suggested some such set-off against good luck to Mark not a week ago, and his chief objection to it was, if I remember right, that there was nothing he should miss sufficiently, except—his wife."

A bright glow of pleasure possessed her face for a second or two. Then it grew pensive again, as she repeated, under her breath,—

"Not a week ago !"

Much to Vere's relief, "Mark over!" came down the wind just then, and stopped the converse for the present.

To chronicle the sport at length, if it did not savor of vain repetition, would be pains thrown away. To such as have approved them, the sketch would seem colorless and faint; to such as know them not, no word-painting would worthily set forth the various delights—never quite, though so nearly, the same—of a clear August day so spent in Wildernesse. The patient upward climb through glen and corrie, till the last brae is breasted and the posts attained; the rest just long enough to steady the nerves again amidst great peace, which is not stillness, for there is never stillness on the moorland while curlew and plover are awake or the western breeze is stirring—the tingle of the pulse at the first whirr of coming wings—the self-approval when each shot is followed by a dull thud, and through the smoke of the second barrel you look for the crumpled heap of feathers that was a brave grouse-cock a second ago—the comparing of notes after the drive is done, when our elaborate defense of that palpable miss finds no favor with a jury of our compeers, who will never allow that sun or cloud could possibly have interfered in any aim but their own—the nooning, in the shadow of a "brindled rock" within reach of the hill-spring that, where it soaks through the moss, makes russet emerald—the conquest over a wolfish appetite and the intense thirst, achieved with a view to straight powder thereafter—then the leisurely walk or ride that brings us home again, when the last pipe is flavored by a comfortable consciousness of having done to death a certain number of one's fellow-creatures in the merciful fashion that leaves few halt or maimed. Looking back on such a day in after-time, from the midst of work or worry, are you not prone to murmur,—

"Quando ullum inveniem parem"?

It is sufficient to say that the drive was voted the completest success by every one concerned therein, either as actor or spectator, and that the whole party returned in great spirit to the castle, where they found the Solitary in a state of tranquil beatitude.

"I'm ashamed to say how much I've enjoyed myself," he said. "I like poking about old places above all things, and I haven't exhausted Kenlis yet."

Perhaps it was on this account that Irving needed so little pressing to prolong his visit. After dinner they had music, of course, of a more desultory kind than on the evening before; and there was a good deal of confidential chat—people pairing off much as they had done on the hill-side. Excitement and unwonted exercise acting on a delicate frame may fairly account for fatigue; but, with all this given in, Blanche wondered, as she laid her head on her pillow that night, why she felt so very, very weary.

CHAPTER XXIV.

Quite half a century back, Mervyne was a seaport of high credit and renown, month by month and year by year forging gradually ahead of her rivals in the colonial trade, and taking the wind out of their sails. Her merchants even then were noted for bold enterprise; albeit rash adventures were the exception rather than the rule, and gambling in stocks was no more in vogue there than French hazard.

In those days there dwelt there a certain hard-working lawyer—James Welsted by name—with sufficient ability to keep together, without greatly adding to, the modest connection he had inherited from his father. His opinion carried some weight with it, even in matters not strictly professional; chiefly because, if he erred, it was sure to be on the side of caution. In truth, if he had sometimes put the drag on wheels rolling to ruin, he had quite as often hindered rapid advance to fortune. Such being the nature of the man, it may be supposed that no little wonder prevailed in Mervyne when it was noised abroad that James Welsted had invested all his savings—more than this, all the cash he could raise on credit—in the purchase of certain waste-lands lying along the farther shore of the estuary of the Mere.

A drearier-looking estate could scarcely be imagined. The hungriest of cattle turned away from the rank, sour pasturage, and from the brackish pools. A feeble attempt had been made at establishing a rabbit-warren; but even the hardy cony declined to colonize the wind-swept hillocks, with naught sweeter than bent-grass to satisfy his cravings. One or two small speculators had tried their hands at draining; but, go as deep as they would, the ooze would soak through and poison the crop before it could sprout. The wiseacres shook their heads as they asked each other what James Welsted could possibly expect to make of his purchase. It was useless asking *him* that question; for he could keep his own counsel not less religiously than that of his clients. Some of his intimates expressed their misgivings aloud, while others bantered him on his proprietary ambition; but the lawyer listened both to chaff and warning with the same saturnine smile. Three years later he was, in outward appearance, the least astonished person in all Mervyne, when it was discovered that every perch of those dreary marishes was worth more than the richest meadow-acre that ever was mown, inasmuch as the site was absolutely necessary for the promotion of a gigantic dock scheme, just then set afoot by a powerful company, with the direct sanction of government. The drainage difficulties, which had exhausted the patience and the purses of the puny capitalists who had hitherto tried experiments here, were mere child's-play to the engineers who had already laid athwart Chat Moss a safe pathway for the "resonant steam-eagles." The water was soon taught to observe order and method in its goings-out and comings-in; the faithless, friable soil was shoveled aside or crushed into consistency by the mere weight of stone. And so the great work went grandly on, whilst the Mervynites rubbed their eyes, scarcely believing in the wonders wrought over against them; much as the idlers may have done when the morning sun shone on the palace built for Aladdin by the cunning architects of Jinnistán.

The wealth that thus flowed into the lawyer's coffers,

if not absolutely colossal—he drove no usurious bargain
with the dock company—was large enough to make him
at once a man of mark; for the days of fabulous speculation were not as yet, and seldom even on the Stock Exchange were there attempts to emulate the *coup* which,
after Waterloo was won, made Rothschild's name scarce
less famous than the Iron Duke's. At any rate, James
Welsted was so content with his gains that he never
strove to augment them. Men who had been used to
pass him by as an honest humdrum plodder bowed themselves now before his shrewd foresight, and besought him
to cast upon their enterprises the light of his countenance.
Without the shadow of risk, he might have made tens of
thousands by simply trafficking on his name. But at
none of those baits, however tempting, did he ever so
much as nibble; and so what was added to his pile was
only the superfluity of income which remained over at
each year's end. Sooth to say, these savings rolled up
apace; for James Welsted was none of those who become spendthrifts after their beards are gray, and the
woman he married somewhat late in life had much the same
homely tastes as her husband. He gave up his profession
at once; for he loved not labor for labor's sake, and, after
due circumspection, once more invested large moneys in
land.

Kincton was a fine place, certainly, but not large enough
to carry with it much territorial influence, and therefore,
perhaps, the better suited to James Welsted's requirements.
Though he was neighborly enough in all essential ways, he
never sought to take rank among the county magnates—as
he might easily have done, without fear of discouragement
on their part—and stood scrupulously aloof from politics.
After he had dwelt there a dozen years or more, his wife
died, and thenceforth his habits were completely changed.
He was one of those plain, practical people who never
gain credit for very deep feelings, but who, nevertheless,
recover more slowly from a home-blow than many senti-
mentalists who establish a claim on our sympathy by dint
of parading their mourning weeds. A stranger walking
by the widower's side as he followed the coffin up the
aisle would scarcely have guessed at the love which

had bound those two together. The haggardness of his
countenance might have been set down to long watching
quite as much as to grief, and there were no tears in his
heavy, downcast eyes; but he never lifted his head or
looked the world fairly in the face again. His only child
was scarcely fourteen, so there was no absolute reason to
drag him into society.

Before four years were passed, James Welsted had
done with his duties toward his neighbor, and had written up his account with God. Besides sorrow for his
dead wife, the old man's latter days were troubled with
misgivings as to the future of his orphan heiress. Of all
the texts in Scripture—and he was a simple, conscientious,
if not a very earnest, Christian—there were none that
carried more thorough conviction to his mind than those
which touched on the snares encompassing the possessors
of great riches. Nevertheless, it must be owned that it
was for his child's worldly welfare he was chiefly concerned. Fond as he was of her—proud, too, in a certain
fashion—he did not invest his daughter with fictitious
personal or mental attractions. He acknowledged to
himself that the suitor who should seek Mary Welsted
without a single mercenary motive was not likely to be
found. His long legal experience had taught him to estimate pretty accurately the chances of happiness where,
on one side at least, the marriage contract is signed in a
purely commercial spirit. However, such of these misgivings as he kept not entirely to himself were confided
only to the trusty friend whom he appointed Mary's chief
guardian; and there were found in his will few harder
conditions than he must needs have insisted on had he
lived to dispose of her hand. And so—having to the best
of his ability made his provisions, and set his house in
order—honest James Welsted went contented to his rest.

Is there any older simile than that one which sym-
bolizes man's strength and woman's weakness by the alliance of the elm and the vine? Perchance years and
years before the battered hull carrying Æneas drifted
landwards under the Iapygian Cape, singers dallied with
the conceit, and maidens smiled assent, nestling closer to
the side of their Pelasgian lovers. Every age since then

must have furnished millions of instances where conversion of. terms would have brought us nearer to the truth. But they have become so multiplied of late, that even the aspirants to the honors of the Eisteddfodd would scarcely venture to repeat the comparison. Putting aside the professional advocates of woman's rights, simply because they represent womanhood no more than the Leaguers represent liberalism, female emancipation has spread so far already that it seems to me the best thing we can do, in presence of these wise virgins and matrons, is to stand aside—proffering neither counsel nor championship till they are absolutely required of us, and hoping that the Lemnian revolution may not repeat itself just yet.

A fitter representative of the independent party than Mary Welsted could scarcely have been found. As the helpmeet of an ambitious business-man she would have been thoroughly in her right place, and would have turned out not only a more useful, but a more agreeable, member of society. As it was, her obstinate energy had nothing substantial to work upon, and, from mere lack of outlet, fermented sometimes angrily. Her faults did not spring from badness of heart, or even from any peculiar infirmity of temper. She was large-handed in her charities, and spent the money of which, long before she came to years of discretion, she had unlimited command, liberally enough as a rule, though, even at that early age, she had very just notions of the value of a pound sterling. She bore herself a little imperiously sometimes, but never tyrannically, toward her dependents, and had fewer caprices than most spoiled children. Nevertheless, it would have been as gross flattery to call Mary Welsted amiable as it would have been to call her beautiful.

She herself was quite conscious of this—painfully conscious, too. Even strong-minded women, until their moral training is perfected, are not always exempt from personal vanity, and it is often the last weakness that they vanquish.

From the time that she could distinguish good from evil, Mary Welsted had seldom looked into her mirror without discontent and envy; and, as she passed from childhood, this feeling was rather embittered than softened. The large, clumsy figure, that no device of millinery could refine; the high, coarse complexion, that no combination of colors could tone down; the pale, dull eyes, that never brightened, even in anger; the wealth that would have enabled her to fill a gallery with masterpieces of modern and ancient art could not alter one of these defects. She had her fair share of natural abilities, but none of the rare talent that often more than supplies the lack of surface-beauty. And so it came to pass, though neither confessed it to the other, that both father and daughter asked of themselves the same dreary question, "Is it likely that any man will come wooing here in truth and honor?" and got from their hearts the same dreary answer.

But, as she could not fret herself thin, Mary Welsted was much too sensible a girl to fret herself to death over any dispensation of Providence. She had a capital constitution, and a keen appreciation of the good things of this life. When the year of mourning for her father had expired—and very sincere mourning it was—she went forth into the world with a firm determination to make the best of it. Her chief guardian was a wise and prudent elder, able and willing to take excellent care of his ward's temporal concerns, but utterly unfitted to escort her in society. Indeed, his name, so honored on 'Change, was scarcely known west of The Bar.

Lady Mandrake was the Welsteds' nearest county neighbor. She was a dame of stainless repute, and had married off both her own daughters creditably. So to her care the orphan heiress was committed, and she readily undertook the charge.

There is not much perhaps of the ancient Roman about the modern fortune-hunter; but Vespasian himself could not be more philosophically indifferent as to the source of the golden stream wherein he would slake his thirst. However, this particular Pactolus might have been traced to its fountain-head without aught being discovered to offend the most squeamish nostrils. Even in point of birth there was not much to quarrel with; Miss Welsted's father, and grandfather to boot, were "esquires by act of Parliament," and her mother sprung, to say the least of it, from the *haute bourgeoisie.* So at the advent of the new heiress there was such a stir among the aspirants and their patronesses as might have been seen in old times on Amsterdam quays as some stately argosy dropped anchor, hailing from Indian seas. Men who, in the days when Lady Mandrake had daughters on hand, had voted her evenings slow and only lounged in there for a few minutes as an act of penance or duty, took pains to make their invitations sure, and never by any chance were engaged elsewhere. The dame herself was much too shrewd and worldly-wise not to be sensible of the difference; but it chafed her not a whit. Her own brood were comfortably settled in their well-feathered nests, and she bore no malice to the stranger for wearing more gorgeous plumage. She estimated the importance of her position aright, and made good use of it, you may be sure. There is always a certain satisfaction in being courted, be the proxy ever so palpable.

In the course of her first season Miss Welsted was credited with three distinct offers, one of which seemed perfectly unexceptionable: all three were declined quite as decisively as was consistent with courtesy. There was a good deal of republicanism in this young person's composition; and for aristocrats, as a class, she had small veneration or liking, though, socially speaking, she found them easier to get on with than the scions of the plutocracy. But partner for a *cotillon*, and partner for life, are two very different things. She had no mind to enter a great family, where she might expect such a welcome as a poor, proud German princeling might accord to some potent Hebrew financier. She did not fancy that the faults of her figure and face could be amended by the wearing of a coronet or peeress's robes, and she thought there were better investments than contingent reversions ever so brilliant and proximate. If it must needs be a question of barter, she was resolved at least to have her money's worth in the ample fulfillment of her own fancy. Moreover, by receiving nothing while she bestowed all, she had at least a chance of securing gratitude, even if she failed in winning love.

Lady Mandrake — a stanch Conservative in all her

ways—had little sympathy with such Radical notions; but, even if she had not been content to prolong her own pleasant responsibility, she was too discreet to urge her charge into matrimony generally, much less to compromise herself by advocating any special suitor's claims. But dark and overcast waxed the brow of the august matron when, early in their second season, she discovered that her heiress was no longer fancy-free, and guessed where the preference had fallen.

Miss Welsted was intensely fond of vocal music, and among her physical defects a weak, intractable organ was the one she regretted most. Just before leaving town in the previous summer, she heard Horace Kendall's voice for the first time. It seemed to her that she had never listened to its equal. Many others sang that night—he, not again—but Mary Welsted went home with certain cadences floating in her ears which haunted them long and often afterward,—cadences of that wonderful love-song, all the more passionate because there mingle in it so many notes of a dirge, the farewell of the doomed troubadour.

She was not one of those who, if a fancy cannot instantly be gratified, straightway forget it and take up a new one. All through the autumn and winter she kept one purpose steadily before her—the becoming acquainted with Horace Kendall. She came to town in the middle of the ensuing April, and before the 1st of May they were almost intimate.

Now, it might reasonably have been supposed that further acquaintance with Horace Kendall would have been the best possible cure for the distemper of her fancy. The stage tricks and mannerisms that might dazzle a romantic school-girl ought surely never to have beguiled plain common sense like Mary Welsted's. There were his voice and face, to be sure; yet one would have thought that something more than mere attraction of eye and ear would have been needed to enthrall such a character as hers. But the fancies of even strong-minded women are not to be measured by any rule, unless it be the rule of contraries. Day by day the preference of the heiress for the penniless adventurer—for such she knew Kendall to be—waxed stronger, nor was she careful to conceal it. While the season was yet young, others besides Tiernan guessed that the "Welsted Cup was not now such an open race," and the attendances at Lady Mandrake's evenings fell off perceptibly.

The strangest thing of all was, that Kendall himself should so far have manifested no great eagerness to profit by his vantage-ground. His wildest dreams of ambition could scarcely have imagined a richer prize than that which seemed hanging within his grasp—a prize, moreover, to which men worthier tenfold than himself were known to aspire; yet he hesitated to pluck it. Was it a cold calculation of the chances that caused him to forbear? Or is there in the old worn adage, *Nemo repente fuit turpissimus,* some truth after all? Selfish and treacherous and cruel as he was, there was, perchance, enough of the red Provençal blood in the veins of Adèle Deshon's son to make him hesitate betwixt such a scanty dowry as Gwendoline Marston could bring, and the horn of plenty held in the larger hands of the Loamshire heiress. Moreover, in the lighter scale there were cast the attractions of title and ancestry —always so tempting to the basely-born. So, for a while, the balance swayed almost evenly.

Miss Welsted was as well aware of the state of things as if Kendall had confessed it in so many words. Matters had not yet come to such a pass betwixt them that she could question his actions, or indeed give any outward sign of jealous discontent. But because she sedulously avoided even the mention of her rival's name, it is not to be supposed that, either waking or sleeping, she ignored the other's existence, or hated her a whit less bitterly. Kendall was, as you know, forced to be very guarded in his bearing toward Nina Marston; but Mary Welsted, short-sighted as she was, saw many things to which the world in general was blind; and often, as she drove homeward through the night, by the side of her dozing chaperon, angry tears wetted, without cooling, her aching eyes.

The heiress, as you will perceive, held undeniably strong cards, but not absolutely a game-hand, unless properly led up to. Such aid was rendered from an un-expected quarter, and quite undesignedly. Lord Daventry —his eldest son being yet of tender years—concerned himself not with the "good things" of the marriage-market, and perhaps had not so much as heard of Miss Welsted's name. If he had been a paid agent, he could not have forwarded her purposes more effectually than he did on a certain morning whereof mention has been made above.

A brave man who, either from force of circumstances or consciousness of being fearfully in the wrong, has en-dured insult without resenting it, may, when the first bitterness is past, bear no malice to his adversary; but very seldom since the world began has a coward forgiven the man that wrought him dishonor, or even those who indirectly had art or part therein. Therefore you may judge in what frame of mind Kendall left Kensington Gardens after his interview with Nina's father. All that day and evening, though he went into society as usual, he brooded over it till he came to look on every one bear-ing the name of Marston as his natural enemy. It was with no gentler feeling that he tore open a note brought by the next morning's post; neither did his heart soften a whit as he read. Thus it ran:—

"I ought to believe that these are the last words I shall ever write to you; yet I cannot believe it. They must be the last for a long, long time to come, for I have promised. It is no use struggling now: perhaps some day I shall not be utterly helpless; and then, if you still care, you shall see. You would not look up as I passed this morning. Even if papa spoke harshly—it would not be like him if he did—you cannot possibly be angry with me. That would be too hard. I don't think you ever guessed—perhaps it is as well you never should guess now—how much I cared for you.

"I do so wish I could make you believe that, till I know for certain that you have quite given me up, I shall never do or say a single thing you need mind. It is very foolish, but I cannot help hoping still that, if we were both patient and true, we might win the battle yet At least, *I* mean to try; and will you not try too? You must not speak to me if we meet, and you must not answer this: it might make more mischief. Nothing that you can write would make me trust you more thoroughly than I do; and I would not fetter you with any promises, even if I could. My fetter has brought bad luck enough already. I send you back the key. Don't throw the poor thing away, though it got us into this scrape, but look at it whenever you want to be reminded of me. And now good-by, dear. I pray—so earnestly—that God will make and keep you happy, even if I never hear you say 'Nina' again."

He unlocked the armlet at once, and flung it from him with a coarse laugh, very unlike that soft, subdued one with which society was familiar.

"'Patient and true!'—that's a modest suggestion. So I am to live a sort of anchorite's life for the next four years, on the off-chance of her people's changing their mind, or of her being in the same when she comes to be her own mistress. *Pas si bête, mademoiselle!* We have had enough of child's-play and sentimentality. I have a much better game to play, and I'll play it out in earnest now, by G—!"

Every word in that letter was natural, and came straight from the heart; yet every word in it was penned with infinite care, in the earnest hope that it would plead for the writer in the after-time, when Gwendoline Marston and Horace Kendall must before the world be strangers. Did it deserve to fare better? For myself, I do not care to answer that question. If damsels of high degree will derogate beyond reasonable limits, perhaps it is as well they should be schooled somewhat sharply.

Years ago I remember assisting at an agricultural meeting in the Weald, which, after the serious toast-business had been got through, resolved itself into a kind of harmonic meeting. Late in the evening a big bass-voiced farmer obliged the company with a song that was evidently a special favorite. Only the first out of some twoscore verses abides in my memory:

> "Come, listen all unto my tale,
> And I'll tell ye how it began:
> It's all along of a lady fair
> That loved her serving-man."

In point of tune it was a very dolorous ditty; but the description of the domestic felicity ensuing on the condescension of the person of quality was cheerful in the extreme.   The stalwart Kentishmen smote on the board till the goblets jingled again—applauding, as it seemed, the sentiment no less than the melody; but if, the next morning, it had been noised abroad that the daughter of a neighboring squire had eloped with her father's bailiff, I believe every man there present would have wagged his head disapprovingly, prophesying all manner of evil concerning the delinquents.   The wedding-garment made up of diverse fabrics, even if it be becoming, is seldom lasting—ay, though the cloth-of-gold be worn by so gracious a lady as the Duchess Mary, and the cloth-of-frieze by so proper a gallant as Charles Brandon.

CHAPTER XXV.

"NOT wish to believe you?   Why, I would give half I am worth—more than that—half my life—to believe!"

Mary Welsted spoke these words with a passion quite foreign to her steady, well-regulated temper.   What had so moved her you shall hear.

Since Horace Kendall resolved within himself to put aside "child's-play," and to follow up in earnest the better thing, he had shown no lack of either tact or energy. Not that there was any great need of either.   Mary Welsted was one of those downright women whose likes and dislikes are not easy to be misinterpreted, and who, however humble in other matters, are apt occasionally to usurp royal privileges, by doing more than the passive share of courtship.   She preferred Horace Kendall to all the world, and was not a whit loath that all the world—including, of course, the object of her preference—should be made aware of the fact.   Whether that preference was wise or no, was quite another matter.   She may possibly have asked herself that question more than once; but for some time past she had ceased to discuss it with herself, much less with others.

It is not to be supposed that a model *chaperon* like Lady Mandrake would approve, or even connive at, such a dereliction in social duty as she was now compelled to witness almost daily. Neither did the august matron confine her protest to dumb-show, but, on one occasion, spoke her mind pretty plainly.

"I am not thinking of money, my dear. If you had decided on marrying poor Hugo Clermont, who is *criblé de dettes*, and never can have more than three hundred a year of his own, I should not have been surprised; for you can perfectly well afford it, and you would have gained something like a Position" (it was quite a treat to hear Lady Mandrake enunciate this word), "at all events. There is no need to look into Burke to find out who the Clermonts are. But here—good gracious!—what do you, what does any one, know about Mr. Kendall, except that he is a clerk in the Rescript Office, with a fine voice and a presentable face? Is that all you look for in a husband? I wonder you don't choose Fiorelli from the Mesopotamian. His singing is infinitely better than the other's, and he's much better-looking, to my mind."

Miss Welsted flushed angrily; yet she chose to answer only the first part of the diatribe.

"There is no accounting for taste, of course; but I wonder you could not suggest somebody more attractive than Hugo Clermont—a creature with a head like a barber's block, and not five ideas inside it."

"I don't know how many ideas he may have," the elder lady retorted; "but he expresses them like a gentleman, at all events, and that is more than can be said of Mr. Kendall. His affectations are the most palpable counterfeits; it quite fidgets me to watch him, sometimes."

"I never denied that Mr. Clermont was a gentleman," the other remarked: "I never supposed a cousin of yours could be anything else. Perhaps it is my fault that we can't get on together. It is only quite lately that I have mixed in good society, remember. I dare say Mr. Kendall's manner is not perfect; but it does not shock or fidget me. It is very true that we know nothing about his family, and perhaps Burke knows nothing either. Well, if I marry him, there will be no one to patronize me ; that's one comfort, and not a small one either."

Lady Mandrake drew herself up majestically. She was a just and upright person in the main, though somewhat of a schemer, and throughout this affair had certainly been innocent of nepotism.

"I think you will regret that taunt about my cousin when you are cooler, Miss Welsted; I have scarcely deserved it. I spoke according to my own ideas of duty. They are old-fashioned, perhaps; but I am not likely to change them. I did not pretend to any authority over you. I am not your guardian, and you are only under my charge so long as it suits your pleasure. I ought to apologize for having spoken to you as if you were my own daughter."

Mary Welsted's temper, although sufficiently obstinate, was not rancorous. When she felt herself in the wrong, she was ready enough to confess it.

"I am sorry already, Lady Mandrake," she said, bluntly, "and of course it's I who ought to apologize. You have been only too kind to me all along, and I am not going to quarrel with you for telling me I am a fool. I dare say I am ; but I can't help it. Isn't there a Fools' Paradise somewhere or other ? Perhaps they will let us in there ; and you will come and see us sometimes, I know, though you do look so grumpy about it. And now you are going to give me a kiss and make it up."

The elder dame did not put back the olive-branch or refuse the salute; but, while she bestowed it, she grumbled something under her breath about such infatuation being perfectly sinful.

" Well, the sin must rest on my own shoulders," Mary Welsted said, with a laugh; "and they can bear it."

As she spoke she glanced, with a kind of quaint humor, at the reflection of her own substantial person in the mirror hard by.

Thus the course of courtship ran on smoothly enough —so smoothly that Horace Kendall, with all his fatuity, was sometimes surprised with the progress he made. It was strange, certainly, that the set speeches, which even in the ears of such a romantic child as Nina Marston did not always ring true, should pass current with one whose sound common sense verged on strong-mindedness. Nor, in very deed, was Miss Welsted always, or even often, imposed upon. She drank the poison—drank it greedily, too—knowing it to be poison all the while. It was the old story of the opium-eater repeating itself, as it will do to the end of time. The warning of all the doctors in Christendom cannot open the victim's eyes more thoroughly than they are opened already to the properties of the fatal herb. He knows better than you can tell him what a price must be paid for each delicious dream; and yet it would be easier to keep the wounded hart away from the water-brook than to teach him to refrain. Nevertheless, the heiress was not so entirely given up to her own devices but that she hesitated a little when she had to answer to a direct question "Yea" or "Nay;" and when Mr. Kendall became plaintive about her not wishing to believe in the disinterestedness of his attachment, it was with a bitterness savoring of self-contempt that she spoke the words set down at the commencement of this chapter.

Kendall was not really much discouraged by this reply; but if his aspirations had been crushed decisively, his tone and manner could not have been more tenderly reproachful.

"Is it so impossible, then, for a poor man to be honest? Will you judge only as the world judges? I thought— I hoped—you would judge differently. Surely it was cruel not to have spared one this."

"There is no cruelty in the case," she retorted, in her abrupt way; "on my side, at least, there have been no false pretenses. To the question you asked me just now, I answer, 'Yes.' Wait; don't come any nearer yet. Having said so much, I say again that I would give half my life to feel quite sure that if I had been portionless— ay, or not richer than Gwendoline Marston—I should have heard you speak as you have spoken to-day."

In the flush of success Kendall had risen to his feet,

with the evident intention of enacting all the forms of gratitude suitable to the circumstances; but that impulse was checked, as you perceive, and as he stood still, at a respectful distance from his affianced, his demeanor was scarcely that of a triumphant lover.

"So you will half trust me in spite of worldly wisdom, Mary?" (A slight pause made the word fall all the more musically.) "Whole trust will come in time, I know; and I will be patient till it does come. I am glad you mentioned that name; for if you have a shadow of suspicion in that quarter henceforth it will be your own fault, not mine. I don't deny that I have admired Lady Gwendoline; but I declare, on my honor, that I ceased to think of her before I ever thought hopefully of winning you."

A dignified disclaimer, was it not, to be uttered by the lips of Adèle Deshon's son? Very rarely, be sure, does even a sensible woman see any outrageous absurdity in the self-assertion of the man she loves, when it is made at the expense of her own sex. Conquests for which Edwin would not gain credit with the most simple-minded of his club-intimates he may parade before Angelina, in the comfortable assurance not only of their being implicitly believed, but of their being retailed afterward, under the strictest seal of secrecy, to Angelina's select circle. And the odd part of it is, that it is not only the lady-paramount of Edwin's affections who is thus jealous of his amative renown. Araminta, whom everybody said he jilted so infamously, when she has finished bewailing her virginity, or widowhood, as the case may be, seems equally anxious to prove that his fascinations have been fatal to others besides her hapless self, and will resent incredulity quite as fiercely.

Her suitor's sultanesque *pose* did not strike Mary Welsted as ridiculous. On the contrary, she felt more satisfied than she had hitherto done that he was speaking truth; and so perhaps he was, or just so much of it as the Father of Lies would choose for the seasoning of his subtlest falsehood. Kendall was indeed definitely severed from Nina Marston before he seriously urged his suit to her rival. How the severance was effected was, of course, beside the question.

"Ceased to think of her ?"

Why, even while he was gazing into the dull, unexpressive orbs, that after his most rapturous tirades scarcely brightened, he remembered what a light and luster used to fill the superb Spanish eyes ; and even while he spoke of trust and patience, he remembered who wrote so lately, " Only be patient and true."

Though she had fair intuitive powers, Miss Welsted guessed at not one syllable of all this. And though the misgiving that she was acting unwisely had not vanished entirely, she had perhaps never felt so happy in her life as when she stretched forth her hand to her lover as he finished speaking.

It was an honest, workaday hand, sufficiently white, but without any pretensions to elegance, and scarcely to be compressed into liberal "sevens." These defects had never been so palpable to Horace as when he stooped and pressed the massive fingers to his lips; but he executed himself bravely, and held them there quite as long as was becoming. Nor was he less successful in the achievement of the betrothal embrace, which shortly afterward ensued. Nevertheless, when Miss Welsted hinted that she would prefer being left alone, he accepted his dismissal very patiently, on the condition of their meeting later in the evening; and if you had crossed him on his way homeward, you would scarcely have guessed that you looked on the winner of the great prize in that season's lottery.

The potent seniors who on summer afternoons congregate in a special window of the Sanctorium are not prone to indulge in idle gossip. The subjects there are for the most part such as are likely to interest, on political or other grounds, men holding a stake in the country. The scandal and chit-chat of the hour they leave to the smoking- and billiard-rooms, where is found the lighter-minded leaven of this august society. Nevertheless, on the following day the Welsted engagement was fully discussed at this conclave, and Lord Nithsdale thought the news of sufficient importance to warrant an inroad into his wife's dressing-room before dinner.

"We need not have been anxious about Nina, after all,"

he observed. "Mr. Kendall had much more substantial objects in view, it seems, than a foolish flirtation."

The Lady Rose bit her lips, as if the intelligence only half pleased her.

"More substantial, certainly, in every way. Well, some people's luck is quite provoking; I have no patience with it."

Lord Nithsdale smiled gravely. Not particularly keen-sighted in ordinary matters, he had begun already to interpret his wife's thoughts very accurately.

"So you had designs on the heiress for one of your *protégés*, Rosie? I am sorry you are disappointed; but it almost serves you right. You should leave match-making to older and wiser heads."

The countess could not deny the imputation. She had never yet mentioned the scheme to the person chiefly interested therein; but she had certainly speculated as to Avenel's chances of success if he could be induced to lay serious siege to the heiress. It was so pleasant to fancy Regy a millionaire, and with such a perfect temper he was sure to make any woman happy. She had laid quite a train of combinations for bringing them together, and here were all these ingenious schemes shivered as hopelessly as Alnaschar's glass.

"Never mind what I meant," she said, rather impatiently. "If I *am* disappointed, I dare say I am not the only one. I suppose one ought to pity poor Miss Welsted; but I have no compassion to spare for people I hardly know. I wonder what Nina will say to it. I have not heard her mention his name lately, and I fancy they have very seldom met. I am to take her to the Martindales' ball to-night. Mamma is still nursing her cold."

The season was thinning out; but the Martindales' entertainment was always crowded. Their rooms were perfect for dancing, and their suppers something to eat, and not to dream of afterward. The drive thither from Carrington Crescent, where Lady Nithsdale picked up her sister, was a very short one. Nevertheless, the countess found time to say,—

"Have you heard the last piece of news, Nina? Miss

Welsted, the great heiress, you know, is engaged at last."

"Engaged? Not to Regy Avenel by any chance?" the other asked, in the listless way that had come over her of late.

"No such luck," the countess retorted, pettishly. "As papa would say, a rank outsider, who ought never to have been in the race. There, you would never guess. It's your friend—not mine, thank goodness!—Mr. Kendall."

Rose Nithsdale was the tenderest-hearted creature breathing. She would not willingly have dealt to her bitterest enemy such a stab as she now dealt to her pet sister; but she was utterly in the dark, you must remember, as to the state of Nina's feelings, and had no reason to suspect that she touched anything more sensitive than a foolish fancy, cured long ago.

Nina Marston reared herself out of the corner where she leant, and sat for a few seconds quite apart without speaking. Then she said, in a slow, measured voice, like a child repeating a lesson painfully learned by rote,—

"Horace—Kendall—and this is true?"

"Perfectly true," Lady Nithsdale returned, indifferently. "Hugh brought it from the Sanctorium this afternoon, and they don't deal in *canards* there. A curious piece of luck, isn't it? But you needn't look so thunderstricken."

A lamp flashed in just then on Nina's wide fixed eyes, and at the same instant there flashed across Lady Nithsdale's mind a vague suspicion of the truth—a suspicion which, had it come a little sooner, would have made her bite her tongue through rather than speak so carelessly.

One word in the last sentence was not so ill chosen, after all. Walking along the conventional paths of society, with no Asmodean advantages, we may be reminded now and then of poor Duchess May, when

> "She stood up in bitter case,
>   With a pale and steadfast face,
>   *Toll slowly.*
>   Like a statue thunderstrook,
>   That, though shivered, seems to look
>   Right against the thunderplace."

But before Lady Nithsdale could put either pity or penitence into words, Nina sunk back into her corner again, closing her eyes.

"We shall see them to-night, I suppose?" she said, quite quietly.

And then Lady Nithsdale knew that, whatever sorrow might be lying at her little sister's heart, there was no fear that the world would be made aware of it. She did not answer the half-question; but her hand somehow stole into Nina's, and the girl held it fast as one who, even with some such help, can scarcely master a paroxysm of pain. She was holding it so still when their carriage stopped at the Martindales' door.

As she followed her sister up the staircase, she overheard a whisper, "Looks wonderfully handsome to-night." She knew perfectly well for whom the remark was meant, and smiled a saucy smile, and lifted her haughty little head like a thorough Marston. We all know their motto —"*Point faillir.*"

As the sisters passed through the first door, they came upon Avenel, who was evidently waiting for them.

"You are engaged to me for the next waltz, Nina, remember," he said.

The girl understood him quite well, and, as she took his arm, looked up into his face gratefully, and Lady Nithsdale did so partly, at least; for she did not feel surprised, much less vexed, at what, under any other circumstances, she would have considered a breach of allegiance.

"Are—are they here?" Nina asked, almost inaudibly, when they had made some way through the throng.

"Yes," he answered. And so they moved on, slowly and silently, till they came over against a group in the second saloon, at which many glances had already been leveled.

By virtue of seniority, Lady Mandrake was the chief personage therein. The aspect of the worthy dame was decidedly lowering. She sat there, upright and grim, with the air of one determined to carry out to the letter a certain duty without dissembling a distaste for it. Close to her stood Horace Kendall, who had scarcely yet learned to bear himself quite as becomes an accepted suitor. He had answered several congratulations—for the engagement was now publicly announced—cleverly enough. Nevertheless, he seemed nervous and ill at ease, and ever and anon glanced over his shoulder, as if he expected something or somebody to appear. Last, though certainly not least, of the trio was Miss Welsted herself. Even a partial friend must have allowed that the heiress was not looking her best that evening. The last few days had been full of excitement, and excitement on sanguine complexions like hers tells very unbecomingly. Somehow, too, her dress—brilliant azure, trimmed with lace—rather seemed to enhance than to tone down this effect.

"I can't look at her without humming 'The Red, White, and Blue,'" Harry Jekyl observed. And truly the parallel, though malicious, was not inapt.

Seeing her chaperon execute a salute *à la commandeur* —Lady Mandrake on this especial evening was chary of even such stony civilities—Miss Welsted looked up to see who was thus favored, and so her eyes and Gwendoline Marston's met. The heiress was as self-possessed and self-reliant a person as you could easily find; but she certainly was not equal to this occasion. She read thoroughly well the meaning of the satiric glance that roved all over her own expansive figure, and she knew quite well that the comparison was not drawn by herself alone betwixt those uncouth contours and the other's lithesome grace. Had she been on speaking terms with her rival, her position would have been less embarrassing. Anything, in fact, would have been better than sitting there helplessly, conscious of growing hotter and redder every instant.

A disinterested bystander might have been provoked if he could have detected the passion working then within those two women—each of them in her own way worthy of honest love—and have realized for whose sake such passion was stirred. Nevertheless, there was nothing strange in this. All who have read *King Lear* of course will remember how the peace and honor of two royal houses were wofully wrecked, only that the false, fair-faced bastard might be able to boast, as he lay a-dying,—

"Yet Edmund was beloved."

Kendall's attention had been called off for a moment; but, turning his head as a person to whom he had been speaking passed on, he saw the disturbance on the face of his betrothed and—its cause.   To say that he was put to confusion very faintly expresses Horace's state of mind. His cunning—or tact, if you like to call it so—could carry him through any small dilemma; but it was quite unequal to any emergency like this.   He was quick-witted enough to comprehend the significance of Nina's appearance, leaning on the arm of the man who had so lately put him to open shame, and to feel that there could no longer be peace, or even a hollow truce, between himself and Lord Daventry's daughter.   Moreover, he saw that Avenel was well aware of his embarrassment and relished it keenly.   A desperate impulse, that he could-not afterward account for, prompted him to take a step forward, half stretching out his hand.   A faint smile showed that the gesture was not lost on Lady Gwendoline Marston; then, with a slight bend of her slender neck, she glided away through an opening in the throng.

No cut direct could have been half so galling as that cold, quiet farewell; and yet farewells less bitter have been spoken on the decks of outward-bound ships by those who could never hope to meet again on earth; ay, and on death-beds, by those who, unless the mercy of Heaven be boundless, could scarcely hope to meet again in eternity!

"You are a trump, Nina!" Avenel muttered; "you did that superbly."

She glanced up at him with the prettiest disdain.

"Did you think I was going to scream, or faint, or amuse all these people with a scene? *Merci!* Did you not tell me not so long ago that I was too young for stage tricks?   I think I am too young to wear willow either, even if wreaths were not out of fashion.   Didn't they look happy?   But if happiness makes one look so hot and red, I think I should prefer a little mild melancholy. I don't wonder quite so much now that Rosie found you intractable. Ah, you needn't look unconscious; I know what has been her pet scheme lately. She certainly *is* overwhelming!"

"It will take a wiser head than Lady Rose's to make my fortune," he answered, gravely. "Though it's very nice to be schemed for, I should make a poor prince-consort for such a tremendous royalty."

Not a word was spoken afterward that the whole world might not have listened to. Her partners—comparing notes at Platt's far into the small hours—agreed unanimously that Gwendoline Marston was in "ripping form" that evening; and Lady Nithsdale, watching her little sister rather anxiously for awhile, felt comfortably sure that no harm had been done beyond a heart-graze—already nearly healed. Let us assume that they all were right. If we can carry our own burdens lightly, without stooping or staggering, there is surely no law that obliges us to lay them in the scale that busybodies may test their weight to a grain.

As the crowd closed in behind Avenel and his companion, Kendall drew his breath hard, like a man relieved of some choking pressure, and, leaning over Miss Welsted, tried to take up the thread of conversation where it had been broken off some minutes before. But that he spoke, and she listened, under a certain constraint was perfectly evident. Lady Mandrake's voice had seldom sounded so pleasantly in Horace's ears as when, after a whispered conversation with her charge, she asked him to see after her carriage.

Soon afterward he found himself in the smoking-room of his club, listening to the comments, wondering or envious, on the brilliant change in his prospects. But all this incense—under the semblance of unconcern, he inhaled it greedily enough, Heaven knows—did not so possess Kendall's brain as to bring placid sleep or to baffle the busy mockeries of Dreamland.

P

CHAPTER XXVI.

WHEN the affianced couple met on the following day, no allusion was made by either to the *rencontre* the previous evening. Kendall, of course, was not likely to broach the subject, and Mary Welsted had tact enough to see that it was best to avoid it. It was abundantly clear that no rivalry or interference was to be apprehended thenceforth from Gwendoline Marston, and, like a sensible woman, she was content to profit by the present without raking up the past. Nevertheless,—much, it must be owned, to Horace's relief,—it was evident that she neither expected nor desired demonstrative love-making, and their common future was discussed in an exceedingly matter-of-fact way. Whatever might have been the heiress's faults, avarice was not among them; and, if her own wishes could have been carried out, there would have been little trouble on the point of settlements. But they were only wishes, after all.

Nearly a year had still to elapse before she would cease to be a minor, and while her wardship lasted she could not, without the consent of her guardians, dispose of the smallest portion of her inheritance. According to the provisions of her father's will, in case of her dying unmarried before attaining her majority, the entire property would pass to her nearest male relative—a Yorkshire clergyman, endowed with a small living and a large family.

The testator hardly knew his cousin by sight; but he knew him to be an honest, honorable man, such a one as might be trusted with the responsibility of founding a family. Though James Welsted had personally no ambition, he was not minded to leave the distribution of his great wealth to chance, or to risk its being dribbled away through many channels; still less did he fancy the idea of its furnishing a *pièce de résistance* for endless legal banquets. This state of things was new, not to say startling, to Horace Kendall, and, though he listened with much outward complacency, the skein of his thoughts was somewhat raveled.

Under the circumstances, would it not be well to defer the marriage some nine months, so that the settlements might be drawn up in accordance with the heiress's own liberal notions, rather than trust to such concessions as might be wrung from the stern probity of her guardian— a stiff customer to deal with, if report spoke truth?

On the other hand was to be taken into consideration the danger of Mary Welsted dying in the interval; but, reviewing the robust proportions of his betrothed, Horace decided within himself that the risk was by no means a formidable one. On the whole, he thought he would prefer to wait. However, as unnecessary delay did not appear to enter into the lady's calculations, he could not decently suggest such a thing, and was fain to accept the position with the best possible grace. The heiress was to have an interview with her guardian that same day, and after this, perhaps, he would see his way somewhat clearer.

"What does your mother say to this?" Miss Welsted asked, all at once. "You have written to her, of course?"

Horace almost started. This was the very first time since he left the bosom of his family that any one had alluded to a single member thereof. But his confusion only lasted a minute or so.

"She is in the seventh heaven, of course," he answered. "How could it be otherwise? I do wish I had brought her letter to show you, though you would have laughed at it, I dare say. My poor mother has not quite forgotten yet that she was bred in Provence, and her fondness for me amounts to infatuation."

"No, I shouldn't have laughed; and I shouldn't have considered her so infatuated as you do. I wonder whether she'll like me? I am not what is called 'a taking person,' I am afraid; but I get on pretty well with some people."

Any other than Horace Kendall would have been moved by the earnestness of the homely face; but his heart turned toward her not a whit more tenderly. Neither then nor thereafter did one better impulse hallow, were it but for an instant, his sordid greed: yet, as you may fancy, not the less profuse was his lip-gratitude.

He would not listen to her if she spoke so unjustly of herself; but before she had known his mother a day, she would have no such misgivings. To make them acquainted was the thing he most wished; only he had scarcely liked to propose it. If she would not think herself neglected, he would run down to Swetenham to-morrow and persuade Mrs. Kendall to come up to town for a week at least. She was a sad stay-at-home; but now she would gladly return with him, he felt sure. He need not be absent twenty-four hours.

His distaste for the unlucky girl to whom he had plighted his troth scarcely amounted to antipathy; yet he caught eagerly at the first excuse for absenting himself from her presence. Before they were riveted, the golden fetters began to gall; and as she laid her hand upon his shoulder, with more of trust and fondness than she had hitherto shown, it was not compunction at the lie he was enacting that caused him to shrink ever so little from the caress.

"That is a good, kind thought," she said, "and I thank you for it. I hope you will persuade your mother to return with you; but don't hurry her off on my account. I promise not to think myself neglected. It will be time enough for you to face this awful guardian of mine when you return. Perhaps his growl will be the worst part of him, after all."

So, on the following day, the affianced suitor betook himself to Swetenham. The fashion of his reception there will be easy to imagine. A quarter of a century's sojourn in the land of fogs and frosts had not sobered down Adèle Deshon to the level of decorous British matronhood, and she could be passionate in her joys and sorrows still, on much lighter provocation than now, when there was a prospect of her Prince Charming being installed in a statelier castle than she had ever dared to build for him in Cloudland. She was half tempted to bribe the church-ringers to welcome her son with the full strength of their chimes, and was only restrained by the fear that such homage might be displeasing to its object, with the uncertainty of whose taste it was not safe to trifle.

Any one who could have assisted invisibly at the family party must have been struck by the extraordinary coolness with which Kendall *père* listened to the details of the rare good fortune that had befallen his only child. The expression of his cold, crafty fox-face could never have been mistaken for sympathy; and his small eyes twinkled rather with malicious cunning than parental pride. Soon after dinner he took himself off on some pretext or other, and left the two to savor their triumph.

The evening—a pleasant one on the whole—did not pass without a slight difference of opinion betwixt the pair. This arose on a suggestion of Mrs. Kendall that her son should write and communicate the brilliant change in his prospects to the squire of Vernon Mallory, who was still in enforced exile.

"He has had nothing but worry of late, poor fellow," Adèle said, with a sigh; "and I know he would be pleased at the news coming directly from you. This is not the time to forget what we owe him."

Men of Kendall's stamp are usually prone to spurn the ladder by which they have mounted, and, when the bridge has once carried them safely over, care not how soon it goes to ruin and wreck.

"You know best what your own debts amount to, mother," he said, sneeringly. "A place in the Rescript Office, and an odd hundred or two to start me, I think about express mine. I don't see why I should trouble myself about it. The news will read quite as pleasantly when it comes from you."

Adèle bit her lip—a bright scarlet lip still—and the color sunk in her face as she pressed her hand on her side.

"Don't speak like that," she said, in a low, tremulous voice. "It hurts me. If you won't do as much on your own account, surely you will not refuse to do it on mine?"

The other, apparently, did not think it worth while to prolong the discussion.

"Very well; I'll see about it," he grumbled. And with this concession his mother was fain to be content.

Early on the following day Dr. Kendall required a private interview on his own account. What he had to say —short, and very much to the point—possibly did more credit to his head than to his heart. There are things so unutterably base that, whether they occur in the course of fact or fiction, they are best left unrecorded. Therefore the arguments with which the elder man enforced his claim—not an exorbitant one, it must be owned—to a share in the advantages of the proposed alliance shall have no place here, specially as their nature may easily be guessed.

In spite of Miss Welsted's freedom from prejudice and large democratic views, it is by no means certain how she would have received a secret that Dr. Kendall might, had he chosen, have revealed. At any rate, Horace did not choose to make the experiment; and he would have purchased silence at a higher price than was now demanded. That he long ago suspected, and more than suspected, the ugly truth, is most probable; but this was the first time it had been placed before him in its bare deformity; and he went out of his reputed father's presence much in the condition of a drummed-out soldier, who, callous to all other ignominy, still winces a little while the smart of the branding lasts.

No very hard words had passed between the two. It was a question of exchange and barter, after all. The younger man was not wont to waste his heroics; and the elder, if you had flung a crown-piece at his head with a curse, would have stooped contentedly to pick up the coin out of the kennel.

Nevertheless, hardly any consideration short of necessity would have tempted Horace Kendall to tarry another night under that roof. He said as much to his mother, indeed; and, if her preparations had not been so simple, she would have made no demur about their hurried departure after looking once into his face.

The journey back to town was not, strictly speaking, a blithesome one. Though Kendall made not the slightest allusion to the subject-matter of the morning's interview,

his sullen silence was significant enough, even without
the scowl that ever and anon shot from under his bent
brows; and Adèle's flushed cheeks and drooping eyelids
showed that there was womanliness enough left in her
warped nature to make her feel ill at ease in the presence
of her son, since she knew him to have been made aware,
beyond the possibility of a doubt, of her ancient shame.

Nothing could have been more radiant than the demeanor of the pair when, on the following morning, they
had audience of Miss Welsted. Certainly the latter need
not have disquieted herself as to how she would be welcomed by her future mother-in-law. Perhaps a person of
more refined taste might have been somewhat oppressed
by Mrs. Kendall's "gushing;" but the heiress rather liked
it than otherwise. It had the charm of novelty; for her
lot had hitherto been cast among staid and steady people,
and anything that was overstrained she set down to Provençal enthusiasm.

So everything went swimmingly on. The formidable
guardian—though he evidently regarded his ward's choice
with no great admiration or favor—showed himself more
tractable than had been expected; and before a week had
passed Horace congratulated himself on not having hinted
at the possibility of delay in completing the contract.

Miss Welsted's presence at Kineton for awhile was
for many reasons desirable; so she proceeded thither—
escorted by Mr. Carden, her guardian, and her quondam
governess, who had for some time past performed such
sheep-dog duty as it was beneath Lady Mandrake's dignity to undertake. That excellent chaperon bade adieu
to her charge with much civility and kindness; but she
did not precisely weep upon her neck, as she would probably have done had the match been of her own making.
It was with a certain reluctance—she was *so* hampered
by engagements, she said—that she promised positively
to be present at the nuptials, that were to take place early
in September.

Although Horace could hardly be said to miss his betrothed, the days ensuing her departure dragged somewhat heavily. They were days of perfect liberty, too,
and the laziest Sybarite would not have murmured at

occasional visits to Lincoln's-inn on such pleasant business. However, he regretted now and then that he had resigned his appointment in the Rescript Office so hastily. He knew himself to be no favorite there, and did not flatter himself that the congratulations of his former fellows would be very sincere ; but, if he had got no sympathy, he would at least have known that he was envied —no mean satisfaction ; it was a capital lounging-place, for the work was nearly always nominal. He had not even his mother to talk to or to tease, for Mrs. Kendall left town the day after Miss Welsted.

The general exodus was now in full progress, and a more popular man than Kendall would not seldom have been condemned to a solitary club-dinner. As he walked home after one of those dreary repasts, he felt inclined to quarrel with the conventionalities which prevented him just now from being a guest at Kineton. If the place were ever so dull it would be his own, or virtually his own, very soon ; and the sense of proprietorship would make his walks abroad there rather pleasant. He was tempted to invent some decent pretext that might excuse his running down, if only for a day. A little solitude will work wonders sometimes, in forcing domestic affections that otherwise would be slow in flowering.

A reading-lamp was burning in his sitting-room when he entered it. He glanced carelessly at his writing-table, where his letters were usually laid, to see if any had come by the last post. There were no letters ; but there was— a telegram.

The feats of the electric battery stand clearly first and foremost among the achievements of this wonder-working century : nevertheless, I have great doubts whether the span of human existence is not materially affected by the additional strain on the nerves. Gamblers on the Turf or Stock Exchange, or even perfectly legitimate speculators, doubtless get used to it. They flinch no more before the dusky-yellow envelopes than others do before the blue-wove packets, directed in a fair clerkly hand, that add so materially to the merriment of each Christmastide. But nine ordinary people out of ten will be sensible of a certain sinking of the heart at first sight of one of these messages, the import whereof they cannot guess—or guess only too truly.

"Ill news travel apace," was a proverb in vogue long before Volta was born; and even nowadays, when our ships come in, our correspondents are content as a rule to advise us thereof by post. It is only when they have a wreck to announce—the wreck perchance of our very last venture—that they work the wires with a will.

Kendall would have treated any possible disaster that could have befallen his neighbor with a calm philosophy; but when it was a question of his own misfortune, his sensibilities were wonderfully keen, and you would not have supposed that a grain of stoicism was to be found in his whole composition. He felt sick and faint as he took up the ominous missive, and his hand shook as he opened it. This is what he read:—

> "*Kineton*, 5.30 *P.M.*
> "*A fearful accident has happened. Come immediately.*
> "J. Carden."

Not a word as to who was the sufferer; but that was quite needless. There was but one life at Kineton in which *he* had any interest, and this life, he knew very well, was the one imperiled, if not already ended. Poring over the paper in a dull, mechanical way, he became at last aware, from the date of its delivery at the London office, that the message must have arrived within a few minutes of the time when he went out after dressing. If he had got it then, he might just have caught the down-mail; now, it was impossible to start before morning.

He had but just sense to realize this: he realized little more as he sat there staring with haggard, vacant eyes. Among all the feelings seething within him there was not one with which an honest man or woman would sympathize; yet if any of you who read these pages have spent one of those awful periods of enforced inaction, when your presence is urgently needed at some tragedy being enacted elsewhere, you may, perchance, hold even such a creature as this not wholly undeserving of pity. The brandy that he drank in the course of the night would have stupefied him at any other time, but now it only steadied his hands enough to enable them to pack a few necessaries that he must take with him ; for before his servant, who slept out of the house, could come in the morning, Horace hoped to be miles away.

He got to the station somehow, and took the first train, though it was one of the slowest, and reached Kineton but little earlier than the express starting two hours later. But motion ever so dilatory was better than sitting still. When he reached his destination at last, he found a dog-cart waiting for him.

"How is your mistress?" he asked of the groom standing at the horse's head.

Kendall's voice was so husky and low that the man had almost to guess at the words ; but, knowing what the first question would be, he had his answer ready.

"Mortal bad, sir.   We all hoped you'd ha' come by the night-mail.   I 'most doubt if you will find her alive now. You had better let me drive, please."—Kendall was fumbling helplessly with the reins.—"The mare's a bit awkward till she gets into your hands, and we haven't a minute to spare."

The distance was not great, and the trotting mare did it in fair match-time ; but before they drew up at Kineton hall-door Horace had heard all the details of the disaster.

Miss Welsted had gone out in her pony-carriage as usual.   The tiger occupying the tiny back-seat was a mere child; and she had no other attendant, for the *gouvernante* who usually accompanied her chanced to be unwell that afternoon.   Her ponies were young and rather hot ; but she had driven them several times before, and they had never shown any symptom of vice.   The flies had fretted them, perhaps, while they were standing, for they pulled more than usual, even at starting ; but Miss Welsted, being strong in the wrist and perfectly fearless,— though by no means a scientific whip,—rather liked this than otherwise.   They were about half-way down the avenue that led to the lodge-gates, when one of the Highland cattle feeding in the park rose suddenly from behind a patch of fern and bolted across the road.   The ponies gave a mad bound that started every bolt in the fore-carriage, and the next instant they were away.

The solitary witness of what happened afterward, besides being stunned at the time, was too stupefied with terror and grief to give a very clear account of it.

"His mistress did not seem much frightened," he said; "and she never screamed out once. But as they tore round the last turn and came in sight of the lodge, he heard her say, quite softly, 'God help us! They are shut!' Then he stood up and screamed with all his might to open the gates; but the lodge-keeper ran out a second too late."

Perhaps the runaways could not have stopped themselves then if they would. At any rate, they never slackened their pace, but crashed full front against the bars. The shock pitched the lad—a mere feather-weight—sheer over the fence among the garden-shrubs. When his senses came back, he saw among the wreck of iron and wood—for the gates too were shattered—one of the ponies stone-dead and the other helplessly maimed, and his mistress in the lodge-keeper's arms—lying white and still.

Mary Welsted was not dead; though when the doctor saw her half an hour afterward he decided it to be a desperate case of brain-concussion, and all the science that was soon summoned to her aid only confirmed that verdict.

Mr. Carden met Kendall in the hall as he entered, and beckoned him into the library. The old man's face was very sorrowful, and his eyelids, perhaps, were heavy with something else besides a long night's watch. His manner was infinitely more cordial now than when, a fortnight ago, he went through the forms of congratulation.

"I pity you from the bottom of my heart," he said. "It may be some slight comfort to know that you have not come too late, and that if you had come last night it would have availed nothing. She has never spoken since, or even opened her eyes."

"Is there no hope?" Horace asked, faintly.

"Absolutely none. Indeed, we ought to hope that the

release will come speedily. You will know why when you have seen her. Will you come at once?"

They went up-stairs together. On the first landing Kendall stood still, listening and trembling.

Down the corridor from a room at the farther end there came a sound such as few can bear for the first time unawed—a sound which, once heard, is not easily forgotten—a sound more terrible in its monotony than any sharp, sudden cry—a sound which, though it savors of both, is neither gasp nor groan—a sound that forces us, in our own despite, to believe that unconsciousness is not insensibility—a sound perhaps more significant than any other of the prolonged agony of a parting soul.

"It has gone on so ever since she was brought in," Mr. Carden said, answering the other's look of frightened inquiry. "They have tried trepanning without the slightest effect. I don't wonder that you are overcome. It has tried us all fearfully."

Kendall paused a minute or two, and then spoke in a weak, hesitating voice:—

"If there is no chance of her knowing me, do you think I had better——"

The elder man's face changed from compassion to contempt.

"Do I think you had better go in at once?" he said, very coldly. "Unquestionably I think so. You will act as you think fit, of course. My duty was clearly to bring you here; and I have done it."

Horace could not for very shame hang back.

"You—quite misunderstand me," he stammered out; and so passed on, and in through the door standing ajar.

The room was darkened; but, as Kendall entered, one of the attendants drew a curtain partly aside, so that a thin column of light streamed in on the death-bed. There was nothing there very shocking to the eye. The fatal blow had left little outward trace, and besides that terrible moaning she gave no signs of life; this—the doctor, standing by the bedside, whispered—was growing fainter and fainter.

Putting great force upon himself, Horace came near and pressed his lips on the pale hands, motionless save for a

THE DEATH-BED OF MARY WELSTED.

Page 236.

slight twitching of the fingers. Even at such a moment he could spare no tenderer caress for the woman who would have given him all. Then he sat down apart, with his face buried in his hand.

All those present, with the exception of Mr. Carden, gave him credit for natural emotion, and pitied him accordingly. If they could have perused his thoughts, perhaps they would not have been so liberal of sympathy. He was utterly crushed by the suddenness and completeness of the blow; but his regrets were almost purely selfish. For the poor girl who lay a-dying he felt much the same vague, careless compassion as a speculator would give to the laborers drowned by the flooding of his favorite mine.

Minutes, under such circumstances, are not counted by the clock. Though the silence, broken only by brief whispers, seemed to Horace endless, it had not perhaps lasted a quarter of an hour when the moaning grew perceptibly fainter, and was succeeded by heavy, labored breathing; and then the doctor said, speaking for the first time above his breath,—

" She is going fast."

The agony, if such it had been, had spent itself; but in the last moments of life a faint gleam of consciousness seemed to cross the poor dizzy brain; for her eyes were half unclosed, though it was evident that she recognized no one, and her right hand groped feebly on the coverlet, as if it searched for some other hand.

Mr. Carden glanced over his shoulder at Kendall, who had drawn near with the rest : then, seeing that Horace stood helpless and irresolute, he bent down and took the quivering fingers into his own.

And so, holding an honest man's hand after all, Mary Welsted passed away, we may hope, into some better abiding-place than the Fools' Paradise whereunto she had aspired.

Kendall's first impulse, when all was over, was to escape as speedily as possible from the scene of the disaster. It was bitterly true that he had no business at Kineton now; neither, truth to speak, did Mr. Carden seem specially anxious to detain him. It was settled, as a matter of course, that Horace should be present at the funeral; and in the course of the same afternoon he took his departure.

Certain half-hours cut a deeper notch in a man's life than the average of years will leave. Horace's drive back to the station was one of such. The soft summer breeze sweeping through the tall elms of the avenue seemed to murmur mockery. There was insolence in the aspect of the ample corn-lands, red-ripe for the sickle, and in the greenery of the broad meadows dotted thickly with fat kine. On all this, one day—and no distant day either —he was to have looked as lord and master. How did he look on them now? His face was so far a tell-tale that even the stolid Loamshire man, sitting by his side, partly guessed at the color of his musings, and was rather inclined to rejoice than to repine when the other dismissed him at their journey's end without any offer of gratuity.

"He looked a precious sight more sulky than sorry," the groom remarked, afterward. "He's a bitter bad devil, I reckon. If the poor missus had lived, she'd ha' repented of her bargain pretty often."

In very truth, it was long before Horace Kendall emerged from that savage desperation which has tempted, or well-nigh tempted, certain professing Christians to "curse God, and die." However, there is method even in the madness of some folk. To the blasphemy our friend was fully equal, but as for the death—— In spite of these losses and reverses, it is probable that this delicate plant will flourish when hardier and nobler trees are dust.

CHAPTER XXVII.

THE glory of autumn was waning in the western high-
lands. The rich contrasts of color—for Wildernesse, like
a mere mortal, seeks ever by gorgeous apparel to dissemble her decline—were giving place rapidly to sober
russets and grays. The wind swept keenly down the
gullies with an ominous whistle, and had had a skirmish
or two already with the pines in prelude to their winter
battle. The loch was seldom calm enough now to mirror
birch or oak, and such shadows were thinner where they
fell. . The grouse-cocks crowed defiantly on the moorland; for, standing erect, each on his own tussock, all
ear and eye, they might afford to set at naught the wiles
of the fowler. A few chances in sheltered hollows where
there was still feeding-ground, or a long-shot in rounding
the shoulder of a hill, were about all you could expect;
and it was a little too early for good cover-shooting as
yet. At such a season a man's thoughts, unless he be
very keen on sport, are apt to follow in the track of the
swallow.

Now, Mark Ramsay was by no means an inveterate
gunner, and when his destructive duties had been duly
performed, one would have thought that his inclinations
would have tended southward; but he seemed perfectly
content to abide at Kenlis. Once, when his wife ventured to question him as to the probable time of their
removing, he contrived to evade a direct reply; and,
though there was no impatience in his manner, it was
evident that he did not choose to be pressed on the subject.

The castle party—speaking of those actually resident
there—was narrowed down to three. Alsager and Vane
had gone their several ways some time ago; and a week
later Mr. Brancepeth, too, had left on a tour of lowland
and north-country visits that would bring him home by

leisurely stages.   Lady Laura was to have borne her
husband company throughout; but though, when her
friends spoke of departure, Blanche made no objection in
words, the piteous pleading in her eyes was quite too
much for La Reine Gaillarde, who without more ado
cast her engagements to the winds, utterly setting at
naught the resentment of her ill-used acquaintance, and
making very light of her lord's grumbling.

"Don't you pretend to be helpless," she said, "but go
off and enjoy yourself like a man—or rather like a single
man.   You don't often get such a chance, you know.   If
you get into any mischief—provided it isn't very bad
mischief—I'll try to forgive you."

Perhaps Mr. Brancepeth was rather flattered at being
still considered capable of a peccadillo, or the very idea
was too much for his gravity.   At any rate—*solutis risu
tabulis*—it was amicably settled that Lady Laura should
remain at Kenlis till the Ramsays could escort her south.

La Reine was by no means an exemplary matron.   I
do not mean to imply that her sins, either of omission or
commission, would have brought her under the ban of
any criminal code; but with her reckless words and actions she very often proved a rock of offense to her weaker
sisters.   As for the strong-minded ones—the stones they
had already would have made a goodly cairn.   Nevertheless, it is probable that certain famous fanatics would
have haggled awhile with their consciences before completing such a self-sacrifice as she now decided on un-
hesitatingly.   She knew perfectly well that at most of the
halting-places above mentioned there would be ample
provision of the amusements in which her soul delighted.
She was sure to foregather there with more than one of
her special favorites—indeed, divers pleasant plans had
been laid already with a view to such meetings: hardest
trial of all, she knew that certain of her rivals, with the
advantage of a start and clear course, would make play,
and want some catching whenever she should take up
the running again.   Yet she accepted quite readily the
prospect of comparative solitude, without a chance of the
mildest flirtation, or of a break to the monotony of the
days following and resembling each other, beyond an

occasional scamper on the back of a hill-pony, or a sail on the loch when the wind was not too wild.

Laura took no credit to herself for all this. To stand by a friend in need seemed to her the simplest thing in nature, and not in any wise to be regarded as a penance, or even as an exceptional duty. Nevertheless, it seems to me that charities less worthy of record have been celebrated in pompous phrase on lettered tombstones.

Certainly, few could have looked in Blanche Ramsay's face without feeling that her need of support, if not of succor, was very sore. The melancholy which had assailed her by fits and starts in the early days of her residence at Kenlis had fairly mastered her now, and seldom loosened its grasp, strive or struggle as she would. But there was a cause for it now—a cause that, ere this, has made braver and brighter birds than this little Oriole sit moping with dull eyes and plumage unpreened, while their mate was soaring apace through all other tracks of air rather than the one which led nestward.

To speak plainly, though she had not as yet made a confidante even of Laura Brancepeth, Blanche had long ago confessed to herself that she was jealous in real earnest. The cause of that jealousy you will easily guess.

I have said that the actual residents of the castle numbered only three; but whether the Irvings could be considered as non-residents might fairly have been questioned. Assuredly, much more of their time was spent at Kenlis than in their own home; and during the brief intervals of their absence, it might have been remarked that some business generally called away Ramsay on such distant expeditions as engrossed all the time betwixt breakfast and dinner. Once, and once only, he had avowedly gone over to Drumour. He went there alone, for a single night, to help to fill some game-boxes that Captain Irving wanted to send off south; but it is to be presumed that the grouse were wilder than usual, for it was the third day before he returned to Kenlis.

Even in his hot youth, Mark had always to a certain extent acted *caute, si non castè*, and he was still less likely to parade his indiscretions now. While conversing with Alice Irving his voice rarely sunk below its ordinary

Q   21

tone, and very rarely were the glances of either more expressive than familiar acquaintance would warrant. He never pretended to engross her attention, or seemed jealous at seeing it bestowed on another. Nevertheless, a mere stranger, after being an hour in their company, would probably have come to the conclusion that a singularly good understanding existed betwixt the two. There is a subtle mesmerism in these affinities that, without being at all contagious, makes others besides those directly influenced by them conscious of their existence.

Laura Brancepeth — neither a stranger nor disinterested—fully appreciated the state of things, and chafed under it hourly; but with all her impulsiveness she was far too well versed in the world's ways to interfere by word or gesture, or to broach the subject till Blanche herself should think fit to do so. Though she had rather a knack at travestying proverbs, she had got that one about a tree and its bark pretty straight, and on more than one similar occasion had found the benefit of acting thereupon. But if it was occasionally pain and grief to the friend to keep silence, how, think you, did it fare with the wife?

A dangerously deep game was being played up yonder, and the players did not start on level terms. Comparing great things with small, any one who has often looked on at really high whist must have seen a parallel case scores of times. Do we not know him—the light-minded gamester, utterly incorrigible in the error of his ways, and proof against reproach or sarcasm—who, having trusted once too often to his luck, accepts the position quite hilariously, treating his blunders as if they were part and parcel of an elaborate joke? And we, the bystanders, laugh with quite as much as at him, and think, "What a good loser he is!" contrasting his bearing very favorably with that of his partner, who, it is evident, does not relish the jest quite so keenly; for every point lost to themselves, or scored by their adversaries, has told on that other face— anxious enough when the play began. Now, it does not follow of necessity that difference of temperament has anything to do with this difference in the demeanor. It may well be that, as they walk homeward to-night, one

man will confess to himself, if he reflects at all, that the
purchase of that peacocky park-hack must be deferred, or
that Coralie must be balked of her latest whim in jewelry;
while the other will be racking his brain, overstrained
already, with reckoning up the resources wherewith he
may once again tempt Fortune. And if he be not quite
case-hardened against remorse, he may perhaps remember
having heard long ago that "it is not meet to take the
children's bread and cast it to dogs."

It was not of her own free will that Blanche Ramsay
was playing so perilously. Her position had been simply
forced upon her; but it was none the less true that her
very last stake was now involved. Considering all things,
her self-possession and self-control were something wonderful. If the tie binding her to Mark grew frailer daily,
no fault of hers brought it to breaking-strain. Peevish,
or plaintive, or sullen she never was, and if her face sometimes looked a little sad or weary, a gentle word from
him would always bring the light back again, if it lasted
not long. So much even he was fain to confess, thinking
over these things in the after-time.

As for Mark, he was simply following up his fancy, as
he had done a score of times before, utterly regardless of
the distinctions between right and wrong, faith and falsehood, cruelty and compassion; it was his fancy so far—
no more. In such a nature as his, love, as honest men
define it, had no more chance of ripening than the golden
grain scattered among desert stones. He had not begun
to dislike Blanche as yet, and found her sufficiently com-
panionable still, when he had time to spare; but such
hours as were spent in the shadow of Fontainebleau rocks
would never come again, and the soft white hand that he
was then so fond of toying with was powerless now to
keep him from straying.

What Alice Irving had at stake would be hard to determine. It is possible, indeed, that she had not yet defined
it to herself. She was no novice at the game, that was
clear; and, being conscious of the strength of her hand,
was content to play it warily without forcing the chances.
With her demeanor toward Blanche, La Reine herself
could not quarrel. Not a single act, or word, or look

could fairly be called presumptuous. She deferred in all things to her hostess beyond what may reasonably be expected from the meekest of guests; and if any point, howsoever trivial, was referred to her decision, she invariably withheld it till she was certain of not running counter to the slightest wish of Mrs. Ramsay. And the other paid her back in kind. No stranger coming to Kenlis would have guessed that Alice Irving's presence was less welcome to its *châtelaine* than it was the first time she set foot therein.

So things went on with admirable surface-smoothness; but, go as smoothly as they would, the time came when Mark could no longer delay a move southward, especially as Laura Brancepeth was waiting for his escort. He said as much to Captain Irving one night as they were finishing their *partie*.

The other shrugged his shoulders rather ruefully.

"I've been expecting this any time these three weeks. You're thoroughly right to go. I wonder at any one staying here after the fall of the first leaves, who isn't shackled down as I am. I should have liked above all things to spend this winter in town with Alice—leaving her at Kenlis alone is out of the question, of course—but I simply can't afford it. The fat kine have never much favored our pastures; and this is one of our famine-years. I'd have strained a point or two for her sake if it had been possible. She'll find the winter very long, I'm afraid."

Now, this speech coming from many people would have meant just this:—"I am very poor, and you are very wealthy. If you happen to have two or three hundreds lying idle at your banker's, the proffer of a six-months' loan would come at this·juncture with peculiar grace, and so neither our party nor our picquet need be broken up." But, like the Castilian beggar who will never overstep a certain line in degradation, Alexander Irving, gambler and profligate to the backbone, had his points of honor. On the present occasion he meant what he said, neither more nor less, and Ramsay, who had exceptional luck in steering clear of *gaucherie*, knew his man far too well to think of suggesting any such aid. He only said,—

"I wish with all my heart you could have managed it, it would have been so pleasant for all of us. Couldn't you venture on a short visit? Perhaps before long we could offer you quarters. At the present moment we're roofless in London, you know."

"Don't tempt me," Irving answered, gravely. "If I've learned nothing else in all these years, I've learned not to trust myself. It wouldn't be a short visit if I once got into the old haunts and among the old faces; and with my habits I would not accept quarters even under your roof. Thanks for the notion all the same. If things should turn out better than I expect, we may possibly meet again before long; if otherwise, I dare say Alice and I will survive till you come north again."

Then the subject dropped.

A word or two about that same picquet-playing will make matters clearer. Mark had adhered fairly enough to the spirit of his promise to Alice to abstain from deep gambling, and the nominal stakes remained much the same as at the beginning; but a fiver on the rubber of three games had become by no means exceptional of late, and they played as often as not according to the Russian rules, where every point scores. One way or another, Irving's winning balance had mounted to no inconsiderable sum; it might be reckoned in hundreds now. The luck had been tolerably equal, but Mark was probably right in giving his opponent credit from the first for superior skill and in predicting that it must tell in the long run. But the superiority was not disagreeably manifest; and it was still so much a question of cards, that a shade of odds would have tempted an ordinary backer to give choice. The subject of profit or loss had never been touched on betwixt them till the very last night. It was much later than usual when they sat down, and their time was limited; for, though neither affected early hours, it was their rule never to break far into the morning.

"Have you any idea how we stand?" Mark asked, as he took up his cards. "You keep a score, I believe?"

"Yes," Irving answered. "I have done so for many years. If my banking-book had been as regularly kept as my play-account, it would have been better for me and mine. I can tell you now, if you wait a minute. I'm just two hundred and eighty to the good," he went on, after adding up a page of his *carnet*. "I didn't think it had been quite so much."

"I thought it was more," the other said, carelessly. "If that's the case, I have seldom had so much amusement for my money—and instruction too, for the matter of that. I flatter myself I have improved several points since our first trial of strength."

"You don't flatter yourself," Irving said. "There can't be a doubt about your playing better than you did at first; and you would play better still—you don't mind my telling you—if you were not quite so quick over your discard. I can afford to give you that hint now, you see."

"I don't know about that," Mark retorted. "You've hit the blot, that's certain, and I'm obliged to you for the hint. I'd rather it had come an hour later, though. Can you guess why? Well, I was going to propose to you one rubber of three—*à l'Anglaise*—absolutely the last for this bout: fifty on the game, and a hundred on *la belle*. There's too much the double or quits about it, isn't there? I don't the least expect you to accept."

The same eagerness came over Irving's face, and the same gleam into his eyes, as was remarked there when picquet was first mentioned at Kenlis. He had none of the small meannesses of the third-rate gambler, and when he erred it was never on the side of timidity. His principle was invariably to *pousser sa masse*—only, unluckily for him, the mass was as often his own as the banker's money.

"And why not accept?" he said, in his softest voice. "It is no great plunge for me. At the very worst, I shall rise a better winner than perhaps I have any right to expect; and if I win, in spite of the famine-year, there'll be a little corn in Egypt."

"We'll have fresh cards, then," Mark observed; and, with no more said on either side, the heavy rubber began.

Irving had it all his own way at first, and scored a game without difficulty; but the second was more evenly contested. The luck seemed to have turned, for Mark scored ninety against his adversary's fifty-five, the latter being eldest hand. A glance at his cards told Mark that there was a heavy point, and in all probability at least one high sequence, against him. Indeed, it might be the taking in of one card only would save the game; but that one would win it—the fourth queen. He held an ace and king of different suits, so the quatorze must needs be good. It seemed as though Irving's hint had not been lost: he pondered long enough over the discard, at all events. Then, laughing to himself a little contemptuously, as men laugh at some trite jest or old-fashioned conceit, he put out the queen of hearts.

The topmost card on his *paquet* was her sister of diamonds.

On Irving's placid face there was, it must be owned, a palpable anxiety as he began to declare. His hand was wonderfully strong: six cards and a quint-major brought him to twenty-one. Then he announced three aces. He glanced sharply at his adversary, evidently not expecting them to pass unchallenged; but Mark only nodded; and now there was nothing to stop the pique, which, with the cards, made the eldest hand game and rubber at once.

"That was a near thing," the conqueror remarked, with the slightest, the very slightest, tremor in his voice. "The quatorze of queens was against me throughout. Is it possible that you didn't go for it?"

"Quite possible," Mark answered, "though I ought to have done so, beyond a doubt, for it was my best chance. If one could only guess what one was going to take in— I don't know that it would improve the game, though; it's pretty enough as it stands."

Whilst he was speaking, he had taken up his discard and mixed it into his hand, shuffling the cards to and fro mechanically, like one whose thoughts are busy elsewhere. Then he rose, and, unlocking an escritoire, took some notes out of it, which he laid upon the card-table. The other let them lie there.

"You don't care for your revenge, then?" he said.

"I have no right to ask it, for that was to be absolutely the last rubber; and if I had, I should waive it:

I should only be following up a bad *veine*. Those unlucky queens ought to be a warning."

With something like a sigh of relief, Irving folded up the notes tenderly and placed them in his pocket-book.

"I think we shall not winter at Drumour, after all," he remarked, after a minute's silence. "To-night has just turned the scale. We shall be boarded and lodged at your expense, after all—Alice and I."

Mark's start of surprise was perfect.

"You don't mean that? Well, I didn't grudge my losing it before, but now I think I seldom or never won to such good purpose. There's one thing I'm going to ask you. Will you tell Miss Irving nothing of to-night's doing, and not let her guess how her winter in town was brought about? It would be a pity to spoil her pleasure, you know; and that it will be pleasure there's little doubt. I don't mind confessing to you that the first time she ever stayed here, certain confidences passed between us on the subject of high play, and that I received a certain warning."

Captain Irving's smile was full of indulgent superiority —such as might become a great philosopher whose abstruse pursuits are sometimes scarcely appreciated as they deserve by his kith and kin.

"Poor Alice!" he said. "Yes, she does torment herself sometimes about these matters—as if self-tormenting ever helped one's self or others. You're quite right, though. There are secrets—quite harmless, of course— of which womankind, ever so trusty or tractable, is not worthy; and this is one of 'em. So about this last rubber —*silence à la mort!*"

After a little more converse of no moment, the two parted for the night on the best possible terms. But Irving knew only half the secret, after all. He had all the worst faults of the inveterate gambler; he would have won a pauper's last shilling with as little scruple or pity as though it belonged to a millionaire; and he would push the advantage of skill to the very verge of honor; nevertheless—let us give the devil his due—if he could have overlooked his opponent's play during that last hand, he would have cast down those notes that he folded so complacently, even as Judas—a thought too late—cast down the blood-money. Ay, more than this ! If he could have guessed at the motive prompting the curious discard, it would have been no fault of his if Mark Ramsay had not had an early opportunity of proving whether Vere Alsager was right or wrong in crediting those delicate white fingers with some skill in the use of hair-triggers.

The Irvings departed after luncheon on the morrow; for on the following day Kenlis Castle was to be left till next summer to the care of two or three Scotch servants, who, for a sufficient " con-sid-er-a-tion," were not afraid to risk an occasional encountering of the Brown Lady. But in the course of the morning Alice Irving found herself in a certain nook of the south terrace, where—by the merest chance in the world—Ramsay was smoking a contemplative cigar. She was radiant with happiness, for she had just heard from her father of the change in their winter quarters.

" I'm sure it's all owing to you. Don't deny it."

And her eyes said, better than the scarlet lips could have done, " I thank you."

" I never deny pleasant imputations," Mark said, with a laugh. " You may give me all the credit you can possibly afford. I deserve a good deal ; for it was so thoroughly disinterested of me to try to persuade Captain Irving that neither of you was quite fitted for an Arctic winter ! Is it treason to mention Drumour and winter in a breath? Never mind; it can't be helped. The die is cast now, and you must make the best of it."

" The best of it !"

She spoke the words almost in a whisper ; but as she spoke she glanced up once in her companion's face. If Vere Alsager had been near enough to look under the long, sweeping lashes, he would have been less likely than ever to alter his opinion as to the " quiet devilry" of the great gray eyes.

CHAPTER XXVIII.

We have almost forgotten George Anstruther. Out of such clay it is difficult assuredly to mould an interesting personage, either in real life or romance: nevertheless, as he played rather an important part in this story, it will be better to go back to him for awhile.

The outward perturbation in which you saw him last —when he made haste to escape out of the sound of Blanche Ramsay's marriage-bells—passed away within the hour; but the methodical routine of his days was not taken up so easily again. It is the same with all machines —alive or dead—working in a deep groove. Hard as it may be to throw them out of gear, when this is once done effectually it is harder yet to set them back on the track. For the first time in all his life Anstruther knew what restlessness meant. Certain tormenting phantoms haunted him—in his laboratory, where he now worked only by fits and starts—in his hours of exercise, ride as sharply as he would—and, most of all, when he lay down and strove to force himself into sleep; and sleep, when it came, was too full of dreams to refresh or restore. Even at the whist-table his thoughts would go wandering far beyond the outer walls of the Orion—sometimes beyond the sea.

The jar on his moral organization told on him physically, too. The fine, regular appetite, that was the envy of all his Indian comrades, began to fail, and more than once an artistic dish sent back untasted gave the *chef* of the Planet occasion to exclaim against insular ingratitude. Divers of his acquaintance noticed the change, and decided that it was "a case of liver," and that George Anstruther, after all, had not fared so much better than other consumers of curry and cayenne. He himself at last inclined to this view of the question, and, after considerable reluctance and delay, consented to a medical inspection.

The famous physician he consulted was a man of the world as well as a man of science: perhaps not a few of his cures might have been attributed to a habit of considering and prescribing for other than mere bodily symptoms of disease. In the present instance he allowed that the liver was partly at fault; but it was not only on this account that he suggested change of scene. A month in Switzerland and another at Wiesbaden, with one or two simple remedies, were all he thought it necessary to prescribe.

Anstruther took both the advice and the physic patiently, and went through the course of travel and the course of waters with exemplary punctuality—feeling, all the while, tolerably sure that neither would do him any material good. In the first fortnight of his sojourn at Wiesbaden there certainly was an improvement, and three or four Orionites who had come thither on a like sanitary mission found him quite as ready as themselves to make up a rubber at club-points—which those decent bodies much preferred to the meretricious *trente et quarante*—and much readier to take exercise either on foot or horseback. But all at once he seemed to fall back again beyond the point from which improvement had begun. There was no rational way of accounting for this, unless a packet of letters forwarded from England had anything to do with it. As for the intelligence they contained, the whole world might have looked over his shoulder as he opened them and been none the wiser; though they included a brief kind note from Blanche Ramsay, asking Mr. Anstruther to spare them a fortnight at Kenlis, or longer if he could contrive it.

Do you remember his behavior some months before, when, walking in his garden, he first read that handwriting? How carefully he opened the dainty envelope? How he lingered over the perusal? How long he mused afterward—frowning the while? Much after the same fashion he bore himself now, only that his feverish fingers did not entreat the note quite so delicately—they rather crushed than toyed with it—and those few lines took thrice as long as the others in reading. His frown too, as he sat a-musing, was heavier tenfold.

Nothing of all this was apparent in the tone of his answer. His regret at being now forced to decline, and hope of being more fortunate hereafter, were perfectly worded. If a fault could have been found, it would have been that the courtesy was a little too formal and cold. But from that day there was a notable change in Anstruther for the worse. Notable it must have been; for each and every one of the Orionist clique was too much engaged in watching the state of his own health to look very keenly after his neighbor's, and yet they all observed and commented on it.

When the appointed time was fully spent, Anstruther drifted listlessly back with the tide—setting homeward now. He took Paris on his way, purposing to spend a week there; but by the third evening he was weary even to death of the noisy, tourist-ridden city, and came straight to town by the night mail.

The autumnal attractions of London to most people are not powerful; but Anstruther was independent of society —or, at least, of all but a very minute portion thereof— so far as his amusements went. He was really glad to find himself within arm's-length of his books and his crucibles again; and a faithful few—loving a square yard of green cloth better than the widest prospect of emerald fields—mustered still in the card-room of the Orion.

Gradually he began to slide back into the old ways; before he had been home a full month he had found quiet again, if not perfect peace, and for awhile the current of his life flowed on much as heretofore. If the tormenting phantoms had not utterly vanished, they kept discreetly in the background for the present; but, in most of these cases, once haunted is always haunted. He knew very well that they were lurking somewhere in the dark, and would appear once more at their own time and season.

One murky afternoon—the November fogs came before their time that autumn—Anstruther went down to his club at the usual hour, and stopped on the steps to exchange salutations with one of his familiars passing out; "familiar" is the proper term, for no one, since Walter Ellerslie's death, had the right to call Anstruther "friend." This man—Thorndyke by name—was among his closest intimates. Both were old bachelors, leading a methodical sort of life; and respect for each other's skill, added to certain gastronomic sympathies, had bred a kind of liking

betwixt them.   Anstruther was rather disappointed at
seeing the other's face turned outward: Mr. Thorndyke's
place at the whist-table could not easily be filled.

"You're off early," he said; "some business, I suppose?"

"You are about right," Thorndyke retorted, turning
up his furred collar with a shiver. "I haven't a hundred
steps to walk; but no man would go that far for his own
pleasure through this infernal fog. There's something
worth looking at up-stairs, too—though it's more in your
line than mine; for I don't appreciate picquet. There's
a fresh hand turned up this afternoon—fresh to most of
us, at least, though he's a very old member. Did you
ever hear of a Captain Irving—no? Well, he has just
sat down to play nine games with Blanchmayne, with
fifty on the rubber. They are ancient antagonists, it seems.
I fancy the viscount must have got a rare dressing once
or twice, or he wouldn't be so civil."

This famous card-room was not an out-of-the-way gar-
ret, or a noisy ground-room—such as may be seen in
other clubs, where whist is subordinate to conviviality—
but a lofty and spacious presence-chamber, wherein
brooded always a solemn stillness, if not a silence that
might be felt. Thick sun-blinds and ample curtains repelled the garish eye of day, and after dusk-fall the sad
mellow light of shaded waxen tapers prevailed. The
wagering, though never desperate, was often deep; but
bets were offered and accepted in a quiet mercantile
fashion. Winners betrayed no noisy exultation, and
losers cursed not their ill luck—aloud. Light-minded
strangers entering there jocund with good cheer—the
cellar of the Orion was proverbial—had scarcely passed
through those august portals before the *religio loci* constrained them to tread softly and speak under their breath;
and they issued forth, as a rule, in a frame of mind befitting those who have sojourned for a space within the Tro-
phonian Cavern.

On the present occasion a couple of rubbers were going
on, neither of which had any special attraction for Anstruther, and he walked straight to the corner where a
knot of spectators were gathered round the picquet-table.

Of the two players, one you are well acquainted with; the other was an oddity in his way—a most disagreeable way, it must be owned.

There was not a shadow of reason or excuse, so far as any one knew, for Lord Blanchmayne's misanthropy. His constitution was as tough as whalebone; his fortune far beyond his needs; and he was hampered by no kind of family duties or cares. Yet he had never been known to waste kindly or courteous word on man, woman, or child. He was a solitary—partly by choice, partly of necessity: for his own order, when the fact of Lord Blanchmayne's confirmed celibacy was once established, cared not to court his society; and when, to suit his own purpose, he mingled with his inferiors, he would never dissemble contempt for his company. He was an adept at all games of chance and skill, and a shrewd though not an energetic or eloquent politician. But he would have been more successful had he had a better opinion of the world in general; and some of his subtlest combinations went awry simply because he would not give his partners credit for common sense, or his adversaries for common honesty. *Parcere devictis* was a maxim that even as a schoolboy he had learned to despise; but he was a good loser—the stake was of no sort of consequence to him, and instead of bearing malice to any man who fairly got the best of him, he rather respected such a one, and treated him accordingly. His sallow, cross-grained face does not lower a whit more than usual now, though the second game has just been scored against him; and with a kind of sullen admiration he growls out,—

"You haven't grown rusty in all these years : plenty of practice, I suppose ? I wish I could say as much for myself; but bad play's catching, and I don't get many chances of improving my game."

The side-blow was meant for certain bystanders who rather fancied themselves at picquet.

"As far as practice goes, you must have had the advantage in point of quality, if not in quantity," Irving answered, with a glance round that took the edge off the other's sarcasm. "I've been playing a good deal lately, it's true ; in Germany, first, with a real professor, who is gone—I'm afraid not to a better world ; Paradise without picquet would be Purgatory to poor Bernsdorff; and lately in Scotland with a near neighbor of mine—Mark Ramsay, of Kenlis Castle—a fine player, too, though a little flashy. He's in town now, and I shouldn't wonder if he were put up here. Does any one know him?"

Blanchmayne grunted out a negative, and it was evident that the name had no interest or significance for any there present—save one.

Anstruther started, and, if you had watched his face narrowly, you would have seen his brow contract and his lips brace themselves ; but he never uttered a syllable till the *partie* was decided easily in Irving's favor. During the buzz of comment that ensued—the viscount chose to défer his revenge—he accosted the conqueror.

"I never had the pleasure of meeting you before to-day. When we're better acquainted, I hope you'll give me some lessons at picquet; but, frankly speaking, that's not my object now. You said that the Ramsays are in town, I think ? I was not aware of it. Perhaps you can tell me where they are staying ? My name is George Anstruther."

"You flatter me," the other said, with a little, deprecating laugh. "One *partie* don't go for much : I'm more likely to learn than to teach here. I remember your name quite well ; for I heard Mrs Ramsay regret that she could not prevail on you to come so far north. Luckily, I can give you their address. For the present they've got rooms at ——'s."

In those days the renown of that famous caravanserai was scarcely limited by the frontier of civilization. Its ancient proprietor—an enterprising cosmopolitan, who, in the pursuit of his profession, soared superbly above prejudice and conscience—has gone to settle his own account, or found a principality, in some far-off clime, and the place is changed—for the better, perhaps. But, even now, few strangers arriving there—hailing from regions howsoever remote, of four continents—need be debarred from their national comforts and delicacies. Prayer-carpets are still provided at a small extra charge, and a space on the house-top is especially set apart for sun-worship. If the heir-apparent of the Cannibal Isles were sojourning there,

I doubt not that *filet de garçon à la Pérouse* would be served at his table as often as it pleased him—always provided that the prince were not terrified by the figures set over against that dish of savory meat in the bill.

"I thought of calling there on my way home," Irving went on,—"only to leave a message, though. Shall I give you a lift so far?"

Anstruther's manner—especially with strangers—was always rather stiff and formal; but it was unusually constrained now, and he seemed to shrink back within himself, as if he regretted having made the first advances toward conversation.

"Thanks! I should be very happy, if I were not otherwise engaged," he said; "but I can't possibly call this afternoon. I shall take an early opportunity of doing so."

The change in the speaker's tone did not escape Irving: very few things passing within his sight or hearing *did* escape him. He thought there was something decidedly eccentric about his new acquaintance; but he simply bowed his head as if accepting the excuse, as he asked, incidentally,—

"Shall I mention that we have met, if I happen to see Mrs. Ramsay? I think, from what I have heard her say at Kenlis, she would be glad to know that you are in town."

"If you—please," Anstruther answered, this time with marked hesitation, and then turned away abruptly.

"A very fair beginning," Irving mused, as he stepped gingerly across the slippery pavement to his cab, and drew up the windows. "I rather believe in auguries, and it's as well to start with something in hand. Blanchmayne was quite right. His game isn't improved since we met last: I think I've got his measure. It remains to be seen what the others are like—it wouldn't be safe to take his estimate of them, that's certain; but with even paper I ought to hold my own. It strikes me my losings to Bernsdorff weren't such a bad investment. I'll take odds that same Anstruther knows a thing or two. I don't fancy those modest people who are so ready to take lessons, particularly when they're my canny countrymen; and there's no doubt on which side of the Border he was begotten. It's a hard-bitten face: but how queer it looked just now! I believe he'd have blushed if he hadn't forgotten the trick; and what made him stammer? It's not his habit, evidently. Mrs. Ramsay spoke of him as a sort of guardian, if I remember right. Can there have been any love-passages? Absurd! *A d'autres, mon bon.*"

A complacent chuckle suggested what sort of comparison he was drawing in his mind just then.

Mrs. Ramsay was not at home when he called; so that evening Irving had no chance of seeing whether her face would have furnished matter for guess-work at the mention of a certain name.

When Anstruther turned away after the colloquy recorded above, he went first to one of the whist-tables, and stood watching the progress of the game; after a minute or two, as if he had suddenly remembered something, he walked quickly through the door leading into a smaller apartment used as a writing-room. It was empty just then, as indeed was generally the case; for very little correspondence was conducted at the Orion, and ink was seldom used save for the drawing of checks. He sat down at one of the tables and took up a pen; but this was a palpable excuse for lingering there, for he never traced a word on the paper before him. His thoughts were in a strange medley, and he himself could hardly have told whether they were more tinged with pleasure or pain.

One thing was certain: the calm of the last few weeks had been utterly broken up within the last half-hour. The phantoms that had kept aloof for awhile were at their old mocks again already, and they were clearer in outline now—more like the reflections in a mirror of forms actually in flesh and blood. So she was in London; within reach—easy reach—of .him at that very moment. To-morrow—this very day, for the matter of that—he might, if he chose, prove whether the soft brown eyes had forgotten to look up pleadingly, and whether the cool white fingers would still send the same feverish thrill through his pulses as when they touched his wrist on a certain afternoon. Was it well to make the trial? Would it not be wiser to fly—ay, even to the uttermost parts of the earth—while he could yet use his wings, than to hover stupidly over the snare? He recognized with self-con-

R   22*

tempt verging on self-loathing—nevertheless he *did* recognize it—that he was being mastered by a passion utterly irrational, hopeless, and guilty. Truth to say, it was not the guilt that made him shrink and waver.

When George Anstruther's character was first sketched, he was set down, as you will remember, as one self-respecting rather than God-fearing; and when a monitor like self-respect calms such a turmoil as was working within him, then flax-withes will bind firebrands. If he had been inclined to boast that he had avoided hitherto gross or overt offense against the written law, he must needs have boasted himself as one whom chance or circumstance has kept clear of the verge of battle, rather than as one putting off harness smirched and dinted by strife. He was virtuous—or what the world calls virtuous—by habit rather than by creed; and he had no sure or abiding principle whereunto to cling when a fierce temptation dragged him down.

Since Phryne, laughing scornfully, shut her door in the face of the poor philosopher who came a-wooing with the dye fresh on his scanty locks, what a many right merry jests have been indited concerning the loves of elders! Yet if the records of crime throughout all nations and all ages were searched narrowly, not many blacker pages would be found than those whereon it is written what befell in the baffling or the accomplishing of these untimely passions.

Young man's love blazeth, and is done;
Old man's love it burneth to the bone.

There is truth enough in that rude couplet to leaven a large lump of Proverbial Philosophy.

The curled darlings, scarcely out of their teens, are prone enough—Heaven knows!—to waste a fair' inheritance and dishonor an ancient name for a harlot's kiss or a coquette's smile; and even the Barnwell tragedy repeats itself only too often. But in sin and shame there is always a deeper depth—well for us and our children that it is so—and the boy will stand shivering and shrinking on the brink of the pit into which the graybeard has plunged headlong at the beck of waving white arms.

Wild tales assuredly might have been told of Antony's youth; but I doubt if, while his brow was brent, he would have followed so fast in the wake of the Egyptian galley while the sea-fight was swaying to and fro off Actium, or have set his breast so straight against his sword's point at the lying rumor of Cleopatra's suicide.

CHAPTER XXIX.

"Perhaps we may meet again before very long."

So much, and no more, said Alice Irving, when she bade adieu to her hostess at Kenlis. She did not deem it necessary to set forth more definitely her father's plans for the winter; and when Blanche a little hesitatingly answered, "I'm sure I hope so," she did not dream the truth of her word would be tested so soon. She counted, not unnaturally, on a brief respite from the anxieties and suspicions that had harassed her of late; and when, on the fourth evening after their arrival in town, Mark observed, carelessly, "I met Irving in St. James's Street this afternoon," her heart gave a painful throb, and then sank within her. If her thoughts had been put into words, she might have murmured, "Hast thou found me, O mine enemy?"

If she manifested no great pleasure at the intelligence, she betrayed no vexation. You would have detected no sarcasm in her placid reply,—

"Indeed! I didn't think they would have followed us so quickly."

But, as she lay awake that night alone, as was usual now—for Mark, since he took to keeping late hours, occupied a separate sleeping-chamber, on the pretext of not breaking his wife's rest—the tears rolled fast down her cheeks, and she did not try to check them. She remembered how she had lain awake musing once before—on the eve of her second marriage-day. That was only a few months ago; yet how far, far off it seemed! Her heart had fluttered then, but not painfully, and she fell asleep smiling. Her smiles now were for the world to see, and it was hard work to find them sometimes ; certainly it was not worth while to force them for her own behalf. And then, in spite of herself—for here she strove hard to turn the current of her thoughts—she remembered Oswald Gauntlet's warning. Would he be glad or sorry if he knew that it had all, or nearly all, come true ? Not glad, she felt right sure of that. Then she fell a-wondering where Oswald was just now. Perhaps he was in town, or at Woolwich—much the same thing. Suppose she were to write a little note to his club, and ask him to call on her, just once, for the sake of old times, letting by-gones be by-gones. Among her conjugal confidences were not included the details of that last interview in Gaunt Square ; but would Mark be likely to object, even if he knew all ? Blanche sighed drearily, as she acknowledged that she need have no scruples on that score. She felt as if the sight of a kind, familiar face, even though it should look on her at first somewhat an-grily, and the clasp of a strong, honest hand (not a white, womanly one, like Captain Irving's), might help to brace her nerves. There were substantial dangers enough around her ; but she had begun to start at the mere shadows of late, and, since she had no longer La Reine to lean upon, the sense of isolation and helplessness dark-ened round her hourly. Yes, she would certainly write. To have settled even so much was some comfort ; never-theless, she fairly cried herself to sleep.

Before noon on the following day the note was duly dispatched ; but the messenger brought word back that Major Gauntlet was still abroad, that it was not known when he would return, and that, till further notice, his letters were to be forwarded to the Poste Restante, Vienna. Mrs. Ramsay was bitterly disappointed. All that morning she had been rehearsing, much to her own satisfaction, an imaginary scene with Oswald, and now it seemed likely to be deferred indefinitely. She could not possibly write and ask him to come back from Vienna. It was provoking, to say the least of it ; and in the first moment of vexation, I fear, she spoke unadvisedly with her lips concerning Commissions, and the War Office to boot. Unless their lovers' or their friends' credit be at stake, very few of our sisters are patriotic or Spartan enough to submit without a murmur to their private arrangements being thwarted by public duty; and betwixt such superior persons and our poor Blanche there was not a single feeling or idea in common.

In this discontented mood—after an utterly abortive attempt at luncheon—Blanche was debating with herself how she should get rid of the afternoon. None of her confidentials were in town, and to general converse she felt by no means equal, when Mr. Anstruther's card was brought up.

"Certainly, I shall be very glad," she said, in answer to the query whether she would receive the visitor. This was not merely a form of words. An old acquaintance was not like an old friend, particularly such an old friend as Oswald Gauntlet; but the homely proverb about half a loaf applies to the *petite maîtresse* sometimes, no less than to the peasant wench, and Blanche just now was not inclined to be dainty.

So this was where his meditations of overnight had led George Anstruther. It could hardly be otherwise. When such a question is once debated, as a rule it is virtually lost. It struck Blanche that he was somewhat altered since they last met. He looked certainly gaunter and more angular, and altogether more precise and formal, than heretofore. He was carefully dressed, as usual; but, abased as the man was already—at all events, in his own eyes—he was still above the devices of elderly foppery, and chose that his face and figure should remain as time and climate had left them. Mrs. Ramsay, it seemed, was quite content to take him as he was, and a more sanguine visitor would have been satisfied with the warmth of her welcome.

"One is never really at home in a hotel," she said, after the first greetings had been exchanged, "even in the way of receiving one's friends; but there are exceptions to all rules, and the week would not have passed without my letting you know our whereabouts. By-the-by, how did you find us out?"

He answered the first part of her speech only, by a stiff bow.

"It was at the Orion,—an old-fashioned club, I dare say, you never heard of. A Captain Irving mentioned Mr. Ramsay's name. From what he said, I fancy he must have been a constant visitor at Kenlis."

Had the room grown darker all of a sudden? or was the fresh shadow only on Blanche's face?

"A very constant visitor," she said, hurriedly. "He was our nearest neighbor, to be sure, and anything like society is at a premium in the far north; but Mark and he have become almost inseparable of . late. They are both devoted to picquet, you know."

She thought afterward he guessed at her embarrassment, and would have helped her out of it.

"Quite enough to account for an intimacy, I think. It's a fascinating game, as I've found to my cost. Yes; it was as a picquet-player your husband was first alluded to. Then I introduced myself to Captain Irving, for the purpose of finding out if you were in town."

"Then you cared to know?" she asked, with one of the shy, eloquent glances that had helped to do much mischief in old times. Anstruther bore it bravely: at least not a muscle in his stolid, rough-hewn face stirred; but the fingers that lay crossed on his knee were locked a little more tightly.

"Undoubtedly I cared," he made answer. "I have not so many friends that I can afford either to forget or neglect them. I assure you I often thought of you at Kenlis, and hoped you were making the most of all that glorious weather. There hasn't been such a Highland autumn for years, they tell me."

"Yes; the weather was perfect. It is a pity you were not with us to enjoy it. I hardly expected a refusal, I own. Did you not give me a half-promise when you gave me—this?"

She drew out of the bodice of her high velvet dress the amulet you wot of, with the fire-opal gleaming in the square of dusky gold.

Anstruther's cheek flushed for a second quite visibly, though in the stiffness of his manner there was no change.

"If I had given a whole instead of a half promise,— and even to that I don't plead guilty," he said,—"I must needs have broken it. I was working out my time at Wiesbaden. I didn't expect much of the waters, luckily, or I should have been disappointed; but I thought them worth a trial. So you wear that trinket sometimes? It is highly honored."

"It's silly to be superstitious, I suppose," she said; "but I never pretended to be wise. I have great faith in talismans. Don't they lose their virtue if they are not *always* worn? Have you been ill, then? I had no idea you were at Wiesbaden for health's sake, or I should not have accused you of playing me false."

"It was nothing worth speaking of," he replied, indifferently; "only the harvest of seed sown long ago in India. But I cannot, to speak truth, congratulate you on the effects of Highland air. Would it be impertinent to ask you the same question?"

"By no means impertinent: my glass tells me the same blunt truth every morning. No; the air certainly didn't brace me as it ought to have done. I think I never knew what it was to be thoroughly tired before, with no sufficient exercise to account for it."

"Had you a very large party to entertain?" he asked. "Because that is fatigue enough in itself, no matter how pleasant the society."

His cold gray eyes were steady, as a rule, rather than piercing; but now she was aware of a scrutiny in them that set her on her guard.

"Not at all a large party: only the Brancepeths and Mr. Alsager—these you know—and Colonel Vane, an old acquaintance of mine and Mark's. To be sure, the Irvings might almost be reckoned in our party, for they were more at Kenlis than at their own place—Drumour."

"Captain Irving is married, then?"

Blanche only half liked the interrogatory, especially as she suspected a purpose in it.

"He has been a widower some years," she replied, with a slight movement of impatience, as if she had had enough of the subject. "He has one daughter—a fascinating person in every way. You can judge of that for yourself, if you'll meet them here at dinner to-morrow. It's difficult to tempt you, I know; but, if you're fond of music, when you have heard them sing together, you won't repent for once breaking your rule.   And we shall be such a small party—only six with yourself."

Anstruther's deliberation was long and grave enough to have suited a weightier question than the acceptance or refusal of a simple invitation.

"Thanks; you are very kind," he said, at last.   "I'm ashamed to say that the music is no great temptation to me.   Putting that aside, I shall be glad to dine with you to-morrow."

Blanche was really pleased.   That his old-fashioned reserve should have yielded to her first word was a triumph in its way, though scarcely one on which she would have plumed herself a year ago; and it was a certain satisfaction to feel that the virtue of persuasion had not wholly gone out of her.

"That is prettily said," she answered.   "The bad habit of always saying 'no' is difficult to cure; but your case cannot be desperate yet.   I shall reckon on you; and, if you fail me this time, don't expect to be forgiven."

"There's no danger of my failing," Anstruther answered, as he rose to take his leave.   "A punctual eight, I suppose?   Don't blame me if your party is spoiled; a stranger coming among intimates is apt to be a kill-joy."

"We'll take our chance of that," she said.   "I wish I were as sure that you wouldn't be bored.   Till to-morrow, then."

It doesn't at all follow that an interview should have been disagreeable, either in anticipation or reality, because we are sensible of a relief when it is over.   There was not the smallest necessity for Anstruther to have presented himself on that day, or, indeed, on any other, before Mrs. Ramsay.   He had taken some pains to ascertain where she was staying, and had mounted those stairs entirely of his own free will; yet he descended them with something like a lightening of spirit.   It may be that he had distrusted his self-command more than he cared to confess to himself, and was proportionately inclined to rejoice that it had carried him through without a stumble. Yet, for all this, he despised himself not a whit less heartily now than he had done when he first recognized his weakness and ceased to fight against it. He was not destitute of a grim sense of humor; and the ridicule of the whole position struck him so forcibly that twice or thrice, as he walked through the streets, he could scarcely forbear laughing aloud. And this man—you will remember—for a score of years past had rarely rewarded any jest, spoken or written, with anything beyond a coldly appreciative smile.

"I wonder what they'd say at the Orion," so his thoughts ran, "if they got an inkling of all this? Much what I should have said last spring, I suppose, if I heard that Blanchmayne had eloped with somebody else's wife, or Thorndyke had taken to the squiring of dames. They are neither of them five years my senior, and I've no doubt they are twice as well preserved. Does it make it any better that I'm going down hill with my eyes open? Better? A thousand times worse. I know so well, too, the very uttermost that I'm likely to win,—a soft, shy look, something like what I saw to-day; or a whisper, —'You're so very kind, Mr. Anstruther; I know you'd help me if you could.' Well, and isn't it enough? And more than enough? Just as if the thing that was George Anstruther a year ago would not pass through fire for a lighter reward than the lightest of these? Help her? So I will, somehow; and perhaps without her leave or license. I half guess already what has made her cheeks so pale and thin. I'll see my way clearer after to-morrow; but, if I would keep my wits about me, I must keep this flutter quiet. I'll have sleep to-night at any price."

Mrs. Ramsay, too, had her little meditation, all to herself, after her visitor had departed.

"There is one, at all events," she thought, "who likes me as well as ever—I almost fancy, better than ever. It's not a very magnificent conquest, to be sure. How Queenie would laugh if she heard of it! I wish she was here all the same; I do miss her dreadfully. I am sure he guessed I had been unhappy, and pitied me in his awkward way. It's very ungrateful to say so, but I'd rather he hadn't done either. There are not above two or three people alive that I should like to be pitied by — much less that I would ask to help me. And, after all, how can any one help? Even I can only wait, and hope against hope. Ah me! It's a weary world, after all; and I used to think it such a pleasant one, and to think, too, how sad it would be to have to leave it before one's time. I don't think so now. If I could have one whole year just like last summer, I'd be content to lie down quietly and trouble no one any more—not that I've been any trouble to Mark as yet. He ought to remember that, whatever happens. Perhaps he does remember it; for he has never spoken unkindly to me yet. I almost wish he would sometimes; anything would be better than being put on one side in that off-hand, good-tempered way. And how well drilled *she* is, too! Even Queenie, though I know she was always on the watch, never could find anything to quarrel with; but how do I know what goes on when she and Mark are alone together, or how often that happens? He's out the whole day long, and it can't be business that keeps him; for I don't believe he's really begun house-hunting yet. There—there—I'm foolish again. I'd better order the carriage before my eyes get red: the air may cure my headache, if it don't my heart-ache."

The dinner next day went off pleasantly enough. Putting Anstruther out of the question, it was almost a family party; for the sixth guest was Vere Alsager, and when people, who have lived for some space in the same country quarters, meet for the first time in town, they generally feel more or less domestic for the moment. Anstruther said but little, and that little chiefly to Mrs. Ramsay, on whose right hand he was placed; but his presence was no constraint on the others, and Mark—who was invariably courteous to each and every one of his wife's friends or acquaintance—soon put the stranger thoroughly at his ease. Prejudiced as he was against Ramsay, and little inclined to appreciate mere outward graces, Anstruther was not thoroughly proof against the charm of the other's manner; and, when the women had departed, he moved —not unwillingly—into the chair next to his host's.

"I was rather disappointed in not seeing you at the

club this afternoon, Mr. Anstruther," Irving remarked. "They tell me you rarely fail to put in an appearance there."

"I had business that detained me," the other answered, rather hesitatingly. He had been so much out of the way of conventionalities, that even an excuse came lamely off his tongue. "I shall take my lesson before long, rely upon it."

"It's the other way, from what I hear," Irving said. "The viscount allowed that 'you were acquainted with the first principles of the game,' so you must be nearly *de la première force ;* but that wasn't why I specially wished to meet you. Ramsay's name was put up there to-day, with Blanchmayne as his proposer, and I meant to ask you to second him. I'd have done it myself, of course, but I've been at the Orion so rarely of late that I'm almost forgotten now ; and you are as one in authority, I understood."

Now, though Anstruther had small liking or esteem for Blanche's husband, the proposal would have been less distasteful coming from any other channel. Long judicial practice, and natural keenness of perception, had made him no mean physiognomist. At all events, he had got accustomed to facial warnings, and to rest a good deal on first impressions; and these had rarely deceived him. He had not watched that *partie* of picquet two days ago for naught. He had begun to distrust from the very first those smooth delicate features and glittering eyes, and guessed that sharp cruel talons could come forth on occasion from the velvet paws. He would never thereafter have met Alexander Irving, in any relation of life where his own or a friend's interest was deeply concerned, without standing somewhat on his guard. In the very proposal that he, George Anstruther, should avouch Mark Ramsay a good man and true, there was something that jarred ; but, coming from that especial quarter, it sounded ominous and unnatural. However, there was no real choice left him.

There are persons, doubtless—luckily their name is not Legion—who, when replete with old wine and fat venison, would decline—without sufficient cause, remember—to requite their entertainer with such a slight service, and depart, pluming themselves on having discharged a social duty rather cleverly. But Anstruther was by no means equal to such an occasion; he hesitated just long enough to prevent the acquiescence being cordial, and then professed his willingness to become Mr. Ramsay's seconder, and forward his election in all reasonable ways—disclaiming, at the same time, anything like influence at the Orion. The obliged person noticed the hesitation, without guessing at its cause: it rather amused him than otherwise, and did not in the least interfere with his expressions of acknowledgment. Irving observed it too, and was con-. siderably puzzled thereby—and gave the puzzle much more thought than Mark had done.

"What the devil was he boggling at ?" said he to himself. "It's just of a piece with his beginning to stammer the other night for no rhyme or reason. People with mysteries have no business in society. He'll bring about an *imbroglio* somehow or other before all's done: see if he don't! But 'it's' not likely to affect me or mine, that's one comfort."

Alexander Irving remembered those last words—and with cause—before all *was* done.

Whatever his private fancies might have been, no sign of suspicion showed itself on the surface, and the flow of desultory talk went smoothly on, till Alsager, whose love of music amounted to a passion, suggested a move. Both father and daughter were in superb voice that night; and even Blanche's admiration was, for the moment, sincere. But to one man there present—though he seemed to listen, in rapt attention, with half-closed eyes—the rich melody was as the flowing of a far-off torrent, without rhythm or distinguishment of sound. With all his vigilance—though neither eyes nor ears had for an instant that evening been off duty—Anstruther had failed to catch a look or word whereon suspicion might be grounded. Nevertheless, he had gained the first letter of the word which, once fully formed, would unlock the secret. Over this he pondered; and, as he drove homeward alone, he murmured, half aloud,—

"A blight on the false, fair face! I know now what makes the other one so wan and pale."

CHAPTER XXX.

When Captain Irving spoke of the current year as one of financial famine, he rather overcolored the state of the case. That he was still suffering, as he had long suffered, from chronic insufficiency of income was perfectly true; for his life-interest in Drumour was heavily encumbered, and never likely to be otherwise; and the sum derived from the letting of the house and shooting was barely sufficient to cover household expenditure, conducted on ever so modest a scale. Unless the cards were kind, luxuries were out of the question. He had grown accustomed to thus living from hand to mouth, from hour to hour, and perhaps did not altogether dislike it. He was such an inveterate gambler, that increase of fortune would only have led to playing for increased stakes; so that a heavy run of ill luck might at any moment have reduced him to his present ebb.

We all know how the Indian "brave"—of the Cooper-type, of course—bears himself when, having lost his last horse at play, so that he can course the buffalo no longer, he sees the keg of fire-water empty and his wigwam-walls bare of meat. He wastes no breath in cursing or praying, but chooses some convenient spot for ambush, and will wait there patiently from dawn to evening, and from evening to dawn—only tightening his belt sometimes to choke the wolf within him—till the Great Spirit shall see fit to send game within reach of his arrow. In Irving, an epicurean by habit and inclination to the tips of his delicate fingers, there was a strong dash of this simple stoicism. When he found that his resources were crippled for a time, he accepted the position with perfect good humor, making a jest of privation and of the shifts that he was compelled to resort to. Alice never complained, to be sure · that was a great point; and, on the whole, the

23*

wheels of their frail chariot rolled on more smoothly than could have been expected.

Fortune had rather smiled than frowned on Captain Irving of late, or he would not have been found that autumn at Drumour, though there were sufficient reasons for his presence there; for the lease of the house and shooting had just expired, and no eligible offer of fresh tenancy had been made up to the time when the absentee resolved to try what a spell of his native air would do toward banishing certain ailments that had begun to trouble him. He was not quite satisfied with the way in which his interests, such as they were, had been looked after there of late; and, though he would have laughed the very idea to scorn, there abode with him, perchance, still some faint tinge of the home-sickness which is found nowhere so strong as in the Scot. Indeed, at first—though out-door pursuits were entirely out of his line, and he set his foot upon his native heath only under protest—it was rather pleasant to loiter about the old haunts, and to throw a fly into the pool out of which his first trout was landed, and to watch the sun go down behind a hill that was, nominally at least, his own. But, as the novelty wore off, Irving began gravely to misdoubt the wisdom of his move from Darmstadt; before the Kenlis-Castle party appeared upon the scene, he had more than once unmistakably regretted it. Afterward it was different, of course, and the autumn passed away quite as rapidly as he could wish; but the prospect of a Highland winter was anything but inviting. Nevertheless, acting up to his principle of "what can't be cured must be endured," the Laird of Drumour had made up his mind to be ice-bound; and it was only the stroke of luck mentioned above that induced him to alter his plans.

Self was bound to stand first and foremost in all Captain Irving's calculations; but he was not positively an unnatural father. Though parental solicitude had really little to do with his move southward, he would never have dreamed of leaving Alice in the North alone; and in his choice of town-quarters her comfort and convenience were certainly more studied than his own. He was not a man of half-measures, and, before he decided to winter in London, had sufficient in hand to make petty economies needless. He had no notion of being cabined in furnished apartments, or of testing his digestion by a lodger-*cuisine*. Three of the Drumour household—the cook, butler, and Alice's own maid—accompanied their master to town ; and before the week was out the Irvings were established in one of the daintiest *maisonnettes* in Mayfair—"absolutely thrown away," according to the pathetic house-agent, at twelve guineas a week.

Captain Irving was very consistent in his habits, though they were the reverse of what are usually called "regular." The time of his going to rest was rather uncertain, to be sure ; about two A.M., rather before than after, would have been a fair average. From that time up to noon the outer world, with the exception of his valet, had no cognizance of or communication with him. Punctually, or almost punctually, at that hour he breakfasted in foreign fashion, and was choice in his light wines. Unless she had some exceptional engagement, which rarely happened, he liked Alice to keep him company at the meal. It was not a heavy tax on filial duty, and was about the only one she was called upon to render. Of the rest of the day she was free to dispose according to her pleasure ; and a brougham with a coachman "warranted steady" was at her service to carry her whither she would. No matter what the weather, her father went forth soon after one, and never by any chance put in an appearance again till close on dressing-time. First he drove, or, if the morning was exceptionally fine, sauntered, down to his club at the corner of Pall Mall, where he usually met three or four ancient comrades, who remembered Alec Irving as "devilish good company" when they were all beardless guardsmen together, and were quite willing to chat with him now, in spite of the scandals that had since attached to his name—scandals almost forgotten by this time, even if they didn't come within the social Statute of Limitations. After lounging away an hour or so here, he went about any business he might have on hand, such as a visit to his banker's ; but by three, or thereabouts, he generally found himself opposite Lord Blanchmayne, or some other antagonist of the like caliber, at the picquet-table. Thence he returned straight home, just in time for a leisurely evening toilet. This ceremonial he was never known to pretermit; and whether he dined alone with Alice or in society made no sort of difference either in the process or the result. In the former case he rather lingered than hurried over his repast, and dallied for at least twenty minutes with his coffee and *chasse;* but it was rarely much past ten when he bade his daughter an affectionate good-night and departed to his club again. When they dined in society, which was seldom, the brougham always left him at the Orion, after dropping Alice at home.

It was a strange, lonely life for a woman in the prime of youth and beauty; for, with the exception of a maiden aunt whom she could not endure, and a couple of cousins whom she hardly knew, Alice had no relatives in town; and, from having sojourned so long abroad, her acquaintance scarcely extended beyond the people she had met at Kenlis.

But was it so certain that her life was lonely?

Most parents, however wrapped up in their own pursuits, would have found time to ask themselves that question, if not of others. But Alice had been so used to be left to her own devices, and her father's conscience had so long ago ceased to prick him on that point, that perhaps it was only likely that the existing state of things should seem, to both, the most natural arrangement possible. What turned Captain Irving's meditations into a particular channel on a particular morning it would be very difficult to say. It so happened that he had won largely over-night; but an equally heavy reverse would not have accounted for his being captious, or fretful, or inclined to disturb the peace of his establishment. In this respect he was a model for better men. Possibly some vision had disquieted him. No philosopher, unless his digestion be faultless, can afford to laugh at dreams. Howsoever this might be, it was clear that something was amiss with Irving just now. He was unusually taciturn at breakfast, and sent away one of his favorite dishes almost untasted. If his brow was not precisely stormy, it was certainly overcast. Alice was not a whit alarmed by these unusual demonstrations, but rather curious to know their meaning. At last, glancing up from her *Post*, she asked her father point-blank what he was thinking about.

"I was thinking," he answered, very deliberately, "what a pity it was your mother died so soon."

Alice opened her great eyes in wonder. Truly, to find grapes growing on thorns, or milk flowing in a barren land, would have seemed likelier than a gush of sentiment from such a source.

"Do you really think it a pity?" she said, placidly. "I always fancied poor mamma was saved so much trouble. It must have been a great loss to you at first; but I fancied you had quite got over it."

The satire was quite sufficiently veiled for Irving to have passed it by at any other time; now, he winced perceptibly.

"I wouldn't sneer, if I were you; it don't suit your style of face; besides, there's no point in it, as it happens. It was for your sake, not for mine, that I thought it was a pity. Your mother was not a clever woman; but she would have been about equal to playing duenna; and it seems to me you want one. Now we are on the subject—What are your engagements this afternoon?"

"Nothing tremendous," she answered. "I think of going to see the pictures at the Winter Exhibition, and then I shall pay a duty-visit to Aunt Caroline. She's quite enough of a bore as it is, without making herself out neglected."

"Do you go to the pictures alone?"

"I go alone, certainly; I believe Mr. Ramsay will meet me there. He has a marked catalogue, which will be very useful."

"Very useful, no doubt. Now, when did you see his wife last?"

The dry, semi-judicial tone of these queries puzzled Alice exceedingly, to say the least of it, and her color began to heighten.

"I forget whether it was on Thursday or Friday. What makes you ask?"

"Never mind what makes me ask; but answer me

S

one more question.   When did you see *him* last?   Perhaps your memory won't fail you there."

"I saw him yesterday," she said, with perfect composure.   "It's quite a new idea, papa, your taking so much interest in my visits and visitors: I suppose I ought to feel flattered."

"You may suppose I have some reason for it, at all events.   Alice, listen to me.   I have a suspicion—only a faint suspicion, mind—that there's some fooling afoot between you and Mark Ramsay.   Now, once for all, I won't have it.   There are people who can carry off such things with a high hand, simply by virtue of their position;   but we're not strong enough to muzzle the scandal-mongers, and I don't intend that half the idle tongues in London should be set wagging at our expense. I don't know what they may do in America; but I do know there's no country in Europe where a girl can carry flirtation with a married man beyond a certain point without risking her reputation.   Do you understand me? or shall I speak plainer?"

The girl drew herself up haughtily.   There was a strong family likeness betwixt the two; though in Alice there were outward signs of an energy of existence, of a *vivida vis*, as the Latins have it, and of a quick energy, that could never have belonged to her father; for, from his youth upward, Irving's demeanor had been marked by a listless indifference—not only to things in general, but to the matter actually in hand; and this had told heavily against him in his by-gone *fredaines*.   People would have it that he sinned not from impulse, but of aforethought,—and gave judgment accordingly.   This outward likeness was never so striking as when their faces hardened.

"Yes, I understand you," she said, low and distinctly. "There's no need for plainer speaking.   Married flirtations are utterly unpardonable, unless they are carried on with a purpose.   Conscientious scruples are always to be respected, of course.   I almost wonder, papa, that these didn't develop themselves eighteen months ago, in dear, dull, respectable Darmstadt.   There, surely, if anywhere, one would have thought we ought to have been

careful about the proprieties. Wasn't it rather impru-
dent to give Vladimir Hunyadi the *entrée* to our house
at all sorts of hours? Perhaps I was dreaming when I
heard him talk about the wife he had left behind in
Hungary? That was in the early part of our acquaintance, to be sure; he didn't mention her often afterward.
The poor Magyar! I hope his *gräfin* was not very un-
forgiving when he went back to confess that he was half
ruined."

"He lost his money fairly," Irving said, without lifting his eyes; "and he was an honest, hot-headed fool;
not a cool, pitiless devil, like this last friend of yours. I
have heard enough about him, if you haven't."

Her laugh was very musical, but not altogether pleasant to hear.

"Lost his money fairly; not a doubt of that: just as
fairly as he would have lost his life, if he had stood opposite you *à la barrière*. It's only just; skill should correct luck, you know. But, papa, that idea about 'this
last friend of mine' is quite *impayable* Perhaps it was
I who proposed that we should accept the first invitation
from Kenlis, and proposed going there each night afterward, and started the idea of our wintering in town instead of at Drumour? It's very odd. I have been
laboring under the delusion it was just the other way. I
suppose you have heard all those dreadful stories about
Mr. Ramsay since you came to town, and they will con-
tinue to torment you till—till next August, let us say;
and you have begun to ponder over them since you found
a better match for you at picquet. Confess, now: isn't
it so?"

It was long since Irving had been so nearly on the
verge of a vulgar outbreak of anger. His face grew
actually paler in the effort he made to repress it.

"Insolence isn't argument, you'll find; and, whether
you comprehend them or not, you'll have to obey
orders."

She answered gently, almost humbly; yet there was
no submission in her eyes.

"I don't mean to be insolent, or rebellious either; but,
papa, before you give your orders, wouldn't it be well we

should understand each other?   Surely it's too soon—or too late—for *us* to quarrel. Have you forgotten the compact we made just a week after I came of age, when I signed away all—it was little enough, Heaven knows—that I had power over? It was agreed then that I should be absolute mistress of my own actions thenceforth, and that I might spend my allowance and my time exactly as it seemed to me good.   I didn't ask for any thanks then, because I considered that I got an equivalent for what I gave.   I bought my freedom with a price ; and it's too much to expect me not to use my own, or to abandon it so soon."

Her father's face had grown darker and darker.

"And do you expect me to sit smiling and blinking, while you walk straight to your shame? Curse your compacts! They wouldn't hoodwink a county bench or a Blankshire jury. Now, Alice, you ought to know me by.this time.   I'm not given to bluster.   I'll watch you both narrowly, and, if I have reason to believe that Mark Ramsay means foul play—whether you are his accomplice or not—I'll give him no more chance than I would a mad dog at large.   Now you can act as you please."

Her courage was beyond that which commonly falls to the lot of woman; and in presence of physical or purely personal danger, many of the ruder sex might have envied her name; but she grew a coward now, all in a moment. Yes, she knew her father only too well: she knew that in those delicate blue veins flowed the bitter Irving blood, which even within her memory, to say nothing of worse deeds in the aforetime, had broken out to deadly effect. She knew that when he had once passed the bounds of cool calculation, neither fear of God nor of man would turn him back from the work whereto his hand was set. It had always been so—in anger as in love—and would be so again. But she was too wise to show one sign of the terror that was mastering her; and she looked straight into her father's eyes—lifted now—smiling.

"We're getting quite melodramatic. What a pity we have no audience! But that tragic pose was unnecessary, papa. So you actually gave me credit for misplaced affection, and unfortunate attachment, and all that sort of thing? How very nice of you! Now, isn't it barely possible that I might flirt for a purpose of my own instead of a purpose of yours?"

"I don't see what you're driving at," he muttered, in a much more placable tone, though.

"Have you ever considered the position in which I should be placed at your death? I have. To be sure, I'm the person most interested in the matter I should be simply penniless—that's all: for every acre of Drumour is entailed; and, if the cards ran ever so luckily, you would never leave a large balance at your banker's. Wouldn't it be a great satisfaction to you in your last moments, papa, if you left me established for life at Kenlis Castle? You needn't lift your eyebrows so contemptuously: more improbable things have come to pass. Mark Ramsay would marry me to-morrow, if anything happened to his wife; and I doubt if hers is a good life— certainly not as good as mine."

Irving was fairly dazzled for the moment by the light that broke in upon him. He rose to his feet with a long, low whistle, and then said softly to himself,—

"The devil!"

It was much as if a devout Catholic had crossed himself, invoking his patron saint—only different people have different ways of expressing surprise.

"And in the mean time—if there is a mean time"—he said, after a pause—"what do you mean to do?"

"I mean to take very good care of myself," she answered, with a sauciness that became her infinitely,— "just as I have done for the last seven years. Don't you think I am still capable of it?"

The father looked down upon the daughter with a benignity beautiful to behold—such as might light up the countenance of a pious parent gathering the first-fruits of good seed sown in early days.

"Yes; I really think you can be trusted."

And he dropped a kiss of peace lightly on her forehead.

"Well, now you're sensible again," Alice remarked, "I don't mind confiding to you that Mr. Alsager is to be there too this afternoon. There's safety in numbers; and if he's not a very efficient chaperon, he can point out what I ought to admire."

Her father's good humor was not to be ruffled again.

"You little plague, why couldn't you say as much at first? You'd have had your lecture some day or another, so it don't much matter. Well, be prudent, and don't give the dowagers a chance. You are too handsome to be let off easily."

Irving went forth in unusually high spirits that day. He had done with moral scruples long ago. But the talons hid in the velvet paws would have sprung out none the less sharply to punish a taint of Alice's good name. Making a jest of most things that good men believe in, he was specially apt to mock at the virtue of womankind; but in this one woman's power to walk unscathed among snares and pitfalls he had implicit belief. He was right—so far.

In those last two syllables is struck the key-note of many threnodies. If the sad old parable of the pitcher carried once too often to the well applies sometimes to those who never sleep or wake without whispering, "Lead us not into temptation," how much more nearly ought it to touch those who, save for certain forms of outward observance, might as well have been born in Heathenesse! Whether the vessel be wrought of coarse delft, or tawdry china, or porcelain more precious than the ancient Myrrhine ware, matters but little, when there remains naught thereof but a heap of shards, unworthy a beggar's gathering.

CHAPTER XXXI.

DAYS, weeks, and months passed on, bringing little outward change to any of the chief actors of this story. The estrangement between Ramsay and his wife continued; and at last even the world began to remark that those two were never, by any chance, seen together, except at some great dinner-party, or other similar ceremonial.

They were established long ago in a furnished house, "adapted," to quote the advertisement, "to the most luxurious requirements." But the great reception-rooms were never used; for Mrs. Ramsay's excuse of "not feeling strong enough to entertain on a large scale" was no false plea; and Mark was not likely to suggest any arrangement that would often have necessitated his presence at home. Blanche never complained, or in any wise took her husband to task for his neglect; but beyond a certain point she would not dissemble. Long before the winter was over, she had ceased to affect any anxiety to keep up an intimacy with the Irvings. She received them at her own house occasionally, and dined at theirs in return in due course; and on these occasions—or the still rarer ones when they met on neutral ground—her manner was courteous, without a spark of cordiality. Once, and once only, she had expressed herself plainly on this subject. It happened thus:

There was a private concert to be given, at which, besides other attractions, a famous cantatrice from La Scala was to appear for the first time in England. For one reason or another, invitations were exceedingly difficult to obtain; and even to Mrs. Ramsay, popular as she was, only two were vouchsafed. By a very rare chance, Mark was lunching at home when these arrived.

"The second one's in blank, I see," he observed, after glancing at the card. "How do you mean to fill it up,

Blanche?　It would be very good-natured of you if you were to take Alice."

Even before they left Kenlis he had begun to speak of her thus.

"Perhaps so," his wife answered, composedly; "but I don't feel particularly good-natured this morning; and Alice has so many opportunities of amusement of one sort or another, from what I hear, that I think she can afford to wait.　Besides, I've settled to take Ida Jocelyn, if I take any one."

An evil change came over Ramsay's face.　It only lasted for a second, and its precise expression could hardly have been defined.　It was not so much anger as surprise, with perhaps a little aversion, and a tinge of vexation, as though he had whispered to himself,—

"*Tu me lo pagherai.*"

But this was what he said aloud, and he said it smiling:—

"Of course you'll do exactly as you please; mine was the merest suggestion.　You can't accuse me of interfering with your arrangements.　But I think you're more good-natured than you take credit for, or you wouldn't have gratified Mrs. Jocelyn.　Next to her husband, she's quite the greatest bore of our acquaintance."

He had risen as he spoke, and was sauntering out of the room when Blanche called him back.

"Wait one moment, Mark: I have never accused you of interfering, and you must do me the same justice.　It's just as well that you should understand that, if I hadn't arranged to take Ida Jocelyn, I should not have taken Alice Irving.　And if at any time she should want a chaperon, she must not reckon on me.　My reason is very simple: I don't like her."

There was nothing in his face now but lazy astonishment.

"Is it possible?　I fancied you got on capitally together.　Now, I rather like her, as it happens. If we ever have a discussion, Blanche, I hope it won't arise from simple variety of taste.　'May difference of opinion'—I forget the rest of the toast or sentiment; but it's much to the same purpose.　You needn't stand too much on the defensive. I don't think there's much fear in that quarter of your being impressed into chaperon-service."

And so Mark effected an orderly and leisurely retreat—having certainly not got the worst of the light skirmish, though Blanche stood on the vantage-ground of one who, having been asked to grant a favor, has declined for good and sufficient cause. A bolder and wiser matron would doubtless have swooped down on the opportunity for the which she had watched all the time she was circling so tranquilly. But this gentle bird had never stooped on anything rougher than a rose-branch—and then with no direr intent than resting there awhile, or, at the very worst, pecking at a petal. If she had acted up to a stern sense of duty, would it have fared better with her then or thereafter? For myself, I doubt it. At any rate, the opening—such as it was—was lost, and did not recur again for many a day.

The Ramsays spent their Christmas at Brancepeth Castle: it was an engagement of some standing, and Mark could not avoid it with any good grace; nor, indeed, did he attempt to do so. La Reine, though she had many guests to attend to, found time to watch both husband and wife narrowly on the first evening of their stay. Her bright eyes grew misty once or twice, and her honest heart burned hotly within her, as she saw how fearfully those few weeks spent in town had told on the one, and how utterly indifferent the other was to the change. It was with great difficulty that she kept her anger in check when her remark, "How very pale and ill Blanche is looking!" was answered by, "Do you really think so? I hadn't noticed it. A little tired with the journey, perhaps."

"Journey!" That was all she said; but the word was like a missile, and she fluttered her fan till the sticks cracked again. If it had been in the old times, when buffets were dealt by soft no less than by horny hands, I think there would have lighted on somebody's cheek, just then, rather a stinging salute.

Blanche herself owned that she felt weaker and duller lately; but beyond this she could not be brought to confession, and Lady Laura had not the heart to press her

"It's no good talking over one's ailments, I know," she said, "so we'll drop the subject altogether; and, while you're here, suppose you've nothing whatever the matter with you.   You sha'n't have a moment's worry, if I can help it; and I mean to send you away in as rude health as it's in your nature to be—as if you could be rude, if you tried."

These sanguine expectations were not exactly realized; but Blanche's state both of body and mind was doubt-less improved by the fortnight's respite.   For that brief space she need not disquiet herself about Mark's goings out and comings in.   There was truce to the jealousies and disappointments, not the less keenly felt because they recurred so incessantly; and she even fancied—it might have been only fancy, poor thing—that there was more of kindness in his manner.   It was the palest image, at best, of the old devotion; but is not even a shadow a relief on a dead, blank wall?

Mark had never been very enthusiastic about field-sports: however, he took to them now with a will, and was seldom to be found within-doors when anything was to be done afield with a gun or in saddle.   But twice or thrice he lounged into his wife's apartment half an hour before dressing-time, and chatted to her about the day's performance.   La Reine always knew when this had happened, by Blanche's appearance when she came down to dinner; and a comparative stranger remarked, on one of these occasions, "What a very variable face it is!   It looked so wan and worn at luncheon, and to-night she's girlishly pretty."   But old Marlshire acquaintances shook their heads as they confided to each other "that they had always thought Mrs. Ramsay delicate.   That clear white complexion often went with heart-disease; and she seemed so strangely out of spirits, too."

One day, when the hounds met within easy distance, Blanche was driven to the meet by her hostess.   Scyton of Warleigh was the master now; and, as soon as the phaeton appeared, he ranged up alongside to exchange greetings with its occupants.

"Why, almost the last time I saw you out," he said to Blanche—"the very last, I do believe—was that famous

Pinkerton day, when Ranksborough and Vane had their swimming-match. Do you remember it, Mrs. Ramsay?"

Her answer was not very distinct, and she drew down her veil, as Seyton turned away, to hide some foolish tears. Yes, she remembered it too well—how, just to pass the time, she coquetted with Leo Armitage, and provoked Vereker Vane's jealous wrath; and how—a little frightened, but scarcely repentant—she had watched him ride down headlong on the Swarle. Was it possible that she was the same Blanche Ellerslie who had played at cup-and-ball with men's hearts, feeling just an idle interest in the game, and a certain pride in her own skill? Something of this, though not in so many words, she hinted to her companion. That the comparison had struck La Reine too was evident, though she endeavored to answer jestingly:—

"We have all grown older, and sadder, and wiser, of course. Why, the Sabreur himself has got almost sober and staid; and as for Leo Armitage, it was only the other day I heard he was going to marry an alderman's daughter with a fathomless *cassette. On s'arrangera!* That's all."

"Don't you think it's possible to grow sadder without growing wiser?" Blanche asked.

Lady Laura did not seem inclined to discuss metaphysics; for, instead of answering, she dropped her hand to her ponies, which were beginning to fidget, and followed in the wake of the crowd toward the cover, into which the hounds had just been thrown.

It was a coffee-house sort of a day, with a bad scent and short-running foxes, but excellently well suited for hunting on wheels. Before lunch-time Mrs. Ramsay looked so tired and pale that La Reine turned back and made the best of her way home. That same afternoon— almost for the first time in her life—Blanche had something unpleasantly like a fainting-fit. She rallied, however, quickly, and made light of it to Mark when he came to inquire after her on his return: indeed, throughout the evening she seemed in rather better spirits than usual

One way or another, the fortnight passed only too

quickly; but, when it was over, Blanche would not hear of prolonging their visit. She knew that her choice lay betwixt the company of her husband and letting him return to town alone, and did not hesitate. And so began again for her the same wearing round of restless nights and unquiet days.

"I never," said a sage matron in my hearing awhile ago, when the griefs of a mutual acquaintance were being discussed—"I never pity any one who is thoroughly inconsistent." If you indorse this opinion—which, by-the-by, I did not venture at the time to controvert—you will henceforth have little compassion to spare for Blanche Ramsay in her troubles.

She had spoken, you may remember, with tolerable plainness concerning Alice Irving, and—making every allowance for female mutability—it was scarce to be expected that, within a month, she would entreat that young person to sojourn as a guest beneath her roof. Under ordinary circumstances, the invitation would have been the most natural conceivable.

Captain Irving was one of those inscrutable people who, having little or no ostensible business to occupy them, are constantly being summoned away on urgent private affairs. Early in the spring it appeared that his presence was needed at Paris—"for a week or ten days," he said, vaguely; but it was evident that the term of absence would be elastic. While it lasted, Alice must either keep house alone, or be committed to the guardianship of the aunt Caroline whom she disliked so cordially. That disinterested regard for the young lady's comfort or convenience did not prompt Mrs. Ramsay's strange offer —it was perfectly voluntary, remember; for Mark never hinted at such an idea—may fairly be assumed. The real reason lay somewhat deep below the surface.

The instances are manifold, both in new and old times, of those who have been so goaded and worked upon by the consciousness of being menaced by a vague danger or followed by an unseen foe, that, instead of seeking any longer to escape, they have turned in their tracks and gone to meet the mischief; and this has been the desperation of cowardice, moral or physical, as a rule. Perhaps

you have read that rattling ballad—one of Thornbury's,
if I mistake not—"The Cavalier's Ride:"

> " Tramp, tramp, came on the heavy roan,
>   Pat, pat, the mettled gray;.
> Five miles of down to Salisbury town,
>   And just an hour to day."

The godless gallant had the heels of the Roundheads,
and might have made good his escape without striking a
blow; but, says he,—

> " They pressed me hard, and my blood grew hot;
>   So I made me ready to turn,
> Just where whitest grew the May,
>   Where thickest grew the fern."

It was a merry bout, be sure—none the less merry that
" chestnut Kate" carried her master safe and sound into
Salisbury after all. But the sport is not quite so rare
when the hunted creature comes to bay, not in anger or
dare-devilry, but because the sharp swift agony that will
end all seems easier to endure than the sickness of doubt
and fear.

The illustration may seem strangely inapplicable to
such "genteel comedy" as this has been hitherto: nevertheless, the parallel does not altogether fail. That there
was a danger, and an enemy to boot, in the background,
Blanche was right well aware. She had never yet questioned her husband as to where a single hour of his long
absences was spent; but, if she had so questioned him,
and he had answered truly, perhaps she would have been
brought not much nearer the mark than she was brought
by her own fancy. She was sufficiently acquainted with
Captain Irving's habits to be certain that during the
afternoon Alice might almost reckon on going whither she
would, or receiving whom she would; but in that " almost" there was a slight safeguard—miserably slight, to
be sure; yet the idea of its being removed was, to Blanche,
simply intolerable. One thing must be clearly borne in
mind : Mrs. Ramsay had never admitted to herself the
possibility of there being actual guilt in her husband's
intimacy with Miss Irving. Though she had lived from

her girlhood upward in an atmosphere of coquetry, and, more or less, iu a fast set, she had never been brought into contact with anything much worse than folly; and her suspicions traveled more slowly than those of the average of prudes. She thought that Alice was daily and hourly stealing from her larger and larger portions of Mark's love, or of the sentiment—no matter what— which she, Blanche, had been too glad to accept in Love's stead. This was all; and it was more than enough to make her hate the beautiful marauder with all the bitterness of which her nature was capable. She had no brain for plotting or counterplotting; but, with a certain shrewdness of reasoning, she told herself that, as her guest, Alice would be less a free agent than under her own father's roof in her father's absence. Mark—however little he might respect his moral obligations—had a decided regard for his social ones, and was likely to be more guarded in his demeanor under his own roof than under any other that could be named. It is not likely that any one of these reasons will exempt our unlucky heroine from the charge of inconsistency above mentioned; but perhaps they may prevent this her act and deed from being set down to mere insane vagary.

The surprise that Alice could not conceal when the invitation came seemed not to be purely pleasurable; indeed, she pouted her lip at first, as if the horizon thus opened to her was not all rose-color. She had not a shadow of excuse for declining it; Captain Irving would not have listened for one moment to such a thing. It was the very arrangement for which he would have schemed; and he could hardly believe in such good luck as that his opponent—for in this light he had begun to consider Mrs. Ramsay of late—should play directly into his hand. It was one of his favorite maxims that it mattered little what a husband or wife did, so that the other party to the marriage-contract took no overt exception to the proceedings.

"I shall go to Paris now with a quiet conscience," he said to his daughter, as if he and his conscience hadn't come to terms a quarter of a century ago; and she answered,—

"Well, there's some comfort in that, at all events," with equal gravity.

Those two were so used to their masks that, even when alone, they did not often lay them aside.

Mark heard of the arrangement with much outward indifference.

"It was very benevolent of you," he remarked to his wife. "I suppose you've thought better of what you said the other day. You needn't take her out more than you like, you know, particularly if it tires you."

Blanche was really glad that he did not thank her. She felt she deserved thanks so little, that she could nardly have listened to them without a disclaimer.

CHAPTER XXXII

A WILD spring morning, with promise of worse weather yet in the keen, sharp wind-gusts and fierce rain-swirls,— a morning utterly abominable to those who are forced, on their own or on others' business, to be abroad, yet not without its merits to such as are permitted

"partem solido demere de die"

at their own fireside, in idleness or in pretense at industry. So thought Vere Alsager, as—after dallying with a late breakfast, and skimming two or three papers—he lounged in the same chair that he occupied on the eve of Blanche's marriage, watching the smoke curl from his pipe with half-shut eyes, while he debated whether he was equal to the labor of putting a few finishing touches to a crayon-sketch, to be matured some day into an oil-painting, if the Fates pleased.

A ring at the outer bell made him turn his head, murmuring, "A dun, I suppose: he almost deserves to be paid for venturing out such weather; but his pluck is likely to be its own reward, I'm afraid. I hope he won't give me the trouble of explaining so much to him."

However, when the door opened, it was no commercial face that appeared. Vere nodded lazily to the new-comer.

"Why, Mark, what brings you out so early? You haven't become a man of business all of a sudden, have you? and you wouldn't have come far out of your way simply for the pleasure of my valuable society."

"I don't know about that," the other answered, as he settled himself into another arm-chair. "You are as good company as anybody else when you take the trouble to talk ; and almost any company in such infernal weather is better than one's own, I suppose. I had something to say to you, though, when I came out,—if I could only remember what it was."

"Don't hurry yourself," the other said, rather dryly: "it will come, I dare say."

And for at least five minutes the two smoked on in silence.

"What are you going to do this afternoon?" Mark asked, at last.

"Well, I hardly know. It's as likely as not that I sha'n't stir out at all till after dark. I have rather a drawing fit on me—at least, it was developing itself when you rang. It's a bad light, to be sure; but that don't matter so much for crayon."

Ramsay bent his brows. "Not going out till dark? That's unlucky."

"Why unlucky?" Vere inquired. "Do you want me to go anywhere particular? Well, the symptoms of industry are not very pronounced. I dare say I can manage it."

"I didn't want you to go anywhere particular," the other answered ; "but I wanted you to be anywhere but here for about a couple of hours this afternoon. I promised to bring some one to look at the carving, and the things I brought from Italy, and all the rest of it."

Still with his eyes half shut, Alsager smoked on.

"Miss Irving, of course," he said, after a moment or two. "Ah! I shouldn't wonder if she's a pretty good judge of Italian art; and you are perfectly well qualified to play the *cicerone*. But whether I'm exactly fitted for the part you want me to play, is another question."

Mark appeared to think the first suggestion not worth answering; the inference was too self-evident; but to the second he was forced to reply.

"What are you dreaming about, Vere? I never asked you to play any part, as you call it. I promised to show Alice my old quarters, and I thought it would be pleasanter *tête-à-tête* than *entière*. I couldn't guess you would be so wedded to your chimney-corner on this particular day."

Alsager's eyes were opened now, and he faced half round on the speaker. "They are your quarters still. Don't suppose I dispute for a moment your right to go in and out and dispose of them as you please; but as for disposing of me—— Look here, Mark; we'll play with cards on the table. I'll go out this afternoon; for of course I have no more right to keep you out of these rooms than to take up your library at Kenlis Castle. It's as well we should understand each other for the future. It's clear you've been counting on me to help you in this affair; and last year you would not have been far out in your reckoning; but I'm not so sure about it now. You are going to remind me of what passed here the night before you were married. You needn't. I remember it all perfectly well—better than you do, perhaps. When I fancied it was impossible you'd ever want these chambers again, you said, 'Highly improbable, certainly; but as for impossible, it's too big a word for my dictionary.' It was a fair warning, I don't deny, and I don't pretend to be taken by surprise now, or that I have not been expecting this—something like this—for weeks past; but I don't seem to care about it a bit the better for that."

Ramsay returned the steady gaze with interest.

"You have scruples, then. I confess I wasn't prepared for this."

"I don't suppose you were," the other retorted, coolly. "It's not a question of scruples, as it happens, but simply of taste,—or of whim, if you like. I dare say there were few pleasanter persons in Troy than Pandarus. Somehow, though, I don't think I should have appreciated him unless I had been in love with Cressida, and I dare say the led-captain's isn't half a bad business when you get used to it : I wasn't broken in young enough, you see. You'll have to look out for some one else to be your house-steward here, Mark. The present man isn't strong enough for the place—that's the long and short of it; and I'll clear out at once, without a month's warning."

Whatever Ramsay may have felt, he certainly kept his temper admirably.

"There's no necessity for heroics," he said, "or for un-savory comparisons, either. I offered you these quarters without condition, and if they'd been any use to you you were just as welcome up to this moment as if you were ready to help me with all your whole heart and soul; and there's no need for you to clear out so suddenly. If I want these chambers, I'll tell you so without the slightest ceremony, you may depend upon it. We needn't make a quarrel of it, unless by your particular desire; but I should like you to answer me one thing—just for curi-osity's sake. We'll suppose that scruples have nothing to do with your squeamishness—you quite misunderstood the help I wanted of you. Never mind that; but I'm certain you are thinking of somebody else besides your-self in all this. Who is it?"

There were few redeeming points in the character of either of those two. Both were endowed almost equally with a certain straightforwardness of speech and action —attributable, probably, to constitutional intrepidity— which saved them from descending to ordinary shifts and subterfuges. Alsager was not a whit disconcerted by the point-blank question, though he pondered for a second or two before he made answer.

"You're quite right: I *am* thinking of some one else —of the only person, perhaps, that is really worth consid-eration. I am thinking of Mrs. Ramsay."

Neither did Mark blench before the *riposte* that would have staggered most men; but his tone—albeit still not provocative—was just a little sneering.

"You do Mrs. Ramsay infinite honor. I dare say, if she knew who was her champion, she would be almost

as much surprised as—her unworthy husband. May I
ask you one more question. Since when have you felt
this vocation to succor the distressed and rescue the innocent?"

Alsager's lip, too, began to curl.

"If you mean by 'the innocent' Alice Irving, you may
make your mind quite easy there. I assure you that I
don't take the faintest interest in her welfare, and I would
not lift my finger to warn her. If you want to know
when I began to pity your wife—to pity her so much that
I will have neither art nor part in working out more sorrow for her—I'll tell you. It was since it became quite
plain to me that she was dying by inches: that's about
two months ago."

A curious expression—or rather a medley of expressions—possessed Mark's face. There was surprise, and
a certain vexation, like that of a man suddenly made
aware that others are cognizant of a secret he would
rather have kept to himself; but Alsager always thought
afterward that there mingled with this a cruel, eager
satisfaction.

"Dying!" he said, almost in a whisper. "You must
be dreaming. Why, I've never heard her complain once;
and I don't believe she's even seen a doctor since we
came to town."

"She's not of the complaining sort," the other answered, with his low laugh; "and I doubt if all the drugs
of the Pharmacy would do her much good, unless they
made her sleep; but I believe that others have seen it
besides me, and that she knows it herself. See, now,
Mark; I'm not given to whining, and it sounds too absurd
for me to be preaching to you; but I do think its d——d
hard on her that she should not have had one year's
grace before she was knocked out of time. You wanted
an ornament for your table: that was all right enough;
but why on earth could not you have picked out one that
would stand careless handling and wouldn't break when
you tossed it aside? Poor little woman! It seems only
yesterday that we were out driving on the hill, and she
asked me if I thought she made you thoroughly happy;
and by way of answer I told her what you had said about

Polycrates' ring. It wasn't a lie then—at least, I suppose it was not."

"And why should it be a lie now?" the other said, doggedly. "You don't suppose I wish the poor little woman—as you call her—any harm? No! It's not come to that yet; though it's quite clear that I made a mistake, and took my leap in the dark just six mouths too soon. We're playing cards on the table, to be sure; but you would read my hand if I didn't show it. I don't mind confessing that I'm fairly bewitched—bewitched as I've never been since I was twenty. Alice is not the least like any woman I have ever met. She seems perfectly reckless at times, and yet I don't believe that any man living would tempt her to go an inch over the line she has drawn. Perhaps that's why she can make me do pretty well as she likes already. I don't know what will come of it "

"Your being in a hurry was not the only mistake," Alsager observed. "According to your own account, you thought of marriage in the first instance as a political necessity. You had much better have kept it on that footing. When private feelings are mixed up with reasons of state, there's certain to be a complication. Why the devil did you take so much trouble to win your wife's heart? That you did take the trouble, is quite clear; for she's not one of the gushing creatures that would give theirs to the first comer. If you had taken things coolly from the first, I dare say she'd have accepted mutual freedom quite pleasantly: it's impossible now. You don't know what will come of it; neither do I. I believe it's a presentiment, as much as anything else, that makes me so loath to meddle with the whole business. Do you remember, when we first talked about her, my wondering whether that girl had ever been the heroine of a sensation story? She will be yet; and of a bitter, bad one, too."

On a certain summer afternoon, long ago,—it was in old Oxford days,—I was riding, with two others, along the skirts of Wychwood Forest—not dis-forested then—and we came suddenly on a gypsy encampment. The Zingara who accosted us in passing was no withered beldame, but a "Nut-brown Maid"—a noted beauty, as we afterward heard, among the Romany Rye. None of us had the heart to refuse the piece of crossing-silver, and our fortunes were told, one by one. Two of us were prophesied unto in terms little varying from the usual trade jargon, and promised our fair ladies and warned against our "dark" rivals, in due course: it is unnecessary to say that both promise and warning impressed us infinitely at the time, and have profited us materially since. But over the third hand the Sibyl pondered much more attentively. It may be that her seeming reluctance to speak was a mere trick of her craft; but I did not suspect this at the time, and I suspect it still less now. She must have been a rare natural actress. if the wistful—almost pitiful—look in her eyes was simulated; and her voice too seemed to have lost much of the traditional whine.

"My pretty gentleman,"—he was a very pretty gentleman in those days, poor fellow,—"you mustn't be angry with the poor gypsy if she talks as the Fates bid her; and wiser than me makes mistakes sometimes—though not so often as you think. You'll have your heart's wish often, and you'll make others' hearts ache, for sure: and, for all you are free-handed, you'll never want for silver or for gold. But, my pretty gentleman, the line of life's crossed deep and early—just for all the world like mine is; and them that have that cross don't often wear gray hairs or die in their beds. You won't slight the poor gypsy's warning because she can't speak to the place nor the hour. You have a bold spirit of your own, a strong hand, and a sharp eye; but, for all that, don't ye ride too far nor too fast."

She fell back, and let us pass, without another word; and I, looking into Nigel Kenward's face, saw a sick change come over it—though when we were out of the gypsy's hearing he laughed out loud.

"I got my money's worth, didn't I?" he said, in his gay, rollicking way—"and a little more than I bargained for. Devilish odd things are coincidences. She could not have guessed that I've dreamt, at least twice every year since I can remember, that I had broken my neck in a 'crumpler.' If her words come true, and either of you fellows meet her afterward, stand her a sovereign for my sake—she deserves it for the shot."

Now, this man was absolutely ignorant of the meaning of fear. In those days not a few of us rode with more courage than judgment; but his dreams did not prevent him from astonishing the rashest of us at times, when he was getting a beaten horse over a stiff country. When his countenance changed, as I have described, it had certainly nothing to do with nerves; but rather it was the natural surprise of one who hears a feeling, hitherto confined to his own breast, suddenly interpreted aloud.

The gypsy's prophecy was fulfilled almost to the letter —for assuredly more hearts than one were set aching when five years later we read in the *Homeward Mail* that Nigel Kenward had been picked up stone dead after a terrible fall into a nullah.

The present was a somewhat parallel case. You may remember that, *insouciant* fatalist as he was, Mark Ramsay had long been haunted by an impression that retributive justice would one day, in some shape or other, overtake him. This had never diverted him a hair's-breadth from any one of his purposes; nor was it likely to do so now. Nevertheless, he scarcely repressed a start when Alsager's random words set the chords of that somber fancy vibrating. He answered in a very grave, gentle voice, without a symptom of resentment at the other's plain speaking.

"It's more than likely you're right; but it's too late to draw back now—and I wouldn't if I could. We must 'dree our weird,' as the auld wives say; but I don't wonder at your wishing to stand aloof, or blame you either; and I don't bear malice for what you've said to-day. You needn't trouble yourself to go out this afternoon, Vere. *On s'arrangera.* Good-by for the present: you can meet Mrs. Ramsay with a clear conscience, at all events."

"A clear conscience," Alsager mused, rather discontentedly, when he was alone. "I wasn't aware that I had a conscience till quite lately; and I don't know that I'm particularly enchanted by the discovery. I wonder if the weather has anything to do with these sudden accesses of virtue? I suppose I shall be found preaching at street-corners next—or lecturing Young Men's Association on Continence. There's no knowing what one may come to in his old age. I've probably done rather more harm than good this morning : that's a satisfactory reflection. Saint Mark behaved better than I expected, certainly ; though there was a quiet look in his eyes when I talked about his wife's dying. Dying? So she is dying. There's not a doubt about it. I'm by no means sure it isn't the best thing that can happen to her. On the whole, I think, I'd better look out for fresh quarters. It's a bore, too, for these suit me down to the ground ; but I can't stand living even rent-free on sufferance, or— what's nearer the truth—on false pretenses."

CHAPTER XXXIII.

It is spring again—not spring only by the calendar, but spring in real earnest, with a broad blue in the sky, and westerly softness in the wind. There is shade now under the trees lining the Row ; and the shade is not unwelcome for an hour before, and after, noon. All the world—according to the Court Newsman's definition of the term—is settled in town for the season, and in the long catalogue might be found almost every name that has hitherto figured in this story.

Major Gauntlet and his fellows in commission were *perfuncti officio* at last, and had laid before the War Office the grapes gathered in Canaan. On the very night of his arrival Oswald found himself—as you may suppose—in the smoking-room of the Bellona.

In the pre-Stephensonian era, when cosy hostelries were to be found all along the King's Highway, there lived an eccentric noble who was so fond of sojourning in such places that, when traveling home to the seat of his ancestors, he invariably slept at an inn within three leagues of his own park-gate. "They are always glad to see me—there," he used to say.

Now, without taking quite such a melancholy view of things, it may fairly be presumed that a man of average popularity, returning after a prolonged absence, is likely to meet with quite as warm a welcome at his club as he can reckon on elsewhere. Gauntlet's popularity was much above the average. He was rather a "Don" in some respects, it is true, and possessed a knack of utterly ignoring the opinion, if not the presence, of confident subalterns—which was disconcerting, to say the least of it; but he had a frank, free way with him which prevented even the repressed person from taking more than momentary umbrage; and, if he did not carry his honors very meekly, his self-assertion never trenched upon the swagger. So there was a kind of stir in the smoking-room when his tawny mustache came floating through its inner doorway; and he had so many greetings to answer that it was a good half-hour before he got into his favorite corner with a quartette of familiars.

"Well, what's the last news?" Oswald inquired, as soon as they were thoroughly settled. "Meriton, suppose you give a short summary for the benefit of the stranger."

The man he addressed was a grizzled old staff-surgeon —slow, but untiring, of speech—who was always a safe draw for the latest intelligence.

"There's nothing to epitomize," he answered, after a little consideration, "or next to nothing. The land is barren, or else it's a backward season. I suppose you've heard that Helvellyn went over the Liverpool—he's been going any time these six months—and Carlyon's wife has bolted with a Frenchman: *she's* been going any time these six years. I don't believe there's anything else that you won't have read in *Galignani;* but everybody you know is in town: so you'll be well posted before long. By-the-by, I saw a very old friend of yours only yesterday—Mrs. Ramsay."

A huge puff of smoke almost hid Oswald Gauntlet's face, as he replied,—

"You saw Mrs. Ramsay yesterday? And how was she looking?"

"Looking devilish ill," was the reply. "Gad! I

almost doubt if you would recognize her. If her carriage
had been on the move, instead of in a lock, and if I
hadn't remembered the horses, I think I should have
passed her—and I wouldn't have done that on any account; I've known her since she was a child, too; and
what a pretty child she was!—and what a pretty woman,
too, for the matter of that! You'd hardly give her credit
for it now."

The three others who sat listening were rough and ready
soldiers, not endowed with any special tact or delicacy; but
each and every one of them chose to look anywhere but into
Gauntlet's face just then. Yet his voice was quite steady.

"I am very sorry for this. Do you think she is as ill
as she looks?"

"Worse," Meriton answered, sententiously. "The
voice is quite as much a symptom as the pulse, sometimes. There was never much of a ring in hers; but I
never heard it weak and hollow till yesterday. That's a
rank bad sign. I'd half a mind to ask her if she'd let me
call and look after her, just for old acquaintance' sake. I
prescribed for her when she was a baby; but somehow
I boggled the words out. The fact was, I felt sure that
neither I nor all the doctors in London would do her
much good. It's mind more than body that's ailing;
unless I'm much mistaken. That's how it began, at all
events; and these atrophies—we're bound to call it by
a professional name—beat the best of us."

"What makes you think so?"

The other lowered his voice a little, though with the
buzz of talk going on all round he was not likely to be
overheard.

"Well, I only speak on conjecture. I don't think that
she made a wise choice in her second husband. Nobody
ever supposed she was in love with poor old Ellerslie;
but if she was not happy it wasn't his fault, God knows;
and I believe she was happy, in a quiet sort of way.
Now, if all tales be true—they're only vague rumors, as
yet—she does love this one, and gets very little thanks
for it."

We need not inquire too curiously into the meaning of
the two short syllables that were scarcely smothered in

Oswald Gauntlet's ponderous mustache; but I fear they were set down broad and black by a certain Recorder; and I fear, moreover, that each of the four listeners said "amen" to the evil litany.

That the spirit of partisanship should have shown itself so strongly in a place where, if conjugal differences were ever discussed, the sympathy would generally be found on the marital side, will not appear so wonderful when we remember that Blanche's surroundings, almost literally from her cradle up to very lately, had been more or less military. Her father and her husband, though both martinets in matters of discipline, were well liked by their comrades and subalterns; and in both homes her gentle and graceful influence had been appreciated—somewhat too thoroughly appreciated, occasionally—by all those who came to eat or to drink or to flirt there. But, if those honest fellows carried away a heart-ache, they took the fault, rightly or wrongly, to themselves, and bore no malice to the fair cause thereof in after-days. Even Harry Armar, you will remember, when he lay a-dying, said, "God bless her." Truly, I think that if the present question had come on for judgment before a jury, packed at random, out of the Bellona, it would have gone somewhat hard with Mark Ramsay.

"Yes, it's a hard case," Meriton went on, without noticing the savage interjection; "cruelly hard, if it is as I fear. I don't know much about these things; for I haven't got tired of my own wife yet, and it's close upon our 'silver wedding.' But I should have thought that a man ever so *blasé* and bad might have lived with that nice little thing for just one year without wearying of her—and showing it. There—it don't bear talking of. Let's change the subject."

Gauntlet seemed to be of the same opinion; for he made no effort to prolong the topic, and the chat thenceforth became general; but when Meriton, who kept regular hours, rose to go, Oswald rose also.

"I'll walk with you," he said. "You are in my line home, and I feel sleepy after my long journey." When they were in the street, Oswald put his arm into his companion's and slackened his pace into a saunter.

"Meriton," he said, and his voice was not quite so steady now,—"you and I have known one another for a good number of years, and it isn't likely I should flatter you at this time of day; but there are one or two points —not professional, mind—on which I'd rather take your opinion than that of any lawyer or parson. I want to ask you a couple of questions now. The first is, Have any of those vague reports that you spoke about coupled Mark Ramsay's name with any woman's except his wife?"

"It's really as I said," the other answered. "There has been no definite scandal; but they are very intimate with some Irvings—country neighbors, I believe. Indeed, the daughter was actually staying with the Ramsays a little while ago, if she's not there still; and that same daughter is remarkably handsome—quite dangerously so—there's no doubt about it. But it's hardly charitable to jump at conclusions."

"Charitable!" the other retorted, savagely. "We needn't trouble ourselves about charity when we're discussing Mark Ramsay. Well, you have answered me one question. Now answer me another. Look here, doctor: you know pretty well how it has been with Blanche and me. You know, or ought to know, that I would have tried to make her my wife long ago if I hadn't been next door to a beggar. I don't like to be a pensioner, even upon her. Whether she would ever have said 'yes' is another matter : I never asked her. But there's something perhaps you don't know. I'm not a saint, and I'm not half fit to die, as I ought to be; but if I'd only got an hour to live, there's not a word that I ever spoke to her I'd wish unsaid—that's true, before God. But I don't know how long that would last if I saw her often—as you saw her yesterday. And so I am come to my second question. Do you advise me to go and call there, or not?"

In cases of conscience, John Meriton, if not an exceeding wise, was a very upright, judge; and, whether he had to decide for himself or for others, he laid down the law according to his light, without fear or favor. He pondered awhile now before he answered; and, when he did so, it was hesitatingly.

" Yes; I think if I were you I should call. She needs all the strengthening that can be given her, poor thing, and perhaps the sight of a kind, honest face would be a better cordial than any I could prescribe; and yours would be an honest one, Gauntlet,—honest to the end. I am inclined to trust you more than you seem to trust yourself. I don't say that there won't be temptation, and I don't say that many men we call devilish good fellows wouldn't drop to it; but I do say that if I thought you'd ever try to make things worse there—and, bad as they are, they might be worse—I'd never touch your hand again, unless it were to feel your pulse; and then I'd make pretty sure first that you weren't malingering."

" Thanks."

That small word on Oswald's lips meant a good deal. Beyond a " good-night," they exchanged no other.

Les pauvres esprits se rencontrent sometimes as well as the finer ones. There could not possibly be any collusion betwixt the two; and, as they were then a mile apart, even mesmeric affinity of thought could have nothing to do with it. Yet you will observe that Meriton's anticipations coincided curiously with those that Blanche had indulged in when she resolved on sending her note to the Bellona.

The next morning was so soft and sunny that Gauntlet thought it not unlikely he would find Mrs. Ramsay already in the double rank of sitters lining the Row. Though he was not the least apprehensive of a scene, he would somehow have preferred that their first meeting should take place under the public eye. He saw scores of fair familiar faces, but not the one he was in search of; and on more than one of these there was a light of welcome in which many men would have been tempted to bask for awhile. But Oswald was in an ungrateful, not to say ungracious, mood just now, and few of his acquaintance got more from him than a word or two in passing. As he was leaving the Park, after a couple of turns to and fro, he came upon a group on the skirts of the crowd, that, if he had felt no special interest in either of the two persons composing it, would probably have attracted his notice. Indeed, the face and figure of the

lady would have attracted attention, if not admiration, anywhere, and her dress, in a quiet style, was absolutely perfect. Who the lady was you may easily divine, and also who was her cavalier. Gauntlet's glance scarcely rested on the pair for a second; but in that second he amply realized the dangerous beauty of which Meriton had spoken. There was nothing *empressé* in Mark's demeanor as he leaning against the rail immediately behind Miss Irving's chair, dropping a careless remark occasionally; but that very carelessness would, to some people, have conveyed an idea of security; and so Oswald Gauntlet interpreted it. The two men exchanged nods, —they were but very slightly acquainted,—and rather an odd smile flickered on Ramsay's lip as he bent down to whisper something to Alice which made her look up quickly. Oswald guessed at once that he was the subject of the whisper, and partly, too, guessed its import. As you may suppose, his feelings toward the speaker did not grow more charitable.

From the Park to the square where the Ramsays were residing was but a stone's-throw; and he found himself at the door before he had time for further reflection.

When her visitor was announced, Blanche rose up from the couch on which she was lying, with a little, startled cry. As she stood up on her feet, Oswald fancied—it might have been only fancy, of course—that he saw her totter; but there could be no question whether the surprise was an agreeable one or not; for there was a flush of pleasure on her face, such as had not been seen there for many a day. While that flush lasted, she looked so like her old self that Gauntlet was half inclined to laugh at Meriton's dismal forebodings; but when it vanished— and it did so vanish, even while he had hold of her hand —her pallor grew even more remarkable: just as the snow never looks so deathly white as instantly after the Alpengluth has faded.

"I thought you were never coming back," she said, as she sank down wearily on the couch again. "When did you return?"

"Only last night: so you see I have lost no time in finding you out."

The effort that it cost him to speak those few words cheerfully, none but those who have put the like force on themselves would understand; for his big brave heart waxed faint within him, as he looked on the ruin that the last few months had made. No need to ask how it had been wrought: he knew that right well.

"How good of you to come so soon, when you must have so many things to do, and so many people to see! And to come unasked, too—that's best of all."

"Well, perhaps I ought to have waited for an invitation," he said, with a poor attempt at a laugh; "but were two old friends to stand on ceremony? and there's no one I want particularly to see—unless it is at the War Office. I must report myself this afternoon. Never mind my affairs, though: they will keep. I want you to talk about yourself. I am afraid you have not been well lately, from what Meriton told me."

"The dear old doctor! Yes, I saw him yesterday, and I meant to have asked him if he had heard anything of you lately; but he went off in such a hurry that I hadn't time. So he thought that I was looking ill? Well, I can hardly tell you what has been the matter with me. I never was very strong, you know; but I seem to have gone down hill very fast lately, and I don't feel as if it was in me to climb up again."

"Don't be so absurd. You have no business with such ideas at your time of life. Now, I dare say you have had no advice all this time? It's just like you: you never would take common care of yourself."

He spoke almost angrily; but Blanche was not deceived for an instant as to the feeling masked by the roughness of speech.

"It seems like old times when you begin to scold me. No, I confess I have seen no doctor. I felt so perfectly sure it would be waste of time and trouble."

The very echo of Meriton's words! No wonder if they sounded in Gauntlet's ears like the strokes of a funeral bell.

"But you will have advice now,—if it's only because I ask you so very earnestly."

"Don't look so piteous about it," she said, with a faint smile. "You haven't asked a favor from me for such ages that I am bound to grant you this one. There, I'll see any doctor that you like to send here, and I'll promise to do as he bids me. Are you satisfied now?"

He took her hand—it lay as light as a snowflake in his broad brown palm—and pressed it by way of answer.

"Do you mean to give any account of yourself?" Blanche asked, when the silence was becoming awkward. "You must have traveled over half Europe, judging from the time you have been away."

"Over most of it, certainly; but there's very little to tell. You would not care for a lecture on fortification, I suppose? I saw three or four reviews, to be sure,—especially at Berlin and Vienna,—that the poor old general would have reveled in, and that I think would have amused you."

"That was the business part; but I want to hear about the amusements. You don't mean me to infer that it was all work and no play? Is the Viennese waltzing as wonderful as it is reported? You must have appreciated *that*, at all events."

"It is very good, but nothing miraculous, so far as I saw. I can't speak from absolute experience; for—you will hardly believe me, I dare say—I haven't had one single spin of any sort since I saw you last."

"I can hardly believe you," Blanche said, with a gleam of mischief in her eyes. "Fancy you as a wall-flower! Why, in the old times you used to think nothing of going a hundred miles to a ball."

"Ah! but it was in the old times, you see; that makes all the difference. One must draw the line of levity somewhere, and I drew mine when I was elected to the Emeritan. I believe if any member of the club were to be found indulging in a round dance it would be a case for the committee at once."

She looked at him, still with that same faint smile; and once again she read him thoroughly. She guessed quite well what had kept his arm from encircling any woman's waist during all those months, and why it was just possible that Oswald Gauntlet never would breathe partner more. Long as she had known and well as she had liked him, she had never till this moment rightly realized the value of the heart she had put aside—for what? Even now there was not within Blanche Ramsay a spark of what we—who are of earth earthy—call Love. Nevertheless, if she could have followed the first promptings of her own heart, she felt half inclined just then to lay her head down on the brave, broad breast and sob herself to sleep, as she had done when she was a small, spoiled child.

Very absurd, was it not, that she should be moved by so slight a sacrifice?

"Life is real, life is earnest,"

as the poet very properly sings; and thoughts ought not to be wasted on treading of measures or twangling of viols. But we are as God made us and as the world has left us, after all,—not a whit better or wiser or stronger; and, with many of us, even such trifles as these go far to complete the sum of weal or woe.

It is unnecessary to remark that Mrs. Ramsay did not commit herself so ridiculously. On the contrary, she was sensible enough to turn the conversation immediately to less dangerous ground,—such as the well or ill faring of their mutual friends, etc., reserving, as she said, the right of questioning Oswald hereafter as to his sayings and doings abroad. And so the dreaded interview passed off very much as Blanche had sketched it out in her mental programme, without a single embarrassing allusion to her past or present domestic relations,—for Mark's name was never mentioned from first to last; but when Gauntlet rose to depart, she as nearly as possible spoiled all by breaking down.

"You'll come again soon—very soon—won't you?" she said, holding his hand fast. "I am *so* lonely."

A whole chapter of lamentations and complaints would not have been so piteously eloquent as that one sentence. It was, indeed, in terrible earnest—"the cry of the helpless and needy in their distress."

"I'll come as often as you like," Oswald said, once more forcing himself to speak cheerily,—it was a harder effort than ever now,—"oftener than you like, perhaps. Now, good-by for the present. Remember your promise about the doctor: it'll be claimed to-morrow."

The pent-up tears flowed apace when Blanche was left alone; nevertheless, she felt glad and grateful beyond words at Oswald Gauntlet's return. As for him—this is what he muttered through his teeth as he strode away, scarcely knowing whither he went:—

"Dying! and dying like that? And they want us to believe in Justice and Mercy?"

Better Christians perhaps than the poor horse-gunner have sinned almost as heavily in thought when such a trial vexed them sore. It is so much easier to recognize that we ourselves are punished according to our deserts, than that the penance of those we love very dearly is merited. The maxim, "Whatever is, is right," dates from old times. It ought to guide us in rough paths no less than in smooth; and others besides complaisant sinecurists are bound to respect it.

It might have seemed to many that Blanche Ramsay was now only expiating the wrong-doing and misdemeanors of Blanche Ellerslie; but, if all the jurists that ever expounded points of law, and all the divines that ever taught submission, had pleaded and preached to this effect till they were hoarse, and even if Oswald Gauntlet had had patience to listen to the end, he would still have reared his rebellious head, and answered,—

"A lie."

CHAPTER XXXIV.

AMONG the many mansions that woke up to life with the spring, Nithsdale House, of course, was numbered. The countess was there, and, if we may be allowed the expression, "all there." Indeed, before the marigolds were in bud, the choir of her adherents had begun to chant in their hearts, if not with their lips,—

> "With everything that pretty bin,
> Our lady sweet, arise."

And she answered blithesomely to the call. Country air and gentle exercise had refreshed her wonderfully, and she came up, as her racing friends would have expressed it, in blooming condition for the season's work. Earl Hugh had left his home-farm and young plantations with less reluctance than heretofore. He grew fonder of his dear little wife every day; and, though he could not enter actually into her favorite amusements, it was such a real pleasure to him to realize that she was enjoying herself, that he began to think London not such a wearisome place after all. A certain carefulness, not to say smartness, was observable in his attire, which had hitherto been of the homeliest. Indeed, some of his cronies at the Sanctorium bantered him on this point; and the earl did not deny, or seem to dislike, the imputation.

The Daventrys, too, were to the front again, though the duties of hereditary legislation sat very lightly on the head of the family. He was generally to be found in his place about the time of the great spring handicaps. If the winter recess had done much for Lady Rose, it had certainly done more for her sister. The slender figure had acquired a richer roundness, and the girlish face a more decided character, without losing any of its delicacy. The startled, anxious look that might have been seen there often enough last summer was never seen now in the Spanish eyes. Of all the lights that shine over this earth of ours, is there one that can compare with the dawn of fair womanhood? In this light Gwendoline Marston just now lived and moved. It was soon beyond dispute that she would rank high among the beauties of that season; and none acknowledged this fact more than another old acquaintance of ours

The world had not gone particularly well with Horace Kendall since the cup of wealth, not to say of happiness, was dashed from his grasp so rudely. The life of an absolutely idle man with small means and with few personal friends is not often enviable. He was not absolutely a pauper, it is true, though the loss of the small salary drawn from the Rescript Office made a material difference to his income; for, though that same mysterious allowance was still continued, he had had a hint—con-

veyed in equally mysterious fashion—that it might lapse
at any time. This, added to a flourishing crop of small
debts, made the lookout ahead rather gloomy. But it
was not only as a profitable speculation that he repented
himself of having lost Nina Marston. Watching her
eagerly—and he never lost an opportunity of so watching
her as she walked or sat in the glory of her beauty—he
was filled with regret and longing, which, if not good and
generous, were at least sincere. All that there was of
manhood in this man's nature was waked at last, and
waked for his punishment. Very often

"His own thought drove him like a goad."

He did not find many distractions in society, either. It
might have been part of his self-tormenting to imagine
this, but somehow people weren't so anxious now to
invite him to their houses as before, and the influx of invitation-cards was not positively overwhelming. With
Lady Longfield, for instance, he was scarcely on speaking
terms; to be sure, he had treated his early patroness with
such insolent neglect, when he was in the zenith of his
prosperity, that it was no wonder she was offended. In
point of fact it was not so. The good lady was incapable
of bearing malice against any one, simply because she
had not memory enough to cherish even an affront; but
her pretty cage would only hold one lion at a time, and
it was fully occupied now by a distinguished foreigner
who had come over from Nordland, with a head of hair
like Absalom's, and a touch on the harp like that of Absalom's sire. She had forgotten Kendall's existence—
that was all; and perhaps society had, to a certain extent, followed her example. When a person with no substantial claims on its attention once loses the world's
ear, it is a chance, as every one knows, if he gets listened
to again. So, by day and by night, Horace went about
discontentedly to each and every place where there was
any likelihood of his meeting his lost love; and when he
did meet her, what did it profit him ? Whether he looked
plaintive or savage—and his eyes were tolerably expressive, you will remember—he was always answered

by the same slight, careless salute before which he had winced as he stood side by side with his betrothed to receive congratulations on his triumph. Twenty times he had gone forth swearing a great oath that he would accost her and know the worst of it, and each time he had come back without having opened his lips, cursing himself as fool and coward. When at last he did speak, it was without premeditation, and it happened in this wise.

It was at a garden-party at Fulham—one of the earliest of the season—and the hostess had invited quite as many people as her grounds would comfortably hold. Nina was too bewitching that day. She wore the peculiar shade of blue which, beyond all other colors, became her. She was in radiant spirits, too; and every now and then you might hear her silvery laugh trilling from among the little crowd that seemed determined to beset her. Horace looked and listened till he grew almost mad; and while the fit was still full upon him, it chanced that Nina stood for a second quite alone: a waltz was just over, and her partner had gone to fetch her something from the *beauffet* close by. She did not notice Horace's approach, till his voice sounded close behind her shoulder.

"Good-morning, Lady Gwendoline; you see I can't keep silence any longer."

She did not start; and, though the laughing light had vanished from the face she turned upon him, there was neither anger nor scorn there,—only perfect calm.

"And why not?" she asked. "Have you anything particular to say?"

He put on his best expression of tender reproach. It was wonderful on what small encouragement the man would grow melodramatic. If he had been on his death-bed, unless distraught with terror, I believe he would have tried for an "effect."

"How can you ask such a question? Can't you guess what I would say?—if you would only listen. Is pardon utterly hopeless? Ah! Have you forgotten your last letter? I read it over daily."

She did start now slightly; there was no denying it, and her color changed withal.

"I have not forgotten it," she said, in a very low, quiet voice.

There was no time for more; for just then Nina's partner returned, and Kendall fell back. He had tact enough to know that, if he had gained any advantage, now was not the time to press it.

"I've made her answer me," he muttered; "that's one point scored; and I've got over my d——d shamefacedness; that's another." He went home better pleased with the world in general and himself in particular than he had felt for a long while past.

Howsoever sanguine may have been the expectation that Horace founded on this incident, he certainly was not prepared for a note that reached him by post the very next morning. It contained one sentence only:—

"*If you can call at Nithsdale House this afternoon, between two and three, I shall be glad to see you.*"

He turned the note over and over, as if he were not sure that he read aright. There was no mistake about the handwriting—he could swear to that anywhere. Why, her last letter—it was an odd coincidence, certainly—had reached him under precisely similar circumstances of place and hour. He fell into a hurly-burly of thought quite bewildering.

What could be the meaning of this sudden relenting? Was it possible that the cold indifferent demeanor had only been a mask, while the willful passionate heart was still more than half his own, and that Nina had only waited for a chance of being reconciled? Very possible, certainly. He would have preferred seeing a little more emotion when he accosted her yesterday; but then she had always wonderful self-command, and plenty of pride too. Doubtless even now much special pleading would be needed to banish her *bouderie.* To this he thought he was fully equal: if he could get her alone for a clear half-hour, he had no fear of failing here. Of course she meant to see him alone; but why at Nithsdale House? Perhaps it was the safest—the only safe place, after all: their last rendezvous in the open air had not come off so successfully as to tempt her to risk another such. Perhaps she had enlisted her sister on her side: there was no telling.   Everybody said the countess was a paragon of good nature,—though he himself could never quite see it,—and if matters were once put straight again they would run more smoothly than ever.   Finally he came to the conclusion that Horace Kendall was a very fascinating person and fully deserved all the luck that could befall him—only henceforth he must throw no chance away. He spent the rest of the morning in sketching forth the line of argument that he meant to adopt, and he had got it all tolerably well cut-and-dried when he started to keep the appointment.

Despite all this, he did not feel quite so satisfied as he stood under the portico of Nithsdale House ; and as he mounted the great staircase his confidence oozed out, much after the fashion of Bob Acre's courage, so that he came into Nina's presence in rather a modest and humble frame of mind.   She was waiting for him—alone, as he had expected—in the first and smallest of four reception-rooms that occupied nearly the whole of that floor, and the folding-doors leading into the next apartment were closed.   She rose as he entered, saying,—

"You are very punctual.   I am glad you have come."

But her hand was not stretched forth to welcome him. It only pointed to a chair close to the sofa on which she had been sitting.   It was not quite the greeting he had reckoned on, and somehow the programme did not look quite so easy as it had done three hours ago.   As he sat down he began to speak hastily—as if he were afraid that, if he hesitated, his nerve or memory, or both, might fail.

" Could I do otherwise than come ?   Cannot you fancy how I have longed for this interview, and how I have hoped, almost against hope, that I should hear you say you forgave me ?   I was in utter despair last year,— despair of ever being able to come near you again,—and half mad with anger too.   You would not wonder, if you had heard the words Lord Daventry said to me that morning.   If it had not been for this, it would never have happened.   You must know that my heart had nothing to say to that unlucky engagement."

If her color had only changed, or if her lip had trembled ever so slightly, or if her eyes had flashed, even in anger! But cheek and lip and eye were as steady as steel.

"I have nothing to forgive," she answered. "There is no use in forgiving dead things, I have always heard; and our past is dead long ago. You gave me a sharp lesson, and it has not been lost on me: that's all. If it please you to give papa the credit of all that was said or done after that morning—very soon after, too—I dare say he would be content to take it. I don't want to hear about your engagement: I was sorry—yes, really sorry—for your sake, and still more for hers, that it ended so terribly. It was for quite another reason that I asked you to come here to-day."

Was this quiet self-possessed woman the same Nina Marston who used to flush and flutter under his glance and shrink before a sharp word? Kendall was bewildered.

"Then what was the reason?"

"It is soon told. You spoke of a letter of mine yesterday,—I suppose you have it still; and there was an armlet, too."

As his golden vision vanished faster and faster, his face began to lower

"So that's your game, my lady," he said to himself; "to get everything back that could compromise you, and then to drop me quietly for good and all. Not a bad game, either; but I'll spoil it yet."

Nevertheless, he answered, in his silkiest voice,—

"Yes, I have it safe, and the armlet too, and every line you ever wrote, and every flower you ever gave me. Is it likely I should ever part with or destroy anything that links me to you?"

"I don't know about it's being likely; I only know that I sent for you here for the one purpose of asking you to give me back—everything."

His eyes grew cunning and malignant, and his tone almost openly defiant.

"I will not part with a scrap of paper or a rose-leaf—to say nothing of the armlet—while I live."

She did not seem a whit vexed or surprised; indeed, she scarcely repressed an evident inclination to smile.

"You can keep the flowers, if you have a fancy for relics; it's the other things I am anxious about—really anxious, I don't mind confessing it, or I should not have sought this interview; but I never quite expected that you would give them back—for nothing. I know exactly how often I wrote to you, and, as you have kept every scrap, there should be no difficulty about the letters. They can't be worth much to you. Now, to me (with the armlet, of course) they would be worth just £500. Will you sell them?"

Horace Kendall, as you know, was not troubled with many of the finer feelings that hamper some people in their pursuit of substantial advantages; but he sprang up from his seat now with his cheeks all aflame, as if a buffet had lighted on them suddenly.

"Did you send for me here to insult me?" he stammered. "It was base—cruel—unwomanly!"

She smiled outright now.

"I thought we had quite done with theatricals. Pray don't excite yourself unnecessarily. It is only a question of buying and selling. There is no insult in a fair proposal. If you won't accept my terms, I'm sorry for it. I'm afraid I can't raise them."

If wishes could wither or kill, Gwendoline Marston's tenure of life and beauty would have been slight indeed just then. After the first outbreak of passion, Kendall had cooled down almost instantly; but his sneer was almost worse to look upon than his scowl.

"You are magnificent in your offers, at all events. It's rather an expensive whim, this last one of yours. Since when have you become a millionaire?"

"Ah! you doubt my power of performing what I promised? Well, you have a perfect right to do so, and ought to be satisfied."

Before he was aware of her intent, she had crossed the room with her swift, springy step, and opened the folding-doors, beckoning to some one within. The some one was no other than the master of the house himself. Now, Lord Nithsdale was not only very kind-hearted and easy-tempered by nature, but showed it in all his bearing toward his fellow-men. Even on the bench he had a way

—as we have hinted before—of looking at criminals, when it was not a case of personal violence, much more compassionately and encouragingly than was becoming in a chairman of Quarter Sessions. Perhaps not twice before in all his life had such an expression been seen on his honest, homely face as it wore when he came forward, taking no sort of notice of Horace's nervous salutation.

"Hugh," Lady Gwendoline said, "I want you to convince Mr. Kendall that the money we have been speaking of will be forthcoming."

The earl nodded to her kindly; but, when he addressed himself to his visitor, John of Somerset himself could not have quarreled with the affability of his manner.

"You can scarcely suppose," he said, "that this interview would have been allowed to take place here unless Lady Gwendoline Marston had previously consulted me and unless I had approved of its object. I decline to discuss for one moment the circumstances under which these letters and other matters came into your hands. It is sufficient to assume that Lady Gwendoline desires to get possession of them,—of everything,—and that she is prepared to pay a fair price for so doing. My guarantee will probably be sufficient; besides, I have my check-book here. It is for you to say whether you accede to our terms, or not. They will not be altered; but you can take time to consider them, of course."

Horace was almost choked by disappointment and rage; but his very passion gave him strength, that he might otherwise have lacked, to make an attempt at self-assertion.

"I don't want an instant to consider," he said, with great heat. "After the words that have been said here, I should despise myself if I kept one thing that could remind me of Lady Gwendoline Marston. All that pertains to her shall be returned within the hour, and without a bribe. I trust that you will both some day repent the insult—utterly uncalled for, and impossible to resent— that you have thought fit to put upon me."

And so Horace Kendall made his exit from this our stage—not so clumsily, after all, if he did not precisely strut off with an air. Let us hope that his small audience

did not begrudge him his little "effects." Lord Nithsdale watched him depart, with a queer expression of
dislike dashed with curiosity, such as might suit an en-
tomologist who has just lighted on a rare but revolting
specimen.   As the door closed, he turned to Nina.

"That's well got rid of, at all events.   We'll send the
check directly we get your packet, of course.   It won't
be returned, you'll see."

She tried to smile up in his face, and to murmur a few
words of thanks; but it was a failure; and then Gwendoline Marston did what, under the circumstances, was perhaps the last thing you would have expected of her—she
sat down and began to cry bitterly.   But her tears were
dry long before the packet arrived; though it came punctually enough, and the messenger took back an envelope
containing a slip of that plain gray paper which, on certain occasions, is apt, more than the most perfect picture,
to wake the "Desire of the Eye."

Horace Kendall cursed the giver freely, as he crumpled
it in his hot fingers; but he took special care not to tear
or destroy it, and he would perhaps have been infinitely disconcerted if the envelope had contained only a
less practical proof that he had been right in trusting to
the other side's liberality.   The £500 in figures looked
fair and round, and the subsidy would help materially to
clear off a crop of ill weeds in the shape of debt.   Why
should he trouble himself to be generous to utter strangers, such as all connected with the Marston name must
henceforth be to him?   If his feelings had been hurt,—
cruelly hurt,—there was the more reason for golden salve.

In fine, he pocketed the check, and cashed it without
delay.

When Gwendoline Marston that night in her prayers
thanked God she was free—quite free—she had as ample
cause for gratitude as ever woman had—be she maid, wife,
or widow—since Eve's first orison.

CHAPTER XXXV.

IF a man, overborne by any grief or pain, not the more endurable because no outward symptoms can be discerned, should go forth into a crowd to seek for solace, the chances are that he will return in a more discontented frame of mind than that in which he set out, simply from realizing the fact how infinitely little his own sufferings affect the rest of the world at its work or play. It seems very hard; and it seems quite as much so to those who would repel rather than solicit verbal condolement as to the tenderer natures who are not too proud to be pitied or petted. Yet there is little reason in this, as in most human repinings. We might just as well expect a darkening on the face of nature, when our own mood is gloomy, as on the face of society. The children may complain to their fellows that these have not danced to their piping nor wept to their mourning; but we, whose beards are grown, if not grizzled, if we have learned nothing more, ought at least to have learned this lesson,—that it is not in the market-place we ought to look for sympathy to lighten the burden or share the joyance of our day. Suppose that, spent with hard struggling for life, we stand on a sinking ship: why should it disquiet our friends ashore, who, if a blast shriller than common should roar round the gable, will only mutter, "A wild night," and then finish their wine with a keener zest; or our warier comrades, who, ere this, have found safe anchorage under the lee of the black headland we shall never weather? Still more, how can it concern the sea-folk down there yonder? A fiercer storm than that in which we are laboring would not trouble the silence and rest

> "Where there is neither moon nor star,
> But the waves make music above them afar—
> Low thunder and light in the magic night."

Nay, if all tales are true, nothing that once was flesh and blood sinks far below the central deeps; and there is no fear that the mermaiden at her play should be frightened by any such ugly sight as the corpse of a drowned man.

So the business and pleasure of this season went on just as if no story could have been written about any one in particular concerned therein. It was a summer, to be sure, somewhat fruitful of misfortune. There was terribly heavy plunging, east as well as west of Temple Bar; and certain disasters caused the most careless of passers-by to stop for a second to listen to the crash and watch the ruin. But when merchant-princes met, haggard and care-worn, in conclave, to discuss whether for the general credit's sake it were not better to avert some great house's downfall by private sacrifices,—not only of money but of principle; for the very indulgence verged on a compromise of crime,—the layers at the Corner were not less busy, nor the backers less bold. And when the heir to a great name and fair estate was found with a bullet through his heart after the St. Maur handicap was won by a "dead outsider," the event was scarcely mentioned on 'Change, and was instantly forgotten in the hubbub of the announcement that Cacus and Co. had failed.

Without this preamble, you would probably have inferred that the drama in which the Ramsays bore principal parts attracted no sort of public attention; nevertheless, the plot thickened daily, simply because it was evident, to any who cared to watch it, that the last scene must be played out ere long.

The Brancepeths came to town rather later than usual; but within an hour of their arrival La Reine was sitting with Blanche. The change in her friend's appearance that she had noticed at Christmas struck her much more forcibly now,—so forcibly that she forgot all her prudent doctrines of non-interference,—and she "freed her soul" abruptly.

"It's no use, Blanche; I dare say I shall only make matters worse; but I can't be a hypocrite any longer. It *is* being a hypocrite to keep on pretending to think there's nothing the matter, when you are fretting yourself to

death under one's eyes, and to pretend, too, that I don't
know what's wrong. Won't you let me talk to you about
it, at all events, and make sure that I can't help you in
any possible way ?   How I do wish I could!"

Lady Laura had nestled down on a low footstool close
to the sofa on which Mrs. Ramsay was lying, and, as in
her eagerness she pressed the other's hand, she felt it grow
cold and tremble.   Nevertheless, Blanche's face lighted
up a little

[illegible] Queenie, do
[illegible] when you
[illegible] confessed to
[illegible] with, 'I told
[illegible] promise, dear,
[illegible] an Oswald
[illegible] warning—
[illegible] perhaps you
[illegible] than I vexed

[illegible] I [illegible] think any
[illegible] believe your
[illegible] has been done, and is
[illegible] so awfully
[illegible] willfully.
[illegible] him ? I don't mean
[illegible] least afraid."

[illegible] with an eagerness

[illegible] Queenie, I wouldn't
[illegible] possibly do
[illegible] more harm than you
[illegible] of such an idea

[illegible] plainly that a super-
[illegible] character was as
[illegible], and seemed in no
[illegible] suggestion unfavor-

[illegible] any one else ?" she

[illegible] between those two.

Blanche knew perfectly whom "any one else" meant, and her own face actually flushed as she answered,—

"Oh, Queenie, that would be worse than all. I never had much 'proper pride,' as they call it; I would go down on my knees this moment to win from Mark one of the old kind looks and words; but to *her*—if I heard that intercession had been made for me there, I should die at once of the shame."

Lady Laura bit her lip; it was not so much the rejection of her good offices as the consciousness of her own inefficiency that chafed her.

"I don't think I should have exactly 'interceded.' There are so many ways of putting things. But perhaps you're right, dear. I'm too much of a blunderer to be trusted.   Is there nothing—absolutely nothing—I can do? It's so provoking to be useless and helpless."

"You can do a great deal," Blanche said, as she laid her cheek against the other's shoulder. "You can come and sit with me when you've nothing better to do. I'm not the least like an invalid; but, somehow, I've got so dreadfully indolent lately, that every afternoon when I've been out for about an hour I always want to creep back here, and if I rest till dinner-time I get through the evening tolerably well."

"Not an invalid!" the other interrupted, impatiently. "I wonder what your doctor would call you? I suppose you've gone through the form of seeing one by this time?"

"Indeed I have," Blanche replied, with her faint smile. "Oswald Gauntlet made such a point of it the first time he called, and he behaved so wonderfully well altogether, that I couldn't refuse him. And a very nice —'motherly person,' I was going to say—that same Dr. Skwilce is. He's a wonderful reputation, and yet I don't exactly believe in him; but his medicines are quite delicious. He's a voice like an elderly turtle-dove: you can't think how soothing it is to hear him cooing away close to your ear. I always feel sleepy after he's gone."

"Well, but what does he say is the matter with you?" Lady Laura persisted. "He must have given a rational opinion some time or another."

"It's something about a sluggish action of the heart," Blanche said, placidly. "I'm sure I don't know what that means; I should have thought mine went fast enough sometimes—not always—to satisfy anybody."

"And what does he tell you to do, or not to do?"

"I'm to never overtire myself, and to be amused as much as possible without being excited, and to eat everything I can fancy. Not a hard regimen, is it? And then, he says, I shall very soon be well. Queenie, dear,"—here her voice sank, but did not tremble in the least,—"I think the doctor's right: I believe I shall be well——very soon."

For a minute or two after that, Laura Brancepeth saw all things through a mist—darkly. She did not trust herself to speak of these things further that day; and it was long before she had courage to broach the subject again.

If Major Gauntlet did not fulfill his threat of coming too often, and never overstayed his welcome, it was not for want of making the experiment. As yet he had never encountered Mark Ramsay in his own house. Twice or thrice they met casually in society; and on one of these occasions Mark said a few polite words about the cheering effect of the other's visits on Blanche's spirits.

"I can always tell when you have been there," he concluded.

It did not seem to strike him that he himself had any business "there," or that he was expected to do anything toward lightening his wife's depression—though he ignored it no longer. Oswald felt much as Laura Brancepeth had done under like circumstances; and, as man talking to man, he found it even more difficult to frame his answer fittingly. It seemed almost intolerable to accept the cool, careless words as a compliment to himself from the author of all the mischief that had been done and never could be undone, and to be conscious the while that the speaker was deliberately trampling under foot a gift that to the other seemed priceless. He did contrive to mutter some meaningless commonplaces; but thenceforth he gave Mark no chance of airing his courtesy.

Before any of the events recorded in the last two chapters occurred, Alice Irving had ceased to be the Ramsays' guest, and had gone back to keep house for her father, who had returned somewhat sooner from Paris than he was expected. During her visit not a word worthy the recording passed between her and Blanche. The gentle deference to her hostess, and utter absence of self-assertion, which had marked the girl's demeanor in the later days at Kenlis, were still unaltered; and her bearing toward Mark—in the presence of a third person, at least—was quite faultless. Their sayings or doings *en champ clos* shall have no place in this story. A few—even if they have not made *nouvellettes* their chief study—will be able to fill up the blank page; and to others let it remain a *tabula rasa.* Licit and lawful love-making, perhaps, is not often brilliant in reality, and not many would have patience to read through one chapter thereof, reported verbatim: yet it is honest bread at all events, if it should be somewhat stale and flavorless; but there was little of the wholesome leaven in such converse as was likely to pass betwixt Blanche Ramsay's husband and Alexander Irving's daughter.

That some such mutual understanding as has been hinted at above—not the less definite, perhaps, because it had never been written down or outspoken—subsisted between them, is certain. Doubtless Alice had good grounds for reckoning on speedy promotion in the event of a death-vacancy.

Now, you will be good enough to remember that in one of our opening chapters it was set down that Ramsay was as far removed from my own personal idea of a hero as it is well possible to conceive: howsoever austerely he may be judged, it is not his biographer who will plead extenuating circumstances or take exception to the verdict. Nevertheless, I should like you to realize that it is a man—perverted and depraved as you will, but still a man, and not a monster—that is here described. It may seem to some almost preposterous that such a compact should exist at all, much less before the ink in the marriage-lines of one of the parties thereto had had time to fade. But as to the fact—I fear one would not have to search far through modern annals to find its parallel; and, if witnesses were to be called as to the mere probability, more than one name not yet erased from visiting-lists would be found on the *sub-pœna.* As to the time—well, there are other ways of reckoning this than by the pendulum.

There is a weird old German story that tells how a student once sold himself to the tempter for a price, in the which length of days was a chief item. How the rest of the juggle was wrought out matters not; but this part of the bargain the fiend evaded by causing his victim every now and then to fall into a trance, which lasted for years instead of hours, in some desert place, so that the dupe reached the extremest limit of man's existence before he had *lived* half its span.

My brother, it might happen to you or to me,—for it has happened to our betters,—without having given bond to Sathanas, on awaking from a lethargy or a dream which seemed only to endure a few seconds' space, to find all around us barren and lonely, and ourselves wrinkled and withered and gray.

It was equally certain that Irving had not been wrong in the confidence that he reposed in his daughter—if the calculation, cruel and base at the best, be worthy of the name. However closely Alice may have walked to the verge of crime, she assuredly had not hitherto forfeited the right to boast that she could take very good care of herself. Mark had no doubt won from her more than any honest man has a right to expect from a woman who cannot bear his name; but he was still more than half baffled by a steady resistance such as he had seldom or never before encountered. In this, perhaps, as much as in anything else, lay the secret of his being so bewitched as he had avowed himself to Alsager. It was in his nature to wait forever, rather than abandon an object on which he had earnestly fixed his desire; but the struggle and strife told on him outwardly, and had you perused his face narrowly you would have found divers lines and hollows that were not there last autumn.

Blanche's bearing toward her guest was perfect too, in its way. She no longer affected cordiality, but in the

V

minutest observances of all courtesy she never failed. The state of her health was quite sufficient excuse for her not chaperoning Alice abroad, even if the latter during her father's absence had not declined almost all invitations. Though the visit had been suggested by Blanche herself, Captain Irving's return was doubtless a relief; and on the day of Alice's departure she felt as if a painful strain had been relaxed, and quite enjoyed the reaction. During Miss Irving's stay Anstruther only called once at the Ramsays', and twice excused himself from dining there. Upon the single occasion when they met, after their first greeting, he scarcely seemed to notice Alice's presence; only once, just before he rose to take leave, he glanced at her askance. His back was turned to Mrs. Ramsay, and Alice's face was averted for a moment; else, perchance, one or both might have been startled, if not warned, by the malevolent meaning of his eyes.

Anstruther had fallen much into his old habits again, and now not a morning passed without his spending two hours at least in his laboratory. The only difference was that now, as a rule, he preferred to work alone, whereas before he had usually been assisted by his servant, Henry Trendall by name. The man was neat-handed and intelligent, and, besides, had a natural fancy for chemistry— so much so that he was inclined to grumble at his services being now so often dispensed with. Also, Anstruther had resumed his regular attendance at the Orion. He had tried his strength at picquet against Irving several times before the other went to Paris, and successfully; though the skill was so nearly balanced that there was no question of losing on either side.

When Mrs. Ramsay was left alone again, Anstruther found his way to her house much oftener, though his visits were still scarcely frequent enough for intimacy, and their conversation never touched upon anything more interesting than the ordinary topics of the day. He was not a brilliant talker, certainly; but there was a dry shrewdness about his remarks that not seldom made Blanche smile, and, before Gauntlet appeared, he was perhaps about the most welcome of her visitors. Afterward things were altered. Of course the two men were bound to meet before long. On Oswald's third visit he found the chair by Blanche's sofa already occupied by Mr. Anstruther. The latter did not take his leave immediately; but he moved from his place at once, as though aware that the new-comer had a better right to it, and he was unusually silent during the remainder of his stay. More than once, when he thought he was unobserved, his eyes peered earnestly from under their shaggy brows into the martial face over against him; but there was no malevolence in them now, only a kind of wistful curiosity. And, as he so gazed, the outlines of a story came upon him clear out of the shadow.

"Ay! you love her dearly," he thought within himself, "and you have loved her for half your life, I dare say; and what have you got for it? A few summer smiles, and a few softer speeches than the other fools; that's all. And she likes you better than the rest, no doubt; and I would give a year or two of life to be in your place now, though while she's looking up into your face she's whispering in her heart, 'If it was only Mark who was sitting there!'

"And yet you would not grudge her a drop of your heart's blood—it's a brave heart, too. You didn't get that cross for nothing; I've heard more than the dispatches ever told. You'd ride with a laugh on your lip into a place that to us poor civilians would seem like the mouth of hell; but I'd do more for her than you would, after all. I'd do for her that which, if it were mentioned in your hearing, would take the color out of your brown cheek and make your great strong pulse stand still. I'll do it, too; and then we'll see which of us stands nearest to her, you or I."

These somber meditations did not prevent Mr. Anstruther from expressing with more than his customary courtesy his pleasure at having been made acquainted with Major Gauntlet. He did not seem much inclined to profit by the chance, though, for it was many a day before his gaunt figure darkened those doors again. Blanche herself remarked upon it at last.

"I do believe he's jealous of you," she remarked to Oswald. "Some people are so exacting, they can't bear to share even their friends with any one.   I'm half sorry you frightened him away; he's rather amusing, with his old-fashioned oddities."

The gunner twirled his mustache somewhat superciliously, as if he thought the subject not worth deep discussion.   However, putting Laura Brancepeth aside, who somehow never was in anybody's way, he would have supported with much equanimity the absence of any person, howsoever agreeable, that was likely to interfere with the *tête-à-tête* upon which he had come to reckon almost daily.

CHAPTER XXXVI.

CAPTAIN IRVING's winter campaign in town stretched into the summer. You may guess that it was both pleasant and profitable, or it would not have been so prolonged. He had a good deal more than held his own at the Orion. Besides Blanchmayne, who took his punishment like a glutton, and one other, few cared to measure their strength against the smooth, smiling champion who seemed to have chained Fortune to his chair.   The second exception was George Anstruther; and this adversary, after awhile, Irving became not over-eager to engage.   He was not precisely afraid either of the other's skill or luck, albeit he recognized both, and—being superstitious, like all thorough-paced gamblers—was rather troubled by a presentiment that he was fighting against heavier metal. But this was not all.   He had an absolute dislike to sitting opposite the cold judicial eyes that while they dwelt on his own face seemed to be searching for something of deeper import than points or sequences.   Somehow he felt certain that this man, for some reason utterly inexplicable, bore him a grudge ; and Alexander Irving—who throughout his life had set at naught enmities, howsoever well deserved—was strangely disquieted by this fancied animosity.   From one cause or another, he never played

quite up to his game against Anstruther; and this in itself chafed him sharply. When a glimmer of the truth crossed his mind, it was unheeded. Even if he had suspected that Anstruther once admired, or even loved, Blanche Ramsay—and he had long since admitted the utter improbability of the hypothesis—he would never have suspected him of partisanship now.

"He must have got hold of one of those cursed stories, I suppose," he said to himself. "That's what makes him look so queer."

Indeed, there were stories enough and to spare abroad, relating to Captain Irving's youth and manhood, that might have accounted for people, not especially scrupulous or sensitive, looking on him rather "queerly." However, in spite of occasional hitches and checks, the sojourn in town turned out anything but an extravagance; and others besides Mark Ramsay contributed to the free maintenance throughout the winter and spring of father and daughter. So satisfied was Irving with the result that he thought he would let well alone. His wary eye had detected divers indications, lately, of a turn in his luck, and he resolved to be beforehand with it.

So one morning at breakfast, without any previous notice of his intention, he bade Alice be ready to return to Drumour the following week. She received the announcement with perfect indifference; and when her father asked her, with a sort of lazy curiosity, "Are you glad or sorry to go?" it seemed as if she were speaking truth when she answered, "Well, I hardly know: on the whole, perhaps I am glad. I'm beginning to get a little tired of the cohue, and of seeing the same faces so often. Drumour will be quite lovely just now."

"I suppose you will see some of the same faces again before long," Irving retorted, with a slight sneer. "Meanwhile, you can be as pastoral as you please. I don't know about Drumour being lovely; it certainly won't be lively; but a little lethargy will do neither of us any harm."

If Mark Ramsay was chagrined or surprised when he heard of the intended departure, he dissembled extremely well. When Blanche was told of it by Alice herself— Miss Irving's conventional calls had never been interrupted—she was fain to turn her face away, lest it should betray her. She would scarcely have felt so exultant had she guessed at certain arrangements that were made that same day; nor perhaps would Mark's equanimity have seemed so very wonderful to any one cognizant thereof.

The respite, while it lasted, was even greater than that which Blanche had enjoyed at Brancepeth; but it lasted hardly so long. The Irvings might have been gone some ten days, when Mark appeared in his wife's dressing-room one morning while she was making an attempt at a late breakfast. He looked graver than usual, and frowned as he glanced at some letters that he held.

"How have you slept, Blanche?" he asked, just touching her brow with his lips before he sat down in an arm-chair on the opposite side of the table to her couch. "You look better this morning."

How even that careless caress made her heart flutter and her cheek glow!

"I slept better, and I feel almost brilliant this morning. But what do those letters mean, Mark? Nothing troublesome, I hope?"

"Nothing terrible; but decidedly troublesome. They seem to have a knack of getting matters into a tangle at Kenlis; and old Menzies has no head to unravel them. We shall have to change our factor soon, I think: he's getting past his work. Indeed, he almost confesses as much. It was a sort of anarchy in Sir Robert's time, and they don't relish the mildest form of regular government. It's a bore to be hampered with business when we have a houseful; and I should like to get everything straight before the shooting begins. Our term here expires on the last of July, you know; but I must go down much sooner than that; indeed, I think of starting by the night-mail to-morrow."

The soft eyes rested on him more steadily than searchingly. It seemed rather as if she were beseeching him not to deceive her, than imputing to him any such intent.

"It *is* troublesome," she said, "and so very sudden, too. You know best what ought to be done, Mark, of course. I could not start quite so soon as that; but there is no-

thing to keep me in town. I could join you next week—
if you wished it."

There was a piteous significance in those last words;
but Mark never noticed it. He was only too content to
see his wife take things so quietly. He had counted on
her submission, but scarcely on such a placid acquiescence.

"If I wished it?" he answered, quite cordially. "Of
course I wish it. The sooner you can come the better,
Blanche. Kenlis is much too large and eerie a place to
make a comfortable hermitage ; and I fancy the change
will do you good. You certainly want bracing."

Bracing? Yes, she did want it, cruelly; but it was
of a kind that never came on the wings of the purest
breeze that ever rustled through heather. Some such
fancy crossed Blanche's mind; but, under the gleam of
kindliness in Mark's manner, her face brightened.

"I have no trouble with household matters, so my
preparations will be soon made," she said. "I don't
know whether the change will do me good; but I shall
like it. Town isn't lively when one only sees one's friends
at home. By-the-by—talking about one's friends—have
you settled who are to be asked to Kenlis in August?"

"No. I have left that to you," he replied; "at least,
nearly so. Alsager's is the only name I'll put down on
my own account. It's no use counting on Vane. He'll
be among the buffaloes about that time, from what I can
hear. Now, Blanche, I want you to understand that
you'll please me best by inviting just the people that
please you best—neither less nor more ; and there's no
reason why they should wait for August. There's very
fair sea-trout fishing, and somehow or other people are
always amused at Kenlis; or seem to be,—which comes
to much the same thing. Couldn't you persuade some
one to escort you down? There's Gauntlet, for instance.
He can get what leave he likes ; if he's no other engagement, I should think he would be charmed."

It was so seldom that Mark, of late, had shown any
such solicitude for his wife's comfort that the novelty
ought to have gratified if it did not surprise her. And
yet Blanche's heightened color sprung more from vexa-

tion than any other cause. She could not help asking herself whether it was likely that, had the positions of the two men been reversed, Oswald would have dreamed of consigning her to the other's escort; and, further, whether Mark himself would have been inclined so trustfully when he and she loitered under the Fontainebleau oaks. It was with a certain constraint she answered,—

"I don't know what Major Gauntlet's engagements may be.; but I can easily ascertain, and ask him to take care of me, as you suggest. I dare say he will be glad to do so: he's one of the few people who like old friends better than new ones, and don't mind trouble. I should have asked you to find room for him at Kenlis, in any case, this autumn. I should like the Brancepeths to come, too, as soon as they can manage it; and, Mark, you don't mind my inviting Mr. Anstruther? He's really been very good-natured, in calling and bringing me books, and in all sorts of ways; and, though he declined last year, I think he'll accept this. He's not a favorite of yours, I know; but he won't be much in the way, for he never shoots, and keeps very early hours."

"I beg your pardon," Mark returned, coolly. "I have no sort of antipathy to Mr. Anstruther: indeed, I rather admire him than otherwise. Judging from the little I have seen of him at the Orion, his whist and picquet are of the first force: besides, it will be great sport to see him and Irving pitted against each other. A professor is an acquisition anywhere. Ask him, by all means."

After this they spoke only of domestic matters of no moment, and Mark departed well satisfied with the manner and result of his interview. Blanche did not see him alone again till the following evening, when he dined early at home, before he started by the North mail.

Not many injured wives, probably, would have let such an opportunity slip of taking a delinquent consort to task, were it ever so gently. But Blanche was not equal to remonstrance—much less to rebuke. There are weaknesses which are unpardonable; and hers was one of such, no doubt. If any excuse could have been alleged for her supineness, it would lie in this:—not only, as aforesaid, did she hold her husband guiltless, so far, of absolute criminality, but a shrewder and bolder legalist than she would have been puzzled to frame definite articles of accusation against either him or his accomplice; for the guarded demeanor of both, if it did not make them safe from suspicion, made them nearly safe from impeachment. Neglect, Blanche might certainly have complained of; but it is very hard to grapple with a negative, and her mignonne hands were not formed to grapple with anything. If her light, tender clasp failed to detain the truant, she could but fold them meekly while she sat and pined. The wiles of light attack and simple ambushment, which helped her only to effectually achieve conquests that she did not care to keep, had failed utterly here; and when they so failed she had no more science or energy in reserve.

During the *tête-à-tête* at dinner, though her eating and drinking were the merest form, she seemed in rather better spirits than usual, and alluded once or twice to the people at Drumour, and the probability of Mark's seeing them so soon, with perfect composure, and mentioned, almost triumphantly, that she had secured Oswald Gauntlet's escort for her journey in the following week.

When it was time for Mark to depart, he came round to where his wife was sitting, saying,—

"Well, good-by for the present, Bianchella. Take care of yourself, and follow soon."

And he meant to seal the adieu with just such a careless salute as that of yesterday. Perhaps, unknown to himself, his tone had softened, or perhaps the pet name, seldom if ever bestowed of late, had its effect; but, as her husband stooped over her, Blanche turned toward him, and her arms were wound round his neck, and his lips were drawn down to hers, while she whispered,—

"Kiss me once, dear—only once—in the old way."

A grain or two of remorseful pity hindered, just for a second or so, the smooth working of the well-ordered machine that served Mark Ramsay for a heart, as he did as he was bidden. He did not grudge the caress, nor seek to shorten it; and, if it were to be exchanged at all, it might well be prolonged. Scarce a year since, those two were formally made one, as firmly as God and man could weld them; and yet, through all the cycles to come, their lips will never be joined again.

CHAPTER XXXVII.

Mr. Anstruther was the earliest arrival at Kenlis; for the Brancepeths could not move northward till after Goodwood, and Alsager was only expected on the eve of the twelfth.. Judging from his demeanor during the first days of his stay, the former personage was not likely to add much to the conviviality of the party. He never fished, or rode, or drove, but seemed to prefer a solitary ramble to any other diversion; and even when he sat down to picquet at Mark's special invitation, it was evidently more to please his host than from any special interest of his own in the game. He played, too, in an odd, absent way, not nearly up to his proper form. There was a haggard look in his eyes, and more than once Blanche was struck by this when, with an instinctive feeling that she was being watched, she looked up and met them. For the first time in their acquaintance, she was rather inclined to avoid than to seek a *tête-à-tête* with Mr. Anstruther, and for a week at least there was little or no opportunity for such a thing; but one day—the day before the Brancepeths' arrival—it could not well be avoided.

Mark had ridden out, as was his custom, alone, immediately after breakfast, and Blanche had insisted on Major Gauntlet's profiting by a morning absolutely made for the destruction of sea-trout. She almost regretted her self-sacrifice—loss of Oswald's company for six hours was nothing short of this—when she saw that Anstruther did not seem inclined to start for his usual ramble, but loitered about like one who has no intention of stirring far afield. Watching him from her boudoir window, she felt certain that he was making up his mind to speak to her.

"I wish he'd make it up quickly and get it over," she said to herself, with something of her old petulance; and it was chiefly with a view to precipitate matters that she left her own room and established herself in the library, which looked out upon the south terrace, where the gaunt figure was still pacing up and down. She was not kept long in suspense; for she had scarcely settled herself on her sofa when the door opened and Anstruther entered. He had evidently not calculated on finding her,—at least so soon; for he started and half drew backward, and advanced at last hesitatingly.

"I came to look for—for the second volume of *Antediluvian Remains*," he muttered.

"That ponderous book!" Blanche answered. "Couldn't you put off poring over it till a rainy day? This one's too delicious to be wasted. I'm ashamed of sitting in-doors myself; and, as it is, I think I shall creep round the garden before lunch." ·

He sat down, resting his elbow on the table that stood betwixt them, and shaded his eyes with his hand.

"The book doesn't matter," he said, absently, " and I suppose the day *is* tempting: I've hardly noticed it. I may as well go out for my walk, after all. At any rate, I won't inflict my company upon you much longer. Don't be complimentary, please. I know it isn't genial company at any time—less than ever now."

"Why now?" Blanche inquired. "Are you beginning to suffer in the same way as you did last year?"

"Likely enough," he answered, with a gruff laugh. "Such things are apt to return even when we think we are rid of them,—which I never did. Will you let me put my ailments aside for the present, and ask about yours? Perhaps I have less reason to say, ' Don't think me impertinent,' now than when I put the question last. You haven't grown stronger since then."

"Not stronger, certainly," Blanche said, with an attempt at cheerfulness. "But who knows what the Highland air will do for me?"

The long, bony fingers clasping his brows contracted a little.

"It did you more harm than good last year, that same air Mrs. Ramsay, I have given offense often enough in my life by being so rough and plain of speech. If I'm to be unlucky again now, I can't help it. I mean what I say, and I never forget what I say. Perhaps you've guessed that I'm going to remind you of something I said not much more than a year ago, when I interpreted the letters engraved on that trinket,—I'm glad to see you haven't got tired of it yet. I said, you may remember, that if you ever needed help I should be ready to serve you in other ways than as adviser or trustee. I think you do need help now; and—I am ready."

Blanche looked at him in utter amazement. Could he possibly imagine that she—who to Laura Brancepeth had given only a half-confidence, to Oswald Gauntlet none— would lay bare to George Anstruther the secret of her heart's bitterness? A grain more of pride would have made her answer haughty. As it was, it was cold.

"Thanks. You mean everything that is kind; but I cannot see how you can give me help ; and I don't know that I need any."

The hand covering his face sank by degrees, till it rested on the table ; but the shaggy brows still shaded the down-cast eyes.

"You do not see ; you do not know," he said. "I both see and know. I see that if it were not for one shadow over your life it might run on smoothly and brightly enough— ay, for years after I am dead and gone; and I know this shadow might be removed. There!—I have no patience to speak in parables : Blanche Ramsay, would not the world look pleasanter if Alice Irving were out of it or out of your way ?"

Her nerves had never been very strong, and weakness and fretting had unstrung them so of late that a very slight shock was enough to break them down. She was dreadfully frightened now. It was not that she had a suspicion of the real import of Anstruther's words. Her only definite idea was that she had fallen on one of the cases of sudden and unaccountable insanity of which she had read and heard, and was alone with a maniac. Look-ing up, with this terror upon her, she met his eyes, lifted now for the first time, gleaming with an eager malice. Blanche shrank back into the farthest corner of her sofa, with a smothered cry. She knew afterward that she had answered quite quietly, and wondered to herself; but at the moment she was scarcely conscious of what she said.

"Don't talk in that strange way, or look at me so strangely. The world is well enough, with its lights and shadows. I have no wish to alter them. If you speak like that again, I shall forget you are an old kind friend, and be very, very angry."

The effort almost exhausted her, and she broke down with a gasp and a sob. Anstruther saw at once the effect of his words, precisely the contrary of what he had intended; and his first impulse was to undo this. He swept his hand quickly across his eyes; and when they met Blanche's again, the evil fire had died out of them, and they were colorless and cold.

"Pray don't disturb yourself," he said, in his most deliberate tones. "You have completely misapprehended my meaning; but let that pass. My intrusion was quite unwarrantable; and I ask your pardon for it humbly. I'll promise never to repeat the offense. It is sufficient for me to know that you don't think fit to trust me. I ought never to have expected otherwise."

The staid sobriety of his manner reassured her at once. "It was only his brusque, awkward way of putting things, after all," she thought to herself. He had meant to console her; there could not be a doubt of it: only, she did not want consolation from that quarter.

"There is no offense," she said, softly, when her breath grew steady again. "I ought to be grateful to any one who takes an interest in my happiness or unhappiness; and I am grateful, believe me. But there are some things one does not talk about, even to one's self. The best way would be to forget everything that has been said this morning: will it not?"

And she held out her hand, still trembling.

"Much the best way," he answered, as he put it to his lips in a dull, mechanical way. The life and heat that were there a few minutes ago seemed utterly to have bored expression of his face, that he had just had an inter-view with his factor.   They had a great deal of music that evening; and, one way or other, everybody was so much engaged that a brief absence of Mr. Anstruther's was not noticed by any one of the party.   He was not away more than a quarter of an hour, and returned just when Alice was beginning her last song.   It was an old Breton *chanson*, very rude in its rhythm and simple in its melody, but with wild thrilling cadences exactly suited to her rich, flexible voice.   The words matter nothing—indeed, they were in *patois;* but the burden of the chant was "farewell."

"I do hope it will be fine to-morrow," Miss Irving said. "If it's very bright and warm, could we not go out with the lunch ?"

She looked rather hesitatingly at Laura Brancepeth ; but the appeal was by no means successful.

"You can do as you please," La Reine answered.   "I shall stay and keep Blanche company."

Alice bit her lip in anger—not more at the rebuff, than because she felt she was coloring.

"Will you take me, papa ?" she asked.   "Of course I can't possibly go alone."

"And why not ?" Lady Laura inquired, coolly.   "*Je n'en vois pas la difficulté.*   Above a certain degree in north latitude, chaperons are not required."

Irving didn't like the turn of the conversation, but did not think fit to take up the glove in his daughter's behalf just then: so he answered, with his placid smile,—

"Certainly, child.   I shall be very glad to squire you, if it's anything like a day."

Then they separated for the night.

Laura Brancepeth, knowing what she knew,—setting all suspicion aside,—owed little charity to Alice Irving ; yet she would never have spoken or looked so hardly if she could have foreseen what one hour would bring forth.

gone out of the man, and, as he rose up, his very limbs seemed to move stiffly.

"It will be much the best so. And now I'll go for my walk. I have done mischief enough for one day."

So, without listening to a faint contradiction from Blanche, he departed. Though she called herself "fool" for having been frightened at all, for a good while after she was left alone she lay fluttering and quaking, like one scarce awake from an ugly dream; and it was with great difficulty that she repressed an inclination to indulge in a hearty crying-fit.

Such temptations were much too frequent of late, it must be owned. When she was a little recovered, she rang and ordered her pony-carriage, and caused herself to be driven down to the nearest point to the trouting-ground. In truth, the fishermen were found, so to speak, almost within hail. Mrs. Ramsay brought with her a much more elaborate lunch than had been carried out in the spare creel, and the two consumed it in great comfort and amity, though the lady's portion would scarcely have overfed a canary.

Often and vividly in after-time will the memory of that scene recur to Oswald Gauntlet. If he should live till his ears wax dull and his eyes dim, he will not forget how the birches whispered then overhead, or how the loch glimmered through the sweeping boughs, nor the velvet sheen on their moss carpet. No wonder if they lingered there till the best of a perfect fishing-day was wasted. And though the gruff old keeper growled under his breath, "It's a sair pity," it was perhaps more as a professional protest than because he thought the Sassenach's laziness unnatural. Probably before

"Grizzling hairs his brain had cleared,"

and before he had learned to value aright the "worth of a lass," Donald himself, at such a place and time, would scarcely have been more keen.

When at last Mrs. Ramsay thought it was time to return, she did not affect to decline Oswald's offer of escort. She had no mind to trust herself alone at Kenlis again. Nevertheless, she seemed to have quite shaken off her fright of the morning. Indeed, her companion flattered himself that she was in rather better spirits than usual; and there was not a trace of consciousness in her manner when she met George Anstruther at dinner. Neither in the latter's manner was there any visible alteration from his usual stiff formality.

The Brancepeths arrived early on the following day; and as soon as she could get Laura to herself in her boudoir, Blanche confided to her as much as she could recollect of the scene enacted in the library on the previous forenoon. La Reine was a good deal puzzled, it must be confessed; though she would by no means allow that Blanche's terrors had been anything but absurd.

"I always fancied he was very fond of you in a fatherly way. Not that I believe much in fatherly attachments: they are very much like cousinly ones—a delusion and a snare. I have no doubt he meant to entrap you into a confidence, only he managed it rather clumsily. As for his going out of his mind, he's no more chance of doing that than you or I, depend upon it. I don't admit that disliking Alice Irving—supposing he does dislike her—is any proof of incipient insanity: if it were, more than one of us will want the *camisole* before long. For my part, I think the world would get on capitally without her; but my thoughts don't much affect the question, and I don't see that Mr. Anstruther's do, either. *Lettres de cachet* are out of fashion nowadays:—I'm not sure that it's altogether a blessing. Can he be thinking of making a raid on Drumour and abducting her with the strong hand? Or, stay: perhaps he meditates marrying her in due form, and getting her out of our way legally. *That* would be something like self-devotion: wouldn't it, dear? Of course he wouldn't reckon—no man ever does—on a certain rejection."

Her reckless rattle was not altogether without a purpose; and it did, indeed, provoke Blanche to smile.

"I shall think *you* mad, Queenie," she said, "if you go on in that strain. As to what he meant, I haven't the slightest idea—nothing, very probably, except to show that he was sorry for me; but—I didn't like his eyes."

She shivered, as she spoke the last words low and hesitatingly.

"I don't suppose any one admires them," the other returned, composedly. "But he can't alter his eyes, any more than he can his nose, or chin, or any other feature in his face; and some eyes have a trick of scowling whenever they want to be expressive. It's not so clear to me that I've been talking such utter nonsense, after all. At any rate, Blanche, I won't have you torment yourself with any ridiculous fancies. I'm certain you look a shade better than when you left town. Oswald Gauntlet must have taken great care of you on the journey, and since. I really think I admire that man more than any one I ever read of. It's so nice to see him with his gentle ways, and to remember that, if he had his deserts, he would be covered with crosses; and, of course,—like all true devotion,—it is unrequited. Often, if I were to hold my tongue, he wouldn't know that I was in the room. It's very good of me never to have a jealous fit."

"You're always good," Blanche said, as she nestled closer to her friend, "and so is he; you can hardly guess how good. Now let us talk of something else. You must have quantities to tell me. Begin about your Goodwood party."

CHAPTER XXXVIII.

"A BAD lookout," said Vere Alsager, as he shut down his window with a shiver betimes on the morning of the 12th—referring, you will understand, not so much to the landscape as to the prospect of sport. The wracks of cloud were drifting in from seaward, broken here and there, but not brightened, by

> "Dreary gleams above the moorland."

By-and-by, perhaps, when the fractious wind had done moaning, blinding mist would drive the keenest homeward; but at present there was not even this excuse for shirking.

"We'll have the hill to ourselves, at all events," he muttered, rather sulkily, as he donned his frieze. "There'll be no luncheon foolery to-day."

It was not often, even in his thoughts, Alsager did the gentler sex discourtesy; but he was in a misogynic, not to say misanthropic, mood that morning, and the state of the weather did not altogether account for this. He had not yet succeeded in laughing himself out of the weakness of pitying Blanche Ramsay. The subject of their conversation on a certain morning that you wot of had never since been broached betwixt him and Mark; and the two, to all outward seeming, were just as good friends as ever; but, though he had received no notice to quit, or even a hint at such a thing, Vere had sought and found fresh quarters. He had not as yet occupied them; but it was understood that he would return to his old ones no more. On his arrival over-night, he had been very much struck with the appearance of his hostess. So far from seeing any such improvement as Lady Laura had fancied, he detected a decisive change for the worse. Not only did Blanche look paler and thinner, but there was a sort of transparency in her complexion, which, even to an unprofessional eye, is of evil augury; and it was evident that the light duties of hospitality among intimates overtaxed her strength.

From the sofa where Blanche reclined—listening to, rather than sharing in, the low *causerie* carried on by Lady Laura and Gauntlet—Alsager's glance turned toward another corner of the same room, where Mark leaned over the back of Miss Irving's chair, commenting on, as it would seem, the contents of a portfolio of Highland photographs that lay on her lap. Alice and her father had arrived the same day, on a week's visit. Alsager perhaps spoke only the simple truth when he said that he would not have chosen the girl for a model. But if he had never been fascinated by her beauty, he had always fully recognized it,—never more fully than now. As she sat so quiet and demure—rarely unveiling her dangerous

eyes, still more rarely smiling with her rich, ripe lips—
the contrast with the pale, listless figure over yonder was
as striking as if she had seemed to exult insolently in
her advantages. So it struck one at least of the spectators: the cold cruel cynic—not greatly changed, perchance, in the main points from the man whom all
Florence cried shame upon, years ago—was conscious
just then of a glow of honest, unselfish anger. Truly,
though she had fared ill in other ways, and though it
helped her not a whit, this poor Blanche had the luck of
awaking sympathy with her sorrows in the unlikeliest
quarters.

This is why the moroseness of Alsager's morning mood
was not entirely to be attributed to a falling glass. Those
whom he met at breakfast seemed scarcely in blither
humor. There were only a quartette of them,—all men,
of course. No one in his senses who had no business
abroad would have made acquaintance with such a day
an hour earlier than usual. However, there was no
talk of staying at home, or giving the weather chance of
clearing. Nothing but rheumatism or Cimmerian darkness would have kept Mr. Brancepeth off the hill on the
12th; Mark, though he shrugged his shoulders very
expressively, took the inevitable bore with his wonted
coolness; and a soaking more or less mattered little to
Gauntlet or Alsager: so they sallied out in pairs, as in
the previous year.

The sport was very much what might have been expected, except that it lacked the excitement of finding the
grouse wild. Even that, nuisance as it is, would have been
better than seeing them get up sulkily and drop down
wearily, as if impressed with a morbid suicidal idea that
life was not worth flying far or fast for. On the whole, it
was dreary work—up-hill in more senses than one—and
the gillies themselves were rather glad when, as the several
parties met for lunch, the thick, white mist-wreaths settled steadily down, with such evident intention of holding
the ground till nightfall that no one controverted Mark's
suggestion that they had done enough for *that* day. As
it was, if the corry beneath them had not been easy and
straight traveling, they might have had some difficulty in

groping their way down to the loch-side and finding the boats that were to ferry them back.

Northern twilight comes late, as you know; but on this afternoon, so far as the sun was concerned, it was a case of dead reckoning, and by six o'clock, any one standing on the terrace at Kenlis might have fancied he was looking over the Thames in November, rather than over a Highland loch in August. If it was dark without, it was darker within doors—darkest of all, in a certain corridor facing north, at the best of times, but gloomily lighted by narrow windows holding scarcely more glass than stone. Like all the rest of the house, it was comfortably carpeted, and the embrasures were all cushioned; yet it was not a place where anybody would be likely to linger. The family pictures lining the walls were not very enticing. No winsome dames or courtly cavaliers were to be found among them. Those austere, hard-visaged worthies were evidently here in a sort of honorable banishment, instead of being actually buried in the lumber-room.

Nevertheless, the north corridor seemed to have certain attractions for certain people at certain seasons. It was nearly half an hour since Mark, passing through,—quite accidentally, of course,—had found Alice Irving sitting in one of the aforesaid embrasures. In that same spot the two still sat, speaking but seldom, and, when they spoke, seldom glancing at each other, but gazing out always on the mist and rain. At length said Mark, after a steadier look in his companion's face than he had indulged in hitherto,—

"Is it my fancy, or is it this dreary half-light, that makes you look so pale? Alice, you are not ill? Your hand is like ice."

The words were simple enough, just such as a man in all innocence might have spoken to any woman his familiar friend. They were quietly uttered, too, and yet they breathed a tender anxiety which, had they been addressed to herself, would have made Blanche Ramsay's heart leap for joy. They were significant enough to Alice herself, even without that other eloquence of the fingers twined in hers.

She was not pale now; but she shivered as she replied,—

"No; I am not ill. Perhaps I have caught a slight cold; or perhaps I have been moping till I have begun to stagnate. I wasn't brilliant when I came down this morning; for I was stupid enough to have a bad dream last night, and not to forget it when I woke."

"A dream?" said Mark, inquiringly.

"A dream, of course: how should it be anything else? I should like to tell it you, though. I thought I was here in Kenlis, but in a part of the castle I had never seen. It was a gallery something like this, only much —much longer; and the walls and ceiling and floor were all of bare gray stone. .I don't know how it was lighted, for there were no windows, that I saw, and no lamps anywhere; but it was not dark, nor anything like dark, for I could see the great door at the farther end. I felt, somehow, that I had no business there, and had lost myself; but if I could only get to the door, and if it were unlocked, I should find my way easily enough. I tried to make haste, but could only creep along, and the door seemed to grow farther off and smaller; but I got to it at last, and it was locked—fast locked—or I could not stir it. I was so frightened that I wanted to scream; but I could only just whisper, 'Help.' Almost before I had spoken the word, I heard a rustle, like the rustle of a woolen dress, outside, and then a laugh—a low, dreadful laugh. I wished—oh, how I wished!—that I had let the door stay locked forever, rather than have called the Brown Lady to open it. I knew it before I saw, as the door swung ajar, the skirt of the dark-brown robe. I fell forward on the flags, my eyes in my hands; for, somehow, I felt they would be blighted if she looked upon my face; but the next moment I knew she was bending over me, and I heard her laugh again, and say,—don't think I am romancing: I can remember every syllable,—

"'Ye've thought to save your bonnie face: peek in the glass when ye rise.'

"It was the agony of fear that woke me then. At first I lay panting and trembling—too thankful to find it was only a dream; but as my breath came back I seemed

to hear that same rustle of woolen stuff, and then my
room-door closing very stealthily. At first I was more
frightened than ever, but then said to myself it was just
the sort of thing one would be likely to imagine after such
a dream. Presently I took courage to draw the curtain
and peep out. The door was fast shut, and everything—
as far as I could see by the lamplight—exactly as Julie
had left it; and so she said when I asked her the question this morning. So it must have been a fancy, and a
very foolish one, too,—not half enough to account for my
bad spirits to-day. I have heard of people playing cruel
tricks; but this is the last place on earth where one
would fear such a thing."

"The very last," Mark answered, frowning. "There's
not a man or woman ·here capable of a vulgar practical
joke — even if they would risk the consequences. But
how came you to dream of such horrors? I was not
aware that you had ever heard of that absurd legend, or
that any one—except an old crone or two—believed in it.
However, all things considered, I don't wonder at it.
No: it must have been pure fancy; but what with that
and the dream, I don't wonder at your looking pale. It's
been such a dreary day for you too, my Alice."

Her hand still rested in his, and she did not resist when
he drew her closer to his side, nor reprove him for those
two last guilty words. She was in one of her reckless
moods just then, and something else besides mere depression of spirits had contributed to this. Alice was still
sensitive in her pride, if not in her conscience, and Laura
Brancepeth's cold civility had galled her all through that
day keenly. It was so very seldom that La Reine Gaillarde kept any one at a distance, that reserve on her part
was more significant than rudeness would have been in
such a woman as Lady Peverell.

"Yes: it was rather a dreary morning," she said, with
a sigh. "I'm very glad you were driven off the hill so
soon; you see, there was no one at home I cared for
much, or—what is, perhaps, more to the purpose—who
cared for me. Papa hasn't shown to-day, and there was
no one else at home."

Mark smiled. He had seen enough of these feminine

reprisals, to guess what Alice had suffered, and at whose hands she had suffered it.

"So they were not hospitable to you within-doors? Now, who was in fault, I wonder?"

She drew her hand away,—though he would still have detained it,—coloring deeply.

"Not Mrs. Ramsay, you may be sure. She's always much gentler and kinder than—than—I deserve."

"Then it was Lady Laura?" Mark said, with a certain contempt. "Nobody ever minds what she says or thinks. She would not have been so warlike if she had a flirtation of her own on hand. But she takes after Cleopatra in more ways than 'in the swarthy cheeks and bold black eyes;' and now, I suppose,

> 'It chafes her that she cannot bend
> One will, nor tame and tutor with her eye
> That dull, cold-blooded gunner.'

Never mind, Alice. Perhaps some day you'll choose your own company at Kenlis; and then you needn't be troubled with people who don't care about you."

She rose up quickly.

"Hush! You know I never like to hear you speak so; and I like it less than ever to-day. It will bring bad luck, if nothing worse. Now I must go: I've stayed too long. I should not like to be missed down-stairs."

"When it's a question of the proprieties, up-stairs, or down-stairs, or in my lady's chamber, there's an end of all argument. It's a pity you have overstayed your time. Perhaps we'd better have kept the hill, after all."

She turned where she stood, and laid her hand on his arm, looking up at him with such a softness in her changeful eyes as he had never seen there yet.

"Unjust!—unkind!"

That was all she said, and then her head drooped and drooped yet lower and lower, till it rested on his shoulder. Mark's arm girt her waist, and he too bent his head till his lips lighted on her brow, and there abode.

I by no means wish to enlist your sympathies for Alice Irving; but in settling her sentence certain things should be considered. That she had acted cruelly and basely in stealing—or in accepting, it matters not which—the treasure of another woman's life,—more basely and cruelly still in founding hopes on that other's death,—no casuist could dispute: yet these hopes were not mercenary. To prevent her father's interference, she had caused him to believe that a calculating ambition, rather than blind impulse, had guided her hitherto; but it was not so. Had Mark been landless and nameless, she would still have been tempted—sorely tempted—to follow him to the world's end. This unholy love of hers was as sincere, except that it was not as abiding, as any that has been blessed at God's altar; and, moreover, it was her first love. Strange enough, was it not, that just the same miracle should have been wrought in her case as in Blanche Ramsay's, and that both should have been wrought by the same hand? And yet not so strange. We should know by this time that *Detur Digniori* is about the last device that should be borne by *celui qu'on aime.* And then remember what Alice's training had been. She had had no mother, since she could lisp the name. Left to run wild in her own fashion, she had been kept ever since girlhood, by her father's negligence, if not by his will, always within the glow of the furnace of temptation. Perhaps she had fared better than many would have done in escaping hitherto—as she had in very truth escaped—without any serious scar. If the smell of fire still clung to her garments, was it wonderful?

The girl had had wonderfully little happiness in her life—perhaps, with all her faults, rather less than her share—so little, indeed, that some charitable Christians, if they knew all, might have held that her resting there contentedly was not absolutely an unpardonable sin. Recovering her self-possession, she withdrew herself from the half embrace, and moved swiftly away. Mark knew better than to attempt to detain her.

When he was alone, he turned again, pressing his forehead against the glass, and his hand against the stone mullion, as though he wished by the cold contact to quiet the fever in his blood; but when shortly after he sauntered into the library, where most of the others were assembled, you would have judged, from the slightly

CHAPTER XXXIX.

ONE of the pleasantest rooms at Kenlis, especially under lamplight, was the smoking-room. It had formerly been used as a second library; but of its studious aspect there were few traces now. A great trophy of Eastern arms hung over the fireplace; two or three bookcases of black oak were evidently left there rather as garnish for the walls than for any studious purposes; and in any of those lazy luxurious chairs work would have been impossible. Anstruther and Irving were playing picquet; and the other three men were discussing the prospect of the morrow, and of the season—glancing from time to time at the progress of the game, on which they had bets. Mr. Brancepeth was not among them, but in his own chamber, already sleeping the sleep of the just.

Though they did not notice it much at the time, both Alsager and Gauntlet remembered afterward how strangely Anstruther looked that evening. He had accepted Irving's challenge in that absent, indifferent way to which reference has been made before; and he had not spoken a syllable since, beyond what was absolutely required in scoring; but that vigilant anxiety in his eyes was more remarkable than ever—only he seemed to be watching not his adversary or the game, but something, as it were, in the distance.

The last hand was almost played, for Irving, with a dash of triumph in his courtly smile, was about to declare a point and sequence that must needs have been decisive in his favor, when he dropped his cards and sprang to his feet, as did every man there present—Anstruther overturning the table as he rose.

From overhead there came a terrible cry—something betwixt shriek and wail—significant, not of physical torture alone, but of utter despair—such a cry as the mere parting of soul and body would scarcely wring even from the weakest—such a cry as, through Heaven's mercy, seldom startles the echoes of this our earth, though it may be familiar to those of the Place of Doom. In that awful utterance, more than one who heard it seemed to recognize a voice that had witched their ears ere now with its glorious flood of melody, and more than one said within himself what Irving's pale lips said aloud,—

"My God! That was Alice's scream."

Little as either of them liked the unhappy girl, as they sprang up the stairs together, Oswald Gauntlet's heart fluttered faster than it had done in its Baptism of Fire; and Vere Alsager felt a quiver of the nerves, such as might affect one forced against his will to witness some ghastly experiment of surgery.

Tottering and stumbling as he went, Irving followed at his best speed. The last to leave the room was George Anstruther. Doré might have caught a fresh idea from his face just then. This man was already numbered among those who are tormented—not before their time. Ramsay himself was across the hall before any others had left the smoking-room; but, before he had mounted the first flight of the great oak stairs, there were hurrying feet in the corridor above, and shrieks of women—not like the cry that had startled them but now, nor uttered by the same voice, but rather of terror than of pain. He knew well enough in what room the tragedy, of whatsoever kind it might have been, was being enacted; and, as he came to the half-open door, he met Laura Brancepeth on the threshold. La Reine looked fairly panic-stricken.

"You mustn't go in," she said, closing the door behind her. "Don't think of it: it is too horrible. Her maid and mine are with her. They will do all that can be done till a surgeon comes. Where does the nearest live? Send for him instantly: you can give no help here."

"What has happened?" Mark asked, in a hard, dry whisper. He had to moisten his lips before he could accomplish even this.

In a very few words she told him.

Alice Irving was not given to cosmetics; nor was there much temptation for such fraud. Paint or pearl-powder could have done little for her clear complexion and delicate coloring, and she could well afford to let them stand on their merits ; but sometimes—especially in the autumn, when she was most exposed to sun and wind—simply as a precaution against tanning, she would bathe her face and neck, before going to rest, with Milk of Roses or some such innocent lotion. She was beginning to do this that night when her maid left her. Before the liquid had time to dry, her cheeks and throat began to smart and burn intolerably, and in a few seconds they were covered with an awful blotchy eruption—like an aggravation of ery-sipelas—that was not only skin-deep, but seemed to cor-rode the flesh. Casting the bottle aside,—it was smashed to atoms where it fell,—she sprang to her mirror. Look-ing on the reflection therein, she cried aloud in her despair as she would never have cried in her pain.

Can you wonder at it? It is well to prate and preach about the worthlessness of surface beauty; but show me the woman who without one instant's preparation will accept the change from fair to foul—from lovesome to laidly—unrepiningly, and I will bow before such a world's-wonder as neither we nor our fathers have known.

Though she knew it was but a disguise that she could doff in her own good time, even Medea could not com-plete without a pang the hideous self-transformation that was to beguile the daughters of Pelias, when

> "she poured,
> Into the hollow of an Indian gourd,
> A pale green liquor; wherefrom there arose
> Such scent as o'er some poisonous valley blows,
> Where naught but dull-scaled. twining serpents dwell.
> Not any more now could the Colchian smell
> The watermint, the pine-trees, or the flower
> Of the heaped-up, sweet, odorous virgin's-bower;
> But shuddering, and with lips grown pale and wan,
> She took the gourd, and with shut eyes began
> Therefrom her body to anoint all o'er;
> And, this being done, she turned not any more
> Unto the woodland brook."

While La Reine was speaking, and while Mark stared at her as if he only half realized her meaning, Irving came up behind them. The other two men had suffered him to pass them at the stair-head, where Anstruther halted, and the others stood aloof in the corridor.

"*You* will go in," Laura said, opening the door wide enough to let the father pass in, and shutting it again behind him.   In that brief instant Mark Ramsay heard and saw more than he was ever likely to forget: he heard a deep, hoarse moaning, like that of one choking in quinsy; he saw Alice Irving groveling prone on her face, as she had groveled in her dream.

If, as they sat in yonder north window together, a jagged rift of flame had shot suddenly out of the low clouds and laid the woman, whose hand he held, dead and black beside him, Mark would not have felt half so horror-stricken and helpless as he now did.   Yet, as he turned to give orders to one of the servants, who were hurrying up by this time, about fetching a surgeon instantly, his face was marvelously calm—only it looked so infinitely older.

"The rest of you go down," he went on.   "This part of the house must be kept perfectly quiet, and all the help that is wanted at present is here; unless—unless—any one knows anything of surgery?"

Rather vacantly, than with any apparent hope, as it seemed, of its being answered, his glance wandered from Alsager to Gauntlet and rested at last upon George Anstruther—standing still at the stair-head.   All three shook their heads; but Anstruther averted his as he did so, and you might have seen the hand behind him clutch the oak balustrade, as though without some such support he would have staggered.   Mark noticed nothing of this; but, as he turned away to the stairs again, he saw Laura Brancepeth start forward from the doorway, and he heard her say,—

"Blanche, how could you be so rash?   You're not fit to leave your room, much less to be here."

The next moment he was looking at his wife, fascinated, so to speak, in spite of himself, by her strange expression.   There had been a kind of horror awhile ago even in Laura Brancepeth's bold black eyes; and, considering the temperament of the two, that this should have appeared in Blanche's intensified, was but natural. But why should they betray a horror of remorse as well as a horror of fear?   And why should they turn with awful questioning toward George Anstruther's still averted face? White, even down to the lips, as the lace on her dressing-robe, Mrs. Ramsay stood panting and quivering; but she never spoke till she drooped her head on La Reine's shoulder, clasping her hands tightly round the other's arm, and only that one caught the whisper,—

"God help us! I know what he meant now."

Laura started violently, and for a second or two she felt fainter than when she first looked on the ruin within. But the very peril of the situation—though she embraced it not wholly—nerved her to an effort. Bad as things were, she felt they might be worse yet.

"Hush!" she murmured, swiftly. "You don't know what mischief you may do." Then she said, aloud, "Let me take you back to your room, Blanche, while you can walk. It is madness to stay, when you can't help; and you know that everything that is possible will be done. I don't answer for keeping my wits about me if you are taken ill to-night."

Mark Ramsay's gaze dwelt upon the two, as they moved slowly away, with a steadiness akin to malignancy; but if he had any suspicions, it was evident that they were still quite vague. Indeed, he was in that state of bewilderment which causes a man, if he has any power of reasoning left, rather to mistrust than rely on his first impressions. After a pause, he said, composedly enough, addressing himself to Alsager,—

"I think you'd better all go down. I will stay here till Irving comes out."

Was it only minutes that Mark sat there staring at the door over against him—listening for a sound, ever so slight, that should break the dead stillness? Would it have been easier for him to bear if he had guessed that the sharpest throe of mental or bodily agony had not wrung one moan from Alice since she knew him to be within hearing? It is satisfactory to reflect that every iota of the punishment meted out to this man now had been thoroughly well earned. I am not sure that there was not in his own mind, just then, a consciousness that the retributive justice which, despite his fatalism, he had foreseen, if not dreaded, had overtaken him at last. But I am quite sure that such a consciousness did not make him more inclined to bow to the chastisement, or a whit less savagely bent on revenge to the uttermost on whoso had art or part therein. His wife knew something of it, he felt sure; and whatever she knew, before the night was out he would know, or——

Before he had thought out the threat, the door opened, and Irving came forth, his face wearing its courtly mask no longer, but almost distorted with grief and rage.

"Can you give no guess at the meaning of this devilry, or the author of it?" he said, hoarsely. "The bottle's smashed to atoms, and the hell-broth spilled, but I rubbed my finger on the carpet where it was soaking. Look at that, and then guess how Alice looks as she lies there!"

On the smooth white flesh there was a swelling like an angry blain, and the inflammation was evidently spreading still.

"Guess?" Mark retorted, shrinking back as he spoke. "Do you suppose if I could guess I should be idling here? But we'll not sleep till we have found out something. That's for ourselves; but can nothing be done for her—nothing?"

"Nothing till the doctor comes," Irving replied. "Cotton-wool dipped in iced water seems to relieve her, and they're trying that now. She'll be in a raging fever before morning, I suppose; perhaps that's the best thing that can happen to her. I'm not to go back till I bring the doctor; and—and she begged of me, so earnestly, to take you down-stairs, anywhere from here. You'll come away, won't you? I'm going to my own room till I'm wanted."

They parted at the stair-head, and Mark went straight to his own apartment, where lights were always burning at this time. He remained there perhaps twenty minutes, evidently in deep thought; then he went up-stairs again, and passed along the main corridor, without lingering for a second to listen at the threshold of Alice's chamber, and so came to a door which he opened softly, without knocking. It led into a room—half dressing-room, half boudoir—where he found, as he had expected, his wife and Laura Brancepeth.

CHAPTER XL.

You may remember that in the early days of their acquaintance La Reine had decided that Mark Ramsay was not so black as he had been painted. But of late she had come to the conclusion that the original coloring of the fancy portrait was about correct; and he was as thoroughly out of favor with her as it is possible to conceive. The reason was simple enough. Her prejudices against Mark only vanished when she saw that he had both the will and the power to make Blanche happy perfectly; and when he ceased to trouble himself about this, they returned with double force; but, for every one's sake, she took special care to conceal her dislike, and before the world they were the best possible friends. With all this, the very last person that Laura would have wished to see enter the room at that moment was Mark Ramsay.

She had been trying her very best to soothe Blanche, telling her that Alice's injuries might, after all, be only superficial and temporary, that at any rate they must have been caused by some terrible mistake in the ingredients of the lotion, and that it was absolute insanity to impute such a crime to George Anstruther. Blanche had listened, and seemed to wish to be persuaded,—perhaps because she was too weak to argue,—and she was lying still now, with her eyes half closed, holding Laura's hand fast. She opened her eyes when her husband entered, and started up with a faint cry.

If you had seen Mark's face just then, you would not have wondered at her alarm; but there was a fell lowering there worse than overt menace, and somehow it was evident that he was here with a purpose—and not a kindly one. It was to La Reine he first addressed himself.

"I am sorry to disturb you; but I want to say a few words to Blanche alone. I won't ask you to leave us for more than ten minutes, or to go farther than the next room."

Laura was sorely tempted to rebel. It seemed to her little less than cruelty to leave that weak, fluttering creature to fight her own battle; for one glance at Mark's face had told her that battle, in one shape or other, was impending. But, unless there is matter for the Divorce Court's handling, it is very hard for any third person to hinder a husband from a private interview with the woman who has sworn to honor and obey him. So even La Reine was constrained to yield to the force of circumstances; but, as she rose, she kissed her friend, whispering,—

"There's nothing to be frightened at, darling. I shall be quite close by."

Then she turned to Mark.

"You will be careful,—won't you? She has been so shaken already to-night."

As she said this, there was a pleading look not often seen in her haughty eyes; but Ramsay did not seem to notice either the glance or the words, as he opened the door for her to pass into the sleeping-room beyond, and closed it behind her carefully. Then he came back, and stood gazing down at his wife as she lay,—always with the same darkness on his face,—till Blanche could bear the suspense no longer.

"What is it, Mark?" she cried out. "What have I done? It is too cruel to frighten me so!"

Was it possible that the hard, icy voice that answered her could ever have whispered "Bianchetta"?

"I do not know what you may have done; I do not say that in your own person you have done anything. But I say that you can help to bring guilt home to others; and this help you will hardly refuse me. I have no time for paltering: will you tell me at once, not what you know, but what you guess, about this affair?"

She trembled in every limb as she turned her face away till it was half hid on the pillow.

"What can I tell you? How could I guess—Oh, Mark, it's not possible you suspect any one here of having contrived this fearful thing? What earthly motive could there have been?"

She had risen up in her eagerness, and would have caught his hand in both her own; but he drew back out of her reach.

"I have come here to *ask* questions, not to answer them; but I will this. Yes, I do suspect—and more than suspect—I have my choice between believing in a miracle and believing that this devil's work was planned and wrought by some one under this roof. No motive—? Is it so unlikely that you should have found a friend shrewd enough to guess that the spoiling of Alice Irving's face would please you, and devoted enough— that's the word, I suppose—to accomplish it?"

Soft and yielding as she was by nature, and weakened by long illness, moreover, there was still enough of woman's dignity in Blanche Ramsay to revolt under the cruel insult.

"I have not deserved this," she said, more firmly. "What right had any one to suppose that I should rejoice in such a crime? And that you, of all people, should hint at it—Ah, Mark!"

She broke down with a sob. He laughed out loud; and Laura Brancepeth, within, hearing that laugh, drew closer to the door dividing them.

"No reason? Not if they guessed that for a year past there has been but one face in all the world for me—the face that has been marred to-night? The end sanctifies the means, you know; and what could be a holier end than bringing husband and wife together again? Why, they put Dunstan in the calendar for searing a woman's face with hot irons. Why should not they do as much for your friend? You will not help him, either, by equivocating, I warn you."

She was fairly roused now. Did not George Anstruther deserve threefold better at her hands than this man, who, not content with neglect and treachery, must flout her with the insolent avowal of his sinful passion? Why should she give up a friend, howsoever guilty, to the tender mercies of one who would not show her even the mercy of allowing her to ignore—or seem to ignore— her wrongs? She looked up at her husband, not quaking or flinching now.

X　　　30*

"Such words, spoken by you to me, are simply cowardly. I never sought your love; but since I accepted it I have tried hard to keep it—how hard, you know as well as I—and when I thought I had lost it, I never reproached you. I only hoped that God would have pity, and give it me back or let me die. And He has had pity; for I believe I am dying—and I believe you know this. You might have had patience a little longer; but, if I were to live to grow old, you and I will be as much apart from this minute as if one of us was buried. There need be no open *esclandre*, unless you wish it: I care little which way you decide. I will never knowingly see Alice Irving again: yet no one can be sorrier than I am for this horrible accident—I believe it is an accident: at least, I cannot help you to any other conclusion."

Her voice never faltered once, though the darkness in Mark Ramsay's face deepened with every word. He strode closer to the sofa, and caught Blanche by the wrist—not crushing it at all, but holding it lightly in his fingers, as if he only wished to fix her attention.

"So you won't turn king's evidence," he said. "Well, I gave you the chance, remember. It'll be time enough to settle our conjugal relations when to-night's work is done. Now I'm going to deal with your champion. Perhaps he'll prove more tractable than his mistress."

The momentary excitement had passed off, and fear—not so much for herself as for others—began to master her again.

"For pity's sake, don't leave me so," she murmured. "You are under some dreadful mistake. I can't even guess whom you are alluding to."

"Not to George Anstruther, of course—Bah! I thought you were better at dissembling. Why, your eyes betrayed you in the corridor, and your pulse convicts you now."

He flung her hand away as he spoke, and turned to go; but Blanche caught him fast, and held him so that he could not wrench himself loose till she had slipped down before him on her knees. She had no breath to speak; but the agony of her upward look ought to have pleaded for her more effectually than any prayer All

at once a change like death swept across her face, and
Mark, stooping, was just in time to catch her before her
head struck the floor.   His own face never softened a
whit; but he laid the senseless form on the sofa as gently
as if he had still loved it—raising his voice, as he did so,
to call Laura Brancepeth.

As La Reine advanced quickly, you might have seen
that she had done with intercession; for her eyes dissembled no longer her aversion and scorn.

"So you have killed her!" she said, low and bitterly;
"and that is what you came to do.   I half suspected it."

They had flung aside conventional courtesies, these
two—as men on the verge of mortal duel cast away cum-
bersome garments.   As Mark lifted his head, their glances
crossed like swords.

"I have done no murder—as yet; and, what is more,
Lady Laura, I have used no poison-practice,—which, considering the fashions of the house, is perhaps remarkable.
You'll find Mrs. Ramsay has only fainted; but I doubt
if I can be of much use in recovering her.   I'll send her
maid here at once.   You need not fear my disturbing
you any more to-night."

And so he went out.

CHAPTER XLI.

WHEN Alsager and Gauntlet got back to the smoking-
room, both were too thoroughly unsettled to think of
going to rest; and it was as well to watch there as elsewhere.   There was no danger of their voices being overheard; and yet it was under their breath that they spoke
of what had happened above.

"It's the most horrible thing I ever heard of," Oswald
said, as he drained a great goblet of iced water; "and it's
so utterly inexplicable.   There's an infernal ingenuity
about it that don't look like a servant's trick.   Her maid

is a Frenchwoman, to be sure; but why should she have borne malice?—such malice, too!"

"Julie's perfectly devoted to her mistress, I believe," Vere answered. "No: it was no servant's work, you may be sure of that."

There was a kind of intelligence in his face that made the other ask, quickly,—

"Then whose work was it? You have a suspicion, I'm certain."

"Scarcely a suspicion—only a vague, dim idea, which I should be sorry to encourage: I don't know that I ought to mention it. Well, if there's no further cause to justify it, you will consider this unsaid. I'm more than half afraid Anstruther knows more of this matter than he would care to confess."

"Anstruther!" Gauntlet repeated, in profound amazement. "What on earth makes you pitch on that quiet, harmless, old-fashioned creature?"

"I'll tell you," Alsager said, sinking his voice still lower. "Did you ever notice all those flecks and stains on his hands? I did long ago, and wondered how they came there,—for his neatness in other respects is quite remarkable,—till Mrs. Ramsay explained it by saying that he was a great chemist. He spent half his life in India; and our poisoners are the merest bunglers, compared with the Easterns. They have all manner of damnable herbs and plants and juices out there, that we know nothing of. The Begums, if I remember right, were often quite as clever at disfiguring as in slaughtering their rivals. You must have heard a dozen such stories yourself."

Gauntlet nodded his head.

"I see your drift now, and there's a shadow of circumstantial evidence, certainly; but then there's an absolute want of motive—unless you hold it to be a case of malignant monomania. We've read of such things: there was a curé in Belgium who used to poison the communion-wine."

Alsager looked searchingly at him for some seconds before he answered.

"An absolute want of motive? And *you* say this? I

confess you surprise me. Perhaps I ought not to have begun such frank speaking; but, as it is begun, surely it isn't worth while beating about the bush. I believe you have known Mrs. Ramsay from her childhood. It is scarcely more than a year since I made her acquaintance; and yet I guessed some months ago that all the grief which is wearing her life out was caused by the face that has been spoiled to-night. Ay! and I guessed, besides, that yonder 'harmless, old-fashioned creature,' to do her a kindness or a pleasure, would execute what neither of us would have nerve to plan."

Oswald Gauntlet leaped up from his chair with a bitter oath.

"And you dare to insinuate that Blanche Ramsay could be privy to such loathsome work, or that it was to serve her that it was done?"

"Sit down," Alsager said, with his *rire sous cape.* "It's pure waste of chivalry. Insinuations are not much in my line, and I'm just as incapable of imputing connivance in such horrors to Mrs. Ramsay as you are; and, even if it had ever been otherwise, I should have done her justice after what I saw to-night. I wonder you didn't see it too: you're not so sharp-sighted as I took you to be. You didn't remark the way she looked at Anstruther in the corridor, or you would have thought, as I did, that her suspicions, at all events, went pretty straight to the mark·and had not far to travel. But there never was such a horror on the face of any accomplice, even so remote, as was written then in hers."

"I beg your pardon," Gauntlet said, rather confusedly. "I totally misunderstood you. But if there was no complicity on her part,—and of course there was none,—why should she have suspected him, more than you or me?"

"Ah! there I'm hopelessly at fault. Some vague threat of his, perhaps, or even a look in his eyes which she remembered and interpreted when it was too late. I told you, from the first, my clue was a very slight one; and it may snap at any moment. I only wish it may. If Mark should get hold of it, and follow it up, there'll be worse work before morning than these old stones have seen for many a day."

"What do you mean?" Oswald asked, with some impatience. "Can't you speak plainer?"

"Well, there'll be murder," the other retorted, "neither more nor less. That's what I mean. I hope that's plain speaking enough for you. Well, we can only wait and see. On the whole, this is a Twelfth that I shall *not* mark with a white stone in my calendar."

Then there ensued a long silence.

*   *   *   *   *   *   *

When those two went down to the smoking-room, Anstruther betook himself to his own chamber, that lay at the end of a passage leading out of the main corridor. He locked the door, as he entered, so hastily that the key was turned before he was aware that he was not alone. Under ordinary circumstances, his valet's presence there would have seemed very natural; but Mr. Anstruther at that moment desired solitude above all things, and he was about to bid the man depart, rather sharply, when a glance at the other's face checked him and changed his intention. It was a countenance of the ordinary plebeian type, not remarkable for intelligence, and rather good-humored than morose in its habitual cast; but it was entirely transfigured now by a strange expression of mingled cunning and fear. The latter seemed at first to predominate; for it was some time before he managed to answer his master's question as to what he wanted.

"I want to speak to you," he said, at last, "about—about——"

He jerked his thumb toward the main corridor. There was a significance about the gesture, which, no more than the omission of all form of address, was not lost on Mr. Anstruther, whose brows, contracted already, were bent a little more heavily; but there was no other sign of emotion as he sat down and, in his curtest manner, bade the man "say out his say, and be quick about it, for he wanted to be alone."

"The sooner the better, as far as I'm concerned," the other retorted. It was quite evident that he was too frightened to be civil, and had been providing himself with Dutch courage to boot. "I've come to give you warning—no month's notice or nonsense of that sort. I wish to go at once, and I mean to."

"Is that all?" Anstruther asked, indifferently. "There need be no difficulty about it. I suppose you know your own mind, though you have been drinking."

"Not all, nor half all," the man rejoined, with a scowl. Anstruther was not popular with his inferiors, and perhaps the valet was not sorry of a chance of venting some suppressed spleen. "I mean to have something more than my wages and my fare back to town. Now, you're going to say that I haven't a claim even to that much in law. Damn the law! I wonder what the law would think of such work as you've been doing to-night."

Always in the same indifferent manner, Anstruther answered,—

"You mean to imply that I am accountable for Miss Irving's accident?"

"Imply?" Prescott snarled. "Yes, I do mean to imply. Do you suppose I'm fool enough to speak as I have now, without proofs? Ah!—proofs enough to bring you to the gallows, if it's a hanging-matter; and if it isn't it ought to be. Would you like to know what they are? Well, bad as you are, you've a right to look at your goods before you buy 'em. I began to suspect there was something up when you got so infernally close and fond of working alone at the chemicals. I wonder you never thought of locking the shop up when you left it. I used to ferret about there when you were out riding, and one day I came on a vial, hid up in a corner, half full of a curious whitish liquor in it with hardly any smell; but what there was was unlike anything I had ever smelled before. I just wetted the tip of my finger with the stopper; and I thought I'd had enough of experiments for one day. I dare say you have guessed why. I put the vial back again; I didn't see it again for ever so long, though I looked often enough; but I'd swear to the smell anywhere, and so you'd find out if you chose to go with me into the poor young lady's room yonder."

"A link of evidence, certainly; but only one, and not enough to convict." Anstruther spoke with the quiet discrimination of one accustomed to weigh the weight of testimony, and with no other interest in the case than the anxiety of an upright judge.

"Ah! But suppose it's not the only one," the other went on, with malignant triumph. "Suppose I'd noticed how queer you looked, and how your hand shook, when you were dressing for dinner, and suspected something was coming off—though I'd forgotten the vial? Suppose, by the merest chance, I had been in this room somewhere between nine and ten, and, when I heard your footsteps in the passage, had hid behind those curtains, and seen you take something devilishly like that same vial out of the dispatch-box that has no key except the one you wear, and that I'd watched you leave the room and come back again in five minutes or so, with a queerer look on your face than I'd ever seen there, and push something into the heart of the fire that cracked and spluttered,—lucky the day turned chilly, wasn't it?—and then pretty nearly empty that pocket-flask—you, who are so mealy-mouthed about a drop of liquor or two? Just suppose all this, and then what do you think of the evidence? I expect you've hung men on less."

Still not a muscle in George Anstruther's face moved; but there came an expression into his eyes that made Prescott resolve henceforth to keep the width of the table, at least, betwixt them.

"The evidence is strong; and you're quite right in supposing that I've been satisfied with less in my time. That's nothing to the point, if this came into court. My line of defense would be very simple and easy. I should affirm that, finding you in my room drunk and insolent, I dismissed you on the spot, and that you had trumped up this charge to revenge yourself. The testimony of a discharged servant is usually sifted rather severely. It would come to a question of character, after all. There has never been a whisper against mine. You know best if your own would bear looking into. From what I've heard of your antecedents, I should think—not. I don't say it would suit me to bring it into court. You want hush-money, of course; but you'd better consider all this in fixing your terms."

Prescott bit his lip sulkily. He was not altogether prepared for the case assuming this complexion; but he could not deny that it was a probable one.

"I don't know about my evidence satisfying a jury," he grumbled; "but Mr. Ramsay, here, is the nearest magistrate, and it's more than likely it would satisfy him."

It was a random shaft; but it told far beyond the expectations of the archer. Whether it was that some natural instinct warned George Anstruther of the deadly peril in which he would stand if he were thus confronted with Mark Ramsay, or whether, having nerved himself to endure a distant though perhaps certain penalty, he shrank appalled before swift and instant retribution, it is hard to say. For myself, I incline to the latter interpretation.

There are numberless instances of hardier criminals than he being utterly cowed by the news that the three days' grace betwixt them and their doom is shortened to one hour. Be this as it may, Anstruther's countenance had lost its judicial calmness, and his voice shook with something else than anger, as he required the other to "name his price at once, without further chaffering."

"It's worth five thousand—well worth it," Prescott rejoined, sulkily; "but, as you're not made of money, and I want it in a hurry, we'll say four. If you haven't got it at your banker's, you can get it fast enough in London; and you'd leave this to-morrow, anyhow. I'll go that far with you for the look of the thing; but another thousand wouldn't tempt me to stop the month out in your service—no, nor hardly to brush your clothes again."

Though for mere greed this man was willing to connive at crime, he spoke those words with a loathing palpably sincere; and, amidst the tumult raging within him, Anstruther was sensible of a sharper pang, as he felt that even such a creature as this had the right to shrink from him now.

"You shall have your money," he said, speaking with an effort. "You'll trust me till I can raise it, I presume?"

"Yes; I'll trust you. You daren't break faith with me; and I believe you are honest in your way. I'd give something to know what set you on this game."

"Will you go?"

That was all Anstruther said; and the words came in-

distinctly through his hands, that covered his face as he
rested his elbows on the table. The valet was only too
glad to find himself safe in the passage outside, with his
object attained.

Long after the echo of his footsteps had died away, his
master sat motionless in that same position. At length
he rose, unlocked the dispatch-box to which Prescott had
alluded, and took out of it a tiny silver tube, scarcely
thicker than a crow-quill. He dropped this into his pocket,
and resumed his seat. It was not till the door opened
again that he lifted his head.

Was it worth while to have endured the agony of his
recent abasement—to have bought shameful safety with
a bribe—to have been made the mock of his own hireling
—only to be set face to face, before the night was out,
with Mark Ramsay?

CHAPTER XLII.

WITH the average of mankind,—to womanhood the
aphorism scarcely applies,—audacity, or even coolness,
under peculiar circumstances, is very much a question of
experience.

There flourishes even now, down in the West, a certain
divine, famous alike for learning and godliness, who
became more famous than ever from the manner in which
he bore himself in time of sore trial. The town in which
he ministered was visited by one of those deadly epi-
demics that are scarcely less dreadful than the ancient
plague. At last there was such a panic in the place that
all who could by any means escape fled therefrom, and
some even among the doctors came reluctantly to their
duties, if they did not absolutely shirk them. Now, this
good parson not only put far away from him all temptation
—and temptations were not lacking—to quit his post, but
labored more strenuously than ever. Late and early he
might have been found, with a countenance, if not cheerful,

always serene, in such fearful strait as was he of old who stood between the dead and the living ere yet the plague was stayed. When at last—partly by fever, partly by fatigue—he was brought so low that all, himself included, believed his hours were numbered, he waited for death, they say, not less composedly than he would have waited for sleep.

Two or three years later, the same divine was involved in a terrible railway-accident, from which he escaped comparatively unhurt, though his situation for some time was critical in the extreme. He preached a very eloquent discourse afterward, wherein he described his own sensations at length; and a more beautiful illustration of submissive trust in Providence could hardly be conceived. He was not apt to vaunt himself, and perchance, by some mysterious process of thought, had come to believe that he had in very truth felt what he described. Nevertheless, according to the testimony of eye-witnesses, during that period of peril he did nothing but wail incoherently —being fairly distraught with fear.

As the strongest antithesis to this godly person, take Cecil Grantley. He would fly like a timid hare from the vicinity of the mildest form of scarlatina, and, when he joins in the pursuit, requires much priming before he will negotiate a sheep-hurdle. Well, not long ago he got into a very awkward scrape, the nature of which matters not. Up to a certain point he had to deal with feminine adversaries, and up to this point his trepidations were simply pusillanimous. Suddenly a fresh personage appeared on the scene,—a most truculent personage, too; but Cecil brightened up directly.

"It's all right now," he said; "we've got a man into the wrangle;" and thenceforth he carried the thing with a high hand.

Now, George Anstruther perhaps was not physically or morally more of a coward than his fellows, but in the even tenor of his life he had hardly ever been proved by anything like personal danger. In those days—it was before the Mutiny—the gentle Hindoo seldom belied his character. For many years the Indian judge had been surrounded by people who would no more have dreamed rent of upbraiding, and of Mark's having listened, gazing at her always in the same dreamy way, as though her bitterest words stung him neither to remorse nor anger. He must have made her understand, somehow, that howsoever accountable he might be for the shortening of the frail life just ended, George Anstruther's blood was not actually on his head; but how he did this she could never recollect. She remembered the maid's rushing in and out again into the corridor to seek for help, and she remembered how a certain relief mingled with her terrors when she found herself watching the corpse alone.

When Laura Brancepeth shall come to that hour when, for her soul's sake, it will behoove her to be in charity with all men, one name assuredly will be excepted from the amnesty. Yet perhaps it is well she never knew that Mark Ramsay went straight from her presence to that of Alice's father.

To give Irving his due, no disaster of his own would have brought such dejection on his face as possessed it while he sat brooding over that which had befallen his daughter; but natures such as his are more often hardened than softened by any great sorrow, and, as he looked up and saw who it was that entered, his brow contracted gloomily. If he did not hold Mark to a certain degree accountable, as it were in the second degree, for Alice's calamity, it had at all events occurred under his roof; and this was quite sufficient to make the sight of him very unwelcome just now.

"The doctor has come, of course?" Irving inquired, with something in his tone which signified that without some such excuse the intrusion was unwarrantable.

"No, he has not come yet," Mark replied; "but it was needful I should see you at once. You asked me, an hour ago, if I could give no guess as to the meaning or author of the devilish work yonder. I could guess at neither then; but both are known to me now. That's what I've come to tell you. Be patient a minute," he went on, as Irving rose up with such a fell menace on his face as would be hard to describe. "I must say out my say, once for all. I'm not going to deny that the scandal-mongers might have found fault with my in-of menacing him, even in gesture, than of insulting a statue of Siva.   A canter across an indifferent road was about the roughest exercise he had ever indulged in.   He considered the honor of first spear by no means worth the risk of broken bones, and would go a mile round sooner than scramble across a moderate nullah, let alone leaping it.   Excitement of any sort he considered unwholesome and irrational,—the excitement of peril most irrational of all.   While his villainous scheme was still in its first germ, he had counted the cost and resolved to pay it; and when he grew familiar with the idea, and shrunk from it no longer, he never lost sight of the probable consequences to himself.   He knew that the mere fact of his predilection for chemistry would be sure to attract suspicion sooner or later ; and, moreover, though difficult, it might not be impossible for an analyst to determine from what precise region the venomous ingredients must have been brought.   Alsager's surmises were right.   It was during his sojourn in India that Anstruther had obtained these.   He had indeed confiscated them after they had been employed in similar disfigurement. He had taken all possible precautions, to be sure ; and, with average luck, the chain of circumstantial evidence linking him with the crime must needs be weak.   At first he thought he had prospered beyond his hopes ; for, though he was last to enter the corridor, he was there soon enough to hear Laura Brancepeth speak of the broken vial.   There was little fear of analytical tests after that.   But then had come the blow which put all his calculations to the rout. It had never entered his head that stolid William Prescott would be shrewd enough and patient enough to play the spy,—and play it to such fatal purpose. But, though he was taken by surprise, he kept his self-possession admirably till he heard that threat—it was only half intended as a threat, after all—about Mark Ramsay. It was not the magistrate that he dreaded, but the man who, if half the tales were true, had trampled under foot written and unwritten laws on less provocation than this ere now, and who would have been scarcely less scrupulous in working out his revenge than he had always shown himself in working out his desire.   It was this which made George Anstruther accept extortion without bargaining, and it was this which sent a shiver through his blood when he looked up and saw who stood on the threshold.

With eyes wide open and vacant like a sleep-walker's, he stared at his visitor as he closed the door softly and turned the key and then came nearer till he stood just where Prescott had been standing awhile ago. There was nothing very alarming in his face : it was scarcely so lowering as when he entered his wife's dressing-room, but it was even more set. The two looked at each other for perhaps half a minute. Mark watched in silence the workings of the other's countenance. They would have told him enough, if his suspicions had slumbered till now. Then he said, with a strange quietness, "You can guess why I have come here."

The first syllables of Anstruther's reply were scarcely intelligible ; but the last were uttered more clearly.

"I cannot guess. Has—has it anything to do with the —the—accident of this evening?"

"Everything to do with the—accident. We'll call it so for the present. You remember I asked in the corridor, just now, whether any one knew anything of surgery ; and you shook your head like the rest. Perhaps you were taken by surprise, and hadn't time to think over your resources. It may be hours before the doctor comes, and every second may be precious. Chemists such as you are often carry about strange drugs with them ; and, if you have no drugs, you have knowledge. They say all poisons have an antidote. Is there none for this ?"

Anstruther could hardly believe his ears. Was it possible that the person he so dreaded had not come to accuse or condemn, but only to ask for such aid as any man has a right to expect from the stranger sojourning within his gates? But the first flush of glad surprise was checked by a cold sense of helplessness,—by a hopeless feeling that, though the door of escape stood wide, he could not pass there. It was not too much to say that George Anstruther would have given up almost everything, short of his heart's blood, to have had the power of undoing his deed. Fear of the consequences, doubtless, chiefly swayed him ; but there was a tinge of remorse too, howsoever faint. Moreover, a dreary consciousness that all had been done to no purpose, and that not one doit of the prize for which he had sold himself would ever be paid, had crept over him since up yonder in the corridor, glancing up once sidelong and stealthily, he met the horror of Blanche Ramsay's eyes. But it was not to be. He knew right well that, though besides the risk of fever there was little danger to life from his devilish drugs, their effects were past the art of man, and that time would never efface, even if it should mitigate, the hideous scars. The face that was so dangerous yesterday, no woman would ever more be jealous of. Never would any man henceforth willingly look on it twice. Though he dared not avow all this, he dared not speak contrariwise.

"I would gladly help you,—most gladly; but I have small skill in such matters, and might do more harm than good in advising. They have tried cold applications, I suppose. That ought to give temporary relief; and I trust the surgeon will be here very soon."

Mark gazed well at the speaker, still rather earnestly than threateningly.

"Are you quite sure you can suggest nothing? Mind, I ask you this, knowing that mere medical skill will avail little. Think again. It's a question of life or death."

The keen perception that had served Anstruther well in ordinary matters quite failed him here; for from that strange quietness of Mark's manner he drew encouragement when he ought to have drawn warning.

"I do not know what others can do," he said, with a certain haughtiness, "but I am quite sure that I can do nothing. If I had any doubt on the subject, I should not have wanted asking twice."

"I'll give you one more chance," Mark said, speaking very low. "Not for your sake, but for hers who lies yonder. I know as well who has done this deed as if I'd watched you drop in the poison. Don't waste time in denial,—it may be shorter than you think,—but listen to me. If you can hold out any certain hope that what has been done can be undone,—quite undone,—you shall go forth from this house harmless, and you shall never be troubled more by me or mine; and, if you bear me any grudge, you may set your foot on my neck now, if you please. Lying won't help you, for I'll look into your eyes while you answer."

All his terrors came back upon Anstruther like a wave in reflux; yet he, too, felt that lying or evasion would be useless, and he spoke like those of old time whose utterances were not according to their own will, but as the Spirit gave it.

"Her life is safe. I can give no other hope."

Mark breathed long and deep, as gymnasts do when preparing for some great feat of strength or skill

"Then half my errand is done. I came to seek help here, as I would have sought it in hell if I had known the road there, and I would sooner have given the devil my soul than you your freedom in exchange; but I would have given it. There was something else, though. If there was no help to be wrung from you, I came—to kill you!"

Mark Ramsay's voice was a proverbially pleasant one. There was nothing jarring or startling in the tone of those last three words. If an actor had delivered them on any stage, the house would have murmured justly enough at a good point being spoiled. A very quiet reading even of Hamlet rarely succeeds; but then, you see, it was a singularly select audience to which Ramsay was playing, and he did not trouble himself to study effects. In sober truth, there was the savage earnestness there that rends a passion to tatters; and so the solitary witness interpreted it as he sprang up with a white terror on his face, glaring round him in a wild, hopeless way—yes, hopeless; for, whether by chance or design, Ramsay had moved during the last two seconds so as to stand directly betwixt the other and the fireplace, where, putting weapons of defense out of the question, the one bell-rope hung. He would have cried for help, but his voice was nearly gone. There was little chance of a shout bringing timely succor; but, even if it had been so, there was manhood enough left in the old civilian to make him loath to cry aloud for help against a single unarmed enemy. Indeed, the physical odds against him were not so great. He had the advantage in height and weight, and probably in strength, if not in activity; and though his gaunt frame had waxed thinner of late, it had not become bent or emaciated, and there was a tough, wiry look about it still.　But there was no question of physique here.　The thirsty eagerness for the struggle on one side was opposed to shuddering reluctance on the other; and had you watched the two you would no more have doubted as to the result than if you had watched a panther crouching for his spring on a buffalo.

"You—you are mad!" Anstruther gasped out.　"Have you forgotten that—that your life is forfeit when you have taken mine?"

The other broke into a ghastly laugh, and drew ever so little nearer, very slowly.　It seemed as though he saw the terror he inspired, and savored it as part of his vengeance.

"Forgotten! No; I have forgotten nothing.　Not that what you have done is a hanging-matter; but what I'm going to do is—that's as clear as day.　It's only a sort of suicide, after all, and it's a pleasanter way than knotting one's own noose.　You'll have made clean work of it between you—you and yonder wife of mine."

A confusion with which animal fear had naught to do rang out in Anstruther's cry.

"My God!　Is it possible you suspect your wife of having art or part in this?　See, I speak as if I were on my death-bed.　By all my hopes of mercy, she's as innocent as any of heaven's angels.　Believe me! you shall, you shall!"

"I believe you," Mark answered; "and she'll have the benefit of her innocence, if that's any consolation to you.　If I'd time to think about such trifles, perhaps I might wonder what has made you so zealous to serve that wife of mine, and so anxious to shield her.　We're past all that now."

And even as he spoke he drew nearer, and the hungry glitter brightened in his eyes.

The bitterness of death comes not always with or just before the death-pang, and those who tottered and stumbled at the entrance of the Dark Valley have been known to walk steadily enough when they were within the shadow. So it was with George Anstruther. Whether it was the mere energy of despair that sustained him, or whether a generous impulse prompting that last intercession abode with him still, no one will never know; but assuredly he did not die a coward.

"I loved your wife," he said, speaking quite firmly now. "Does not that account for all? I loved her that day when you and I first met. I've loved her since, so well that I repent to-night's work no more than if I'd set my heel on an adder in her path. I love her so well that I'll save her, in spite of you, from the shame of having married a felon. You thought I was afraid of death. So I was; but it was death in your fashion—not in my own. Before I knew you were coming, I was ready with—this."

He had felt in his pocket ere this, and now, with the quickness of thought, drew forth the tiny silver tube and crushed it betwixt his strong white teeth.

With a spring like a wild cat's, Mark Ramsay cleared the distance betwixt them; but his fingers gripped a throat that never felt the pressure, and of the two bodies that crashed on the floor together the life was in only one.

The fury of baffled revenge mingled with a natural horror in the survivor's face as he shook himself clear of the corpse and arose; but, as he grew calmer, he began to debate with himself what was best to be done. After two or three minutes spent in deep thought, he walked to the door and unlocked it, then rang the bell twice or thrice violently. Not for one instant while he waited did he avert his gaze, nor did his eyes alter their expression of hate and loathing. Two or three servants came hurrying up, Prescott the foremost. It was to this man Ramsay addressed himself.

"Your master has taken poison. He took it too suddenly for me to stop him; though, of course, I tried. He did it to save himself from being arrested for the crime committed here to-night."

The valet was too utterly prostrated by the annihilation of his golden dreams to do other than repeat, helplessly, "Poisoned himself!"

"There is no doubt about it," Mark replied. "There will be an inquest, I suppose; and it will be well for you, and you, and you" (he glanced from one to the other of the servants as he spoke) "to take notice of *this.*"

Y

Shuddering and shrinking, they followed the direction of his finger: it pointed to the silver tube still crushed between the clinched teeth. All human help was so palpably hopeless that no one thought of rendering it; and each followed Ramsay out of the room in silence.

"Speak about this as little as can be helped, or, at any rate, speak low. Keep this door locked till the doctor comes," Mark said to Prescott. "He can go in, if he likes, after he has visited Miss Irving." And so he walked slowly away—whither, you will presently see.

"What a big dashed fool I was to trust him!" the valet muttered to himself, disconsolately. This, setting aside a few exclamations of wonderment among his acquaintance when the news was bruited at the Orion, and the self-congratulation of the civilian who succeeded to his pension, was the only funeral oration pronounced over a man who, in his time, had filled high places with honor; whose word was as his bond, and whom Walter Ellerslie trusted like a brother; who, if not a model of Christianity, had seldom willfully or wittingly broken one of God's laws or injured onè of God's creatures, till the night when, having sinned heavily in both wise, he died unrepentant.

"*Finis coronat opus.*"

The dullest schoolboy has that by heart before he has got half through his rudiments; but sometimes wise elders will be very near the End before they are assured whether the Crown will be one of shame or of glory.

CHAPTER XLIII.

IT was, in truth, only a fainting-fit into which Blanche had fallen awhile ago, but it lasted long; and, when she partially recovered her senses, she seemed to be wandering. Her first intelligible words signified a wish to be left alone again with Laura Brancepeth: so the maid was dismissed, and betook herself to wait in the sleeping-chamber till she should be required.

"Now, you mustn't excite yourself, dear," La Reine said, with authority. "And, whatever you do, lie still for the present."

"Lie still!" Blanche moaned. "How is it possible? Oh, Laura, if you knew! if you knew!"

"Well, but I do know," the other retorted, in her impetuous way. "It's not hard to guess that your husband's furious at what has happened to-night, and came to vent his wrath on you. That's so like a man, and especially like a husband: even Henry does it, sometimes, —though he's rather afraid of me. He didn't say it was your fault, I suppose?"

"No," Blanche murmured. "He didn't say it was my fault; though he said many cruel words—such as I could never forget, even if I forgave them. But, Queenie, he suspects the same person as I did; and I think he's gone there now. What will happen to us all?"

La Reine looked somewhat blank at this, though she made shift to answer, carelessly,—

"Happen to us! Nothing worse than has happened already, you may depend upon it. Mark knows better than to bring such a charge against one of his guests on mere suspicion; and more than suspicion there could not be. If he were mad enough to do such a thing, Mr. Anstruther would not condescend to plead guilty or not guilty, but would leave the house at once. It's the only thing he could do. Every one will be going to-morrow, as it is, I should think, except me. Of course I shall stay till I take you South."

Her assumed cheerfulness had small effect. It could not bring back the light on Blanche's face, nor still the tremors that shook her almost incessantly.

"You don't know Mark," she panted. "I never knew him myself, before to-night. I wish—yes, I do wish—that I had died yesterday. No, I'm not wandering, Queenie—nor dreaming. If one could only wake and find all this a dream! I feel that some worse horror will happen yet, and it will be all—all through me."

Laura Brancepeth's wits were good, strong, serviceable ones, not easily to be scattered, but they were getting into sore confusion. It was useless to argue with Blanche in her present state ; and yet, if she could not be pacified, serious harm must needs ensue.

"What can I do, dear ?" she said, half despairingly. "Shall I call in Wright to take care of you, and go and find Mark myself and bring him here? Anything would be better than your torturing yourself so."

For the first time since her swoon, Blanche opened her eyes and fixed them upon her friend eagerly.

"Ah ! if you could do this, Queenie,—if—if you were not afraid"—

"Afraid !" Laura retorted, in supreme scorn. But her dauntlessness was not put to the proof, at least in the way she had intended ; for, as she rose up to call in the maid from the adjoining chamber, the door of the dressing-room opened, and Ramsay entered once more.

It was recorded, long ago, that the best point in Mark's rare personal beauty was the soft richness of his coloring. This would certainly have never been noticed now ; for the color seemed to have faded in some strange way out of his eyes and lips, and the clear olive cheeks looked sickly and wan. The malignant lowering was no longer on his face ; he only looked intensely weary. He did not speak till he came quite close to the two women, and then it was in a subdued tone.

"I did not mean to disturb you again to-night, but I have no choice. Something has happened since I saw you last."

La Reine had risen, and stood betwixt husband and wife, holding Blanche's hand fast, as though she would have shielded her from some bodily harm.

"Good heavens! what is it?" she cried out, angrily. "Surely we have no fresh disaster to hear of!"

"Why not?" Mark answered, still in the same slow, deliberate voice. "Would you call it a disaster if the author of all this crime had been discovered and made a confession?"

Laura's hand was wrung till she could scarcely bear the pressure, as Blanche started almost upright with a piteous wail.

"Mark! Mark! You will—you will—have mercy."

He never blenched before that agony : indeed, you might have fancied there hovered round his lips the shadow of a smile.

"Are you interceding for George Anstruther? You may spare your breath. A priest's prayers might help him now, if priests can help the dead."

Cruel as this man was by nature—tenfold crueler now in the bitterness of half-slaked revenge—I believe had he guessed at the effect of his words he would no more have uttered them in that shape than he would have driven a knife straight to his wife's heart then and there. Had he done so, it would scarce have been quicker work.

While the last syllable lingered on his lips, Blanche stood upright upon her feet, clasping both hands tightly on her side, staring at him with wild, haggard eyes. And then a change—other than he had seen there lately— such a change as can come but once on any human face —swept across hers, and she sank back on her couch with a long, gasping sob. Her hands dropped idly down, and she lay quite still.

The kind old physician's prophecy had come true, though not in the sense in which it was spoken, and sooner than he had reckoned on. It was well with Blanche Ramsay at last.

What passed during the next quarter of an hour that ensued, Laura Brancepeth could never distinctly recall. Perhaps she did not care to tax her memory too closely. She had a hazy impression of having poured forth a tor

timacy with Alice; and I'm not going to prove to you that it was innocent, at this time of day. If you had thought otherwise, I should have heard of it long ago. It's sufficient to know that some people looked on Alice as my wife's worst enemy, and that this thought was uppermost in George Anstruther's mind when he mixed his poison to-night."

"You know all this," the father said, in a savage whisper, "and you mean to hold your hand and to ask me to hold mine?"

"What would you do?" said Mark Ramsay, drearily. "They are both dead."

Irving staggered a full pace backward, with a dreadful question in his eyes that to save his life he could not then have put into words. Once again the other laughed in that same ghastly fashion as he had done in Anstruther's chamber.

"You think I killed them. I don't wonder. Well, I went to kill him; but—curse him!—he was too quick for me. And she died five minutes ago, in a heart-spasm."

"Tell me more," Irving said, under his breath. The first horror had left him, and all the pity he had to spare was engrossed by his own daughter. Nevertheless, it was with an awe such as he had never known that he listened to the brief story of what you have just read,— such an awe as the flintiest-hearted skeptics have felt when the air around them was heavy with death. But always in his mind the thought was uppermost of how on the first hour of their meeting he had conceived a vague dislike and apprehension of George Anstruther, and how in his own folly he had thought, "He cannot harm me and mine."

Moreover, though he himself would have scoffed at the idea, or at the most would only have admitted fatality, he was overborne by a strong sense of helplessness, by a consciousness that all the rough-hewn ends had been shaped by other hands than those that first fashioned them—perchance by the hands of Him who said, so many ages ago, "Vengeance is mine." There is a weak point in almost all infidelities; and many, before their atheism was put to the last crucial test, have cried in their hearts, if not aloud, *Vicisti, Galilæe!*

And what were Alice Irving's thoughts, when she heard how swiftly and completely she was avenged? It was one of her attendants brought the news. The woman was too frightened to speak coherently; but Alice divined all the tragedy as completely as if it had been enacted before her eyes. The cruel calculation had been right to the letter. Her life had outlasted—perhaps was likely far to outlast—her rival's; and what did that profit her? She knew, not less surely than if a hundred surgeons had sentenced her, that her beauty was marred, not for a season, but for evermore. She knew, not less surely than if his own lips had uttered the bitter words, that henceforth pity was the uttermost she could expect from Mark Ramsay. Though his love, in spite of the guilt that loaded it, had been so precious to her, she had always recognized it as a passion strong chiefly in its sensuousness, and one that would prove weak and unstable as water under such a trial as this. There was the stale formula of consolation:—they might be friends still. Friends! Alice almost gnashed her teeth as she thought what a horrible hypocrisy such a pretense would be betwixt herself and the man who that day had kissed her brow. Amidst all those burning pains, she felt the print of his lips.

CHAPTER XLIV.

The smoking-room lay at the extreme end of one of the wings of the castle, and it was too remote for many sounds from the other parts of the house to penetrate there—unless it were such a cry as had startled the occupants an hour ago. The servants who were cognizant of Anstruther's death obeyed orders, and discussed it among themselves. Neither of this nor of the other tragedy were Alsager and Gauntlet made aware, till the door opened and Ramsay appeared. There were no signs of passion on his face, nor any marked signs of pain—only that weary look of exhaustion. And yet both guessed, before he spoke a word, that he had blacker news to tell than any they had already listened to.

"Is she much worse?" Alsager asked.

"You mean Alice Irving?" Mark replied, after he had filled and drained a great goblet of iced water. "Not that I know of. When last I heard of her, she was in rather less pain. But I have heavy news for you. Anstruther has committed suicide, after confessing himself the cause of yonder disfigurement. I was present, but not near enough to prevent him. The poison did its work quicker than a bullet. There! you needn't waste pity on such a hound as that. There's worse behind. Not a quarter of an hour ago, I broke the news to Blanche as cautiously as I could, and—Lady Laura was there with her—her fright brought on a spasm of the heart, and she died almost instantaneously."

"Dead!"

The word broke from the lips of both; but in the one case there was only the shock of surprise; in the other there was the climax of a strong heart-agony. As Gauntlet covered his face with his hand, he groaned aloud.

During the minutes that ensued, there was waged in Oswald's breast such a struggle as must need leave traces long after it is ended. He was beset by a fiercer temptation than he had ever yet passed through; and, though he mastered it at last, the wrestle was sore. Perhaps you cannot guess at the nature of the temptation. It was no other than a longing to add another crime to the catalogue of that night,—black enough already,—if indeed it were a crime to grapple Mark Ramsay's throat, as he would have done any felon's, and to require of him life for life. For then assuredly—even if he grew more charitable in the after-time—he held this man no less accountable for the death of the woman that he, Oswald Gauntlet, had loved so dearly, than if the murder had been wrought by a downright brutal blow. It was because he loved her so dearly that he restrained himself. If Blanche's name must needs be mixed up in this sorrowful and shameful story, it was not for him to add thereunto another ghastly chapter. Had she been living still, her thin, wan hand would have been surely raised to warn him from reprisals, and he would surely have obeyed the beckon: so—now as then—let her have her will. But, albeit he prevailed in wrestle over the devil that fought savagely within him, he prevailed not so far as to endure Mark's presence. When he rose up, it was with averted face, and their eyes never met, as he walked out silently and swiftly.

For months past he had seen the end coming nearer and nearer, and he had known that nothing short of a miracle could avert or, perhaps, much delay it; and, now that it had come, it seemed to him like some hideous nightmare. He could not realize at first that the delicate mobile lips, whose smile when it lost its mirth did not lose its pleasantness, were now still and set, or that the eyes which had never looked on him unkindly were luster-less and dim, or that the voice which when he last heard it had stirred his pulse not less powerfully than in the old days was dumb for evermore. But, as he began to realize all this, there began a struggle in this man's breast, and he was beset by a temptation the like of which he had never encountered.

And the other two kept silence likewise for a full minute after the door had closed behind Gauntlet, till Ramsay broke it impatiently.

"What are you thinking of? I'd rather hear you speak than watch you stare."

"Is it worth while to ask?" the other said, bitterly. "If my thoughts ever mattered much, it's rather late in the day to ask for them. Besides, if I were to tell you, it might only breed a quarrel; and, somehow, I don't feel up to that. We had best let ill alone. After all, I've no right to judge you."

"I understand. You'll write down every item of what has happened here to my account. You are not unjust, I dare say."

There was a helpless depression in his manner that moved the other to answer less harshly.

"I don't know that. The fatalists—I'm more than half a fatalist—would say you were only an instrument.

If it is so, I am selfish enough to be glad you were picked out instead of me. Mark, I'd have changed places with you pretty often within the last two years. I wouldn't do that to-night; and I wish the night was over, with all my heart and soul."

"Do you think to-morrow will be any better?" Mark asked, wearily, "or the next day, or the next? Do you remember what I said when we talked it over in my chambers? We have 'dreed our weird' with a vengeance.

"You've never asked me how it all happened. I'd rather tell you at once and get it over; though I've told it once already."

As Alsager listened to much the same story as Irving had heard but now, it was evident that his interest in the first catastrophe did not go beyond wonder and curiosity. He was not in the habit of scattering his sympathy broadcast; and George Anstruther's suicide moved him very little more than if he had read it in the public prints.

"That was a devilish narrow escape of yours," he remarked, coolly, when he heard how Mark's murderous intent had been anticipated. "It was a very natural impulse, I'll allow; but at our time of life we ought to have got beyond such things; and so you'd have thought when you found yourself in the dock. I doubt if they'd have brought it in even manslaughter, unless Nevis had tried you. It's very odd I should have always suspected him; and I told Gauntlet so. He wouldn't have it at first. I wonder what he thinks of it now?—or of anything else, for that matter? I never saw any man more thoroughly knocked out of time. Go on now: it's no use halting when you've got so far."

But as Alsager listened to the details, still more brief, of the second calamity, the hard cynicism vanished from his face, and when all was told he drew a long breath very like a sigh.

"If it was over so quickly, she couldn't have suffered much," he said. "I'm glad of that,—poor thing! She'd had her share of it before. That was the time to pity her; and I did, and told you so. It's absurd to pity her now. Do you know, Mark, I believe in many more things than people give me credit for? and I like to fancy that she'll find a pleasant berth somewhere,—a real pleasant one,—such a long way off from yours or mine. Well, heart-complaints are curious things. Hers might have killed her without any meddling of yours. Perhaps that's the best way of looking at it."

The other shook his head, as though putting aside the crumb of comfort, if it was so meant. He made no answer, and then again silence ensued. At last said Alsager, abruptly,—

"What do you wish every one to do? I don't think Lady Laura will move before the—the funeral; and I'll stay too, if I can help you Whatever you've done or left undone, you've stood by me pretty stanchly since that morning in Florence; and I'll stand by you now, even if we cry 'quits' after this."

Seldom—perhaps never—had any of his own sex seen such an eager, beseeching look in Mark Ramsay's eyes as glistened in them then.

"For God's sake, don't go," he muttered, hurriedly; "I'm so nearly beat as it is; much more than I was after that jungle-fever. I rather prided myself on my nerve. I shall never do that again."

"That's settled, then," the other answered, with his wonted composure. "I stay. And now,—how about the Irvings?"

Mark started, just as he had done once before when Alsager set a chord in his musings tingling, and from just the same cause. Amidst all the turmoil through which he had lately passed, be sure he had found time to ask of himself that question more than once. Alice had judged very accurately the length and breadth and depth of his love. No more life lingered in it now than was in the dead corpse of his wife up-stairs. It was but the spectral semblance of love that he had to face now and henceforth. A man of his temperament had better tenfold be haunted by any "dull, mechanic ghost" than by such a one as this. He had not yet confessed as much to himself, and he certainly was not prepared to confess it to even such an old friend as Alsager. Nevertheless, he shifted his posture uneasily, as he answered,—

"The Irvings? They must stay here for the present,

of course. She could not possibly be moved in her present state; though, if the dead dog yonder did not lie, her life is not in danger."

"They must remain here for the present, naturally," Vere persisted; "but afterwards?"

Vere had not any intention of tormenting; but compassion for Blanche Ramsay was still strong enough within him to make him behold with some satisfaction the other's embarrassment.

"Afterwards!" Mark retorted, angrily. "Didn't I tell you my nerve was gone for the moment?"

It was a relief to one of those two when, at last, a servant came into that room to say that the doctor had arrived.

Mr. Brancepeth was one of those whose very existence, in times of great emergency, their fellows are apt to ignore.

No one, from first to last, had thought of rousing him; but he was waked from a placid and not unstertorous slumber by a light touch on his shoulder and by a warm drop falling on his brow. Without being intrepid, he was a very self-possessed person: nevertheless, during his first waking moments he felt a slight tremor, as he doubted whether he saw a vision or no. That white, tear-stained face ought rather to have belonged to the Brown Ladye who was said to walk at Kenlis, than to his gay, daring wife. But it was Laura, and no other, who stood sobbing there, so utterly broken down that it was some time before she could give any rational account to her husband of what had happened. To say that Brancepeth was panic-stricken only faintly expresses the state of mind in which he was thrown. It was not only the intrinsic horror of the events themselves that affected him so strongly. If they had occurred in a sphere of life removed from his own, and they had been brought before him in his official capacity, he would have looked into them with magisterial calmness; but their having been enacted not only under his very eyes—though those eyes chanced to be closed—and all the actors and sufferers therein being his own intimate acquaintance, if not familiar friends, seemed to him to involve such an awful incongruity, that for the moment he was fairly unhinged, and was almost as incoherent in his questions as Laura was in her answers.

Now, it is possible that some who read these pages may partly indorse the opinion of Mr. Brancepeth, and consider such passions and calamities as have been just narrated well suited to mediæval melodrama, but singularly improbable in a modern country-house inhabited entirely by members of the upper ten thousand.

The objection does not sound hypercritical; yet, when there is fever or venom in the blood, it matters but little whether its color as it ran in health was imperial purple or murky red. Furthermore, I will make bold to suggest that we are in no material respects much politer than our nearest neighbors beyond seas, and that, before all things went awry, Choiseul-Praslin · had no mean rank among the ancient names of France, and that the tragedy wherewith Europe rang from west to east was wrought just twenty-two years ago.

A very heavy heart that night was Laura Brancepeth's; but it would have been heavier far if the last thought on her mind, before she sank into a feverish sleep of utter exhaustion, had not been that, prosy and precise, and grotesque in some points, as he might be, it was an honest, honorable man, at least, that lay beside her. Ay! and, with all her recklessness, she had never said or done aught that need shame him.

CHAPTER XLV.

THE doctor who had been summoned to Kenlis was a favorable specimen of a country practitioner, and, when he was walking the hospitals, had been rather celebrated for nerve and cleverness in the accident-ward; but the case he had now to deal with was far beyond his skill, and, though, after hearing the nature of the calamity, he had come provided with divers lenitives and emollients, he could only succeed in mitigating the torture she was still enduring. With respect to a permanent cure he could hold out little more comfort than Anstruther had given. Those fearful seams and scars were surely indelible; and, even though the sight might be saved, there was little chance that the deep-set gray eyes would ever regain their lustrous softness. As a matter of form, without the faintest idea of being useful, he visited the scenes of both the other catastrophes. He was tolerably callous both from habit and temperament; but it was not without out a certain emotion that he laid down Blanche Ramsay's hand after searching for a pulse in vain, and it was not without a certain relief that he closed the door again on the corpse of the suicide.

Few in Kenlis Castle, either gentle or simple, closed their eyes that night in more than brief, broken sleep; and all were glad to see day break, though it broke but gloomily.

Laura Brancepeth was up and dressed betimes. It was not that she had anything special to do, but when once awake she could not bear to lie still. She did not think of leaving her room, and had just been trying to swallow some slight refreshment, when her husband, who had risen still earlier, came in.

"I didn't mean to disturb you, but Major Gauntlet is so very anxious to see you, I could not refuse to ask whether you were equal to it. If you are, I do think it would be a kindness."

"Certainly I will," she said; "and I am not a bit surprised at his wishing to see me."

Mr. Brancepeth bent his head in acknowledgment, and withdrew.

A few minutes afterward, Gauntlet entered alone. His face was very pale, but perfectly composed, as were his voice and manner.

"You will guess that I should not have intruded on you at such a time without a purpose. I have come to ask of you a great kindness: I do not think you will refuse it; though if you should do so I shall not take it in ill part. Before I leave this place—and I do so within the hour—I should like to see *her* just once; and I want you to go with me as far as the door. Wait: don't decide till you have listened a minute longer. If I had ever spoken one word to her who is an angel now, that could shame her where she is gone, either in jest or seriously, I would not ask you this. Ah! I see you believe me without an oath; but, if I swore it on my death-bed, perhaps the world would only half believe. What has happened here will be more than a nine-days' wonder, and the scandal-mongers won't leave a blank in their romance, if they can help it. I would not have one stone to be cast at her on my account. They may say I loved her,—so I did: God alone knows how dearly,—but they can hardly say that I meant dishonor, if my last visit to her is sanctioned by the brave, kind woman who was her nearest friend."

The earnestness with which they were uttered made the simple words almost eloquent, and Laura Brancepeth's heart glowed as she held out her hand frankly.

"I do believe you; and I never hesitated even from the first, though I am glad you spoke to the end. I will come with you at once."

So those two went together, treading softly, though on the thick carpet their steps made no echo, to the door of the chamber where the remains of Blanche Ramsay lay; and Laura stood and watched without, while the other went in, closing the door behind him. Through that door it is not needful we should follow.

Many years ago, walking after nightfall through the

streets of a town in Northern Italy, I came upon an open porch, through which poured a flood of light from many tapers. On a couch just within, in an attitude not of death, but of sleep,—for the head was propped up by a silken pillow,—lay a corpse—the corpse of a young, fair woman. There was a bright garland on the deftly-braided hair, round the neck a golden chain, and on the waxen arms and fingers jewels not a few. I have looked upon some gruesome sights since, but never on one that shocked me so thoroughly. I thought then—and I think now—that of all this earth's pomps and vanities the least pardonable are funeral parades. While the world lasts, ceremonials will endure; and when great men fall in Israel, perhaps there needs must be lyings-in-state. Yet those of lowlier degree may well hope for peace and privacy on their bier, if they had found them not elsewhere. So, even in this our marionette-show, it is well to cover decorously, if not tenderly, the face of the puppet corpse.

The minutes that she watched seemed to La Reine almost endless; yet probably not ten had elapsed when the door opened again and Gauntlet came out. His countenance was not more disturbed than it had been when he entered; but as he closed his lips quickly, after a vain effort to speak, even under his thick mustache they could be seen quivering and trembling; and deathly cold those same lips felt when, a second later, they were pressed on Laura's hand in grateful and reverent farewell. Neither could she repress a slight shiver as she guessed *where* they had caught their chill.

That silent leave-taking was the only one that Gauntlet exchanged with any soul at Kenlis. He walked straight from the spot, down the staircase, out into the open air, leaving word, as he passed through the hall, that his servant was to follow him with the carriage that was to take them to the nearest station. Neither did he turn his head or look once backward till Kenlis Castle was hidden behind a ridge of hills.

It was long before Laura Brancepeth could muster courage to enter the chamber at the threshold of which she had been watching, but, having once entered, she was in no haste to leave it. When she did so, it was with a

calm on her spirit which was not afterward violently disturbed.

The master of Kenlis shut himself up in his own apartments after an interview with the doctor, and would see
no one but Alsager: to the latter fell the direction of the
funeral arrangements.   Only on one point did Mark interfere; but there he was stubborn.   Vere's suggestion that
it might stifle much scandal if Anstruther's body were
allowed to remain where it lay, to await the coroner's
inquest, he utterly set at naught, and was scarcely induced to grant it shelter in a disused outbuilding.   The
other went so far as to hint that there might be difficulty
in finding bearers willing to carry forth the ghastly burden;
for, putting Scotch superstition out of the question, the
servants were fairly unnerved by the events of last night;
but the next minute he repented of his caution, and was
haunted long afterward by the expression on Ramsay's
face as he made answer,—

"You had better find them soon, as you are so squeamish about scandal; or I'll cast the carrion out with my
own hands."

After this one outbreak, he relapsed into sullen silence.
When he was advertised of Gauntlet's abrupt departure,
he shrugged his shoulders, as if to imply that it was just
what he had expected, and did not concern him in the
least.   Yet, in the midst of this apathy, he seemed to be
waiting for something—not with any eagerness or impatience, but with the expectation of one who knows that,
sooner or later, it must come.

Though she was anything but robust in appearance,
Alice Irving must have possessed an exceptional good
constitution.   Her system had so far resisted a shock
that would have shattered many an athletic one.   She
had kept her consciousness throughout, and, as the pain
abated, it seemed as if she might even escape the serious
danger of fever.   Neither was her strength materially
prostrated.   The fingers only of one of her hands were
slightly injured where they had touched the sponge
scarcely soaked in the lotion; and she could use her
hand perfectly.   Her sight was not at all affected, though
her eyes suffered somewhat from the inflammation around.

So, when she begged to be allowed to write a short note, the doctor, who remained in attendance, objected only faintly. Indeed, he thought the risk thus incurred would be a less one than that of the irritation and anxiety which might follow on prohibition.

This is what Alice Irving wrote, and what a few minutes later Mark Ramsay read:—

"They say my life is safe; and I am glad—or I ought to be glad: I am so little fit to die; but there is still danger of nervous fever; and, while I am sure of my senses, I will write. Perhaps I shall be quieter when it is done. Before you opened this note you guessed it came to say 'good-by,'—not good-by for a little while, or for so many months or years, but for ever and ever.

"It is not an easy word to write, and it does not make it easier that we have both well deserved what has come upon us. Yes, upon us; for I know that your sufferings, in another way, are not much lighter than mine. I am not, and never shall be, a good Christian. It was a sin to listen as I have listened to much that you have said, and yet I scarcely repent it, even now: nevertheless, I know, and you know, that if I could have foreseen the least fearful of the consequences I never should have listened. Even if I were the same Alice that stood by your side yesterday, I hope—I cannot be sure; but I do hope—that I should still be able to say that with my free will you and I shall never meet again. If no judgment had fallen upon me, there never could have been happiness for us two, after last night.

"If you ever cared for me at all, you will help me now. For pity's sake, do not prevent my going home as soon as I can be moved: to lie *here* is worse than the burning. And do not let your eyes rest upon me, even for a second. *That* I could not bear.

"And now we will go our several ways. In spite of all, I will believe yours will not always be dark and lonely. As for me, I shall, at least, never again have to struggle with temptation; and I trust the time may yet come when, without blasphemy, I may pray God to for-give us both and to bless you always.   A. I."

With a strange medley of emotions Mark pondered over the almost illegible lines. The ensuing horrors had not abated the bitterness of the wrath and disappointment aroused in him by the first disaster. Nevertheless, the beauty that had bewitched him seemed already a thing of the past; and, though he chafed savagely over the loss thereof, he coveted it no longer. He had worked himself into such a dread of an interview with Alice that the certainty of its being deferred indefinitely, if not forever, was an intense relief. There was no pain or peril that this man would not have incurred in pursuit of his heart's desire; but he shrank like the merest coward from the lightest annoyance that must needs be profitless. Selfishness in this man was sublimated. If he could have followed his strongest impulse, he would have set a hundred leagues betwixt himself and Kenlis, and he would have tried whether distraction were not to be found on earth,—whether somewhere there could not, even for such a blow as that which had smitten him, be found anodynes.

His meditations, whatsoever they were, were brief, and his answer certainly was not long in penning:—

"You are far stronger than I if you can hope, and far braver if you dare to look forward or backward; but you shall have your will now and henceforth, neither less nor more than you should have had it yesterday. Our ways shall be apart while it pleases you. Only remember this: while I have strength and sense left, wherever I may be, if you say, 'Come,' there is no power short of a miracle shall hold me back from you an hour."

Was the curtness of the farewell designed in kindness, or in cruelty? Were the words, as they were written, sincere, or designed to lie?

How often Alice Irving asked those questions to herself in the dreary after-time may hardly be imagined. She seldom dared listen to her own heart's reply,—much less put the doubt to the proof. But perchance Mark Ramsay may yet have to answer them in a court where casuistry has never yet availed, and where the stubbornest criminal has never yet declined to plead.

CHAPTER XLVI.

WITH Blanche Ellerslie's ending it is fitting this tale should end; neither, concerning the events immediately connected therewith, is much more to be recorded.

Only one inquest was held at the castle. Its mistress had notoriously so long been ailing, and there was so little mystery about her death,—especially as it happened in Laura Brancepeth's presence,—that they forbore to disquiet her remains. With no pomp, yet with all decent observance, they laid her in the family vault, over whose rusty doors a great birch keeps guard. And let us hope she rests there not less peacefully because none of her kith or kin sleep near; for never before within man's memory had any strange coffin been lowered among those bearing the name and scutcheon of Kenlis.

With George Anstruther it was different. Of the circumstances of his miserable end one witness only could speak; and from this one he could expect no more mercy dead than he would have met with living. If Mark Ramsay did not stoop to exaggeration, that he extenuated nothing is most sure; and, albeit his testimony was delivered with perfect calmness, more than one of his hearers were aware of the scarcely suppressed rancor. While the jury were deliberating on their verdict, one of the number—a shrewd Aberdonian—put into words a thought that was probably in the minds of more than one of his fellows.

"He was ower quick for ye?" quoth David Anderson, quoting Ramsay's words. "Eh! mon, I sair misdoot there are twa sides to that. It was written that there suld be murder in this hoose the nicht; gin it wad be self-murder was nae sae sure. Guid save us a'! The auld Enemy has been recht busy here, and aiblins mair souls than his that lies streekit yonder hae fallen into his net."

But those who were bold enough to impute malice to the Laird of Kenlis acquitted him at least of bearing false witness.   Indeed, his evidence, even if it had not been amply corroborated by that of the surgeon, bore too palpably the stamp of truth to be set aside. One or two timid or charitable jurors, insisting on the utter absence of motive in Anstruther's first crime, were for the milder verdict of insanity; but the majority—made up chiefly of austere elders and men of standing in their kirk—would hear of no such compromise. If crime had been committed in high places, the more reason it should be fittingly branded and not be wrapped up delicately.

So over George Anstruther no burial-service was read; and few of those dwelling in or near Kenlis know the place of his sepulture.

When these things were reported in town, that same verdict caused more scandal at the Orion than any of the other horrors. Even an Orionite could not be considered exempt from mental aberration, any more than any any of the other ills that flesh is heir to. To the steady, responsible bodies—who, even when they plunged, did so too methodically to ruffle the surface of propriety—it was monstrously incredible that their associate whom they had been used to revere as a club authority (Anstruther was actually on the Committee) should have been attainted, even after death, with felony.

"He *must* have been mad," they agreed, almost unanimously. Many had noticed—though they had never chosen to mention it till now—a very queer look in his eyes, and for a full year past a strange abruptness in his manner and—there were fewer still that could remember this—signs of weakness in his play.

"Insane? Of course it was insanity!" Lord Blanchmayne growled. "Any decent jury would have brought it in so, if it had been on a shopkeeper or a deacon; but there's no such d—d democrat as your free-kirk deacon. They never miss a chance of snapping at a gentleman, alive or dead."

Truly, so far as his observance or devotion to any form of doctrine, established or disestablished, was concerned, the viscount might be presumed to speak impartially.

Before either the funeral or the inquest took place, the Irvings had returned to Drumour.

The doctor decided that there would be less danger in the move than in the strain to which Alice's nerves must needs be subject if she remained at Kenlis. Her strength still kept up wonderfully, and she walked to the carriage that was to take her home, without faltering; but as she passed out through the great gloomy hall there broke from under her triple veil, that fell to her knees, one dreadful sob, scarcely less piteous than the first wail of her despairing agony. Among those who watched that departure, Mark Ramsay was not numbered. The subject had not once been broached betwixt father and daughter, yet both were perfectly aware that after that evening they would set foot in Kenlis no more.

Irving had assented at once to the removal, and had made no attempt to take any formal leave of Mark Ramsay, contenting himself with a verbal message to the effect that he would not intrude himself there till after the funeral. He was indeed more crushed by this blow than by any which had yet reached him,—not so much, perhaps, on account of its weight as of its exceeding strangeness. The more he pondered, the less he saw his way through the future. It seemed to him that to be constantly in the presence of such a calamity as had befallen his daughter would be more than he could endure; for you must remember that, without being in the least sensitive, he was wonderfully fastidious: to look on any physical deformity whatsoever, even if he had no special interest therein, was even more disagreeable than singing or playing out of tune. To send her from him, even if it were practicable, was a barbarity of which even he was incapable. In justice to him, it should be recorded that he gave no outward signs of these misgivings, but then, and long afterward, behaved himself toward his daughter with a tact, if not tenderness, that would have done credit to a more perfect parent.

Through that autumn and the ensuing winter the two remained at Drumour. In the spring they went abroad again, and have not since returned. It is leased to a wealthy Glaswegian, who, having no more eyes for

the beauties of nature than for the points of a picture,
looks on the place as a mere shooting-lodge, and neg-
lects it accordingly. The lawn has lost its soft velvet
sheen; the parterres glisten no longer like *plaques* of
ruby or *turquoise* enamel; and the creepers that twined
lovingly round Alice's casement flaunt or trail at their
own will or the caprice of wind and rain. But, desolate
as the house may be, it is bright and cheerful, compared
with the castle you wot of hard by. At Drumour at
least there are signs of life sometimes, though of a rough,
boisterous sort; while at Keulis there broods always a
stillness that is worse than the stillness of death,—the
stillness of a curse.

The moors were caught up directly they appeared in
the market; but, if residence at the castle had been thrown
in, it would have hindered rather than advanced the hiring,
for a very simple reason. The place has such an evil
name now that, if a tenant could be found hardy enough
to inhabit it, it would be next to impossible to find a household to minister to him there. There is nothing more infectious than superstition; and the skeptical Southron
serving-men, when they have once succumbed to terror,
visible or invisible, are more helplessly subdued than the
most credulous Highland crones. The Brown Ladye
might roam at her will through the echoing corridors;
and it was whispered that now she walked not always
alone. Strange things were reported to have been seen
and heard by those who tarried behind to set the castle
in order after both host and guest had departed. The
people who were left in charge to keep the furniture from
falling to decay, slept without the walls, and performed
their duties always betwixt dawn and sunset. Scarce
one of them, even at high noon, could have been bribed
to go down the dark passage at the end of which was a
room fast locked and barred,—the room where George
Anstruther escaped out of Mark Ramsay's hands, to fall
into those of a mightier, if not a more merciful, Judge.

As for the master of Keulis, though his wanderings
since then have led him far and wide, they have never
brought him home. It is this constant restlessness that
is the most remarkable change in the man. He was

always fond of traveling, but he had taken it in the same listless, easy-going way that marked his pursuit of all other amusements ; but now he was incapable of abiding more than the shortest space in any one spot, and this anxiety to be gone is not affected by the liveliness or dullness of the place of sojourn. After the first year— during which time no one knew much of his movements— he did not affect to shun society,—that is, foreign society ; for England and he have been strangers since the events recorded above, — and *outre-mer* society receives him amiably enough, if with no cordial welcome. He had been unhappy in his conjugal relations, of course: the same thing applies to so many *Milors*. If Mark's story was a little worse than those of others, it might be imputed to his having a little less than his share of the *phlegm Britannique*.

Does he himself look so lightly on his path? That is a question no one could answer,—not even Vere Alsager. Indeed, though there is nothing like enmity, overt or covert, betwixt the two, they have seldom been seen together since they parted at Kenlis; no man or woman could now be said to be in Ramsay's confidence ; neither can it be known whether he would have had the courage to keep the promise conveyed in his last message to Alice, for she has never written to say, " Come," and I think never will.

It is probable that this thread has been plucked out forever from the woof of Mark Ramsay's life : yet in the plucking forth the whole fabric was frayed and tangled past mending.

He and Irving have met since, once only,—at Baden. Both parties would have avoided the encounter, had it been possible; but to the latter it seemed especially unwelcome. His courtesy was of the coldest, and his answers to the other's inquiries· of the briefest description. He simply said that Alice was as well as she ever would be, and then changed the subject decisively. Neither did he mention that meeting when, after his gambling-bout, he went back to the hamlet, far up the Schwarzwald, where he had left his daughter. They lived at Baden during the winter, but before the earliest visitors appeared retired to their quiet abode, where even yet the peasantry have not ceased to gaze wonderingly after the graceful lady whose face has never been seen unveiled.

We will leave them there.

La Reine Gaillarde had not yet abdicated her sovereignty; but if her laugh rings out joyously at times, it rings not so often as heretofore, and she has never quite shaken off the weight that settled down on her spirits that terrible night at Kenlis. Some of her many friends like her the better for the chastening of her reckless mood: chiefest among these is Major Gauntlet. Oddly enough, even the scandal-mongers have forborne to cavil at their intimacy. Yet there is a secret betwixt those two, of which the world knows nothing, and of which they seldom care to speak. It may be that the big, brave heart might be open some day still to receive with due honor one worthy to be enthroned there; but, thus far, Oswald has never murmured in any woman's ear even such words as he was not ashamed to speak to Mark Ramsay's wife.

Lady Nithsdale is as light of heart and of foot as ever; Regy Avenel is still her prime minister and celibate; and though Nina Marston too keeps her maiden name, she will be Nina Hampton, they say, before long; and, though a few may envy, not many begrudge her the drawing a *quaterne* in the matrimonial *tombola*.

It will not interest you to hear that Horace Kendall has had no chance of repeating the bold stroke for fortune that he missed so narrowly. He is reported to be studying hard in Italy now, with a view to turn his voice to substantial account; and perhaps he may emulate Camille Desmoulins before all is done in this weak, erring world of ours.

Desiderium tam cari capitis is not always measured by intrinsic worth. Often to the wisest and most virtuous, after their decease, more justice is done by those strangers who only knew them by repute, than by those who have known them familiarly.

In ancient time there lived a pious person who, having walked long before the Lord blamelessly, was duly cau-

onized.   Concerning the new-made saint, thus spoke a
man scarcely less pious, if less illustrious :—

"Let us intercede yet more earnestly for the dead, now
that Cyril hath gone among them !" '

When Lady Peverell is removed to a better—it can
scarcely be a higher—sphere, not even, I think, among the
children that she has dragooned into helplessness, if they
were not goaded to rebellion, or among the poor who
have eaten the acrid bread of her charity, will there be
found regard so lasting and sincere as was wasted—if
you will have it so—on frail, faulty Blanche Ellerslie.

Though the loss left its mark on none so deeply as on
Gauntlet and Vane, there are others besides—not a whit
given to the melting mood—who never remember without bitterness the progress of her punishment, and who ·
never without a sinking at heart see the years bring
round the day on which the grace-blow was dealt to
BLANCHE ELLERSLIE.

THE END.

"MAPLE RANGE."

THE RED ACORN.

By JOHN McELROY,

Editor *Toledo Blade*, and Author of "Andersonville, etc., etc.

An elegant 12mo., of 322 pages. Black and gold side and back stamp. Cloth. Price, $1.

READ THE PRESS NOTICES.

The Red Acorn.

"It is a bright, humorous and attractive story of the late war."—*Chronicle-Herald* (Philadelphia).

The Red Acorn.

"The book is rich in incident, and gives a very faithful picture of army life."—*National Tribune* (Washington, D. C.)

The Red Acorn.

"It is a wonderfully realistic story, so true to life in its descriptions, and in the naturalness of its characters, as to lead the reader to believe it was history and biography, and not romance. It is the unusual realistic character of the book which gives it prominence above books of its kind."—*Inter-Ocean* (Chicago).

The Red Acorn.

"*An admirable novel*, called by a name made glorious as the badge of the First Division of the Fourteenth Army Corps, 'The Red Acorn.' * * * Each is a strongly marked and individual creation, who contributes not a little to the thrilling interest of the story."—*Tribune* (Chicago).

The Red Acorn.

"The characters love, laugh, fight and endure in much the same rollicking, devil-may-care style which makes the soldier-life in *Charles O'Malley* so enlivening."—*American Bookseller* (New York).

The Red Acorn.

"The book is a realistic story of real people, who bore the heat and burden of the late war. It is carefully and gracefully written, and the characters become live men and women to the reader. The book will become popular with those fond of fiction which is true to life."—*Daily News* (Denver).

The Red Acorn.

"The way John McElroy in his new story, 'The Red Acorn,' sets his people to love-making and talking about it, is very refreshing. It is a story of the war; brimful of realism and right smart talk. * * * There is snap in Rachel Bond; something winning about Aunt Debby. It *is not* a dull book."—*Times* (Philadelphia).

The Red Acorn.

"The romantic element is the most prominent in the tale; the historic is woven in in such a manner as to be highly attractive, enlivened by pungent dialogues and amusing incidents, and some really stirring descriptions."—*Times* (Denver).

Mailed, postage paid, to any address, on receipt of price, $1. by

HENRY A. SUMNER & COMPANY,

205 Wabash Avenue, Chicago.